The Emissary
Charity Mae

KNIGHTED PHOENIX PUBLISHING

Contents

Map of Purerah	VII
Chapter 1	1
Chapter 2	11
Chapter 3	24
Chapter 4	38
Chapter 5	51
Chapter 6	57
Chapter 7	73
Chapter 8	77
Chapter 9	89
Chapter 10	99
Chapter 11	109
Chapter 12	123
Chapter 13	135
Chapter 14	149
Chapter 15	163

Chapter 16	174
Chapter 17	189
Chapter 18	201
Chapter 19	217
Chapter 20	236
Chapter 21	248
Chapter 22	256
Chapter 23	264
Chapter 24	281
Chapter 25	296
Chapter 26	304
Chapter 27	307
Chapter 28	320
Chapter 29	342
Chapter 30	349
Chapter 31	365
Chapter 32	384
Character Guide	401
Other Books by Charity Mae	407
About the Author	409
Copyright	411

One evening a terrible storm came on; there was thunder and lightning, and the rain poured down in torrents. Suddenly a knocking was heard at the city gate, and the old king went to open it.

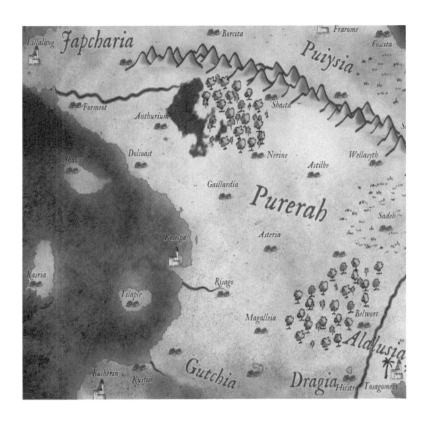

Chapter 1

I never thought I'd be here, with him, wanting him. Our breath hovers in the chilly ocean air as we finally pull away, the mist blurring together before vanishing up towards the falling snow. I take a moment to take in the sound of Prince Gavril's steady breathing, the feel of his gentle yet firm grip.

I can hardly believe this moment is real. I know they say Christmas has a romantic magic, but I never really believed it. After all I'd done to fight for this moment, I cannot process it's real. That this isn't just another dream. Each little soft caress of the snow feels like little butterfly kisses blessing this moment and drawing us closer together as if begging us to see that this was meant to be.

But we're not the ones who decide that. The prince doesn't pick his bride. The Enthronement does. And I'm only one of fifteen other girls trying to prove to be his true princess. And though many of them thought me in the lead, I'd fallen from that place spectacularly, at least in the Prince's favor. But this magical night, I won it back, or so I hoped.

I'm so happy I'm certain if I turned and tried to dance into the sky on the snowflakes, I could. A cold breeze cuts across us, and Prince Gavril pulls me up and steps back to adjust his jacket on my shoulders to make sure I'm kept warm.

I can't help but smile. I watch as his amber eyes focus on securing the jacket, his dark curly hair falling a little from its proper styling to hang on his forehead. I'd likely knocked the lock loose as we'd kissed. In the darkness, his chocolate milk tones are made to look more like milk chocolate as he lifts his head and meets my eyes.

He gives me a half smile that makes my heart flutter, tender, intense. I know what he wants to do and lean closer to let him when there's an odd splash from the ocean behind us. Gavril can't help but check it out. He loves the ocean and what lives in it. I'm curious what sea creature would jump up to enjoy the snow too.

It's lucky, because as we do, we hear voices from the ajar glass door back into the ballroom. They must have spotted the snow at last. Snow is a short pleasure in Purerah. It snows most of the month of January but clears up by mid-February. I blame it on our unique coasts, surprisingly cold in the winter, but not too hot in the summers, kept cool by the cold seas.

Lilly, the youngest of the chosen girls and one of my best friends, pops her head out to see the snow. I'm surprised Gavril doesn't step away until others come out behind her. Her pale skin matches the snow as her dark, sloped eyes gaze up to the sky at the heavily falling snow.

It's not long before the others are pushing the doors wide and getting a view at the fresh snow. There is already a good coating on the ground. It is turning into a thick flurry quickly.

Ericka, the blondest of the girls, hesitates before stepping out. She's wearing one of the most lavish dresses of all the guests at the ball with a long, full skirt with a bit of a train, a flutter overskirt and off-the-shoulder-sleeves, all a striking red and pink.

Dahlia, one of her "friends" in the "elite" group, laughs at her hesitation. Ericka's dress is so large it's making it hard for anyone else to get a look, so Dahlia shoves Ericka out into the snow to make room. Her strength as a professional athlete made it easy for her to push Ericka out of the way. Her natural, coiled hair is pulled into a stunning bun on the top of her head, almost the exact size of her head. She hugs herself to keep her exposed arms warm as she joins us in the snow.

Not all the girls come out though. Those unsure make way for the king and queen to come out. "I thought it might be a snowless year," the king says. His bright blue eyes looking up at the snow, crinkling in happiness the way they do.

The queen smiles, clearly trying to hide her happiness to see the snow. She is the perfect contrast to her husband. His fair warm tones, graying hair, and large happy smile are balanced by her chestnut tones, perfectly dark coils pulled up from her face and down her back, and elegant expression make them quite the happy opposites, yin and yang.

Though the queen surprises me. Just as I just as I admire her composed nature, the queen looks around before she tries to grab a snowflake on her tongue. I'm surprised but happy, letting out a smile. The ever proper and formal queen does have a fun side she's hiding from us somewhere. It's comforting.

"It's a good thick snow too," the king says as his wife lets go of his arm, and he runs his hand along the railing of the balcony.

I know the king well enough to know it's a trap, and I immediately duck to avoid the snowball he throws my way, striking his son's arm instead. The king laughs as does Gavril.

"That was rude," I inform the king.

"I knew you'd take it best." The king grins. Though I'd gotten into trouble for almost revealing my rebel heritage to the royal family, the king has always found me a fun subject to tease.

"Aster." The queen hits his arm, her expression appalled by his playful behavior as always.

"Hey! Have to keep the tradition." Gavril smiles. They must have a snowball fight when it snows. Gavril had just mentioned to me his parents let him outside to see the snow each year, though for his safety they normally keep him inside.

"Not with so many ladies," the queen objects.

But the other ladies don't have the same restraint. Princess Zelda from Hyvil, one of the born princesses, has already formed a snowball and strikes the king with it. The king immediately starts to prepare a counterattack.

Zelda is not the only one who joins in the game. Dahlia joins in as well as Princess Laurina, Bella, Azalea, Forsythia, and Kamala. Princess Rose, Jonquil, Ericka, Isla, and Florence retreat inside to keep from being pelted with snow.

But it isn't just some of the chosen girls of the Enthronement who join in. Nippers, the black stray cat who wanders the palace, has somehow not only gotten into the ballroom but onto the balcony to leap up at the snowballs playfully. If only one of us could tame him.

The king is happy to throw snow at most of us girls and goes after his son with childlike excitement. He does not, however, dare hit his wife.

The chosen girls hiding inside laugh to watch us play. I notice Fabian, the lead reporter for the local paper and courtier, watching with amusement. His wife clearly was not allowing him to join in the game. I think what he really wants is to grab a snowball and throw it at his cousin, Godwin, who is Prince Gavril's attendant.

This snowball fight lasts a good ten minutes or so when the queen's shriek makes us all jump. "Gavril!"

I whirl around to check on Gavril. With how the queen had screamed, I worried the rebels had somehow used the ball to break in like they had at the Harvest and managed to hurt him. A flash of the protestor's indignant face just moments before he was shot off the fountain on Restoration Day races through my mind. I shudder to picture that as Gavril. I was haunted by that image enough.

I'd not put it past my father. He was the leader of the Custod rebellion, the same group I had once thought would be the heroes of Purerah after five-hundred years of civil war. But after being forced to join the Enthronement to help them assassinate the royal family, I'd slowly learned the truth that this civil war was far less about nobility against their people and more the people against the people. I'd tried to stop their attack at the Harvest and almost failed. Did I just fail to stop father's rebels getting in tonight? If I failed...

But Gavril doesn't look hurt or panicked. He clearly is more startled than all of us put together at his mother's shriek.

"Where is your jacket?" the queen demands as if asking why the cookie jar was missing.

We all breathe a sigh of relief it wasn't anything worse. The king and a few others even laugh in relief.

Gavril looks around as if trying to find a way to reverse time and retrieve the jacket before she noticed. My cheeks are red as I quickly take his jacket off and try to slip it back to him. The chill on my exposed arms is suddenly even colder than it had been.

"Well... I..." Gavril stammers as I try to give him his jacket from behind his back, not that it would really help as, of course, the queen saw me hand it to him. I can feel the other girls glaring at me, likely wondering when I'd gotten his jacket. "She-she has no sleeves," Gavril tries to defend himself as he puts his jacket back on. The poor boy was likely closer to thirty than twenty, but his mother still treated him like he was five, and this was a perfect example of it. "Well, just... you know those little cap ones," Gavril tries to excuse.

"You don't go out into the snow without a jacket," the queen continues the scolding. Other girls are rolling their eyes and muttering. This behavior from the queen was a problem in many ways, but to us ladies, it's irritating in our attempts to date the Prince.

"Um... I was wearing it when I went out there," Gavril explains.

"Dalilly, relax," the king says, putting an arm around his wife, "it's all in good fun. We're all cold and wet. He's fine." He chuckles. "He's not going to get the measles or Leafrick fever."

"I know, but it's still not a good idea." The queen sighs.

"I'm just glad you aren't hurt or something," I whisper to Gavril.

He fights not to laugh as the king calms his wife, and we all head back into the ballroom to warm up. Most girls do not have ways to keep warm, so the servants grab towels and blankets to warm us up. I notice Fabian now is helping warm up the cold girls. The prince isn't too wet thankfully, but we both have to take off our shoes to let them dry. My tights are also wet, so I use the convertible opening in the tights to roll them to my knee to help that section dry.

I'm hoping these shoes won't be too uncomfortable without the tights. I dry one shoe and slip it on, but Gavril snatches the second from me.

"Hey," I laugh.

"Uh, red glass?" he jokes.

I flush. *Why, Damian? Why?* My attendant is the best here, and there isn't an event I'm not the best-dressed for, but at times like this... Not that I mind Gavril's attention, but with all the girls watching... Not to mention they knew I'd had the Prince's jacket for unknown reasons. I try not to smirk thinking about how envious they'd be if they knew what we'd really been doing.

"I guess. I hadn't noticed," I pretend I do not know what he is saying.

Gavril smirks. He bends as if to ask to put it on, when one of the towels flops onto his side.

We look over to see Forsythia. "Oh sorry." She frowns. "I just kicked it off. Didn't mean to hit you."

Which is nowhere near true. That horrible, conniving little snake disguised as a woman was trying to ruin my moment and likely steal it. She looks as snake-like as ever in a lithe green dress that shows off her curves, her straight black hair fluttering around her as she covers her mouth as if in an apology, her fair skin as clean as the snow outside. As always, she's trying to be more appealing than me.

Not long before, she planned a stunt for half of us Chosen girls to see her kissing Gavril rather aggressively. She's a sneaky little Jezebel, and for some stupid reason, Gavril isn't able to see through her or at least doesn't want to.

"It's fine." Gavril laughs and tosses the towel back to her. He smirks slightly. He knows Forsythia was trying to break the moment. He doesn't care. It makes my heart beat faster in hope.

I can't help but notice her face reddens slightly as Gavril still helps me with my shoe then helps me stand by taking both of my hands in his. The temptation to kiss him as he pulls me up is overwhelming, but I'm not ready for the pressure of that public of a display. I see the desire for it in Gavril's eyes though, but he wisely doesn't try either. At least they hadn't seen us on the balcony.

"Let's bring out the punch," the king says cheerfully.

The servants bring out two large bowls of drinks: one clearly the smoking bishop and the other a softer Christmas punch. Both were part of the traditional way to end the holiday since the very first Christmas was held in Emilimoh. "You can administer the punch," the king says to Gavril as they get the traditional pokers from their heating place in the fire.

The king takes one and Gavril the other. The smoking bishop is set off by the king while Gavril does the punch. As I watch the softer drink bubble at the heat, I wonder what they put in it to make it bubble the same as the smoking bishop. As a Custod, I am not allowed to drink strong drinks because of my oath.

A sickly bubbling enters my stomach, just like the one in the punch bowls. I am not a Custod. I had been raised to believe so, but my father had been disowned by them before I was born. My mother had been forced to say nothing until I escaped my father's net. She'd explained it all just the night before. I'm still digesting the truth of it and trying to accept it.

But rather than letting my father's lies and tricks break me, I have found hope in all I've done without the Custod magic I thought I had. I intend to use it to help empower and free me, and not let all of it drag me down like it had since the moment I realized the rebels were wrong. Though I still can't prove it, I know it's the truth. I will prove my faith is not misplaced and be the one who will win this and make things right. If I don't, I'll have wasted my life for nothing. The haunting of that man who'd been shot will be nothing more than a never-ending nightmare.

I'm snapped back to reality as they ask which drink I would like. I still prefer the softer one. I am not ready to throw off the oaths I'd thought I'd made that quickly. Not within twenty-four hours.

Small social circles start to form as we all enjoy our drinks. Fabian is chatting with a group a few paces away in a lively mood, laughing with a few of the girls, Forsythia among them.

"Would you like to—" Gavril starts to ask me when Forsythia steps between the two of us and takes his arm.

"Prince Gavril, dear," she says, her voice dripping with false honey that makes me angry, "I was just telling Fabian about what we were talking about the other day." She starts to pull him away.

Gavril puts on the typical fake smile he wears. He doesn't pick the winner of the Enthronement. He just has to marry whoever it is, so there are times, like this, when he just has to endure being dragged around.

But I'm done being dragged around. I am not going to be bullied into being less than I want to be by these girls anymore, and I am not letting that snake do that to Gavril or me anymore.

I stop Forsythia by putting my hand on her other arm. "Sorry Gavril, I didn't hear what you said." Forsythia is forced to stop or look incredibly rude for cutting me off. And she doesn't dare embarrass herself with the king and queen watching the exchange, as we know them to be the only judges of the Enthronement.

Forsythia glares daggers at me, but I'm done being intimidated. If I want to win this and him, I have to stop letting her proclaim her spot on the top and how she pushes off anyone who gets close.

"Oh yes. I was asking if you'd like to settle on the sofa as it's far more comfortable than standing on the dance floor when the dancing is paused," Gavril says.

"What a lovely idea," I agree, gently pulling Gavril's arm that way, forcing Forsythia to let go or she would be seen as the troublemaker. The anger in her eyes is unmistakable, blazing like a dark fire in her dark, narrow, hooded eyes.

"We'll join you," Forsythia says brightly as if that was an invitation for anyone and a lovely idea I'd given.

As she leaves to try to draw the crowd towards where Gavril was leading me to sit, he smiles at me. "I'm impressed. Christmas magic?" I had never fought back against the other girls for my own sake. I'd defended Lilly and my other friends zealously, but when it was at me, until recently, unsure how to fight back, I'd crumpled like a house of cards.

"New perspective magic."

"There's a difference?"

I think about that a moment, looking at Gavril as I thought. "I suppose we'll find out."

The group joins us over on the sofa. I think Fabian had too much of the smoking bishop because he seems happily tipsy. I'm not sure what Forsythia had hoped this would do. Gavril stays seated next to me, and Fabian sat on my other side, complementing the ballet piece I'd done at the start of the night in a rather haphazard speech. His wife rolls her eyes at him many times.

Not long after, several girls are too sleepy to go on, so they head up to bed. Fabian asks me for a dance which is rather funny with his slurred movements. It makes it easier for Prince Gavril to slip in a few more dances with me.

As the prima actress of the royal theater, I am a master dancer, and Gavril had found it the one thing his mother would let him learn as exercise, so we both love to dance and can do things most other people don't have a clue how to do. We have a great time doing ballroom dances most casual social dancers couldn't dream of.

But it is getting late, and with the end of the night, the end of the holiday. And that means this little bubble I've made can just pop. I pray not, but the fear certainly starts to settle into my stomach.

It must be close to midnight, if not past it, when Gavril asks if he can escort me to bed. His parents and everyone but Zelda have already gone to bed. She's laughing and trying to get Sage, the Prince's Custod guard, to eat more treats.

Sage seems offended, but he's had enough sugar to make him a bit sillier than normal. He's a high ranked assassin Custod, how high I don't know, but really high. His normally dull expression (used to hide his emotions) are slacking as he fights little smiles and reveals his irritation at Zelda trying so hard to get him to smile.

I can't resist smiling myself. Someone can loosen Sage up at least. Zelda is one of only four born princesses left in the Enthronement. He must be afraid to disobey royal orders.

"We'll let him enjoy," Gavril whispers.

"Um..." I did promise Sage I'd not be alone with the Prince without his permission. Sage had caught on to the hints of my rebel past before anyone else, and though he could never prove anything, he disliked me and was wary of me. I think he fully suspects I'm a plant, though I'd rejected the role.

Lucky for me, Sage notices. "Ready for bed?" he calls to Gavril, standing up quickly. His dark cloak flutters as he stands. He wears all black, even his hair is black and normally brushed back from his pale face, making his deep green eyes stand out more than ever in his eagerness to escape.

"I'm just going to escort her up." Gavril nods.

"Oh alright." Sage gets up to join us.

"Would you like us to take you to your room?" Gavril asks Zelda.

"Sure." Zelda gets up, her long blonde hair falling over her shoulder as she looks down to brush off her white and gold dress.

"Sage, you can take her, and I'll take Kascia," Gavril hints heavily.

Sage narrows his eyes at the Prince then looks at me. I mouth a promise not to hurt him. Sage sighs and agrees, giving me a look that says, "just this once". I guess there are Christmas miracles.

Gavril smiles and offers me his arm. I take it, and we walk back to my room quietly. When we arrive, he kisses my hand. "Well, enjoy the rest days until the tests start again. Thank you for your time tonight."

"And thank you for... well, everything. This may have been one of the most magical Christmases I've ever had," I confess. There is hope. It is working, and I couldn't have asked for a more perfect holiday, a more perfect man, and a more hopeful outlook. Whenever the new tests start, I'll be ready for them.

Gavril beams. "Good. Perhaps we can top it next year."

Next year. My heart flutters in hope at the idea. "Perhaps," I agree uneasily. Do I dare dream of it?

"Merry Christmas, Lady Kascia. Sleep well." And the look in his eyes tells me much more. I smile wider than I likely should.

"Merry Christmas, Gavril." And perhaps much more.

I'm giddy with happiness as I slip into my warm sheets that night. I'm not sure I need my normal sleep tea tonight, but I take it anyway, as I fear my nightmares returning, but they don't. Instead, I dream I'm back at the royal theater where I've worked in my whole life. I'm changing out of an assassin outfit when my father's voice cuts across me.

"What are you doing?" My father appears behind me. I can see him in the mirror I'd been changing in front of.

"Changing," I reply as I finish securing the strings of my fine blue dress.

"How do you expect to do your Custod duty dressed like that?" Father demands of me.

"I'm not." I pick up the tiara I'd worn a million times playing various princesses in our shows, both musicals and ballets.

Father tenses in anger at me. I look up at his reflection in the mirror. He's dressed differently than I remember. His dark hair and well-trimmed goatee look smoother than I recall. It fits the dark uniform he wore; an assassin uniform like the one I was discarding.

"How can you abandon your calling?"

"Because it's just a role. I'm not being whatever you want me to be anymore." I put on the tiara and make sure it's in my hair properly.

I always thought that my attendant and maids made me look perfect, but now, I look particularly beautiful. I'm wearing the starlight dress my maids had put me in earlier in the Enthronement. It's one of the most beautiful dresses I have and one of my favorites. The fluttering sleeves like stars, the perfect corset top, dark blue with dark golden patterns around the bust like dark wings. Speckles of light twinkle across the top and down the skirt like the dark sky at midnight over Purerah's seas. In this dream, they are just like real stars.

The tiara is made up of the same stars. It fits perfectly into my chestnut brown hair that shows hints of red and blonde I got from my mother, showing in the perfectly done curls that cascade down my back, pulled back at the sides to help fit the tiara more perfectly.

"You're my daughter. It's your duty to assassinate the royal family and replace them, not join them!" Father rages at me. "You're my assassin, my spy. You're no true princess. They won't fall for it. You can't pass."

"Of course, I can." The firmness in my voice impresses even me as I say it.

I turn to my father. He tries to stop me, but something stops him.

"Come, my princess." It's Prince Gavril's voice.

I smile as I turn to him. He's holding out his hand to me with a gentle smile that's far more comforting than anything. His dark curly hair isn't perfectly set like my father's is, but his genuine appearance only makes it all the more perfect. His amber eyes meet mine with perfect trust, almost glowing against his chocolate milk skin.

I ignore Father's demands. I turn my back to him as I reach for the Prince's hand.

Without warning, a faceless person comes up to me and takes my hand before I reach Gavril. "Must assure you're a true princess," he says and pulls out a tab to test my blood with.

As he pricks my finger, I wake up, blinking in the sunlight that's gently filtering into my room.

Chapter 2

It's a cool crisp morning. Snow has piled on my balcony from our sudden snowstorm last night. The sky is clear and blue. It must be freezing out there. Perhaps that's why as I look around, I feel like something is missing. Perhaps it's just the empty feeling of the holiday being over. Normally, that was what I looked forward to. Having done two to three shows simultaneously at the Christmas season every year of my life made the end a relief.

Perhaps it was just the emptiness of the dream. The faceless entity oddly hadn't frightened me though I know I'm little more than a plant, an attempt by the rebels to assassinate the royal family. I thought I'd panic at someone testing my legitimacy by taking blood, but... I don't. I should, but I don't. Why don't I react to the dream more?

I'm looking around, taking in this odd feeling, when my maids quietly slip into the room to see if I'm awake. Vivian, my lead maid, spots me up first and smiles. "Good morning, my lady."

"Good morning, Vivian. Did you have a good Christmas?" I ask as Flur, my second maid, follows with a shy smile.

"It was lovely. And it looks like yours went well," Vivian says, going over to my vanity to get started on the morning preparations. "I've heard the prince's puppy is as happy as ever, if his current staff is to be believed."

I smile. "I'm glad Joy is adjusting well." I'd given the prince a rather energetic husky puppy for Christmas. Partly, I'd chosen Joy to show that I knew him and what he'd want for Christmas. And I wanted to prove I didn't think him the spoiled brat of a prince anymore that I thought he was before I knew him.

I take a moment to daydream of the moment I learned that I'd somehow proven it to the prince before then, and my perfect gift only cemented his certainty in me. It's amazing I pulled it off when I came here to be Father's infiltrator to let them in to assassinate him and his parents. It's such a foreign world to think about, but I'm painfully aware anyone learning the truth would be serious trouble for me.

"It's a late start for everyone, but we'll have breakfast for you shortly then you can go about your dance routine if you like," Vivian offers in her normal friendly, yet formal way. That's even how she dresses. The maid uniform is Purerahian blue with a small white apron, comfortable pants that are easy to move in, and a button up work shirt, mostly covered by the apron. It's simple and uniform and yet has room to be personalized.

Even Flur and Vivian's uniforms are distinct to me. Though the same color, Vivian has a notebook and pen protruding from her apron pockets which is always perfectly clean, wrinkle free, just like her dark hair is always perfectly smoothed back into the low uniform bun.

Flur's pockets carry sewing tools in one pocket and her other is open for putting other things she might need into them, hair pieces, makeup brushes when working on my appearance, and cleaning gear when she's cleaning. Her apron strings aren't as perfectly tight and orderly as Vivian's. Her straight blond hair doesn't stay in the uniform bun as well as Vivian's either and often has soft little whisps at the back of her neck and face.

It makes my heart ache to think of Ro, my third maid who'd been taken by the rebels during one of their attacks. Her apron was often coming loose, pockets full of who knew what as she carried around anything and everything, and her fringe was always falling out of its bun which Vivian was often getting on her for. She was the boldest of my maids. I miss her a lot.

I stand to let Vivian and Flur help me get ready for the day and into my dance gear to do my normal exercises after breakfast when my attendant, Damian Lexus, walks in with a warm smile. He's dressed as perfectly as ever, not a hair out of place. His jet-black hair is pulled into a ponytail at the base of his neck with a seafoam green ribbon that matches his waistcoat. The whole suit fits him perfectly with a matching winter gray that brings his whole look together handsomely and helps his emerald eyes pop against his pale skin. He holds his cane in one hand as he adjusts his cuffs, though as always, they were hardly less than perfect.

"Good morning, ladies," he greets us with his heavy Englarish accent. "I have something for you, Lady Kascia." And he offers me a small, thin envelope.

I frown and open it up. My brows pinch in confusion. It's an invitation from the queen to join her for an afternoon in the spa. I'd never gotten such an invitation before, and as far as I knew, none of the Enthronement candidates ever had.

We'd started with fifty girls, forty-four common natives of Purerah, and six born princesses back in the late summer. Each of us took the same series of tests to prove ourselves a true princess to marry Gavril. There are only fifteen of us left, and in all that time, I'm almost certain not one of us Chosen have gotten such an invitation.

If I'd gotten an invite to meet with both the king and queen, perhaps it wouldn't be so strange. Not only had we all spoken to them two-on-one during the testing process for the Enthronement, but the king seems to be genuinely fond of me. The queen, on the other hand, makes me nervous.

When I'd driven my father out of the castle at the Harvest Ball, she was easily the most spooked when they found me armed outside the saferoom and almost threw me out when I killed the rebel who'd tried to assault Lilly. An invite for an afternoon alone with her was... intimidating.

I try to think if perhaps I'd done anything that would earn me this extra attention from the queen. I couldn't think of anything I'd done over Christmas. Her husband would be the one to get in trouble for allowing me to give Prince Gavril a dog for Christmas, so it isn't that. And though Prince Gavril and I certainly had gotten closer last night, nothing happened that would get me this attention.

And it's not like she's asking me to tea to discuss something. She is inviting me to a spa day. I almost forgot the palace had one. I'd not seen it since the first day in the palace when they did our makeovers. We'd already resolved her concerns about my acts of violence trying to keep the rebels out so there's just nothing I could see her being angry or insisting to see me for.

Had she heard about what happened between Gavril and I in the gym? No. The prince knows she bans him from the gym. We'd both be called in if it were that. Though it was a painful disaster for me, it's nothing she'd be upset about. And if it was over our Christmas kiss, then Forsythia needed a talking to as well.

And if she had found out my father sent me here to kill her family, or that he was the Custod rebellion leader, or that I had been engaged to the Loyalist's choice for king, I'd be in for a trial, not a spa day. What had spurred this?

I frown and look back at the invitation, a simple handwritten note. I can't think of a single reason she'd call for this, but I can't say no. I'd run the risk of being eliminated from the Enthronement. And I can't risk that. Not only had I just finally worked out the problem I'd started in the gym with the prince, but who knew what my father would do to me if I was sent home? I'd rejected his rebel ways. I hadn't spoken to him since I drove him away from the royal family at the Harvest.

Home is damnation. Sure, I knew my mother would accept me, but Father?

I'd have to run the risk of accepting the invitation.

"That sounds nice," Flur says when I accept the invitation and hand it to Flur to return.

"She loves using that room," Vivian agrees. "That's a good sign."

"I hope so." I'd only *just* gotten Gavril to trust me again after our mishap in the gym when he thought I was upset that I kept losing to him because I thought him a wimpy, spoiled prince, when in reality it was because I thought I was failing as a Custod. I'm not sure I'm ready for another drama *right* after I fixed the first.

"I doubt it's that severe, Kascia," Damian correctly reads my worry, assuring me with that fatherly assurance in his eyes. "I'd tell you if it was a danger, wouldn't I?"

I nod. Damian was one of the very few things I could be sure of in this wild game. He had helped me sneak out to find the truth behind the rebellions I once thought the heroes of Purerah. He'd kept true to his word and not told a soul the Custod rebellion sent me here to let them in during the Harvest or that my father is the leader of the Custod rebellion, and a disowned Custod as I only learned two days before. But, I suppose I hadn't had a chance to tell him over the rush of Christmas Day, so he didn't know yet.

"Then trust me, it will be just fine." Damian smiles. "I thought you'd enjoy the idea of a day to relax."

"You think an afternoon with the anxious queen will be relaxing?" I joke. She's a beautiful queen, but a far cry from being a calm or relaxed woman. I've never met anyone so anxious. It's why her stealing a snowflake on her tongue last night was so impressive.

Damian chuckles. "Well, I assure you it's meant to be. We'll just be going about our normal work. So simply try to enjoy it."

"Lunch will be brought up. That's the order for the rest days," Vivian lets me know.

I nod. So, I'd come here after my ballet and vocal practice and have lunch and go right to the spa to meet with the queen. I wish I wasn't a bundle of nerves. I'm able to forget about it, at least a little, as I start on my dance routines in the practice room next to the Ladies' Chamber.

It's so different than my life as a prima actress where my dance and vocal practices were done in a group first thing in the morning before a short break, rehearsals, lunch, then another round of rehearsals until the end of the day. Unless there was a show, then we'd have our lessons and warm-ups start about two hours before the show, with an hour between to get our heads in the game, and of course, change into costume on time. I doubt I'll ever get to enjoy rehearsals again, even if I can't win the Enthronement.

My maids try to help me be excited, but honestly, I'm nervous and reserved, unsure what the day is going to be like not only because I'll be with the queen, but I've never had a spa day before.

When I arrive at the spa, the queen's appearance surprises me more than anything. Though she's an older woman, the queen always looks beautiful and graceful. Her voluminous coils are normally pulled into stunning manes or braided. Today, they're just pulled into a bun out of the way, the flattest I'd ever seen it. I also realize I've never seen her without makeup. Her skin is slightly duller, not as vibrant of a mahogany color as it normally was. Her dress is also simpler. Like mine, it's easy to take on and off. However, her dark eyes carry the same elegance, grace, and beauty they always did.

I curtsy to the queen as I should when I reach her.

"Welcome, Lady Kascia. I'm glad you could join me," the queen says.

"Is it just us?" I ask, looking around. Perhaps more of us had been invited.

"For today, dear," the queen says and leads me into the spa.

It's a large room with many sections that were separated mostly by curtains, all of which are pulled back at the moment. Three maids I don't know are attending the room. The queen's lady-in-waiting, Maryum I think is her name, follows us and takes the lead in handling our activities.

"I thought I... oh, there she is." The queen smiles as the door opens again behind us.

Vivian smiles at me a bit sheepishly. She's wearing the same uniform the other spa attendants are wearing instead of her normal maid's uniform. I smile back.

"I realized you might be more comfortable with your head maid, as of course your attendant is male." The queen chuckles. "Most of them were to start, actually."

I didn't know that. You'd think they'd avoid that with a group of girls who are supposed to be the prince's alone, but for a kingdom that's been war-torn for five-hundred years, perhaps it was less about being picky and just taking what you could get. I doubt many would work for such low wages in a place often attacked by violent rebels.

"I think it's about half men and half women now. Have you done this before?" the queen asks me.

"No, Your Majesty."

"Well, to start, we'll have a full body scrub which we'll do in our own partitions before we'll go to the main spa to enjoy the rest together.

Should be fun." The queen smiles at me encouragingly. It does seem like this is meant to just be fun.

The unique bath experience feels odd, good and bad. How hard they scrub is a bit uncomfortable, but the results feel amazing. I'm then put into a simple bathing costume that leaves more of my body exposed for understandable reasons, with just enough concealment to allow privacy.

Then they have me slip into one of the most luxurious robes I'd ever worn before I'm led into one of the same kind of chairs they'd put us in on the first day to have our makeovers.

Vivian mostly directs the other servants. Two had gone with the queen and two had gone with me. But once I'm in the chair beside the queen, the spa attendants move around between the queen and I more.

The first thing they do is lean the chair back and wash our hair in the most relaxing wash I'd ever felt. It feels more like a scalp massage than anything. They scrub and clean the scalp and hair carefully. Then while it's damp, they put some creams and oils into it before pinning it up to let it sit.

"Your treatment smells not that different from mine," the queen teases warmly. I'd been enjoying the experience so much I'd forgotten to even bother figuring out what to talk about. "Though with how thick your curls are, perhaps they aren't that different."

"I'm sure they must be. Your coils are so much tighter and more beautiful than mine." I turn a bit pink.

"Simply different, dear. I could never get my hair as smooth as yours," the queen points out as the staff start washing and exfoliating our faces.

"I suppose that's true." My chestnut brown hair was nothing to her royal mane. It's thick and curly and does pretty much whatever my maids want it to do when it's damp (other than be perfectly straight). It does have more variants than the queen's dark hair. My complexion is also a bit unusual as it's a bit paler than the common dark tones of traditional royals. My skin is more of a light olive that likely has lightened with how much we're confined to the palace. I'd rarely been outside since late summer.

"And you do look splendid in the royal colors," the queen teases, closing her eyes as the staff work on her facial.

That is also true; Purerahian yellow and blue go well with my skin tones, brown hair, and blue eyes that hold a hazel ring at the center. Like my hair, my eyes are a blend of my parents': my mother's hazel and Father's deep blue. In fact, not too different from the prince, I'm pretty much a perfect blend of my parents. He is not dark toned nor too pale, and I am not blonde but not full dark brown either.

"That's because the staff you gave me is brilliant and knows how to help me pull it off," I compliment her while also deflecting it has anything to do with anything I did.

"Nonsense," the queen chuckles. "You are a lovely girl. All of you ladies are, just in vastly different ways."

"Though Princess Rose must have loved being in here with you. You're so alike," I try to change the topic.

The queen chuckles lightly again. "Lady Kascia, so far, you're the only one apart from my husband and son to join me in here. I have to drag Aster most of the time, and though I tried to get Gavril to enjoy it, I don't think it ever stuck."

I can't help but smile. No, I imagine Prince Gavril, ever treated by his mother as a child, would hate having to spend the day just sitting there relaxing next to her. I know he loves her because he's so patient with how she babies him, but I also know it drives him absolutely insane.

"Well, now you have fifteen girls to choose from. At least fifteen for now." Now the holiday is over, I'm sure tests will resume in earnest. I imagine they're anxious to have it over with and move on to handling the war and the many crises it brings up.

"I suppose I do. I've avoided getting too attached to anyone. After all, who knows which girls will pass or fail? We can guess, but it's hard to know. It's safer that way. It's been hard, but in the long term, I think we'll be better for it."

So she and the king can avoid it, but poor Gavril has to date and get to know us all as if we're his only girlfriend until the girl is eliminated. As I know he hates this, it doesn't seem fair. This whole game isn't fair. The prince has no choice, but the king and queen talk like they don't either.

"Are you looking forward to it being over then?" I ask tentatively.

The queen sighs, relaxing as they start putting serum on her face. "It will be nice to have this stress over with," she admits.

"And someone who will do this with you," I try to make it sound less like work.

The queen smiles. "I certainly hope so. We'll have to see."

"You don't think the winner will want to?" I frown. "Is that why you're inviting us all to do this?"

"Actually, that wasn't my intent at all," the queen admits.

"Pardon?"

"I wasn't planning on doing this with one girl after another. It would take far too long as you can't do these every day," says the queen.

My face falls, or it would have if someone wasn't rubbing serum on it that smells good and yet bad at the same time. Then why did she ask me? There has to be something she is going to drop on me at any moment.

The queen, however, proves she's not just an overly anxious personality. "I asked you because I thought you needed it." I have never heard her tone be so soft and gentle before.

What does that mean? Is she saying I could use polishing, or she needed to make sure I'm worthy of still being here? I'd assured the prince, but I'm far from assuring her.

"I didn't forget what you told us about your father not approving. It was likely hard to see your mother go when you don't know when you'll see her again."

It was hard. My mother had been able to join me for Christmas because the royal family hired my acting troupe to perform two shows before the holiday. It's also how she got the chance to tell me the truth about my father being disinherited as a Custod.

"So, I thought perhaps some girl time would help comfort you. Nothing fancy."

I couldn't help but chuckle. To the queen, this is nothing fancy, but it is to most of us.

"Do you enjoy this often on your own then? If the boys don't like it as much?" I ask.

"From time to time. I try not to go overboard. There are times it helps, and other times, the silence makes it hard not to overthink."

"About the Enthronement?" I guess.

"And other things. I recall it being a great comfort after a miscarriage." The queen stops rather suddenly as if realizing what she'd admitted.

"I can't even imagine how hard all of that must have been." I frown. Gavril said she's lost five? Was it before he was born or five in total? He'd mentioned at least one or two after he was born. He said something about recalling his mother squeezing him extra tight.

"It was. But when my rainbow boy came along it helped a little. I still am in awe when I see him every day." She smiles a warm, watery smile. "He truly is the miracle I prayed for. I thank the Maker for him every day."

"You have raised a fine man." I don't want to take that from her, but she also may want to learn to let up. We'd all seen how, in many ways, she still treats her son like he's a toddler. I recall how nervous she got when he climbed the ladder to put the star on top of the Christmas tree, or how she'd fret he wasn't eating enough, or the few times I'd caught her trying to wipe food off his face — half the time it wasn't even really there. "And soon you'll get a daughter too then hopefully more after." First comes love, then comes marriage, then for her, grandbabies in the baby carriage.

"I try not to think about it." The queen sighs as they put a mask on us.

We're quiet for a moment as they work, and we let the masks settle. Eventually, the queen speaks again. "It's just getting through one thing at a time. This is about far more than what I'd like."

"Meaning you try not to have a favorite?" I ask.

"I suppose that is part of it. I may have started out with a favorite, but with all that's happened, I couldn't begin to guess who the true princess is."

True princess is? The way she said it made it sound like she's trying to find the one authentic piece in a sea of copies. As if there is one in particular that they are looking for. It reminds me of what Zelda and I spoke about a while back. That this test feels less about finding a true princess and more finding some mythical "the one" they are measuring by some standards no one can figure out or understand.

"Well, there could be more than one girl who is a true princess," I test, "though of course only one who can pass all your tests to win."

"Right." The queen must have realized her mistake because she has to mentally shake herself. "You know what I mean." She gives me a smile that doesn't look right with the mask on, making me giggle.

The queen laughs at my amusement. "You really aren't used to this."

"I've never done this before," I admit.

"Well, we're not even to the best part." The queen smiles as they start to comb and wash the thick creams out of our hair.

Once that's done, they bring us to lie on two tables and put a kind of mud like cream across our bodies. It feels kind of messy at first, but as it settles, there's a warm sensation to it that feels wonderful.

"This was one of my favorite parts when recovering." The queen sighs after we switch from lying on our backs to our stomachs for the second half. "It just felt healing."

"We could all use that now and again." I sigh. "You're sure the king and prince don't like this?"

"They always fuss and seem grumpy when I bring them in here." The queen smiles.

"I'll have to make them both join us one day."

"I'd really enjoy that." The queen and I laugh.

Then I realize what I'd said. I was talking like I was the other girl in the family to drag them into it. I might not be, but I could be.

I flush and go quiet. The queen is simply smiling to herself; I wonder if it's at the idea of my suggestion.

We then go and rinse off the mud mask then slip into a large spa with water that's slightly brown. It smells amazing though it has an odd kind of kick to the smell. I can smell lavender, chamomile, and perhaps peppermint. It's a wonderful mix. It's not half as wonderful as the hot water feels on my body. I slip in up to my neck and rest my head back on a pillow. There are jets of water that keep a nice bubble effect that massages my whole body and makes me relax pleasantly. It's like floating on the best cloud ever. I let out a sigh as I settle into the cradling waves.

"This is the best part," the queen agrees. "Sometimes when recovering, I'd do it twice."

I giggle. "Think you should make the king do it more." After all, when he has his "lung attacks" he needs to recover too, right?

"I'd not thought of that excuse." The queen's brown eyes go wide and then she laughs. I don't think I'd ever heard her laugh like that, open and clear. "I'll try it if I ever need to."

"Who cares if they join us. This feels fine to me." I let out another sigh as I let the water hold me up. "As long as we get to enjoy it."

"I suppose so." The queen chuckles, smiling at me. She's watching me with a look like she's surprised by something, pleasantly so, but I hardly notice, just enjoying the water.

"And what we've enjoyed today isn't even all this spa can provide. I have staff preparing treatments to prepare the bride for the big day. That's when I fell in love with the spa. I hardly noticed it until then. I've been blessed with the chance to use this now and then."

"How many wedding plans do you already have?" I ask, amused. I suppose that can help her have something to be excited about in the whole thing.

"I try not to have too many. We don't know for sure when it will be. Depends on how long the tests take to whittle it down," the queen explains settling happily into the water. "But there are little things we can do, like making sure the spa is prepped." The queen smiles at me. "What did you hope to have for your wedding?"

"Oh... I don't know." With my secret marriage to Jake to unite rebellions, I'd known we'd have little resources, and it would be so much politics I'd get very little say anyway, so I'd never really thought about it. I'd grown up knowing I'd marry the son of the Loyalist rebel leader. At first I'd hated it but knew it was my duty. When we both agreed we hated it, we saw we finally agreed on something. One thing led to another, and we fell in love. But when he told me to join the Enthronement, I was shattered. He didn't love me enough to hate sending me into the enemy's arms. What a foolish girl I'd been.

"I never thought of anything I 'wanted'." I frown. "I had things I expected. Like my father to give me away, that it would be small. I guess I wanted my friends there. Call me odd, but I've never thought much about it."

"I can understand being unsure what you could even ask for." The queen's sympathetic smile is genuine. How did the queen who takes in so much from the taxes know what that feels like? "And you fear your father may not approve now?"

"I don't think he'll ever approve. I don't know if he'd give up the chance to give me away though. I'm his only child." I'm lying. Father wouldn't ever be willing to do that if I won. He's deluded himself so much he still thinks he's a Custod after losing his Custod blessing and retraining himself to fight. He'd not care enough for me to get over his delusions.

I don't want to dwell on that, so try to change the topic. "What are you hoping for?"

"Just that it all happens as it should." The queen sighs. "As long as it happens properly."

"It has been a long time."

The queen shrugs. "Perhaps it has." I should have expected that answer. She still sees her son as her little baby. He doesn't seem too old to her. Most crown royals were engaged by sixteen and married by eighteen. Gavril is much older, and that is quite rare.

"You don't think so?" I dare see if I can learn more.

"Perhaps it has been, but this must be done delicately." The queen shakes her head. "And the rebels like to remind us time is short." Like the protester the guards had shot. He sure didn't let them forget.

I frown. "Is it hard having them getting into the palace more often now?"

"It does remind me of when they first started getting onto the grounds regularly. You have to adjust. The saferooms were added after that. Well, the extra ones. The one in the throne room was made when the palace was first built. The one in the dining hall and Covere room too. The rest we added after..."

"After they reached your sister." I frown. I'd seen her sister, Princess Cyrissa, in an impression I'd used as inspiration for my own when we did the vanity test. After I'd seen what the rebels could do, I wasn't surprised.

The queen nods sadly. "We thought she might get over it, you know, but then she fell ill."

I frown. "What happened?" I thought they'd simply assassinated her, stabbed her, slit her throat, or something.

The queen looks at me with sad eyes. "They... assaulted her. She was hurt, but not that badly, but whoever attacked must have been ill or had some illness or just used filthy weapons. She died of whatever he gave her."

"I'm so sorry." It was bad enough they killed her, but they had to make her suffer so much too. Why? I thought they wanted them dead to take the throne. I can't understand why they'd want to do that. They aren't merciful in any way.

"If you can't kill them, just dethrone them. Much like a Custod, rights can be lost if the process of gaining an heir is corrupted," the queen explains.

I sit up, afraid I'm going to vomit. "They what?"

The queen smiles understandingly at me, even nodding at the nearest bin if I needed. "Forgive me. I thought you knew how she died in more detail."

"I just knew you had a sister who the rebels killed. I had no idea." I really do feel sick. Vivian comes over with some peppermint tea which helps a little.

"I think all sides have suffered far too much in this war." The queen looks down sadly. I swear I see a tear drop into the water. "Our family, the people, the rebels themselves, it's done nothing but scar and hurt everyone."

"Then why let it keep going?" I can't help but ask. Why don't they just lift the tax?

"I wish it were that simple, but today is supposed to be fun. There will be more time for this talk later if it's needed." The queen's tone reminds me of the one she uses to soothe Gavril when he's trying to help with something she feels is too big for him.

I'm insulted only a little. Actually, having her speak to me like she would one of her children is slightly comforting. It's like she's accepted me without meaning to. I'm too scared to trust that though.

"Aster was helpful after. I think that really helped draw us close. I blamed myself, as you young ones do. You start to think 'it was me they wanted'. The rebels likely didn't care. They may have even hoped that perhaps she'd have a child, and they could use that child to try to achieve their own goals. Who knows." An aching smile crosses her lips. "Much like whoever wins this will have quite the ordeal to struggle through with him."

"You can say that again," I mutter. The Enthronement has all but torn me apart.

"Even if Aster's playfulness can be annoying. I apologize again for how he teases and leers." She tries to brighten the mood with a smile. "And please forgive whatever leering he's taught Gavril to do."

"Gavril is not like his father in that regard. He's been a perfect gentleman to me," I assure the queen.

"Thank heavens. It is nice to know I don't have to pester him nearly as much about being a proper prince."

"Heaven knows you have to pester the king all day." I smile.

"It's alright in private, but he has no filter." The queen shakes her head in amusement. I could tell it was annoying, but at the same time, something she loves about him.

"He has a bit."

"He called you 'sexy' when you first met."

The queen and I laugh as the staff come over to do a manicure as we enjoy the bath and then a pedicure.

The spa day ends with the most luxurious massage I'd ever had, so warm and the oils they use smell so soothing. I wish I could name the scent. It is flowery, and yet, like peppermint or oranges. It is hard to decipher exactly what it is.

The queen thanks me for spending the afternoon with her and hopes it helped. I assure her it did, though I'm not sure I was feeling that bad beforehand.

I hardly recall dinner other than it was amazingly delicious and had me happily full as I settle into bed, watching a fresh blanket of snow start to fall out the door with the heated blanket keeping me warm. And I thought the Christmas magic ended last night.

Chapter 3

The next day is a happy blur too. We have normal rest day services which Prince Gavril runs. He seems in a good mood, though under his amber eyes are shadows darker than normal. I can't help but wonder if Joy, the red husky puppy I'd given him, has something to do with that. Other than those shadows, he looks as handsome as ever.

Normally, I'd not be so fixated on looking at him, but after my success and the lessening of my stress at Christmas, it's hard not to feel a little giddy and enjoy the eye candy. I'd not seen him since that night after all. I expect I still won't as meals are still being taken in our rooms until the workdays resume tomorrow.

I'm correct, but I still enjoy a relaxing day in my room for the rest of the day, wetting tea with my maids and chatting happily, mostly about Flur's impending wedding to one of the palace guards. The date is still unsure because he was wounded during a rebel attack, but now he's cleared for duty, Flur is trying to talk him into doing it sooner.

But this happy bubble couldn't last forever, and before I know it, my maids are helping me into my uniform for morning lessons. Though it is only the next day, it is like a trigger to my mind. It is time to return back to work.

There are still fifteen girls left in the Enthronement. And now the holiday is over, we're sure to have the tests resume in earnest. At the Christmas ball, Gavril had hinted to me they'd announce the next test soon. So I'm expecting the king to stand and give an announcement any moment.

The rest of the girls look tense too. Princess Rose, at the number one spot at the Chosen girls' table, is oddly stiff and proper, even for her. She mirrors the queen in looks though they're not related. She was the queen's favorite to win when this started. But if what the queen said is true, not anymore. I wonder if something changed.

Lilly, sitting next to me, is rubbing her cuff the way she does when anxious. I try to pull her elbow under the table to remind her to be composed. A little color flushes her pale cheeks. She brushes some of her straight black hair from her face as her dark, sloped eyes vanish as she looks down to get control of herself.

We're halfway through breakfast when the king stands. My heart clenches, ready for it. Azalea, sitting on my other side, also tenses. We aren't alone. Isla, Jonquil, and Florence all tense. Dahlia, ever competitive, doesn't show her nerves at all, but Ericka looks too bubbly, even for her. Forsythia might be the only one who looks as calm as she is, that snake-like little jerk is sure she's already won this game.

"Thank you, ladies, for your patience," he says, coughing into a handkerchief. I tense again, but this time to his cough. I'd accidently seen when the king had what I called a 'lung attack' for lack of a better term. I hadn't told a soul, but I start every time he coughs like that. (Which is really annoying because he does it a lot.)

"I hope you all enjoyed the Christmas festivities. But now it's time to set back to work as you all likely expected. And the next test is the kind you need to prepare for." The king smiles gently at the tension that sweeps the table.

"A true princess and future queen will need to handle visitors to the palace and be able to plan, prepare, and execute various events. You will be tested to prove yourself excellent hostesses, and more importantly, have the necessary diplomacy skills. Starting a week from now, we will host different delegations for summit meetings. Your teachers will break you up into groups to prepare the welcome reception, opening feast, agenda meeting, and farewell feast and party for each delegation. Each group will prepare for one of these four kingdoms: Purysia, Alalusia, Japcharia, and Dragia."

My gasp isn't the only one that sweeps around the table. Japcharia has been our rival nation since it was formed. We'd warred perhaps as much as Englaria and Spearim. And Dragia... their princess had been dismissed early on, an insult to be sure. They would have every reason to try to pick a fight. I wouldn't want to handle either delegation.

"And though you will be working in a team, you will be judged on your part, not how it all turns out as a whole," the king says reassuringly. "Anyone found trying to sabotage another lady will be judged accordingly. I hope this goes without saying, but this is about far more than the Enthronement, ladies. Please remember that and do your best for your kingdom, win or lose."

He sits back down to finish. The queen leans over and whispers something to him. Gavril's expression causes me to almost spit out my mouthful of food, fighting to restrain my laughter. I don't know what they are talking about, but it is not going Gavril's way.

I could use the laugh. This test is the most intimidating yet. It is not just failure we might face. If we do a bad job, we may bring a second war, or worse a cold war, with one of these nations. I'd never planned a feast before. I'd never planned a party before. Mother did the cast parties and fundraising events. I helped, but I'd never planned such a thing before. I'm not sure any other test could have frightened me more.

I'm not the only one. We're all filled with anxiety as we go into our lessons. Lady Keva and Lady Hydrengia, our etiquette and diplomacy teachers respectively, decide to share the time to help us better prepare for the event. The room has been rearranged so each team can sit at a table to begin preparations.

"Lady Keva will call your name, and you will come sit at the table prepared for you," Lady Hydrengia calls. She looks down at us through her spectacles. She always reminds me of an owl looking down from her tower with dark hair pulled into a high bun, large eyes, beak like mouth, and long, thin clothes all looking like a tower.

Lady Keva smiles at us soothingly. I still have trouble believing she's not the queen's sister with the same perfect dark skin and hair. Lady Keva dresses like we do for lessons: heels, stockings, knee length skirt (though hers is straight while ours are pleated), button up shirt, and waistcoat. Though she also wears a blazer, which in this winter weather is likely a blessing.

"I'll call you in order. There will be one born princess on each team who will help lead it as they should already have experience in this work," Lady Keva says. She then pulls up her list on her clipboard. My stomach knots.

"Princess Rose, Purysia." Lady Keva indicates the table up towards the front on her right, our left. Princess Rose stands up, the pinnacle of calm grace, and joins that table.

"Princess Amapola, Alalusia." Princess Amapola stands up. She looks as Spearimish as she is, pale skin, dark wavy hair, dark eyes and spicy accident and attitude. She walks up with all her elegance and confidence to join the table on Lady Keva's left, our right.

"Princess Laurina, Dragia." Lady Keva points at the far table on our right.

Princess Laurina stands up, her long red hair pulled into a braid out of her freckled face as she takes her seat with her normal bravado. She did come from the land with the most dragons.

"Princess Zelda, Japcharia."

Princess Zelda, easily one of my best friends in the Enthronement, stands up. She is the most unique of the Princesses, and not just because she's got golden blonde hair and emerald green eyes, but her ears are ever so slightly pointed. They are visible with her braid as she gets up and takes the last table on our left.

"Bella," Lady Keva calls, "Alalusia."

Bella, another one of my dear friends, gets up to join Princess Amapola. I don't know if I'd want to work under Princess Amapola, but I'd not mind being on Bella's team. She flips her dark black hair over her shoulder. I had never noticed she and Princess Amapola could be cousins. Bella has blue eyes and is not as porcelain skinned, but they're close.

"Dahlia, Japcharia."

Poor Zelda. Dahlia stands up, a slight smirk on her almond face. She's the most competitive of the girls. Her former job as a Sparkleball captain of the national team was obvious when you dealt with her competitive attitude. Her coils are pulled into a short ponytail at the crown of her head and bounces as she almost flounces to her seat.

"Jonquil, Japcharia."

Wow, Jonquil gets stuck with Dahlia too? Jonquil's caramel skin is a perfect middle for Zelda's fair skin and Dahlia's dark tones, even her less severely coiled hair is a blend between the two. Perhaps the teachers hoped that with her in the middle, her attitude would help them do well.

"Lilly, Alalusia."

Lilly stands up next to me, shaking a little as she joins Amapola and Bella. At least both of those girls are nice. That will help with Lilly's nerves. She is a sweet, anxious girl, the youngest of all of us. She'd confided in me she did not want the crown or to marry the prince, but pressure from her family had made her stay, but at Christmas, they seemed to lighten up. Now she was just trying to get her into the top ten to make sure her father didn't drive her out for failing.

"Kascia, Japcharia."

I stand, unsure if this is good or bad. I get along well with Zelda of course, and Jonquil I think of as a friend, but Dahlia? This will be interesting. I sit on Zelda's other side. Dahlia smirks at me. Zelda and Jonquil smile warmly though.

"Azalea, Dragia."

Poor Azalea stands up. A slight hint of pink flushes her beige cheeks as she joins that dreaded table. Princess Laurina pats her shoulder comfortingly. Azalea just forces a smile and tosses her brown waves from her face. Those waves often make us joke to one another that we look like sisters. Though I'm more tanned and my hair is more curls rather than waves. I notice Bella exchanges an apologetic smile with Azalea, liking wishing they were together.

"Ericka, Alalusia."

Ericka pops from her chair like a bit of popcorn. Her blonde curls bounce off her shoulders like little bubbles as she almost skips to her seat, beaming at the others. Her confidence in her ability to handle this as the mayor's daughter all but beams off her. She may seem sweet, but she thinks herself the queen of all of us already, and we all know it.

"Forsythia, Purysia."

Forsythia stands up, looking as cool and coy as ever. Her heavy-lidded eyes look down at me as she passes with the normal condescending look. She is pretty if you think a snake pretty. Her black hair is done into an elaborate twist to show off her perfectly contoured makeup against her praline tones. Her dark eyes meet the eyes of her team, friendly enough, but I know better. She's a cheating little snake.

"Isla, Dragia."

Poor Isla's large eyes grow wider as she stands. She's a sweet, shy girl: pale with dark hair and a soft voice. She is known as the most faithful and peacemaking of the girls. Perhaps they think those skills will help with the toughest delegation.

"Kamala, Dragia."

Kamala does not look intimidated at all. She leaps up from her seat, her impressive mane of hair bouncing as she struts to her table, her big islander smile on her face as she settles with her new team. We'll hear her voice all across the room.

"And Florence, Purysia."

Florence stands last of all. Her expression is hard to read as she pushes her warm brown hair from her face and joins her table. She has a hard team. Rose is strict and unyielding, and Forsythia a little snake charmer. I don't envy her, but her lawyer background may help her.

"We'll use lesson times to help you prepare," Lady Keva says, putting down her clipboard. "We'll focus on Purysia as they are coming in just a week. We will not have lessons during the delegation visits."

"In an attempt to make it fairer so you have equal class time to work on it." Lady Hydrengia explains. "And of course, we put off the harder teams for later. We hope that evens out the groups as much as possible."

"We apologize it can't be more even and easy, but real life is rarely so fair," Lady Keva tries to comfort us. "Now, we put down materials about the nations themselves on each table as well as their history with us in negotiations. We hope that helps you prepare. Let us know if you have any questions. You may set to work."

Jonquil looks at Princess Zelda like she's going to know exactly how to get started. Dahlia sighs as she watches Princess Zelda and I go over our references. Jonquil eventually joins me. "And how does this help?" Dahlia asks.

"Knowing their history helps understand their culture," I say.

"So?"

"Easier to not offend them," Zelda points out.

Jonquil frowns. "None of these notes say what they are coming here to discuss. Shouldn't we know that?"

"We're not in the policy meetings," Zelda says.

"Not ones that matter," Dahlia complains.

Zelda gives her a look. "Perhaps it's because too many voices muffle the music," she retorts.

"But sometimes don't you need to offend people to fix things?" Jonquil asks.

This is off to a great start. Dahlia is complaining about us being just pretty decorations. Jonquil is already suggesting we challenge all our relations with them, and I'm just trying to make sure I know how to keep on good terms instead of making them declare war.

"If you're princess, then you get to make those kinds of choices," Zelda says. "But not as just a girl in a competition for the prince's hand. What authority do we have to back up our words? Right now, none. No reason for us to be in those meetings. They'd not respect us now, and if you did win, it would make it hard for them to recall you have authority when the first time you spoke you didn't. It's kind of a delicate balance." Zelda raises her brows to remind Jonquil of how delicate that balance is.

Jonquil huffs but keeps reading the overview. I sigh. We're going to be in more trouble than just being failed if we do this wrong. The only two nations who might actually be offended enough to go to battle are Dragia and ours. We can't afford the "shake it up" and "it doesn't matter" attitudes. We don't want them thinking the "it" that doesn't matter is their kingdom, not that the ladies just think their part in it doesn't matter.

Lady Hydrengia comes over to give us a history overview, and I find it helpful. She explains how the high king set the Japcharian nation apart when the northern areas past Merlake were explored. So we'd never owned any part of the original kingdom, but in many wars where they tried to take control of Merlake, we won more land to try to defend it from more incoming attacks.

I try to recall everything I'd heard at the Court Christmas Dinner about the struggles of dealing with the Japcharians. They'd talked about having trouble communicating with them to arrange something. I imagine it was this. I wish I had committed more of it to memory.

Lady Keva covers their culture's etiquette when Lady Hydrengia finishes. Their etiquette is slightly more formal than ours with very strict rules about how to bow to each level of nobility. There are very little unique points on traditions we need to worry about, thankfully. Though, we are given lists of popular and traditional dishes and flowers as well as colors we may want to use in our hosting. I feel better after Lady Keva's instruction.

"So, we need to prepare the reception," Zelda goes on, writing down all the events Lady Keva told us we needed to run, "prepare the menu for the welcome and departure feasts. And then prepare the room and lead the creation of the main talking points for the following meetings the rest of their stay. I suppose four days does seem short when you look at it that way." It does seem short on paper, but forever long in planning.

"Why don't the cooks handle that?" Dahlia asks.

"Because they aren't trying to please the guests and aren't trained like we are," Zelda says. "I have had to prepare or assign someone to make sure favored dishes were ready for our guests. It's harder when they're part bird." I hold in laughter. The way Zelda said it made it sound like she was snapping at Dahlia to be grateful it wasn't harder.

"So you're saying we don't serve the right food, they declare war?" Dahlia asks sarcastically.

Zelda sighs. Jonquil nods her agreement with Dahlia though the worry in her eyes says she doesn't like agreeing with Dahlia.

"Well no," I try. "But if we don't at least try to show we want to make them comfortable and have what they'd like, they may think we don't care at all. Or, even if they don't, the fact they're dealing with foods they're not used to and don't like and are away from home may put them in a less than happy mood which might affect how they handle disagreements in a meeting. They may not declare war, but it makes your job easier."

Zelda smiles her approval. "Exactly."

"How would you feel if you were them? I'm sure you'd be annoyed that they didn't take a thought for you as their guest, and it would make you irritable. So let's avoid that," I suggest.

"Why is the reception such a big deal?" Jonquil asks.

"First impressions," Zelda says. "And it's supposed to be a small party. It helps them be happy to be here. It makes the difference between them feeling like this is a second home or a fancy glass palace where one step makes the floor crack. I don't know if I'd have agreed to stay if the reception wasn't good."

"What did they do for you?" I ask.

"It was simple. They met me at the dock, escorted me to my room while we chatted, so I could rest and settle in after a month-long trip. Then we had a nice dinner where they tried to have the foods I'd be more familiar with. It made it much easier," Zelda says. "So let's help our delegation feel the same. Most of all, if they assume we just want to crush them out of existence."

"Why would they think that?" Dahlia rolls her eyes.

"Were you not listening to Lady Keva?" Jonquil demands. "They have warred with us more than any other nation. It's a smaller version of Spearim and Englaria."

"Alright, alright." Dahlia sighs. "So where do we start?"

"I think the reception is key," Zelda says. "Then we can plan out the agenda meeting. Menus for the feasts are important, but I think that will be easy once the other two are in place."

"And so now we have to balance this and his birthday?" Jonquil mutters as she looks over her sheet.

"What?" I frown and look up.

"Didn't you know? Prince Gavril's birthday is the nineteenth," Jonquil says, thoroughly irritated.

"I suppose they plan to celebrate after," Zelda says calmly as she looks over the notes the king and queen gave us about talking points they want in the agenda meeting.

"But we have to plan this delegation and a gift, which is hard enough with it being right after Christmas, but now this is on top of it, there's no time for anything," Jonquil complains.

"I feel like he's the kind that won't mind," Dahlia says, also reviewing her papers.

"All the more reason he should have something nice," Jonquil argues.

I personally agree. I'm sure whatever his parents have done in the past is the kind of thing he'd dread. He deserves a more… well, mature birthday for once. But she has a point. With my last gift, I doubt I could top it. Not without time, and these delegations will make that hard.

"Either way, it's the life of a royal. My family has had to forgo or even skip some personal celebrations. My father has been away at battle or summits for his birthday or ours," Zelda says, still not at all bothered, eyes on her papers still.

"All the more reason to do something," Jonquil insists, looking at the others as if they're nuts. "Don't you care about him?"

"Honestly, he's a prince. It's normal." Zelda shrugs.

"And it's not like he'll be disappointed at the lack of attention," Dahlia agrees, both focused on their work.

I'm conflicted. Though I can respect Gavril may want to just forget all about it, I also feel he should be celebrated. He may not mind, but doesn't he deserve to feel special? But what if the best gift really is leaving him alone?

Why not just ask him? That would be the better option.

Now I just have to figure out how to ask for his attention without getting into trouble. The rules say we can't seek out time with him. He has to ask us.

I'll have to try to catch him after lunch. I do my best, but it's not easy. His eyes are mostly on his plate and now and then he'll glance at Sage. I can tell he wants to discuss something with him. Perhaps I should wait.

But just as I think this, Gavril looks up and sees me watching. I give him a small smile and nod at the door, hoping he'd get the hint. He does. He nods shortly, and when I'm finished, he follows me out into the hall then off to the side, so others wouldn't notice so easily.

"Why so secret? Could have just asked," Gavril teases.

"No, I can't. It's against the rules," I remind him.

"Is it?" He frowns. "I know you can't ask me out, but…"

"They said we can't seek out time with you. You can ask us but not the other way around. It wasn't just dates." I shake my head.

Gavril blinks a few times. "Oh, well, asking for a moment to talk is fine. You are asking. Perhaps I need to give you a signal to let me know we need to talk."

"Like what?" I raise a brow. "Tugging my ear?"

"No, no. That's my father's cue he's struggling and to get him out of a meeting." Gavril shakes his head.

"You're not serious?" Is he really trying to think of a signal? "I think what I just did today works fine."

"No, no. We should have something better," Gavril insists, thinking. He was looking up as he thought but then his eyes come back down to me. "Do you sign?"

"What?"

"You know." He moves his hands in an odd way as if communicating with the movements. "Sign language."

"No." I'd heard of it but never done it.

"Oh, hmm, that won't work then." He frowns, thinking. "Should learn," he mutters but doesn't look down as he thinks.

He runs through a few movements, still thinking before he nods. "How about this? You act like you're brushing your hair back like this." He puts the tips of two of his fingers together then runs it from the corner of his lips to his temple. It did look like he was brushing hair back.

"Um, sure." I still find the whole thing silly.

"You try it," Gavril says.

I sigh and do, moving into it as if I was tossing hair over my shoulder.

"Perfect!" Gavril beams, oddly delighted with himself. "But what did you want to talk about?"

"Well, this may be an odd question so soon after Christmas," I begin. "But as I know I can't top my Christmas gift, what would you like for your birthday?"

Gavril huffs. "Oh that," he says, sounding bored and annoyed at the idea.

"You really want us to ignore it?" I can't keep the disappointment from my voice.

"You really rather do something? You know it's mid-delegation."

"It's the day my delegation arrives." I nod.

"Ah, you got Japcharia, hmm. Did Lilly?" he asks.

"No, she's in the Alalusian team."

"Hmm." Gavril nods slowly. "But either way, it's far too busy."

"And I couldn't make it worth it?" I ask teasingly.

The challenge makes his eyes sparkle. "You really don't think you could top it?"

"How do I do better than a dog?"

The glitter in Gavril's eyes looks like trouble. "If I could ask anything."

"Anything." Then I immediately regret it.

"Turn back the clock, so I can see you perform. I've heard you and seen you. You're amazing. But I never got to see the full thing on stage. Show me that, and you'd top your Christmas gift. I want to see you perform in your favorite show as your favorite part."

I bite my lips. "You have any idea what it is?"

"I have a few guesses. Either *The Witches*, *Twelve Dancing Princess*, or most likely, *The Phantom*."

He listed my top three in reverse order. "You do know me."

"I hope so." Something softer enters Gavril's eyes. He clears his throat. "Anyway, if I could have anything, that's what I'd ask from you."

"Oh, just me?" I smile.

"Well, I don't think you can do a one lady show, can you?" he teases me back. Normally, I find his teasing annoying, but something about this one, this challenge actually excites me. There's a kind of electricity between the banter as we crossed each other.

"Maybe."

"Hmm, not the same." Gavril shakes his head. "But not even that magician could pull that off so soon."

"We take a month to prep a show."

"And run a delegation?" Gavril raises a brow.

"We can do anything."

"What can we do?" Damian asks, coming casually over with his brow arched and his hands clasped behind him as usual.

"Kascia asked how she could top what she gave me for Christmas, and I said she could." Gavril's tone indicates he doesn't believe it for a second. Now he's actually putting it to Damian. I'm starting to question it and wish I hadn't gotten caught up in the game. "*If* she could somehow let me see her perform her favorite show as her favorite part." The challenge to Damian in his tone is unmistakable.

I really shouldn't have started this.

Damian blinks as if he's not sure he heard that right. "Excuse me?"

I open my mouth to cover, but Gavril is having too much fun now. "I said if she wanted to top her Christmas gift for my birthday, you'd have to let me see her perform her favorite part in her favorite show." Gavril folds his arms, getting comfortable as he enjoys the challenge. Damian's face falls. "But I'm sure that's just far out of the question."

I shut my eyes. What did I just start?

Damian blinks hard and shakes his head as if he's still trying to grasp what Gavril said. "I should say so," he says indignantly then looks at Gavril hard and speaks slowly as if to make sure he understands. "You want her to star in a live performance of *The Phantom*, with little less than a month's preparation?" He frowns at the idea.

"Well, with the delegations, that might be hard, but sure, that's what I asked for. *If* you can do it." Gavril is smirking. I sigh. This was more fun as a joke between us. Of course, he wants to challenge Damian.

Damian's brow pinches together as his frown deepens. "Who do you think I am? I'm not a magician," he says, sounding aghast.

"I suppose you're not." Gavril is still smirking. I sigh and give Damian an apologetic look. I don't know why he's so set on challenging Damian right now, but he is quite happy to do so.

Damian frowns as he rights his head and folds his arms. "I know what you're doing, and it's *not* going to work."

"Alright, if you can't do it, you can't. I didn't expect you would." He smiles at Damian then looks at me. "Anything else you wanted to talk about?" I shake my head. "Other questions, Damian?" His smirk is too big.

Damian rolls his eyes. "I'm leaving." He shakes his head as he turns and walks away.

Gavril chuckles. "Good luck," he wishes me, kissing me on the cheek— the way my father pecked my mother before they went to work or the way I saw the king kiss the queen when he left a meal— then he and Sage leave.

I pause, surprised by the gesture. I touch the spot he'd kissed, trying to get over my surprise before I turn to start on my work. I have a meal to plan.

I spend the rest of my day after my workouts in my room working on the delegation preparations. I'm not sure how much time I'll have once the first delegation arrives next week.

Damian, on the other hand, is standing over the workbench, ranting to himself about how impossible Gavril's request is and listing all the things he'd have to prepare. For the first time since I've known him, his hair isn't perfect. He keeps running his hands through it, pulling it loose from his ponytail. The ribbon looks ready to fall out.

Maybe this is not the best place to work. I bite my lips, wondering what to say. "Damian, you know you don't have to do it."

"I know that." He half turns to me. "But then what else would you give him for his birthday?"

"A music box with themes from the play," I shrug. "I'll think of something. I never expected to top what I did for Christmas. Besides, I know he'd rather just ignore it."

"I'm not sure I can do that. My brother *loves* to ignore his birthday, and I never let him," Damian reasons to himself.

"Why not?" I ask.

"He hates the attention, and I love to give it." Damian smiles a little as he finally pulls the ribbon out of his hair then combs it with his fingers and ties it back again.

"Well, that's certainly Gavril's point of view." I smile a little. "I'm sure it's fine. One of us will make up for it next year. He really won't mind. He's teasing us; you know that."

"I do know that." Damian finally takes a seat. "He doesn't think I can do it. Part of me wants to prove him wrong. The other half knows I'd be mad to try."

"Sorry you got caught in our silliness." I smile a little.

"It was my fault for walking over uninvited." Damian smiles.

I sigh. "Well, it's alright. Don't worry. I'll figure it out."

"I'm sure you will." Damian smiles then sighs and stands. "I think I'm going to go for a walk," he says, picking up his cane. "Do you need anything before I leave?"

I shake my head while my mind runs through a million things Damian could do, but that feels like cheating. I need to plan this delegation. Damian tips his imaginary hat before leaving. The silence that follows allows me to take a deep breath and return to my work.

That night, I notice a note out of place at my desk. I go to put it into the proper pile and pause. It's not my handwriting.

I couldn't be prouder. Keep it up. You'll be queen in no time.

A sliver of fear makes me shudder. What are these notes? And why wasn't Damian more worried about them?

"Would you mind getting your mail, Miss?" Flur asks in a timid voice.

I turn and see Marlon the falcon is waiting patiently at the window. I smile and walk over to him, opening the balcony door, so he can fly in. He lands on my desk and caws at me.

I love this little bird. It was the way Mother and I exchanged letters without Father knowing. Marlon actually belongs to the Loyalist rebel leader, but he often used Marlon to send messages to my father. Mother found a way to charm him into sending me letters without them knowing. I had always liked the bird and because he likes me it is easy for Mother to lure him into seeing me.

I smile and take the message Marlon offers me then treat him with a few of the bugs I'd gotten for him. He nuzzles my cheek, nibbles at my ear affectionately before resting at the edge of my desk, so I can write the reply.

"Did he bring this too?" I ask, showing my maids the note.

"No miss, I was too scared to let him in," Flur admits.

"Oh," I frown and look at the note. I put it with the other note in a drawer. I'd gotten one before and not even Damian seemed to know where it came from, but he didn't seem to be worried, so I try not to be either. I sit down at my vanity to read my mother's letter as Vivian starts on my hair.

There isn't a lot to say with so little time passed since I saw her. Father is fine, up to normal trouble, but she does not know much about his exact plans. She does hint that it seems the Loyalists are not cooperating with his rebellion anymore. I hope that doesn't mean fighting. She also sends a list of plays they are debating doing for the later season and asks for my opinion.

I write a quick letter letting her know what happened at the ball after she left and about our next test, venting my worries a little before I vote on her next play and put the message back into Marlon's pouch.

I give him one more treat before he takes off out the balcony door again. Flur locks it behind him, slightly relieved.

"Afraid of birds?" I ask gently.

"No, he's just... quite a big bird," Flur says. "I never knew they were so big."

"Kerrigan will save you," Vivian teases. Flur giggles, her face brightening right away.

"That's right. It's after Christmas," I beam at her. "So, when is it?"

"If all goes well, after the last of the delegations leave." Flur is pink, but she looks happy too.

"So that's February..." I urge her on.

"First..." she squeaks.

"A workday?" I frown. "Why not the rest day before?"

"The delegations would have just left. I didn't want..."

"Want what? Vivian and Damian will be more than enough to assist me. If you want to do it on the first, I won't stop you, but don't let me make it harder either," I insist.

"We'll think about it. He should be more than well by then," Flur smiles nervously.

"Worried he'll back out?" Vivian asks.

"If he's not sure he's healed, he may. The doctor cleared him for duty, so I'm hoping after a week he'll relax about it."

"We'll have to wait and see, but if pressure from me helps, I'll tell him to hurry the vene up," I say, making us all break into giggles. I'm sure Damian is glad he's not there.

Chapter 4

After days of stressing over the delegations, I'd love nothing more than a distraction. The other girls feel the same. We sit in the Ladies' Chamber, and Bella, Lilly, and I try playing a game. The game we play isn't quite as interesting as the exchange of points on the Nippers' board.

Nippers is a black stray cat that the staff can't seem to keep out of the palace. He's oddly attached to Damian, but the girls have made it a game to try to score points on the Nippers' board that someone used to replace Dahlia's board for keeping score of how each of us is doing with the prince. Bella and Lilly in particular enjoy trying to earn points on the board and are trying to lure the cat into their laps.

At one point, Jonquil tries to see if the cat is just happy going back and forth or is actually coming when called. When Nippers doesn't move for her, rude laughter erupts from the three "elite" girls as they call themselves: Dahlia, Forsythia, and Ericka.

"You have just as many points on the Nippers' board as you did on the proper scoreboard," Dahlia mocks. "Not that good at getting the boys to like you, are you?"

Nippers' blue eyes slide open from where he's sitting on Lilly's lap and glares at them in annoyance. He must not like the noise.

"Just because someone has a good sense of humor about the board instead of being competitive brats doesn't mean you have to get snippy." I frown at them. This taunting came out of nowhere.

Jonquil frowns. I know she'd felt low on the prince's list, but that didn't mean these girls had a right to be rude.

"Or just bad taste in pets," Ericka taunts, stroking her own little rat of a dog, Cuppy. Nippers lifts his head in offense to that.

"I don't think that's what she's lacking." Forsythia smirks, and the three of them giggle.

"I think we can *all* see what you're lacking." I frown at them. "You don't want to get eliminated for being too competitive. The prince wouldn't approve."

"Like he'd trust you over us." Dahlia shakes her head.

"I think he's proven he trusts us over you." Jonquil glares back at them. "It's not like Kascia hasn't been able to prove he trusts her. She has just as much as you have."

"You mean because she won a kiss in the safe room?" Ericka huffs. "So what? We've all seen he'll do that for anyone who can excite him."

"You're so shallow when it comes to dating," Bella gripes. "How ever did you make it this far?"

"Because we know what they truly want." Forsythia rolls her eyes.

"It isn't you." Jonquil gives me a small smile, indicating she's defending me.

"And it's not you." Dahlia laughs at the idea.

"She has more of a chance than you." Gavril may not be as open about his dislike of Dahlia, but I think her competitiveness intimidates him or at least worries him.

"And you're only here because you turned him on," Dahlia accuses me.

"At least she brings more to the relationship than flattery," Jonquil pounces back.

"And you call us skanky." Ericka rolls her eyes.

"Your language proves us right," I retort.

"Ladies, please, we're trying to relax before the drama," Azalea complains. "Please, just go back to your games."

Jonquil and I do with glares at the other three as they turn back to their own bubble. Bella mutters some comments about the other girls under her breath as she resumes her turn. Nippers meows loudly in complaint at their rudeness. Lilly scratches his chin to soothe him.

The cat isn't the only one who needs it, but none of us are getting it any time soon. It's a lot of stress working out dividing up the work for the next week without the drama: making lists, working with a very frazzled staff taking directions from all of us at once, I'd *really* love a break.

It doesn't help when we all see Rose getting asked out on another date. We all suspect she gets more than the rest of us just because she's the heir to the high throne. Most of all when Gavril's nickname for her, "Swan", may sound sweet, but as Damian had explained, swans are pretty from afar but quite aggressive up close. I doubt Gavril meant only the pretty half of the name.

When Gavril uses the nickname, those who had been in the room when Damian explained have to hide snorts and giggles as they exchange glances. I'm not in the mood. I don't find it as funny as they do. I really could use that distraction right about now.

But it comes in a way I didn't expect. I come back from lunch, and Damian offers me a paper booklet I would recognize anywhere: a script.

"I'm sure you know your part already, but I'd like you to review," Damian says as he glances down at his leather-bound notebook.

My mouth opens a little, and I look up at him. "You're... serious?"

"As the plague." He glances up with a smile then his eyes roll back and meet the ceiling. "Good God, I must be mad."

"Maybe." I look down and open up the script. It is indeed the script for Miss Daae in *The Phantom*. There are notes here and there; it's not my handwriting, so it's not my old script. I stand in shock. I can't believe he's doing this. Shock and excitement battle in my chest.

"I don't believe we'll manage his actual birthday, nor the rest day after. The coordination needed with the delegations being here would simply be too horrendous." Damian shakes his head as he flips through his notebook, so it's unclear if he's talking to himself or me.

"How are you going to do this?" I ask, thinking over all I'd need to do to be ready. "How are you collecting a cast?"

Damian glances back and smiles at me. "I thought your old troupe could be of service. I've already asked your mother, and she didn't disagree."

I can hardly take that in. One last show, the one I loved most. "How are you going to put this production on that makeshift stage?" The one they made here could never handle the grand scenes needed for this production.

He smiles wider. "We're not." He turns his body to face me. "As I always say, anything worth doing is worth doing well, and the Phantom demands grandeur. So that is exactly what we're going to give it. The prince wants a performance? Then he shall have it, the way it should be seen in the Royal Theatre." His eyes sparkle at the thought.

I gape at him. "How did you get this approved?" I thought a dog was hard.

He grins in a way that reminds me of his brother. "I have my ways," he says with a cocky tilt of his head as he folds his arms.

I laugh a little. "Apparently. They really said it was alright? You'll use a big empty theater?"

"Who says it's going to be empty?" He grins again. "One night only, Lady Kascia Thorapple stars as Miss Daae in *The Phantom*," he says as he waves his hand slowly through the air as if he were painting them there, speaking them into existence.

"Why are you here again?" He clearly is more than ready to run his own theater. He could take over his namesake's theater.

Damian laughs. "To help my brother and you." He beams at me.

I shake my head. "I think you were supposed to run the theater instead of my mother." I look at the script again. I honestly can't believe it's real; I'm so stunned I can't fully feel how excited I am.

"I'm not a civilian of Purerah." He smiles then looks at me. "But before I go any further, I should ask. Are you alright with this? It is asking a lot of you."

"Of course!" I couldn't believe it was going to happen. I bite my lips. "Last I'll get if..." if this works out. Or perhaps even if it doesn't. Not like I could go home. I hug the script to my chest without realizing it. Damian's smile becomes warm and gentle as he takes me into his arms. I smile and accept it. "Be nice to actually get to say goodbye."

"I understand." Something in his eye tells me he knows exactly how I feel.

I smile a little. "I doubt I'll ever step on a stage again otherwise." I start fiddling with the corner of the script.

"Perhaps not. But should you win, perhaps you could convince the Prince of a public performance. After all, royals are not unknown for taking part in the arts. The first King Roxorim had his time on the stage." Damian smiles softly.

"This royal family hasn't touched the theater in generations," I huff.

"Perhaps it's time for a change?" Damian shrugs. "But that is for another day. For now, I am simply glad I can give you this." He bows his head a little with a smile.

I nod. "So what's the schedule?" I need to work around it. Damian runs over his idea for how we'll break up my time, telling me to not let him run me ragged as he's known to do. I assure him I won't let him push me around as I finish getting ready for lunch.

When I go down to lunch, I notice a lot of the girls are looking towards the royal table and whispering to each other, but I don't notice anything at first when I look over. It's Zelda's concerned look that helped me catch on. Sage is missing.

In his place in the corner is a larger man with dark hair and brooding eyes. He's standing back like Sage did, keeping an almost comically sharp eye out, his eyes going to every sudden movement.

"Where's Sage?" I ask Azalea.

"No idea." She frowns. "We've all been talking about it."

Had something happened to Sage? I look at the man then at Gavril. I can't see them just suddenly firing Sage. I hadn't noticed if he was there at breakfast. Had he been missing then too? With Zelda's worried look, I can't help but wonder if he'd been dismissed.

But Gavril catches me looking and just shrugs, reading my question correctly. He glances at the guard and uses our signal. I roll my eyes, making him smile. I'll make it quick. I want to review my script while I'm still excited.

Though, I am worried about what happened to Sage. Is he alright? Is he ill? It would be one impressive bug to get to him. The phrasing makes my skin go cold. There wasn't an attack, was there? He hadn't been hurt or worse defending Gavril, had he? The only group capable of that was the Custod rebellion. Gavril said they were direct and only caused the needed damage to try to reach their target. Had my father or one of his men tried something?

Gavril gets up to leave which snaps me out of my thoughts, and I hurry to follow. The large man follows Gavril as Sage did.

I don't get the chance to ask anything with the man standing over Gavril as if trying to intimidate me. He may be much taller than I, but not enough to scare me. As I walk up to them, I realize he's not as tall as he seems.

I open my mouth to ask Gavril what he wants when I spot Sage bounding down the stairs towards us.

He glares at the larger man. "Happy?"

"Yeah, you seem to have gotten proper sleep." The man nods back. "That's a good lad." Sage rolls his eyes.

Gavril frowns. "So, who's in charge here?"

"I am," Sage insists, but the large man just chuckles. Sage sighs heavily.

"You know he is right," Damian says as he approaches the group, casually twirling his cane between his fingers. "Sage is the Senior Custod in this situation. He's been here longer, and he was appointed while *you* merely assigned yourself," he says, giving the larger man a cocky smile.

The man gives Damian a look. "And whose underling are you?" He speaks to him like the Custods speak to one another, so he must be a Custod too. Wow, it's odd I think of them as other than myself so easily.

Damian grins. "Wouldn't you like to know." His smile softens a little. "I'm here with my brother, Cedrick. I'm also an attendant to one of the ladies in this competition. My name is Damian. And you are?"

"Gentian," he says, looking Damian over. "And it sounds like it's none of your business. You keep to guarding your girl. I'll keep guarding mine."

Sage holds in a laugh as Gavril gives Gentian a look. "If I were a girl, this commission would be much different."

"Sorry, Your Highness. That's not what I meant." The large man flushes. I hold in a chuckle to see such a man blush.

"I would hope not." Damian smiles. "And I'm no guard. I only offer my skills where they are needed. Though I believe your son has this situation handled without further meddling." He smiles at the man. "You should trust him to do his job."

"I'm sure he does it fine. But I'm here to help. I've seen enough worry signs to see he needs back up," Gentian says.

Son? Oh, so he's Sage's father. He's here to give Sage backup? As far as I knew, he didn't seem to need it, though I always wondered when the man slept.

"If you are the backup, that still makes him in charge." Damian smiles.

But Gentian just chuckles as if amused by Damian's comment. Maybe it is just part of their family culture.

"Think what you want, sir. But if you really want to be a help to Sage, you'll honor his rank. Though I doubt anything I say will convince you. You already think you know it all. So Sage, I wish you luck." Damian nods to him.

Sage sighs. "Thanks." Then he looks at his father. "Just... make sure you trade off tonight on time. Do whatever else you like." He does not sound like he wants his father's help.

"Indeed, I will." Gentian's tone said it is because he wants to and has nothing to do with Sage's order. Sage sighs again as his father leaves.

"Pleasant fellow, isn't he?" Damian watches the man leave.

"He can be if he wants to," Sage says.

"How was he ever an assassin?" Gavril wonders.

"Oh, he wasn't. My mother was. He married in," Sage says casually as he and the Prince start off. Gavril pauses then starts to laugh to himself.

Damian chuckles. "Well, Cedrick is bound to have plenty of fun with him."

I laugh at the idea, drawing the others' attention.

Damian smiles at me. "Seems I'm not the only one who thinks so."

Gavril smiles at me too. Sage sighs tiredly. "That will be lovely," he says and nods at the Prince to remind him where they should be.

Gavril frowns and gives me an apologetic look. "Sorry. I'll catch you later?"

I nod, nervous about what it was all about. Maybe he is just getting over himself to ask me out. I'll hold to that, so I don't get too anxious.

"Well, as fun as that was, I have something I need to attend to. I'll be in your room later if you need me, my lady." Damian bows his head to me.

I bow my head back. "Don't worry; I'll be working on it," I tease.

He chuckles. "I'm glad you're excited. I'll see you this evening."

I nod back and turn to head up to my room to collect my script. I'm rudely interrupted along the way.

Gentian steps from the side and blocks my path. I frown. It's like he is trying to copy what his son did, but badly. It's more like the troll emerging from the toll bridge to demand his payment than an assassin from the shadows.

"So, you're Lady Kascia." He looks me over. I don't like how his eyes linger at my chest and legs, though the dress Damian has me in today is not really tight-fitting. I presume he's looking to see if I'm hiding a weapon.

I snap to get his attention away from my chest. "You better not let the Prince catch you doing that," I say.

"I suppose he would have spotted the weapon if you did keep it there," Gentian admits and starts to circle me.

That makes an angry spark go off in my chest. "You think so little of him?"

"No, I think so little of you and how you've bewitched him. My son is sure you're the source of the danger here. He can't prove it. But I will." Gentian gives me a glare.

"What makes you think Sage is right?" I demand.

"Because he's the best for a reason. They never should have sent him here. You're driving them both mad." Gentian glares at me with deeper animosity. "And I won't stand around and let you. You're up to something, and I will find it."

I shake my head. "I'm not afraid of you." I can tell he's trying to create the spooky vibe his son does. He's not very good at it.

"You're snippier than the others," Gentian comments, still circling. I do my best to keep my eyes on him.

"I doubt Ericka was as patient," I reply. I also doubt he's had time to talk to the others. He's targeted me. Why do Custods target me? I thought it would be bad if they knew I was a Custod. If they find out who my father is, a disinherited Custod, it will be even worse.

"Something about you is wrong. They never should have let you stay after what happened at the Harvest Ball." Gentian steps close to me, too close. He must know about how I was found armed defending the royal family that night. Though some doubt remains whether I was really defending them. Truth was, I'd been desperate to keep my father or his men from hurting them.

I back away from Gentian, not wanting to let him tower over me, but he keeps moving closer until he backs me into the wall. I wince as he studies me carefully. "I have my eye on you," he threatens me.

I stand to my fullest — though not very tall — height and shove him off me. Thankfully, my action surprises him enough that I am able to. "Watch all you want. I have nothing to hide," I state firmly.

I glare at him and turn to go. But he's still close enough, he cuts me off.

I take a cue from one of our plays and jam my heel into his foot with a sharp stomp. The yelp of pain is quite satisfying as I march away, thankful for my lovely heels that make my determined march all the more powerful.

I march right to my room and shut the door behind me, fuming in frustration. I'm not only tired of all these people targeting me, but angry at my father's lies for putting me in this position.

Vivian notices I'm in a bit of a mood. "Anything wrong, my lady?"

"I don't appreciate the Prince's new second guard accusing me and very rudely trying to detain me," I say, still trying to keep my temper. "I mean, who does he think he is? He thinks he can just waltz in here and know better than his son? That he can walk in and just get me to confess something I didn't even do?"

I don't know why this makes me so angry. I don't normally vent out anger like this to anyone but my mother and best friend. And even then, I try to keep it in, but I'm so fed up and I know I can trust my maids, so it just comes out. "I have more important things to do."

"What did you do?" Flur frowns.

"What? Oh, I just stepped on his foot to make him to move, and then I left," I say as more of a throw off.

"You stepped on a Custod's foot when they tried to detain you?" Flur looks terrified.

"Oh please, what is he going to do? The king and queen don't listen to Sage, let alone his puppet father." I wave her off, pacing a bit in my agitation. "And he has nothing. I've done nothing wrong. And I'm tired of everyone acting like I did: Sage, Gentius or whatever his name is, the cursed rebels, all of them. I didn't do anything wrong." Though I feel like I'm telling myself that as much as them.

Vivian is smiling at me as I pace the room. Flur looks nervous. "What?" I finally ask as they keep watching me pace.

"You stomped on a Custod's foot," Flur says.

"And?"

"And you're not even phased." Flur frowns.

But Vivian smiles. "You'll be the queen in no time, milady."

I flush. I suppose if I look back, I was pretty snippy with the guard. I don't know if I'd have dared stomp on his foot a few months ago. My change of attitude around Christmas did more to help my confidence than I realized.

"Well, I have rehearsals to get to if you ladies don't mind," I say, changing the topic.

My maids help me change into my gear, and I plan on being in the dance hall as long as the other girls don't complain. I stay in my dance gear as I'm used to rehearsing in that, and once I'm warmed up, I read through the script and do the blocking as I remember it and as is written in the notes. I mostly am just trying to awaken my memory of it today.

Diving back into this world I'd known and loved so well relieves so much stress! This is my favorite show for a reason: the music, the dance, the mysterious and romantic nature of the odd love triangle, and something about Christine feels familiar to me, like she's a part of me I love to unlock and live in from time to time.

It puts me in a much better mood when I'm finished and change into my day dress to work on the menu preparations for the delegation.

I asked Damian for help learning what wines were good, but to my shock, the lord of elegance doesn't drink but assures me he'll find someone who can help him find what we need.

He even comes into my room that evening with a crate of wines in his hands and explains how I can taste them without drinking it. But rather than feel better, I feel guilty at not having the courage to tell him what I'd learned.

Damian notices my mood. "What's the matter? I thought you'd be relieved you'd not have to drink it."

"Yes, that is helpful," I say, unsure how to bring it up. "It's just... that may not be as big of a problem as I thought." I feel the heat rise to my face.

Instead of his face pinching in confusion like I thought it would, Damian relaxes. "Your mother told you, didn't she?"

I blink and look at him. "What?" How did he know?

He gives me a weak smile. "She told you about your father and the ultimatum the Custod Council gave him?"

My mouth hangs open a little then I bow my head in shame and nod.

"I am truly sorry, Kascia," Damian says sorrowfully as he tries to meet my eyes.

I can't meet his though. "It's alright." Even though it means all I've done with my life has been a good-for-nothing lie. I'd wasted everything for a duty I didn't have and one I'd never wanted.

Damian pulls me in his arms. "No, it isn't. Nothing is right about what he did to you."

"No, but I'll figure it out."

"Yes, I'm sure you will, but that doesn't mean it doesn't hurt. If it were me, I'd be furious."

I scowl. "That isn't too far from true." Angry, sad, hurt, it's so much to take in.

Damian holds me a little tighter to comfort me. "Let it out if you need to."

I force myself not to push him away. "Not sure it's something I can just let out." It's not exactly like one moment will heal a broken lifetime.

"I understand. Just know I am here," he says as he lets me go, "should you need me."

I smile weakly. "I know." I sigh. He deserves more, but I don't know what more there is. "It's just all been a lie. It's hard to take in."

Damian nods. "To be fair, I didn't know either. Not at first, though I had my suspicions."

"I have a feeling everyone who knew anything did," I say bitterly. Jake is too dumb, as blind as I was. But everyone else must have known.

"No." Damian shakes his head. "Custods don't like to talk about it, so they don't spread it around. I'm sure other people choose not to think about it. Or like your father, they believe he is right."

"But anyone who knows about what I thought I was and what's going on knows it was all a lie. I'm the only one too trusting, stupid and blind," I say. "I didn't have to come here... be in that one stupid raid. Any of it." None of it was up to me. But I'd made it so, and I can't escape it. My life has been for nothing.

"But would you be better for it?" Damian asks. "Would Gavril? Kascia, he has said time and time again, that no one else talks to him about the world outside these walls. You are the only one who is willing to discuss with him a world he has been forbidden to see. And you are the only person to see him as an equal that his parents will actually listen to. The king certainly took your discussion with him about his son to heart. The progress may be slow with everything else going on, but it is there. And you are the one who opened the king's eyes to his son, no one else. Perhaps how you got here was not favorable, and my heart bleeds for you. But I fully believe that you are here for a reason, regardless of what anyone else thinks."

"Even if I'm nothing but a lie to them and myself." What I came here for was a double lie. I am not even a Custod, so my stupid rebellion is not getting them what they want anyway.

"You are not a lie, not to me," Damian says firmly. "They say that The Father works in mysterious ways, and perhaps you aren't what you thought yourself to be, but that doesn't make you of any less worth. You are a beautiful, talented, brilliant young woman with a fiery spirit and a heart and mind that is open and willing to see the truth that others have shunned. Your father blinded you to it, but that does not make you a lie. Kascia, I look at you, and I see a world of possibilities. You are a hope to this people. Proof that people can change once they learn the truth enough to stop fighting and unite with those who were once their enemies. You asked me once who I would choose to lead this people. Well... I would choose you."

I meet his eyes; unsure I dare believe it. "Really?" Or does he just not want me to feel worthless?

"With all my being," he says firmly. "I would want no one else." There is a serenity in his eyes that is impossible to deny.

I bite my lips and look down. "What have I done to prove I could do this?" Other than get Damian to trust me.

"You listened. You listened to the people and wanted to help. You listened to Lilly and sought to comfort and protect her. You listened to Gavril and understood his pain then showed him his own worth. A leader is nothing if they do not listen to their people as well as their friends. And people listen when they know that their complaints are heard and understood."

"How does that help when I'm still not able to do what they ask? I'm not even what the people who sent me here think I am. I came here to kill the royal family. What am I supposed to do?" I look down. "I really have been nothing but an actress playing a role even when I thought I was me."

"I am truly sorry you think that way because that couldn't be further from the truth." He sighs. "Kascia, people, in the general sense, don't fight against the government and join a rebellion because they hate royalty. They do it because they don't like their current situation, and they believe a change of power will get them the results they want. But the fighting has lessened at the capital and other surrounding areas since the Enthronement started. Do you know why?"

"Distraction." It's what they've all been saying. But I also recall Fabian had a different thought but I am not brave enough to guess Fabian is right. Distraction seems more likely.

"No." Damian shakes his head. "It's because like Fabian, they can see history being made. You remember in the story of the chocolate factory that when the news broke out that the factory would be opened to five lucky winners, everyone got excited about it? Even people who didn't like chocolate started buying chocolate bars."

I nod. I recall the play.

"Well, it's because they wanted to feel included. And that is what the Enthronement has done. In a similar manner to the candy maker, the royal family opened their home to the people and invited them in. Every young maiden rushed to be included in the biggest event in recent history. And again, when they started doing the polls, people went to put in their opinion, and for the first time in five hundred years, people started to feel like the royals cared about what they had to say. I know this whole thing has been a nightmare for you, Gavril, and the other contestants, but it has been a blessing for the people. It's the hope that change is coming. And getting some to realize that maybe they don't have to fight to get it."

I wish I could see what he sees. That sounds true, and I trust him, but I am still unsure I can help with that much at all. "I have nowhere else to go, and I want to win. I want to be that person. I just can't believe it would be the best thing."

"I know, and with all the doubt and fear that has filled your life, I can't fault you for that. Frankly, I believe that is something you and Gavril have in common. Sometimes, I feel as though the Merlin himself could show up and tell him he is going to end this war, and he wouldn't believe it," Damian says in a half jest.

I laugh at the idea. "He has more faith than me," I jest back.

"Perhaps." Damian smiles. "But do you see my point? Your father's lies and your past don't devalue your worth. Your worth is infinitely more than all of that. It took me a long time to learn that," he says with a sympathetic smile.

"It just makes me wonder what my place is," I admit.

"Well, perhaps we'll figure it out together." He gives me another smile.

I sigh. "I hope so." I look at the crate. "Though not being able to drink is no longer a problem." My stomach knots.

"True." Damian nods and looks at the crate as well. "But I've heard it's quite enjoyable. At least, my brother-in-law seemed to think so."

"I hope he's right." My face falls a little. "I'm... not sure I'm ready for this." Then again, it is expected for a royal to drink, right?

"Well, lucky, we don't have to go there yet if you don't want to as this is wine tasting, not wine drinking," he assures me with a smile.

I nod, ready to get this over with.

But I'm surprised. It's quite fun. Oh no, I like the taste. I'm not sure that's a good sign. I do not drink any, but I love all the varieties in the wines: white and red, different styles and years. It's like a game.

My maids come in and enjoy watching, though Vivian points out the delegations will likely try to get me drunk to loosen my tongue. "You may want to know your limit."

With a wince of sympathy, Damian agrees. I nod and decide I might as well get that over with as well. Damian puts himself in charge of watching my intake and tries to instigate small talk by asking how my other preparations for my delegation are going.

I'm able to hold more than I expect, but I'm giggly and uncoordinated by the time Damian feels confident I'm drunk enough to call the experiment done, most of all, when I go from giggles to tears in about five seconds flat. I think it took a whole bottle.

That night, I struggle to sleep through an odd headache. Damian asks his brother for something to help, and Cedrick comes into my room to give me some kind of sweet liquid and see how else he can help.

"Should have brought your violin," Cedrick teases Damian. Damian chuckles and offers to get it. "Works on me." Cedrick shrugs.

"Alright, but don't you fall asleep," Damian teases back and moves to leave.

"Fine, I won't," Cedrick play complains. While Damian is gone he keeps me busy with small talk about the show before his brother returns.

Damian puts the instrument under his chin and starts to play a soft lullaby tune. One I know. It's the one my parents used to hum all the time. It sounds so good on the violin. Cedrick is sleepy before I am, but I'm just about ready to drop off when Damian finishes.

"See? I'm up." Cedrick yawns then fake falls asleep as if he's going to fall onto Damian.

I giggle tiredly and yawn and shut my eyes. "Thanks for that, brother." Damian rolls his eyes as he pushes him off then looks at me with concern. That's the last thing I remember before falling asleep.

Chapter 5

Damian is kind enough to let me rest before we do our first script reading. I was worried about being late, but even with letting me sleep in to get rid of the drink in my system, I'm not last to show up. Cedrick is.

Damian smiles at me as I come into the practice room. He asks how I slept and feel now, but I can hear a slight undertone of irritation as he pulls out his gold watch and checks the time then sighs and throws the door an irritated look.

"Well, is it going to just be the three of us?" I ask.

He turns back to me with a gentle smile and nods. "I have laid out instructions for your mother, and your troupe will be rehearsing with stand ins for now. Once it is closer to the performance, we will join them each day to rehearse. I have already cleared it with the king and queen, and you will be excused from lessons starting two lessons prior." Then he glances up to the ceiling and starts speaking to himself. "Though I suppose with the delegations, you'll only be missing one week of lessons."

"Makes sense." I nod. "You really are good at everything."

He gives me an amused smile. "Not nearly, but I thank you for the compliment."

"You're somehow making this work?" I raise a brow. "I think that proves my point."

"True, but I still go to Jashon to make your pointe shoes." He smiles, holding up a finger.

I chuckle. "Well, I suppose that is a unique branch of cobbler work," I admit.

That's when the door opens and Cedrick finally joins us, his anxiously charming smile in place. "We ready?' he asks, his electric blue eyes alight with energy.

"You're late." Damian gives his brother a dirty look.

"What? We have a fluid schedule today," Cedrick excuses, running his fingers through his dark hair before joining us in his seat.

"That doesn't excuse tardiness to a rehearsal. But come on. Let's not waste time," Damian says, handing Cedrick his script as he crosses one leg over the other.

Cedrick accepts it. "No piano?" He raises a brow at his brother. "We're going to just... acapella today?"

"It's only a read through, Cedrick," Damian says, glancing at him over his script held neatly on his lap.

"But... the whole thing is pretty much singing," Cedrick points out.

Damian sighs then looks at me. "Do you mind? I know you haven't had a chance to warm up today."

"No, I don't mind." I chuckle.

"We can warm-up if you're that scared." Cedrick teases his brother. Damian rolls his eyes then whaps his brother over the head with his script.

I giggle as Cedrick almost ignores the action. "Hm... guess no fears then. Just pride." And he uses his own script to mess up Damian's ponytail.

"Cedrick C-" Damian lets out a frustrated sigh. "Curse you." He takes out the ribbon, combs his hair with his fingers then ties it back again. Then he stands, giving Cedrick another look. "Behave."

"Fine. So do you have a music player or just memory today?" Cedrick smiles smartly.

"There's a piano in the corner, you twit." Damian hits him over the head again then moves to pull the piano out so we can use it. Cedrick helps move our seats over to make it easier.

"Are you going to read off the sheet music?" I ask, wondering how Damian would read and play at once.

"I'll manage." He smiles at me then pulls out the sheet music and sets it and his script on the piano. He takes a seat on the piano bench then turns to me. "As your part isn't in the first scene would you rather skip it, or have Cedrick read his lines?"

"His lines?" I realized I don't know his part.

"Oh, I suppose I didn't tell you." Damian frowns. "But he'll be playing Raul."

"Oh..." That seemed fitting. He had done amazingly at playing Bob Cratchit in the Christmas Carol. I can see him doing well at this too. "Well, do you want to?" I ask Cedrick.

He waves it off. "I can work on it later."

"Very well. Then we skip to your opening number," Damian says as he flips a few pages.

"Okay." I nod, clearing my throat to get ready, smiling a little. It was like going home to be back at this work. Damian smiles gently and nods then starts playing the music for me to sing to.

I follow the music, reminding myself of the part as I go, mentally coming back into this world. Cedrick sounds even more sure than me at his short piece.

Damian finishes his play with my last note, and we move into the dialogue. He reads through the other character's lines, but it is rather quick and monotone.

Cedrick on the other hand, plays his assigned side parts way over the top. I figured it is just his energy level, but when he starts singing the other parts, most of all Meg, in a hilarious falsetto I can't stop giggling.

Even Damian has to stop for a bit to control his laughter. "Cedrick, really?" He gives him a disbelieving look.

"What? It helps," Cedrick insists.

Damian chuckles. "Alright." And he lets him have that one.

I still find it hard not to giggle as we go through it. "What if we get mixed up on your real lines or your filler lines?" Cedrick teases Damian. "With all the notes and stuff later."

"Damian's part?" I thought he'd just direct.

Damian smiles slightly and nods humbly. "But we'll get to that in a moment. If Cedrick can drop the falsetto long enough to let us get through this scene."

"I'm helping," Cedrick insists.

"Not when she's laughing too hard to sing." Damian tilts his head and arches his brow.

Cedrick laughs. "But it helps."

Damian rolls his eyes. "Cedrick. No."

"Giggles good," Cedrick insists with a mischievous grin.

"Did you have coffee this morning?" Damian arches a brow.

"You don't let me drink coffee," Cedrick points out.

"Because you go berserk every time you've tried it."

"So what do you think the answer is?" Cedrick grins. I laugh, watching them. They really are siblings.

Damian lets out a verbal sigh and shakes his head. "I'm not playing this game with you."

"So did he have coffee?" I ask, honestly curious.

"If he did, he snuck it behind my back. But I don't know why you would because as far as I recall, you hated the flavor." He looks at Cedrick.

"Yeah, prince and I can't stand the stuff." Cedrick smiles. "I prefer chocolate."

The doors open and Flur comes in with a fresh tea tray for Damian I'm sure. He loves tea.

"Oh, thank heavens." Damian smiles at her. "You are a blessing."

Cedrick sticks out his tongue. He is surely Damian's brother, but they also are opposites in so many ways. Cedrick does not like tea. If I recall right, he calls it "leaf juice".

Damian takes the tea from Flur and takes a sip. Immediately, he starts to relax as he closes his eyes and breathes in the steam.

"And that's how you get his guard down for the attack. Carlos did that once," Cedrick play whispers to me.

Damian gives his brother a side eye then smiles at Flur. "Thank you. Though, I have one more favor to ask."

"Of course." She smiles.

"Do you think you could sing this part?" He points to the lines Cedrick had been reading.

"Oh." Her cheeks go pink. "Sure."

"It's just for the rehearsal so we can get through this scene," Damian says.

"I understood." She smiles. "I couldn't go on stage."

"She'd make a good phantom," Cedrick jokes.

Flur gives him a look in perfect sync with Damian.

"Why are you such a nuance today? Do you need tea?" Damian half jokes.

"No. It's fun." Cedrick play pouts in a baby voice.

"Well, I'm putting your fun on a timeout," Damian says firmly.

"Oh-row," Cedrick says, copying how Joy says it.

Damian rubs his face then takes a breath and looks to Flur and me. "We'll start from the top of the song," he says as he puts his tea down and rests his hands lightly on the keys of the piano.

"Okay." Flur sounds nervous. I smile to assure her it would be fine. It was for practice. Damian gives us a little intro then nods to Flur. She is quiet in her shyness, but she doesn't do badly. I smile reassuringly once more when I get into my part. I think at that point Flur starts to enjoy it. Our short duet is lovely, and we manage to get through the scene without trouble.

"Thank you, Flur." Damian nods his head to her once we finish. "Really, you were wonderful; you have quite a lovely voice."

"Thanks." Flur really turns pink.

"Stunning, you're hired," Cedrick jokes. Flur laughs.

Damian chuckles. "I would, but I wouldn't want to deny Kascia the chance to act on stage with her best friend one more time." He smiles at me.

"Fair enough. She can have your role." Cedrick taunts Damian. I sigh and roll my eyes as Flur giggles.

Damian copies me then turns to Flur again. "Though, if you don't mind, it would help to have a female stand in for the side roles. We could even invite Miss Vivian to join in, and the two of you can alternate roles if you like."

"If you'd like, I can see if she's free," Flur agrees.

"Would you, please? That would be most helpful." Damian smiles at her. "Then maybe we can actually accomplish something today." He gives his brother a side eye.

"We've done great work today," Cedrick insists.

"We're not even a fourth way through the read-through of the play. We have a month, Cedrick," Damian stresses.

"It's a long show," Cedrick defends as Flur leaves to get Vivian.

"Which is why we have to get through the read-through today," Damian says. "Or at least act one."

"I think you can share." I smile at Cedrick who pouts and complains in the baby voice again.

"Perhaps. But shall we get into the next scene as we wait for Flur to come back?" Damian asks as he flips the page.

"Yes. Let's focus." I give Cedrick a look. He pouts once more, but corporates.

"Cedrick, this is your scene," Damian says, putting his hands to the piano again.

Cedrick nods and goes into it, finally behaving professionally. He's fun to go back and forth with for sure. But as the last line is read, Damian stands up from the piano. I look up in surprise at his reaction.

Cedrick gets up too and swaps places. Cedrick plays the piano?

Suddenly, Damian comes in strong with the Phantom's line. His tone is indignant and annoyed as he mocks Christine's lover. He's not gotten into any characters like this. Is he playing the phantom? It would explain the jokes Cedrick was making.

Honestly, the idea of seeing him as the mentor who taught me music is so natural it's not hard to roll right into the performance of the scene. The only real distraction is Cedrick's little smirks as he plays the piano.

Damian becomes soft in his next lines as he assures Christine. He does not sit down. Instead, he remains standing though distant. His hands and arms gesture to me as if to compelling me to follow his command. I can't repress the smile as I play along with the same amount of energy. It's exhilarating. I notice Damian fighting a smile as he steps away, gesturing in a fluid movement for me to follow. His voice is rhythmic and hypnotic as he sings the Phantom's words.

He's perfect at the role. I'd never seen better. This show was sure to be unique and spectacular. He then comes to me and offers to help me out of my chair. I follow along, letting it go past a read through to a mini blocking session.

He leads me at first by the hand, but his grip loosens and gets lighter as we play out the title song. Soon, he's guiding me with nothing more than by the touch on the tip of my fingers, until it is only the entrancing wave of his hand that beckons me to follow him down into the depths of our fictional opera house.

I follow the lead, performing the piece as deeply as I ever had on stage. Damian certainly seems to be having fun as we finish out the song.

That's when Flur and Vivian arrive to help us go through the rest. They may have watched part of it, but I'm not sure as I was enjoying the moment.

When Damian notices them in the room, he becomes flustered and clears his throat saying, "we'll skip the next song because we have to pick up the pace."

I don't mind, as it's his solo anyway, and we try to get through more of the run though. We read through the next scene and song to make sure Cedrick has his lines. Damian skips the play-within-a-play as he is the only one of us that has lines there, which means the romantic song was next.

Which I'll admit Cedrick might actually be too good at, but the fact I find his charms annoying helps me not get too swept into it. He really does have an impressive voice.

The rest is smooth sailing as I've done the show many times, and I'm beginning to think Damian may have as well. The brothers do enjoy their back and forth quite a bit for someone who'd never done it before.

To Damian's relief, we manage to get through the whole show today. Damian makes plans for the rest of our rehearsals to start on the next work day in the afternoons. He assures me, they will try not to go as long as today because I will need plenty of time for my group meetings and planning for my delegation.

I smile, trusting him and thank him for the work we'd done so far. Cedrick insists Flur should be the phantom still just to bother Damian as we pack up. I'm surprised Damian doesn't tackle him or something. He does at least whap him again on the head.

I giggle at them both. I wonder how many brain cells Cedrick will have left with how often Damian is going to have to thwack him over the head during this performance.

Chapter 6

The tension leading up to the delegations' arrival isn't just felt by the Chosen girls. I notice the king and queen are more agitated in their conversations at meals. The Grand Duke will often be waiting outside the dining hall for them to get right to work.

It makes me anxious every time I see him. I can't really explain why, but the Grand Duke creeps me out. Perhaps it's just how he pretended to be the prince at the welcome ball (not that he said he was the prince, but he led the girls to think he was), how he seemed so keen on me — giving me advice on winning — or perhaps too many plays have bad court advisors, but regardless, the man makes me nervous.

Perhaps he's the reason things are still so bad. Though I'm confident the royal family wants to stop the war, the over taxation hasn't ceased. And if the royal family isn't so bad, then how did this all start? Why had the royals set such a high tax that sent their people into revolt five hundred years ago? And more daunting to answer, was the prophecy my father warned me of true? At the Harvest, my father said the Merlin prophesied if the prince married, the kingdom would fall. I'd not found any record of it yet, but I certainly keep trying. I need that proof.

I have spent a lot of time in the royal library trying to find answers to these questions. So, when I have to be in the library learning more about my delegation, it's just second nature. The only real struggle is not trying to find answers about that past, most of all because the wars on and off with Japcharia may play a role in the high tax.

I'd never thought of that possibility, not until I noticed the last official war with Japcharia was only twenty years before the civil war started. Perhaps some fall out from that war or an attempt to retaliate had caused the tax spike? Might that be part of why they want to meet with the nation now?

These lines of thought distract me from the studying I should be doing and lead me down different path. I wonder how the rebels' fighting up north affects Japcharia. Japcharia is on our northern border. Perhaps there was a connection there.

I get up to check what reports I could find on more recent battles in the archives (which I learned is updated once a month). Sadly, the reports in the newspapers aren't much, but I know an insider.

Fabian, the point reporter for the local paper, had been reporting in-person about the war up north. Perhaps I could catch him and ask him about it. I had managed to form a kind of friendship with him because he enjoys interviewing me so much and because we were once stuck in a safe room during an attack.

During that time, he mentioned he often used his brother's office in the palace as his brother so rarely did. His brother is a count in the royal court. Perhaps if Fabian is working there today, I could ask him.

I don't know which office would be the one he uses, but I imagine the doors note which member of the court works where. I know where the offices are because Fabian had mentioned the safe room we'd gone into was near that area.

I put away the books I'd been using. The other girls are too engrossed in their own studies to notice me leaving. I hug myself against the cold hallway. The snow outside hasn't increased since Christmas, but it is plenty cold anyway and the lack of cloud cover doesn't help.

I reach the correct floor and wing, passing the wall that I know hides the safe room. I look at the doors. Sure enough, they are marked with the title and position of their corresponding courtier. However, finding the regional representative of Rosepla is harder than I thought it would be.

In fact, I get completely turned around. I never realized this part of the palace was so large. I end up wandering deeper into the mess of court offices, some doors without any markings at all. I end up checking the whole second floor before I find a staircase I've never seen before. It leads me to a section of the first floor, also unfamiliar to me, but decorated in the same style as the floor above.

By now, I just want to get unlost. I thought I knew the palace well. Now I'm questioning the whole layout of the palace. Perhaps if I'd seen the outside enough, I'd know where I am, but I'd not really gotten a good look at the palace's overall shape since my first day here.

I spot a door more decorated than the others. I presume that means it's a main room of some kind I'll recognize. I find myself in a vaguely familiar hallway. The hallways stretch left and right from me with another door straight ahead of me. There are many doors on either side with a sharp turn on my right where the hall continues.

I step into the hall and close the door behind me, looking left and right to decide which way to go. Deciding I'd rather not have more doors to confuse me, I go right.

Something comes over me, compelling me to try the door on my left. I hesitate and try to open it, but it's locked. The feeling reminds me of my nightmare where I was searching the palace for some unknown something.

I yank my hand away and take the sharp left turn. There's a set of double doors on the right-hand side, but no other doors in sight. The double doors are locked.

The walls are decorated with paintings or impressions of past kings, queens, and courtiers of various merits. There's also a chart of everyone in the court — their elected position and their assigned committees. I retrace my steps to pass through the other door, and I find another long hall with a door on right hand side, likely parallel to the hallway I'd just stood in, but this time I notice three doors on the left evenly spaced across the hall.

I try the first door I come to on the left, but it's locked too. Just as I'm about to pull my hand away to give up, the door next to it opens, and a very disgruntled looking Gavril steps out with Sage behind him.

"What's the point of having me in there if they don't care about a word I have to say?" Gavril is complaining as Sage closes the door behind him. "Could just tell me over a meal they don't need me there as normal."

"I had rather hoped it meant they had assignments for you." Sage frowns in disappointment. I'd never heard him speak so warmly or casually.

"It looks like it will be down to us." Gavril shakes his head. "You know I'm right."

"Of course, I do. And they are going to regret that later, but by the time they realize it, it will be too late." Sage looks deeply annoyed. He looks more human in his expression than I'd ever seen. "Either way, I am going around her. Your office *will* be ready before they arrive. You are going to need it no matter what they say."

"My suite has worked until now. I see no reason not to keep using it." Gavril shakes his head. In the movement, he must have caught a glimpse of me because he pauses and turns to look at me.

I'd been frozen in place, half hoping he'd turn the other way and not see me at all. My cheeks flush pink as he spots me, my hand still on the doorknob.

"Kascia, what are you doing in here?" Gavril asks in a tone of pleasant surprise. Sage on the other hand had gone dark and cold again, glaring at me, clearly more tense. I never realized how tense he is around me until I saw him relaxed with Gavril.

"I got lost," I confess, my hand still on the door.

"Not trying to break into the prince's office?" Gavril smiles rather playfully.

I quickly pull my hand away from the door, turning red. "Oh grace, is that what that is?"

"Yes, have you been trying to find an unlocked door?" Gavril is still smiling as if it's hilarious. "How did you get lost in the royals' offices?"

I swallow. "Honestly?" I glance at Sage. "I was trying to find Earl Fabian. I wanted to ask him a question about an old article of his, and he told me he used his brother's office when his brother isn't there, so I thought I'd see if he was in today. And... well, I didn't know the court offices were so complicated."

"Well, you could see the change of color on this little sign to know if it's being used," Gavril teases. "Let alone smell."

"Smell?" I frown. This hall smelled fresher than that of the court floor sure, but it didn't seem that different. Though he was right about the color. The court floors were decorated a little differently, with less color and darker wood.

"I find the court area smells mustier than these rooms. Like a moist gym while this section is like opening the window to a cool sea breeze." Gavril shakes his head in amusement. I laugh.

The door Sage and Gavril had come from opens. Sage's dark expression stays the same, though perhaps he glares a bit more at the group of people leaving. Gavril keeps his expression neutral and proper, but that tells me he's not willing to show his emotion to these people.

They're all various members of court. I spot Duke Quincy, and his wife, Duchess Catherine who I'd sat with during the Court Christmas Dinner. The rest I'd been introduced to in the reception line at the Christmas Dinner, but it's hard to recall who they are and what positions they hold. I'm pretty sure all are in committees or groups the king assembles. The duke and duchess oversee state affairs.

They mostly ignore Gavril, though a few bow their heads to him or nod a friendly hello, Duchess Catherine among them. None spot me thankfully.

I hear the Grand Duke's voice and the king's replying before the door finally shuts behind everyone.

I immediately notice Gavril's scowl. Sage looks quite displeased too, but I don't think he's willing to voice it with me there. I am afraid to ask, but at the same time, I honestly want to know. "Gavril, why did you leave earlier than the others?"

"I wasn't needed," Gavril says bitterly. "Then why invite me?" he mutters under his breath.

Sage is looking down the hall the opposite way from me as if longing to attack someone there. I assume the Grand Duke as I don't think he has a problem with the king or queen.

My heart sinks. I have full faith Gavril is beyond prepared to help with royal affairs, helping to rule and handle the troubles of state, but his parents still see him as only a child. I'd even pleaded with the king to give his son a chance, but I suppose the word of one girl assumed to be love-smitten doesn't mean much.

"They kicked you out? Your parents are at least softening if they invited you," I attempt to cheer him up.

"I wish they'd kicked me out of their own idea," Gavril half answers, but he also seems to be muttering to himself.

I'm flooded with pain and sympathy for him. Without thinking, I go up to him and put a hand on his arm comfortingly. I pause.

Yes, we'd gotten over a lot of our problems recently, but that was during the magic rush of Christmas. Had it lasted long enough for us to have a relationship close enough for that movement not to irritate him? He has an impressive temper. I'd seen him dent wood when he's frustrated. He'd never shown a sign of hurting me, but when he gets angry, the memory and fear crosses my mind. I'm sure he won't now, but had I crossed a line I was not allowed to anymore?

But Gavril's face doesn't fill with anger or resentment or get that hint of annoyance in his eyes that sparks when Ericka or the other girls do something to annoy him that he must pretend not to be annoyed by. His face fills with shock as if he can't believe I'd touched him.

He looks at my hand, but the shock doesn't turn to anger or even horror, more like surprised something good happened. He looks at my hand long enough to confirm I really am touching him before looking up at me with a soft smile under his slightly bowed head.

"I'm sorry." Considering what happened and how I'd touched him when perhaps I shouldn't, but his reaction didn't seem bad, so fearing he'd think I was withdrawing my sympathies, I keep my hand on his arm. "You should have been a real part of it."

"Should have known you would understand," Gavril says gently with gratitude in his voice before he surprises me further by fully accepting my touch; he moves so we're arm in arm as if to start on a walk around the garden. "Perhaps you have an opinion. Sage thinks I should refuse the directive not to bother setting up my office here, but I think it's a pointless fight as I've been able to fulfil my current duties in my suite just fine."

"Why wouldn't you want an office here?" I frown in confusion.

"I won't need it. It's a longer trip down here when I won't need to meet with anyone and disobeying the direct order for something I won't even need to use feels silly to me," Gavril explains.

"It also means any court members you see have to come up to the royal floor," Sage reminds Gavril as if they were continuing a conversation that was already happening.

"And they'll want to meet with you more if you're closer, right?" I ask. Gavril and Sage look down at me. I fight the flush, reminding myself of my resolve not to be ashamed of what I can offer and how I have to fight to become the true princess they want. "And it's symbolic. Even if you don't use it, having it there shows the court you are ready to deal, and with how your parents treat you, perhaps if they saw you were your own man and use what is rightfully yours, even if they try to belittle you, it may help them take you more seriously."

"Hm, I suppose you have a point there." Gavril nods, studying me carefully. I stupidly wish I looked more royal or courtly, so he'd take me seriously. My day dress is pretty, but mostly for keeping comfortable and warm as I study. It's a lovely boysenberry purple silk or satin (I'm terrible with fabric types) with a matching shade gem at the center of the gathered bust, leaving the rest of the skirt to flow out with a transparent material making a type of cape at my shoulders with an ice-like shimmer. I suppose the cape may help, but it mostly looks comfortable.

He starts to walk, and I follow him without really thinking about it. "Well, perhaps for once Sage has a point." Gavril gives his guard a slight smile. "Just doesn't phrase it as well."

Sage gives him a dirty look as we walk to the door I'd tried to open. Gavril unlocks the door with a key from his pocket before he opens the door and directs me in first then follows, flipping on the light.

The room is a bit dingy and surprisingly small. There's a desk, a chair, and a few other things covered with dust protectors in the room. But Gavril doesn't linger here. He moves to a door on the other side, unlocks that with a different key, and we step inside.

The smell of dust makes me want to sneeze. The carpet is so dusty I'm not sure of the color. The floor underneath is that sandy color much of the palace has. The walls are a darker ocean blue or would be once dusted. Veins of gold form onion dome shapes along the walls, also faded with a layer of dust. There is plenty of space for paintings or other decorations. There is a bookshelf on the left wall. The three door frames (the one we came in through, and one each on the right and left sides of the room) were also a golden color.

The furniture is all covered with dust sheets. There's what I presume is a desk towards the back of the room with a chair, what looks like two armchairs, two sofas, and two more armchairs making a kind of huddle circle closer to our side of the room. A few side tables and two what I presume are decorative tables stand along the right-hand wall with a few random chairs.

Gavril smiles as Sage closes the door behind us. "Well, they weren't kidding when they said it needed work." He walks over to the desk and yanks the cover off. I wave away the cloud of dust that's expelled into the air. Sage covers his mouth and nose with his arm lightning quick, like an instinct, eyeing the cloud with mistrust.

My mouth falls open to see the desk. It's stunning. It has what looks like a stone top that's mostly a deep blue/green with golden veins running through it. The body of the desk is outlined with gold wave patterns against white and blue painted wood backing like the ocean and sky at midday. I walk over to see the front of the drawers are that same stone with golden hardware.

"The covers did a good job," Gavril comments, bending to get a good look. Gavril looks up and smiles. "Though the gold lining will need to be polished, and I'll have to see if we can find how to slip the cover off the dome light."

"Set Godwin on it," Sage mutters.

"Ah, we should do that." Gavril steps out and calls a guard over to send a servant to fetch Godwin.

"Easier having your valet on it," Gavril says as he joins me.

"This is your court office?" I ask in awe.

"Is now." Gavril smiles at me. "Not that it will get much use, but you made a good point." He then starts to take the covers off the rest of the furniture, revealing all the tables had that stone top with white wood, but none as well done as the desk. The armchairs and sofas are the same Purerahian blue just in different tones: some more blueish and some more greenish. But even with all the furniture uncovered, the office looks rather bland.

"We'll need to get tools in here," Gavril notes, opening a desk drawer and finding it empty. "And keys for the drawers…"

"I'm not taking notes for you," Sage says with a slightly playful smile. I'm shocked to see it.

"I know." Gavril waves him off. "Well, what do you think?" He looks at me.

"What?"

"It's rather dull. What would you suggest?" Gavril asks, standing up right and brushing dust off his hands by smacking them together.

"I wouldn't begin to know, Your Highness." I look around, unsure why he's asking me.

Gavril smiles softly and walks over to me, taking both my hands and bringing them to his lips to place a gentle kiss on them. "No titles between us, remember?"

I smile before I can stop it, a little light returning to my eyes. Were we really back to this place of safety? I can't reply for the happy bubble in my chest.

The door opens, and Godwin steps in; his light brown hair looks particularly dark with the dusty light, and I can't even see his freckles in the dark. I can see his bright brown eyes though and smile. "You called?" he addresses Gavril.

"Yes, we need to get this room usable," Gavril's tone becomes a tad more formal. "The desk needs to be stocked for one, and I'd like to make sure we can let the dome light lit. Also, a deep clean is in order." Gavril looks at all the dust.

"I think that is first," Godwin agrees, pulling a small notepad from his pocket and scribbles some notes. "This room hasn't been used in what, twenty years?"

"At least thirty, since my father took office." Gavril looks at our footprints in the dust. "Carpet will need a deep wash."

"Staff will love that," Godwin sighs, still writing. "And that mirror polished." He pulls a cover off one near the door we'd entered from. Its frame is a stunning gold with ocean carvings leading to the Purerah emblem of dolphin, shark, and rose at the top.

"Also need to get some decorative touches." Gavril looks around again then at me.

"Oh, I..." I stumble, wanting to impress him. I think of the paintings he'd shown me on one of our dates. "I'd think a painting of the Great White would look wonderful behind your desk." And might remind those coming in of the power the prince has.

"I like it." Gavril smiles, approving and impressed.

"And if you want Joy to guard you in here, you could set out a crate and dishes for her in the corner behind you." I point out the spot. "Would make her comfortable and looks more impressive. She is a Custod Husky, after all." I assume so anyway. Damian would insist on the best.

Sage nods his begrudging approval. I smile a little, feeling more confident by the second. "And perhaps some yellow roses if floral arrangements are traditional. This room has stunning gold and blue coloring, maybe some more bright yellow would help bring it together."

I bite my lips, trying to think what else. "I don't know what you normally like for your desk or bookshelf, but I perhaps you could hang a few art pieces you like or were gifted."

"The Hyvian ship would look good there," Gavril indicates one of the tables along the wall and looks at Godwin. He's quickly making notes.

"And something with stars," I add. Gavril had said if he wasn't crown prince, he'd want to be a sailor, so I know his passion for the ocean and the nautical, but he also is a star gazer. I'd seen it firsthand. I think that should be represented too. "Perhaps something from your star collection?"

"I'd put 'The Stargazers' Dream' on that wall." Godwin points to the space on the other side of the door with the mirror.

"Excellent," Gavril agrees.

"What about that sculpture of the dancers?" I point at a still unappointed tabletop.

"I'll get suggestions on which and size." Godwin looks at Gavril to approve. Gavril nods, smiling slightly as his amber eyes study me. I flush in pleasure and look away.

"What? Don't like decorating a space together?" The way he says it makes goosebumps rise across my arms. It sounded more intimate than it was.

"Not really my place. I just got lost," I point out. If Forsythia had come down here, she'd have been in my place.

"You think so?" Gavril raises a brow in a teasing question, making me giggle.

"Your Highness," Sage says warningly.

Gavril ignores him. "I thought your opinions would be the most helpful. What else?" He nods to the room.

"Oh... I don't know. It sounds like you have it covered." I look around as I think, but nothing comes.

I turn back to Gavril and jump to see him so close. Did he mean to do that? "We'll see when it's done. At least it makes it feel like doing this has a purpose more than 'symbolic'."

My cheeks flush. "I didn't mean offense by it."

"I know." Gavril's eyes watch me with more tenderness, a hint of concern in his brows. "You don't have to be so worried. It's just us."

"Of course, Your..." I catch myself.

A slight smile crosses Gavril's face. "You don't have to fight to win in here, you know."

"Don't I?"

"Might want to have this chat somewhere else though. I have to send an impressive crew in here to clean up," Godwin points out.

Gavril's shoulders drop, and his stunning eyes meet the ceiling before giving Godwin an exasperated look.

"What? I have just about no time to get this done." Godwin defends, pointing at the filthy carpet.

"Alright." Gavril sighs, clearly still annoyed. He offers me his arm, and I take it.

We step out, leaving Godwin inspecting the room. Sage kicks some of the dust off his boots.

Gavril chuckles at Sage and opens his mouth to speak when I hear a voice I know down the hall ask a guard, "Did my cousin come through here?"

It is Fabian.

"Oh vene." Gavril suddenly realizes it might be bad to have the scandalous reporter spot him and me coming out of the "unused" office. Who knows what he'd make of that. Gavril moves to go back into the room, but then he stops, likely realizing if he's looking for Godwin that's where he'd go.

I open my mouth to ask him what he expects to do, but he quickly covers my mouth with a playful smile before taking my hand and pulling me down the hall and opens the last door on the left. We slip inside just before Fabian rounds the corner.

It's another small room, this one clearly used, with a desk, chair, chest of drawers, and a sofa all clearly in use and well decorated.

Gavril moves to the door on the opposite side, and we quickly go inside. "No way he'll find us in here," Gavril says.

"Wow." The room is stunning. I let go of Gavril's hand to get a closer look. The room is mostly a seashell white and lined with shelves, the borders of which are carved with stunning wave designs and painted gold. A desk much like the one in the prince's study is the main fixture, made of the same stone top but with white wood and gold. It's larger and curved around the comfortable looking work chair which allows more workspace as well as drawers and storage.

The round pillars between each of the shelves are made of a similar stone with that blue and gold color that draw my eyes to the second floor which are lined with more shelves which only lead my eyes up to the stunningly painted ceiling which frames the main glass dome that's the glory of the palace, letting light into the room though there are no windows along the walls.

Much like in the prince's office, there is a set of chairs and sofas around a table, and just past them, a spiral staircase that leads to the second floor and beyond. I wonder if it goes all the way up to the dome.

The room likely feels larger than it is, though it is large, with the high ceiling and the powerful white, gold, and blue colors making it feel open. That's a bright power about the design of this room. I also notice this room has many doors too, in addition to the one we'd used.

Gavril smiles slightly at my reaction. "Surprised?"

"Where are we?" I ask.

"Where do you think we are?"

"I don't know... Covere room?" I hazard a guess.

"No. That's where we interviewed all you ladies after the Harvest. You couldn't fit a full Covere in here. It's the king's office. It's not locked when Father's working but isn't using it."

Now the Prince says it, and I'm over my awe of the room, I see little signs it's the king's office. A little dish of candies on the desk, the little music box I gave him for Christmas sitting closed next to it, and an array of framed impressions. I take a closer look. I also take the excuse to run my hand along the stone desktop, which is as smooth as glass, though I can also tell that's had to be refinished to keep it that way with how not all of it feels exactly the same.

The images are all family impressions. One of the king and queen on their wedding day, a Christmas family portrait, and two that make me smile: a toddler-aged Gavril trying to put the king's crown on his head though it's far too big. It looks like he was sitting on the carpet in this room when the impression was taken. The second is one from the day Gavril was born with a tired-looking queen, a rather grumpy looking baby, and a beaming king.

There is one of them actually outside at the beach and another one of the king and Gavril when Gavril was likely about sixteen, looking like they're in the middle of a playful wrestling match or something.

Gavril doesn't notice I'd taken to looking at the family impressions. He notices some papers left out on the center of the meeting table. He picks them up and looks them over with a slight frown on his face.

"You may want to make sure no one notices they've been looked at." Sage's voice makes me jump.

Gavril sighs and puts down the papers as I turn to look at them. "Good point. They'll worry some intruder got in or something."

"We shouldn't be in here." I'm still looking around. Why did Gavril think this was a good idea when the Covere room is likely as secure?

"I get in here all the time; Father's never cared." Gavril rolls his eyes. "It's Mother who will mind. It's her fault I can't confess it was me if anyone worried." His tone is bitter again.

"Gavril, no matter what she says, one day this is going to be your job. Don't let her make you feel like you'll never reach it," I try to comfort, walking back over to him.

"It's not never getting the job." He looks around the room, a hint of the bitterness back in his eyes. "It's not having a clue what the job is like when I do." He looks back at the papers. It must be a bad report if it put him in such a mood.

"They will. Sooner or later, they'll figure it out." I walk over to look, but the papers are too confusing for me to understand. They look like some kind of map, but I don't know the locations, or the legends used to mark the map. "You can handle any of... this." Even if I can't.

"Just be nice if they, you know, let me help when they invite me in the room." Gavril puts his hands into his pockets, looking up at the ceiling as he thought.

"That's why you need an office. You need to show them you are ready to do this and capable of it." I take his arm to try to comfort him, still unsure I should.

I don't miss the flicker of a smile that crosses Gavril's face. "See, you two do have a point." He looks over at Sage. "How long before Fabian is clear?"

"I'm listening to see if they're done arguing in the hall. It could be a few minutes."

"Well, you can't leave me here. I'll get lost," I joke.

"You'll learn them in no time," Gavril assures me, making me turn pink. I'd never be here again unless I'm on trial or I win. "When he's gone, I can show you around if you want."

"I'd like that," I admit before I can decide if that's a good idea. Sage looks unsure whether he likes that idea either, but Gavril ignores him. He always has ignored Sage's unease about me.

"Well, this room has doors to most everywhere," Gavril jokes. "We came through the reception room, where his valet works, keeping meetings flowing on time and the like. That door there." He points to the one on the right-hand side of the room from the door we'd entered from. "Goes right into the Covere room. The opposite door," he points to the left side one, "goes to the main meeting room. That's where you saw everyone come out." It's also where the king, queen, and Grand Duke were meeting right now. "And that one in the back goes right into Mother's office." Gavril points to one at the back left corner.

"And you say you never use this area," I tease.

"Well, as a child, this was kind of my playground as Mother never wanted me too far away. If she couldn't work in the nursery, I was with her or father in these rooms. When I was younger, I heard more of the day-to-day ruling of the kingdom than I ever do now. Mother never liked me too far away until I was about fifteen."

"You must have hated it."

"Well, I fought more for a voice as a teenager until—" Gavril stops himself. "Anyway, I still had morning lessons, but if I wasn't in lessons,

Mother wanted me nearby. She finally stopped when courtiers complained. While other princes my age were coming into meetings for the first time to listen and observe, I was forced into all-day lessons. I'm sure I could school my parents on law by now, at least what's actually written in it with weekly law reviews and all that."

"You still have them?"

He nods. "The Enthronement made them pause for a while, but I have a review most mornings while you all in your lessons."

"But they let you in a meeting today."

"Then kicked me out," Gavril points out.

"Well, don't do whatever it is again."

"I asked a question."

I pause. What would be wrong with asking a question in a meeting you were invited to? "Was it an offensive question?"

"No. I should have asked it as an offensive question though for the reaction I got. Grand Duke's—" Gavril stops himself again. I get plenty of hints that the prince does not like the Grand Duke. He sent Godwin to keep him away from me at least twice if not more, and now this. "Sorry. I shouldn't spread such gossip."

I frown. "I'd not tell a soul."

"Still, not wise for me to just... I mean, whatever job you get, don't want to twist things."

I bow my head. I rather just listen to his struggles, honestly wanting to understand his feelings and his struggle and world. But he has a point. It's not like I'm his real girlfriend or anything. I'm one of his fifteen contestants.

"I think you're clear." Sage checks the hall.

"Then let's show her around." Gavril smiles and offers me his arm again. I notice he's wearing a purple waistcoat without a jacket. We oddly match.

We go back through the valet's office to the hall. Gavril takes me back down to the hall I'd entered from. He passes the first two doors and goes to the one at the end. He slides a small piece of the wall away next to it, about the size of a recipe card, to reveal a strip of yellow. It's like that color tells him something because he responds by opening the door on our right instead of the one at the end of the wall. "You know this room, but for context. This is the Covere room."

I didn't notice the door on this side of the room. It's the room with the large oval table in the middle where the royal family had interviewed me after the Harvest attack.

"And the door at the end goes into the hall you used to enter it before," Gavril says as we pull back and close the door. "As you've seen it, we won't take a ton of time, and a meeting is due to start in there any moment."

Gavril pulls back and nods at the last door. "That door leads into Mother's office, but I'm pretty sure Maryum is in there, so we won't dare cross her," Gavril jokes.

I giggle a little. "I wouldn't know. I think the only time I've seen her was at the first public event."

"Really?" Gavril thinks it over. "I suppose they are in the background but hard to spot. She and Porteous are as present as Sage or Godwin. Almost as good at hiding it seems." He smiles at a rather bored looking Sage, but he always uses that expression to hide his real feelings.

We reach the second door. "That's the second entrance to the main meeting room. I believe my parents are still using it, so we won't—"

"You should," Sage cuts him off.

Gavril pauses and looks at him.

"They're surely discussing you. Show the Grand Duke you're not afraid of him."

"It's not him I'm afraid of; it's the scandal of being viewed overbearing and demanding." Gavril's looking at Sage as if worried for his sanity.

"But also shows you are active and not pouting. You were dismissed, and you started a date."

"It's not a date," Gavril and I say at the same time, though me with pink cheeks and Gavril with a happy smile.

"Impromptu date, true, but still proves my point." Sage's expression doesn't change. The twinge of annoyance in Gavril's expression tells me he's not used to that, and it annoys him. "Could it really make anything worse?"

Gavril raises his brows and nods as if he couldn't deny that. "Well then..." And to my horror, he does put his hand on the doorknob.

I open my mouth to protest, but I'm not fast enough. "This is the main meeting room," he says as he opens the door then pauses as if surprised to see his parents and the Grand Duke standing near one of the side doors while talking. "Oh, my apologies. I thought you were getting ready for your meeting in the Covere room," Gavril apologizes with perfect acting.

"It's not an official talk," the king insists, giving the Grand Duke a look. "And changes nothing."

"I must point out—" the Grand Duke starts.

"Aster, perhaps—" the queen begins.

"It changes nothing of my opinions. We are sticking with the plan," the king insists. "And did you need the room, Gavril?"

"No. Not without your permission. I thought it would be empty. I was giving Kascia a tour." Gavril smiles and looks at me. "Thought it could be helpful for her."

"The main court offices would be more helpful," the queen points out. So odd how she goes right into being formal as if we had no personal connection even after our time together. I wonder if I'd ever master that skill.

"We'll see those too," Gavril assures.

The Grand Duke gives me a smile as if in congratulations. I force one back, using my acting to make it look happy. He always was cheering for me behind everyone's back, but I also wonder if he's doing that for other girls too.

"I think it's a fine idea." The king smiles. "You two enjoy. We're done here." And his tone tells me he's signaling to the other two that they are done discussing whatever they were talking about. "Let's move into my office."

Gavril watches them carefully. They all go into the door that leads into the king's office, but the king dismisses the Grand Duke. I don't miss the queen looking uneasy about it as the door closes behind them.

"Your father was glad for the excuse," Sage observes.

"And Mother wasn't." Gavril sighs. "Something has to shake that up."

"What up?" I'm so lost.

"Nothing you need to worry about." Gavril takes both my hands and kisses them. "Let's be about our tour."

And Gavril shows me the room, which is beautiful pine wood, white with many ocean scenes and seashells decorating it with some hints of our lovely northern mountain ranges which I'd only seen in person once on my national tour of *The Phantom*. There is a large white pine table in the center of the room, an oval like the one in the Covere Room. But smaller tables were tucked away with their own sets of armchairs and sofas for smaller gatherings. I presume, the staff can move into more prominence if needed. I also notice there are dividers hidden in the walls with latched panels. I knew them from how many we have in the theater.

"And the last room has nothing to see," Sage points out as Gavril turns off the lights as we leave the room.

"I suppose that's true. Boarded up like mine. But..."

"No." Sage gives Gavril a look.

"What's the last room?" I look at the door, the one I'd felt drawn to try to open before.

"Princess's office."

My stomach drops.

"Nothing interesting. It's been empty as long as yours." Sage gives the prince a pointed look.

"Alright, alright." I can see the disappointment in Gavril's eyes. But the symbolism of letting me see the room is obvious, and there is no way I'd dare cross that line.

Gavril does show me the rest of the court rooms, where the offices are. He jokes we should prank the Grand Duke's office, but he likely was back there now, and even if not, I'm sure he's the kind who locks his office tightly behind him.

We're finishing up just before lunch, so Gavril walks me back to my room to dress. To my disappointment, several girls see us. They'll be talking and glaring at me all through meals.

"Thank you for humoring me. I know you had other plans." Gavril smiles at me.

"I enjoyed it." I couldn't lie about that.

"I'll have to show it to you when it's done."

My cheeks turn deep pink. "I'd like that." But alone in his office… almost as bad as his bedroom. Almost.

"I'll see you at dinner." Gavril kisses my hand, but I see the desire for more in his eyes.

I look up to see if any of the girls had followed us. I don't see any.

Gavril straightens up. "Good evening, Lady Kascia."

"Good evening, Your Highness," I say automatically. Gavril turns to leave, and I realize he may have chosen not to go for more after half of the girls witnessed him kissing Forsythia in the hall. I am terrified of what the girls might do if I had the same scene. Forsythia likely would mock me for copying her while the others would hate me more than ever. But I'd have to take it. If I want to end this war, I am going to have to get used to it.

Chapter 7

When I finally reach the library, a hand glides along my arm making me start as I turn away from the bookshelf where I'd wanted to look for a book on the history of Japcharia during the last five hundred years. I turn to see the Grand Duke smiling gently. "My apologies. I did not mean to startle you."

I very much doubt that. I'd have thought he was just one of the other girls if it wasn't for his hand that had cupped my shoulder then down my arm in a way I'd only ever allowed Jake or a fellow actor in a romance scene to do. I don't like how he touches me. He was smiling that smile that looked charming and should be charming. After all, he is tall, dark, and handsome with well-trimmed coiling hair and beard. He's a handsome courtier for sure and one of the finest dressed at all times, but something about him always unsettles me. It didn't help seeing how much the Prince and Sage dislike him, most of all when Gavril won't fully explain it all.

"What did you mean to do?" I ask, folding my arms defensively.

"Nothing for you to worry about," he assures me in his charming manner.

I highly doubt that and look around, wondering if we're alone. The other girls are likely still in the main area studying, so I suppose he can't be up to anything too horrible. He never has though. In reality, he's really not done anything to me other than give me the creeps. No matter how I tell myself all is fine, I still feel nervous and anxious that he's up to something when he's around.

"I simply was hoping to request your help."

"Help?" I frown and look up at him. "You know full well I am not in any kind of position to help you."

"On the contrary, many will see what you already have." The Grand Duke smiles.

"Which is?" I question.

"Well, it can't mean nothing, you are the only lady he's shown around the royal offices and courtrooms." He gives me a half smile that makes me feel sick. "And we all know you're a good choice, though perhaps inexperienced in the royal or court way of life. What I am asking is not hard for even the most inexperienced to do."

"There really isn't anything I can help you with," I insist, picking a random book on Japcharian history as if that's what I'd been looking for and making as if to return to the reading section.

"Oh, but there is." The Grand Duke stands in front of me to stop me. I stop but don't make an effort to hide that I'm annoyed by it as I hold the book against my chest and look up at him, waiting for him to go on without hiding my impatience. "You see, you're about to play a big role with your delegations," he says.

"I'm not in any talks. I just prepare the hosting events. You know this." I try once again to step past him, but he blocks me again.

"I am not asking for any help with the talks. Rest assured I have that well in hand. You have no need to fear that." He smiles once more. I tap my foot in impatience. "No. What I need from you is information."

"About?"

"Each delegation is going to play favorites with the girls. They may even show signs of trying to get the royal family to pick one lady over another. I am simply asking, if they happen to say anything to you, if you'd please let me know. You don't have to seek out the information," he adds quickly when he sees I'm still not convinced. "I am in charge of all foreign relations, you see. And it helps me understanding their frame of mind as well as how they are viewing our... unique situation." He smiles once more. "If they just so happen to hint anything to you, please, let me know."

"I really don't think it will matter to you either way. Unless you're helping judge the Enthronement now," I say, managing to get around him this time, deciding studying in my room may be in my best interest.

"Of course not. That is a family matter." The Grand Duke follows me out of the library, apparently not caring if other girls see him with me. I guess if he doesn't judge, animosity between the girls will mean little to him. "I assure you it's only to support me in doing my duty in assisting the royal family in handling the proceedings with the visiting officials. The royal family will want to know how their constituents react to this event and how it may affect their future dealings with them."

"Perhaps," I reply curtly, wishing he wouldn't follow me up the hallway, but he does.

"My lady." He gets in front of me to stop me once more. "Please, let me assure you this is not meant to show favoritism or let the nations have any influence on the Enthronement. On the contrary, it's meant to assist in making it fair."

"Then reporting it directly to the royal family will cause no harm then," I point out. "Either way, I see no reason to promise either way when it's more likely nothing will happen. Now if you'll excuse me."

"No, no, it's important I report to them." The Grand Duke stops me once more. "You see, it's my job. If they think I'm unable to do it on my own I could be in a… delicate situation."

"Delicate? You seem to have their full trust. Surely nothing shakes their faith in how well you help them." I'm mocking him. I know Gavril trusts him as far as he can throw him.

But the Grand Duke flushes in pleasure at the perceived complement. "Thank you, but it's not just their trust. I want to fulfill my duty as asked. Surely you can understand that. I don't want to let them down." He's a good actor, but my gut tells me the sincerity in his eyes is only to get my sympathy.

"Then you shouldn't need my help either," I say politely and try once more to step around him only to be blocked yet again. I take a deep breath and am about to demand he let me through when a voice comes from behind me.

"Fancy seeing you here, Grand Duke Aldgrone. Just the man I wanted to talk to." Fabian with his wind-swept blond hair, pops out of seemingly nowhere, beaming at us. His bright hazel eyes glint with trouble as he beams at both of us like he'd just uncovered a rare treasure. "I was looking for a quick Q&A with you about the upcoming visits," he says to the Grand Duke. "Does seem the ladies have quite a big part in it if you're talking to them."

Fabian turns to me. "Are you helping with all the delegations or just one?"

"Need I remind you, without direct royal permission, you are not to interview or question them?" the Grand Duke says in playful warning, but I see the threat in his eyes. I'd rather be on Fabian's side than the Grand Duke's, however.

"Forgive me, forgive me. I should ask you," Fabian agrees. "It's so hard not to speak with them. They're so lovely, and this one a great interviewee, isn't she?" he twinkles at the Grand Duke. I'm almost positive Fabian is trying to get the Grand Duke to leave me alone. He likely saw the Grand Duke stop my path forward.

"That she is. Most talented," the Grand Duke praises.

"So, one of your favorites to win?" Fabian latches onto it.

"How about we conduct a proper conversation in my office?" the Grand Duke deflects the question.

"Most excellent plan!" Fabian then turns to me. "I hope you have a lovely rest of your day, and best of luck with your work." He kisses my hand before going right up to the Grand Duke to let him lead. I swear if he could have gotten away with it, he'd have taken the Grand Duke's arm.

The Grand Duke nods to Fabian, bows to me, then leads the excited reporter off.

I sigh and shake my head. Fabian can be a handful, but at least he got me out of that. I look down at the book I am holding and fiddle with the corner of it. But at least this incident reminds me of that uncomfortable political situation I'm going to face in the next few weeks because before I know it, my delegation will arrive.

Chapter 8

The day before the Purysian delegation arrives, everyone is a bundle of nerves. It's not my delegation, yet I'm nervous too. Damian helps by making me fit the Purysian style. They are known to pride their fashion. It's a stylish purple dress with a gathered skirt and butterfly sleeves with a sight gather at the center of my chest. He tops it off with the first hat I'd ever worn in the Enthronement; it's round and makes a cute little shape as I pull it over my head. I have never seen anything like it. They finish it off with a belt in the middle that sets the outfit off nicely and helps add more volume to the skirt. I look as Purysian as any Purerahian could.

Because of Damian's skill, I study the Purysian fashion more closely when we receive them in the reception room. The men and the women are dressed in fashionable but more simple outfits. We wear more dresses in Purerah, but the ladies of Purysia wear more shirt and skirt combinations which shows how well my outfit blends Purerahian and Purysian styles.

I thought I'd be prepared, but I experience my first culture shock almost right away. I'd never bumped cheeks in little air kisses with a stranger before. The closeness told me that Purysians wear heavy perfume or cologne. They don't all smell exactly the same, but lavender is a popular scent I detect in most of the perfumes. I receive lots of compliments on my outfit and even more on my hat. I am happy to let the girls in the Purysian group try it on and pass it around before they return it to me.

All of the nobles of Purysia are friendly and warm, but there is a clear formality in how they interact with us and even each other. Gavril impresses me with how well he handles greeting them and being sociable over the different foods the girls have prepared for this little greeting party.

The decorations are a wise choice, mixing Purysian purple and blue with Purerah's yellow. The Purysian emblem of sword, pen, mask, and flute in a lavender circle is displayed alongside the dolphin, shark, and rose of Purerah.

The biggest hit of the party has to be when Nippers suddenly jumps onto the table to steal a treat. The Purysian ladies all lose their minds wanting to pet and feed the little cat. Sadly, Nippers isn't that friendly of a cat, so he jumps and runs from the attention.

Gavril has a solution though. He brings Joy down to cheer up the saddened delegation. She's gotten bigger since last I saw her, standing almost to Gavril's knee.

She's a beautiful dog. A Custod husky with red on her face and down her back, white belly and undertail, and the brightest blue eyes. She's named Joy for her happy disposition and the fact she was a Christmas gift.

Joy also is odd in that she "talks", huffing and making little noises as if speaking. She can do an almost perfect "hello" and a cute little growl to say Gavril's name. She sits perfectly and lets the ladies pet her, and they coo at her like she's a baby. Joy does her talking tricks for them. The visiting ladies try hard to get her to mimic their names, but it mostly ends up with a confused dog getting treats for making cute sounds. She still sounds like a puppy, her tail wagging so hard her whole back end moved sometimes. I think the dog is a better hit than the rest of the reception.

I expect now the reception is over, I'll fade into the background, but thanks to Damian, even at dinner I stand out. Our visitors love the outfit. It's a shirt and skirt combination, all black, and the top is form-fitting with a black transparent loose shirt with polka dots on it. The final touch is an ascot which I have never worn before or seen any woman wear before I met the Purysians. My maids also darkened my makeup to match and have me wear a similar hat. The four women in the delegation can't stop admiring the whole look.

The food we eat is different too. I'm used to more dumplings, noodle dishes, seafood, and rice. The dinner we have is clearly mimicking the Purysians' food styles. The first course is little carrot cakes, or that's what they taste like, having that sweet yet carroty and nutty taste. Then we have a simple and bland onion soup with socca bread which I have also never had before. It's a little dry with the power on top, but so soft it almost melts in my mouth. The next course is fish in a fine butter sauce before the main course which is some kind of fowl with a seared wine sauce and vegetables of the kind we don't often have, such as carrots. I have to admit, the main course is much blander than the most spiced and soy flavored meats I'm used to.

This is also when the first round of wine is served. Our guests enjoy themselves to the fullest, but I'm much slower to enjoy my drink.

Though I have to admit, the wine pairs nicely with the meal, whatever kind it is. It also goes well with the salad that smells strongly of lemon but tasted more like oil. Then we're given a new kind of wine to pair with a small sampling of cheeses which I enjoy far more than I should before we get to dessert which is one of my favorite things: éclairs.

I try not to smile too much as I enjoy mine, thinking I could enjoy the last two courses more often. I notice Gavril is looking over at me with a slight smile. He knows how much I like this kind of food. I bite my lips with a smile as my eyes sparkle back at him.

A giggle nearby draws my attention. Two of the Purysian ladies are giggling to one another. One of them leans to the man on her other side and whispers to him. He glances at the prince before looking back at me. My eyes dart to Gavril before looking back at the two of them, their eyes fixed on the prince. The man nods firmly and smiles a little to himself before he returns to his own éclair.

My stomach drops as I look at my plate. Why does that make me suddenly nervous? It was just a look. But I feel like a bright spotlight is on my head, and I do all I can to ignore it. It doesn't help I can hear the Grand Duke's bugging me to know who the delegates favored, and all I want is to ignore it.

The Purysians don't look ready to dissipate for the night, even when all the plates are empty. They chatter quickly and happily with the royal family, the ladies, and one another. The king suggests we retire to our more comfortable reception room, and the delegation is delighted by the idea.

Staff bring in tea and more wine for us to enjoy as we sit around on the comfortable sofas and armchairs that have been brought into the room during the meal. I decide I'm not ready for more wine and pour myself some tea and sit and hide in a corner sofa. This isn't my delegation, so I feel no need to be overly anxious to make an impression.

But the delegation takes an interest. The lady I recall being introduced as Duchess Clarisse — I believe she's the crown prince's cousin or something like it — sits beside me with a friendly, yet formal smile. That is how we were taught to act around the Purysians, formal yet friendly.

Her perfume overwhelms me for a moment. I had noticed all the delegates are wearing heavy perfume or cologne. The duchess' smells strongly of lavender and sunflowers.

I stir in some honey into my tea, which is a ginger and ginseng tea that we don't often serve but is a nice relief after the meal.

"You don't want another drink?" the duchess asks me in a strong Purysian accent which is nasally and spicy.

I shake my head politely. "No thank you. It's kind of you as a guest to offer."

"You sure? Your organizers picked a real good quality," she praises, swirling her glass as I had when wine tasting.

"They did," I have to agree. "But I've had plenty." I sip my tea.

"Not used to it?" Duchess Clarisse guesses.

"Not much reason at home." I shrug.

That catches the duchess' interest. "You were not in court before?"

"No. By trade, I'm a prima actress."

"Do you enjoy the castle life?" the duchess asks.

I nod. "I do. It's like a second home. Wouldn't you agree?"

"Oh, I would. You expect to be able to stay then?"

I read through her question. She's fishing. "I hope so."

"And you still do?"

"Would I be here if I didn't?"

The duchess laughs. "I suppose not, at least when you signed up. But do you still feel that way?"

"Yes, I do. I hope to get that far." I fight not to glance over at Gavril. "As the other ladies do." I remind myself not to say girls. "But there are things all of them could bring to the kingdom."

"But do you want him or the throne?" The duchess lightens up almost instantly, getting more comfortable and sipping her wine with a happier air.

I smile. I don't know if she's acting to get me to relax or if she really is relaxing at the idea of girl talk. I have to step carefully though. I saw her reporting at dinner. "When I think about it, most of the time I think him, but yes, I'd like the throne. But that's about helping my people."

"People who want to behead you." The duchess sips more wine.

I frown a bit. "They don't all want to see the royal family gone, and even those that do just want peace in the kingdom again. Peace and prosperity just like your people desire it."

"That is true." She swirls her wine a bit before taking another sip. "Do any of the other girls frighten you?"

I shake my head. "No. Once I think they did, but I'm used to them all now."

"Any you worry will outshine you?" she asks.

I can't help but glance at Zelda who is pink in the cheeks from drinking, talking with two of the other ladies of the delegation. I think she's had a bit too much by how her hand motions are more exasperated. I see a small frown on the younger lady's face, but the elder doesn't seem to mind at all as she sips her own tea.

"Not really. I wouldn't say I'm in the lead." I shrug. "But I wouldn't say I worry about any of them beating me. It's about passing the tests, not about beating each other."

"I suppose not." The duchess nods her agreement.

Then the man sitting with Gavril calls the duchess over. "Pardon me." She bows her head to me.

"Not at all." I bow my head back.

I let out a sigh of relief and finish my tea. I think I'm done for the night. I stand and brush off my skirt. I glance at Gavril. He notices my look and gives me a small smile and nods, letting me know it's fine. I return the smile to wish him a good night and good luck before I head up to my room.

The next day is easier. We only see the delegations at mealtimes. We are excused from lessons as the girls who are in the agenda meeting will not be able to attend, so it gives us an excuse to have the day off. Damian and I use it to rehearse. It's a struggle to juggle rehearsing with Damian and Cedrick and preparing for the delegation.

At dinner, the duchess is friendly and tries to chat with me over yet another glass of wine. I remain friendly but avoid giving her any clues or giving any false impressions about how the Enthronement is going.

On the third day, they have a small... well, for lack of a better term, exhibition where the Chosen girls, royal family, and delegates enjoy the small art display in the palace and allow the Purysians to show off some of their art. A few of the men in the delegation boast that to really show off Purysian skill, they would have to fence.

To the queen's horror, Sage suggests they try their hand against the prince. The king has to hold her by the arm and squeeze her hand to keep her calm as the prince happily accepts the challenge.

When I'd been embarrassed that I mostly lost to him, I really was being prideful. The prince beats the first far too easily. I can tell even he feels like it might have been insulting by his excusing it on the delegate's being polite and lets him have another round. I think we all know the prince let him win that one. The only one who doesn't is the delegate.

But it is the only one Gavril loses, taking it slower than the others, but now I'm simply admiring him, I should have known he was good. His form is solid, his movements elegant and fluid, his eyes sharp and quick to reply. He really has a skill for observation and deduction. He is unmatched, and I am proud, not only to have beaten him as many times as I did, but how easily he makes Purerah proud.

"What do you expect of a nation in such a long war and such a powerful prince?" The Purysian delegate leader, the duchess' husband, laughs. I hope it was meant as a compliment. But our guests enjoy themselves much and compliment us much. The discussions must have gone swimmingly.

The night of their farewell ball goes smoothly. The visitors are in good spirits and so are the king and queen. Gavril might be as well, but I have noticed over the course of the week that the delegation wants his attention most. I hope that helps his parents see how valuable and ready he really is to join in on the work of running the kingdom.

Tonight's outfit is yet another hit. Damian puts me in all white. The skirt goes just past my knees and flutters stunningly as I dance. The wrap bow and flower details on the bodice and sleeves are highly admired by our visiting ladies. Damian also gives me a shrug I can wear if it gets cold. I wear it over dinner, but once the ball starts, I take it off.

The leaving feast is much like the welcoming feast, only finer with a cheese pastry to start, a garlic soup, salmon in a cream sauce, lamb chops with a spicy sauce, another salad, the cheese and wine platter, and finishing with another cream pastry that is shaped like candles with chocolate drizzled across the top. I could get used to Purysian food. Though I'd miss the spices of Purerahian food.

In the ball that follows, Gavril handles the attention he's getting well. He gives each Purysian lady a dance which they all enjoy and say he's the best dancer in all of Purerah. I wonder if that might be true, at least in ballroom dances.

It's nice to just enjoy the party instead of stressing. Gavril is too busy playing the courting game, leaving me free to enjoy myself. I dance with Damian and Cedrick. Apart from Gavril, they are some of the best dancers I'd ever danced with. Cedrick has a fluidity to his movements that makes you forget there are separate steps put together, like a bird in flight or water in motion.

I even get to finally meet Kerrigan. He's handsome, rather like Damian, pale with dark hair, but Kerrigan's eyes are a soft gray. I imagine he's the kind of guy who would spot someone sitting alone across the room and gently lure them into his group of friends.

Turns out, I'm spot on. "We met at a party like this," Flur tells me, holding onto Kerrigan's arm. "I was shy and hiding though I was permitted to join in, and he noticed me."

"Everyone was looking," Kerrigan excuses.

"No one else was brave enough," Vivian teases. I laugh my agreement.

"Well, the rest is history." Flur's cheeks turn a lovely shade of pink.

"You better hurry up. I want to be at the wedding," I tease Kerrigan.

"I understand. It would be an honor, but I... well, with my injury."

"I take you as you are," Flur insists.

Kerrigan smiles. "I know." And he gives her a kiss that makes my heart melt, and Vivian teases them to get a room.

I like Kerrigan. He's exactly what I expect for Flur, at least in personality: pleasant and quiet but amazingly friendly, not shy like Flur.

I'm able to enjoy the festivities until the Grand Duke asks me for a dance. I can't politely say no, so I have to let him pull me onto the floor. He's a dreadful dancer: his footwork heavy and clunky, his leading heavy and stiff. "It's nice to have a moment. You ladies are amazingly busy," he compliments. "You look ravishing as always."

I'm not sure I like his phrasing. I try not to look directly at him, using the pretense of the dance, but he leads me into positions where I can't help it. "Thank you. I've said it many times; my team is the best." I put on a smile.

"It's not just them. You catch everyone's attention. The Purysians seem to love you. You've won the press; that's for sure." The Grand Duke smiles.

"Have I?" I say conversationally. I mentally fight not to give him any of what he asked for the last time we spoke. I pray he doesn't bring it up.

The Grand Duke smiles that grin that makes my skin crawl. "Have you not seen?"

"Seen what?"

"The poll came out this morning. I thought you ladies all got a copy of the paper after the features." The Grand Duke sounds delighted to have surprised me with the news. "You did quite well."

The way his dark eyes look down at me makes my stomach squirm. He's dressed impeccably tonight, wearing the purple and blue of Purysia in honor of them.

"I'm surely the best dressed," I joke.

"It wasn't that type of poll." The Grand Duke smiles again.

I want away from him, and now, but leaving mid-dance would be tantamount to slapping him in the face, and I have no excuse for that.

"I'm sure it's all very nice." I struggle for what to say. "I'm surprised you're taking such an interest. My understanding is you have very little part in the Enthronement."

I might have touched a nerve with how he tenses. "No, but the future queen does interest me quite a bit." I shudder at what that might mean, feeling more ill. "After all, she's the one I'll have the pleasure of working with, is she not?"

"I suppose."

"You seem nervous. Do you fear taking the throne?" he asks me, still smiling, but his eyes are cold and calculating.

"No," I say firmly, hoping I don't come off prideful or cocky.

"You should. You have little idea of the kind of tensions that lie on the other side of the job. You do a magnificent job at the outward appearances, even the political talk for the public, but the public is the least of your worries on the throne. As we discussed before."

"On the contrary, that's whom a queen serves," I say stubbornly. "They are the ones she should be concerned with." Part of me questions if I should argue. Maybe I should keep silent.

"That is how it appears and sounds good in quotes, but the real task lies in working with the court. It's not an easy task, and one I find you are ill prepared for. I'm still ready to help. My offer always stands." He frowns as if in concern.

"I'm sure I'll learn just fine." I wish I'd kept my mouth shut. There's something here that frightens me. I don't like being this close to him. I try to be as far as I can in the dance, but he doesn't let me. Why can't Godwin save me now? He did last time.

"If you hope to win and succeed, you'll need help. With how well you're doing with the rest of it, I will be happy to be that support for you if it came to it," he offers once again.

"I'll worry about that when I need to. No point getting stressed over a problem I may not have to deal with," I deflect best I can.

My heart races as the Grand Duke's face darkens. "You're a foolish one, but stubborn, I'll grant you. You'll never get far with that kind of attitude, my lady. You really think you're so good and perfect for this, don't you?"

"I never said that." I try to keep up my defenses, but the truth is, I feel so imperfect, it's suffocating.

"You don't have to say it." When did his tone grow so dark? "You're pretty, sure; not the most beautiful, but you can play with the best of them. If not for that attendant, you'd be as forgotten as Florence by now. If you want to get anywhere after this, you'll need my help. I wouldn't take such offers lightly."

"I'm not." I try once again to get some distance, but he uses the dance as an excuse to keep me closer than I'd like. "I just won't make a promise I can't keep."

"I'm not asking you to do anything you would be bound to if you didn't join the court." He smiles that smile I hate. I can't help but contrast it with the dozens of smiles I love from Gavril. This is like a twisted version. "And let's face it, you've been good enough to ensure yourself at least that. You'll need me."

"I'm sure I'll manage." Why is this song so long?

"You really don't see how ill-prepared you are, do you?" He sighs as if in sympathy, but the anger I feel from his tight grip says differently. "You're good at being pleasing, but you can't convince anyone of anything. The prince ignores your desire to keep affection private. No matter how you tell people why you look so good, no one believes you, and you can't even convince the other girls you're not trying to outdo them. You are hopelessly lost on persuading anyone of anything."

I swallow to hide how that stung. He has a point. I have not gotten anyone to change their minds. I am always the one changing. I may have learned to defend myself, but I hadn't learned to make anyone else see things my way.

"You're good at getting your complacent followers to act, but if you want to have any power or place in a court, you need to command respect. You can't command a horse."

"The guard does a fine job making sure I don't need to." I put on a smile.

"Don't think I don't see through those performances you put on. You're a wonderful actress, but you need to become more than a girl acting royal. You need to become royal and command that respect, so people will follow those orders. When you finally are ready to realize this, I'll be happy to help you."

But at what cost? What if he's right and if I don't and I can't be helpful to Gavril if I win? Let alone if it stops me from winning.

"Perhaps the likes of Princess Zelda could teach you, but they want to win just like you. You can't trust those girls, even the ones you may think are friends. Give it time, they'll turn on you. But I'm not going anywhere." He gives me that creepy smile again.

Suddenly, we stop as someone taps him on the shoulder. We turn, and I feel a wave of relief rush over me as I see Damian standing there.

"Mind if I cut in?" he asks politely, but the look in his eyes says he would even if the Grand Duke disagreed.

"But of course." The Grand Duke bows his head to him.

Damian smiles then leans closer to him, touching his shoulder, talking low as if only to him. "Between you and me, I would take the chance to go have a sweet. It may help wash some of the foulness off your breath." He then claps his shoulder and turns to me.

I smile my gratitude and take the position with much relief. The Grand Duke keeps his face natural as he leaves us to our dance. Damian seems to take little notice of him as he leads me into the next turn with smooth, exact form. It's a relief after the Grand Duke's clunkiness.

"Sorry about that. I hope he didn't upset you." Damian frowns.

I put on a smile. "I'm alright. An unpleasant way to go when the night was so lovely. You met Kerrigan, I imagine?"

Damian nods. "I did. I was actually in mid-conversation with them when I noticed his grace was taking far too much of your night. I'm sorry I didn't notice sooner."

"It's alright. You deserve some fun too." I smile for real. "I'll be fine." The Grand Duke just wants me to let him have his way. I cannot take him seriously. Or so I tell myself.

"Yes, you will, and do not let *anyone* tell you differently. You have a power in you that scares people like him." Damian gives me a dangerous smile. "That's why being your attendant is so fun. Every moment is another exciting adventure. Like this one." He grins then twirls me twice; first, one way, then the other.

I giggle and smile at his analogy. "That it is," I agree. "But that's why we have a lead and help."

"All too true, my lady. That is why I am always a call away," he promises with a smile and leads me more into the dance.

I enjoy the break. It brings back the fun I was having until the song finally ends. Damian leads me back to Flur and her fiancé, making sure the Grand Duke is far away from me.

Part of me wishes I could get Gavril to dance just to help me relax and remember why I'm enduring this. Instead, I get annoyed, watching him dance with Forsythia.

But then the duke from Purysia asks me to dance. Once again, I don't dare say no, but I'm also not afraid of him. He's formal but polite and smiles friendly enough.

All I can remember is he is the duchess' husband. I think he is one of those names that is like Cedrick as the Merlin is a popular person to name your son after. But there are so many I can't recall which is the name of this man, if any. Cerill? Cedree? Cerick?

"You're a stunning dancer," he compliments me enthusiastically.

"Thank you. I would hope so," I reply before he gives me a twirl. "I did do it for a living all of my life."

"Ah yes, that was what it was." He nods. "Is it odd not to dance anymore?"

"I dance all the time. I practice after lunch when I like, and of course, there are plenty of balls like tonight," I say as we spin about the dance floor. It's not hard to keep up with him.

"That must help." He nods slowly. "Well, it shows. You are a stunning dancer." He spins me about again, trying something a little harder. "And better than me." He laughs when I nail it without even a hesitation. "I'm not that good."

"You are just fine," I assure him.

"Good. You are too kind. You also are quite lovely. You fit right in here with the royalty," he praises. "Our king and queen will look forward to meeting you. Perhaps if you can't win this prince, you can win another." He winks.

I flush. "That's kind of you to say." I don't know why he's going out of his way to say so.

"It may be kind, but it is also true. You fit right in. You are stunning," he says.

I hold back my normal rebuttal. Damian makes me look lovely. Without him, I'd be burned in gaudy orange still. "Thank you. You and your delegation are always lovely. Your ascots are particularly unique," I compliment.

"I'll be sure a box of the finest assortment is sent to you," he promises me as we dance on.

I chuckle a little. "Sweet of you to say." But there's not a chance they'd send a girl with only a chance to the throne such a gift, but his flattery is sweet.

"You'll make them all look ten times better," he assures me.

We talk about theatre the rest of the dance which feels forever long. He declares he loves all of my top choices before he bows to kiss my hand and takes me back to my spot. "You are too kind to share your talent with me," he says as we finish. "It was my pleasure, Lady Kascia." He bows to me.

"And mine." I curtsy back before he leaves.

"I hope he didn't step on your toes." The duchess comes over to me.

"Not at all," I assure her. Why are they all giving me such attention? I notice the Delegation Head speaking to the king.

"Good. He has gotten better over the years," she says. "But I wanted to give you a parting gift before I go."

My cheeks go pink. "There was no need."

"Oh, I wanted to," she insists and offers me a small box.

I can't say no. That would be even more rude. I open it and find a fine teacup, saucer, and matching spoon. I realize she recalled I chose tea instead of a stronger drink that first night.

I manage a smile. "Thank you. It's beautiful." And it is. It's painted with delicate watercolors to look like a quiet night in the countryside along the sea. I admire the stars showing in the careful artwork. The saucer matches and the spoon is made with stars in the design and waves as well.

"Made in my homeland." She smiles. "I hope you keep it for a long time and remember the small friendship we made."

"I will," I promise, feeling my stomach drop. I really hope I'm not the only one getting this kind of attention, but I also don't want to know. If I am, I'm terrified. If I'm not, I don't want to know who else Gavril is favoring.

I attempt to hide the rest of the night. The delegation leaves the next morning. I use the madness to get some extra sleep and try to ignore my stress. I put the box on my desk, unsure what else I could or should do with it.

Chapter 9

Damian congratulates me on doing so well with the first delegation as I prepare for rehearsals the next morning.

"It wasn't even my delegation." I sigh.

"Which gives you that much more practice for when yours turns up." He smiles.

I chuckle. "That is a good point." I glance nervously at the box the delegation leader gave me. Flur is eyeing it with curiosity.

Damian follows my eye. "What is that?"

"Um well." I flush. "A teacup."

"Really?" Damian smiles. "That from them?"

"Yes," I confess quickly, as if getting out fast made it less bad.

Damian nods. "May I?"

"Go ahead." I smile.

Damian opens the box and carefully takes the teacup out, holding it up to examine it. As quite the tea conqueror, I'm sure he'd know a good teacup when he sees one. "Exquisite," he says with a smile then sets it back in the box and looks back at me. "They want your favor."

I swallow and nod. "I think so."

Damian seems to notice my nervousness. "Is that a bad thing?"

"What?"

"You seem to not like the simple fact that they like you."

I sigh. "I don't think it's that they 'like' me," I say carefully.

"It's that they believe you will win," he surmises.

I nod. "I think so."

He arches a brow. "So why is that a bad thing?"

"I just... am nervous I'm the only one," I try to explain.

"Why? Did you want someone else to win?"

"Well, no."

"So why are you nervous about winning and others clearly wanting you to win?"

I pause. "You think they want me to win?"

"They did like your hat." He smiles.

"Great, they should elect you." I roll my eyes.

"It wasn't just the hat." Damian reads my thoughts correctly. "But in all seriousness, I think they both want you to win and see you may be the favorite to win. The latter being affected by the former."

"They only noticed because they saw we met eyes," I admit.

"But they saw you met eyes because they were looking at you to begin with," Damian points out. "How many other people were in that same room but didn't notice that interaction?"

I shrug. "No one mentions it."

"Most don't see it. They saw it because of you. I know because I was watching them."

I force a small smile. "That's good, I suppose."

Damian rolls his eyes. "If you want it that way. But enough of that. We have rehearsals."

All too soon, it's time for the next delegation to arrive: Alalusia. This delegation is even more friendly than the Purysians and even more of a culture shock for me. Their dress is vastly different from ours as well as their behavior.

The men and women stay in their own groups. The men wear fine thin suits with shockingly long, pointed tailcoats that make them look stunningly thin and tall. They all sport mustaches in various shapes from impressive handlebars to thin and curled ones, walrus mustaches, and even an impressive horseshoe mustache. It looks like the thicker the mustache, the more stylish. One mustache has such a heavy curl it makes a spiral on either end. The men are aloof and spend most of the welcome party looking through small round glasses or monocles disapprovingly at the ladies.

The ladies cannot be more different from us, wearing dresses with skirts so large they cannot enter side by side, entering one at a time and then immediately linking arms with another lady in their party. The skirts are highly decorated with countless ruffles, gathers, satin dresses, lacy layers, and all have a gathered hem at the end of the skirt. Some wear long satin gloves; many have lace parasols, likely used to ward off any snow when they arrived. Their hairstyles are pinned up with tight curls in dozens of configurations. Like the mustaches, it seems the thicker and curlier, the more in fashion.

The Alalusian ladies are as bright, bubbly, and chatty as their male counterparts are aloof and cold. They go right up to the royal family in their pairs, greeting them in their relaxed accent. Their "th"s become "d"s and long vowels are substituted for easier ones. "Are" sounds like "our". I have to hide my smile and giggle as I hear the girls repeatedly fawn over Gavril, or rather "Ga'al"

Bella notices the women are overly friendly, yet the men are keeping their distance. She tries to go over to invite the men into the festivities as the Alalusian ladies fawn over Ericka's pink dress that matches their over-the-top style with what looks like bouquets of pink roses sewn at the point of each curling ruffle. The men do not respond well to Bella. I can't help but wonder if it's because she's a girl because when Gavril comes over and takes Bella's arm and addresses the group, they instantly become as friendly to him as the ladies were with the rest of us. They become equally as chatty but speak in more dignified tones.

Though my dress is simple in comparison to the visiting ladies, it matches their style with a large round skirt with one more subtle gathering with black lace lining and soft gathered sleeves and black gloves of my own, matching the soft yellow of my dress. Though I am *no* expert on fabrics, I think mine is silk while their dresses are all satin. The colors work. My maids used my natural curls to make ringlets like the ones the Alalusian ladies have with plenty of volume.

The Alalusian ladies love them so much, they have to feel they are real for themselves. It's the longest examination of my hair I have ever had, and I did theater. They are convinced there is something in my hair to give it that volume. Might explain why the ladies smell like hairspray.

Bella has to step out to handle preparations with something which leaves Gavril open, and being the little troublemaker he is, he decides keeping me on his arm is his next best escape. I think he just wants to watch the show. He's very amused.

"Guess Damian is too good at something," he says so only I can hear as the girls coo. If looks could burn, Gavril would have a burn right on his nose.

"This is just amazin'. We need to know the name of that product," Marquise Loretta insists as her well-painted pink nails fiddle with my hair.

"You'd have to ask my maids," I admit.

"It's not at all stiff." She smiles at me.

I shrug. "It's mostly natural," I admit.

"Amazin'." Marquise Loretta nods. "Some gi'ls got it, I guess." I manage a weak smile. This is going to be a long reception if Gavril does not let me off the hook, literally if you consider his arm a hook.

But thankfully, it's not too long before the rest of the girls join in enjoying all the fancy outfits and jewelry we have on. It is easy to please Alalusian girls, I suppose.

Before dinner, I get another letter from my mother, wishing me luck and saying she's excited to see me soon. She must know how stressed I am about these visits from what I wrote to her and she just knows how I am.

Dinner that night is another surprise. I don't have anyone fawn over my outfit or hair this time. But I thank the Maker for that because I'm too full to be tolerant of such attention. The first course is corn bread that the Alalusians insist must be slathered in butter and/or honey. The soup is heavy with beans, rabbit, and so many vegetables I lose track, though I notice the corn. There is corn in almost everything. The fish course helps calm things down, though like much of this meal, it's a tad oily. Fried chicken is served as the main course with fried tomatoes. Then we have mashed cream potatoes and corn and finish with a sweet potato pie.

I have never felt so sick. I look over at the high table. Our guests are as happy as baby gargoyles with a pile of gems. The king looks just slightly green while the queen is a stunning shade of puce. Gavril looks how I feel. He meets my eyes, and we both fight not to laugh as we instantly know we both agree on how much we like this meal. The leaving feast is going to be even more interesting.

The men of the delegation are louder over the meal than they had been at the party and ask where to blow off some steam around here. I suppose sports will be in order shortly, perhaps more fencing.

The next day, between their meetings, they do indeed have a sporting event. They arrange a friendly game of sparkleball, Alalusia versus Purerah, to be played outside which is interesting in the snow. Sparkleball is a cultural fixture in Alalusia apparently. The women insist on watching the match even in the snow. They look all prim and proper as they sit to watch. They wear thick fur capes on their shoulders, making them look even more round and poofy than normal. The men wear jackets that still make them look as thin and straight as a pole. They wear the Alalusian colors: yellow and navy-blue highlights. The Chosen girls stand out sharply next to them in our simpler jackets and less vibrant colors.

Forsythia can't miss the chance to try to look important when she wishes Gavril good luck. To my annoyance, he smiles and replies, "Thank you, fox." She smirks at the rest of us. She'd wanted her nickname to be said in front of the visitors. I fight not to lose my cool.

The only lady not watching is Dahlia who cannot resist getting in on the game. Gavril is quick to put her on our team. The visitors don't mind. They snort as if thinking Gavril foolish for choosing her. I can't help but notice none of the visiting ladies want to play. I even hear a few jokes about how easy it will be to win with us having a lady on our team. I'm actually rooting for Dahlia for once.

I try to sit away from the main events for a break, but Damian has done a good job again, and the Alalusian ladies can't resist admiring it. He'd made me a golden/brown cape jacket with a stunning hoop hood that keeps the hood up and off my hair, so it isn't ruined. The gathering work is stunning. While the others prep for the game, the ladies spend ten minutes admiring it, Marquise Loretta leading the pack as always.

I'm wondering if I can fain ill to leave when a bark gets my attention. Joy runs up to me, spraying me and the visiting ladies in snow, making them cry out in shock though Marquise Loretta laughs.

"Hello Joy." I smile and bend down to stroke her.

"Re-row!" she howls to the sky as her tail does its normal happy, frantic dance. She then makes her adorable squeak that sounds like my name and lies down in the snow, snuffing at it as she looks up at me in pure happiness. Her red fur contrasts the snow beautifully.

"Happy for snow?" I ask her as I stroke her back, knocking snowflakes from it.

She yips the happiest "yeah" ever and rushes back and forth across the snow, making more of it fly up. The visitors laugh and do their best to knock the snow from their huge skirts.

Joy is leashed to the spectator area near me, but it doesn't stop her running across the side of the field, trying to jump up and retrieve the ball from whoever has it.

I don't know who screams more, Joy or the Alalusian ladies. They are all perfect, friendly ladies until the game starts, and then some rather rude and impressively angry words come from their mouths. It is a comical contrast.

They have reason to scream though. Dahlia is helping our team win almost single handedly. But having the king play (which I'm sure they couldn't avoid without raising questions) gives us a disadvantage as he tries to look like he is playing but does as little as possible.

Gavril and Dahlia do make a good team. The biggest problem ends up being when Joy manages to steal the ball, and she refuses to give it back. But at the promise of waffles later, she gives the ball to Gavril, refusing to give it to anyone else.

When our team wins, thankfully, the visiting gentlemen apologize to Dahlia for doubting her ability. They are truly impressed.

"Never thought I'd see it." They shake their heads.

Dahlia, as cocky as ever, gives them a smirk and a nod as she accepts their apology. Her little half smile of a smirk doesn't leave her face. She looks as proud as a peacock. She stands straight, chest out, with the ball under one arm. She sure looks as proud and powerful as a queen until Joy ruins it by running up and snatching the ball right out from under Dahlia's arm.

Gavril swears under his breath before he yells at her to give it back. We all rather enjoy watching Sage, Godwin, and Gavril struggle to get the ball back. There's something satisfying about watching the three of them run from one end of the field, kicking up snow, fail to catch the puppy, then run to the other side as Joy races away until her lead stops her. She dodges them and does it again. But eventually, Gavril threatens no waffles which finally gets Joy to give the ball back, but not before Gavril, Sage, Godwin, and Joy are so covered in snow, they could be snowmen.

The rest of their visit runs smoothly though. At meals, the ladies are trying to get my attention much like the Purysians did. This time, I look to see who else is getting attention. Zelda, Dahlia, and Ericka all appear to be favorites of this delegation.

I'm nervous for their farewell feast and ball. I tentatively ask my maids if the dress for the farewell ball can handle a too-full-stomach and not make me look like a blimp. Flur laughs as if it's a joke. Vivian shrugs. "Good corset will hide it, but it won't feel great."

"Any way to throw up in a corner without being seen?" I ask dully.

"Doubt it." Vivian finishes tying up my dress.

"I just hope the Japcharians and Dragians aren't as heavy eaters," I sigh, "or I'm going to not only lose my dance figure, I'll offend them by vomiting."

"We can set you to a run tomorrow after they leave," Vivian tries to cheer me up.

But it isn't just being so full I'm afraid of, though that does frighten me. I also know tonight the Grand Duke will be there once again. I will have to stay close to Cedrick, Damian, or Gavril to keep him away. I'm not sure I can handle another attack from him.

At least the dress is beautiful. It's done in Alalusian style but with a simple twist. It's a stunning white and gold with only two layers at the large round skirt. The gathered fabric at the bottom, which I've come to just call an Alalusian gather, makes the gold really pop. The large round sleeves are the most perfect blend of the simple style I like and the big statement the Alalusians like. My Chosen necklace I use to perfectly frame the well-fitting top and the pearl earrings are set off by my full bun perfectly.

Though my skirt seems small compared to the visitor's skirts (that are so big, they have to make more room at the table for them) the ladies don't seem to mind as they chat more loudly than ever. They are delighted even if the rest of us are not. This meal is even worse than the last.

They start with biscuits which are followed by, I kid you not, macaroni and cheese with extra cheese and breadcrumbs on top (and grease of course). At least they are small bowls. We then have a seafood boil with stunning spices on it. I could have had this the rest of the night though it's so oily, it's a tad slippery. The main course is a fine, spicy soup with shellfish, celery, bell peppers, and onions. The fact it is a soup makes it a bit easier to take in. The next dish is a rich mix of various meats and the same vegetable mix from before. I think this one is the hardest course to keep down so far, and we're not done yet. At least the wine helps with how spicy this meal is. The spice level cools down with the chicken and dumpling dish. We finish with a dessert that is fried bread topped with a fine sugar. I manage to get my small piece down, but I'm sure if I try to eat one more bite, I will explode. And we are expected to socialize and dance now?

The king is doing better this time. He looks quite happy as he talks with Marquis Holt. The queen is laughing with Marquise Loretta though I think I see a hint of red around her neck, but if that's from feeling ill from food or something else I can't tell. Gavril is talking with another visiting couple and has a unique way of coping with all he's eating. I think he's had more to drink than normal. He is talking rather animatedly and is a bit pink in the cheeks.

The servants begin to clear up as we stand. It helps my stomach a bit. I try to keep down any signs of how full I am. Because I'm fighting so hard, I don't notice I'm one of the last in the room. "We might be able to hide and empty our stomachs if we're quick," Gavril jokes to me.

"How do they all do it?" I demand. "How are those men so thin?"

"Evil magic," Gavril says. I am not sure if he's serious or not.

"So how do we handle it?" I ask, trying to hold in the sick feeling.

"We pretend we don't feel it. It's how I get through most everything." I swear if he had been holding a drink, he'd have just finished it with how he said that. I'm not sure how I feel about any of what he just said. I just am too full to process it.

Gavril sighs and offers me a hand. "At least if one of us falls on our faces the other will keep the attention away," he jokes.

I give him a look before accepting it. He's got a point, sadly enough. We join the others, and somehow many of them are already dancing. The king tries to talk the queen into it, but like me, I think she's worried the spinning will make something escape. The visitors are dancing like nothing happened. I look around, wondering if Cedrick is doing the same. I can't imagine Damian got through all of that feeling normal, but his superhuman monster of a brother likely did.

I am right. Cedrick is dancing with a group of the ladies, trading between them with impressive speed. The little cheat. I have never seen such heavy flirting in my life, poor Cedrick. The Alalusian ladies' fans are going mad in their hands. But I can't blame them, Cedrick is handsome and charming. His black hair, just curly enough to make a mess, is somehow still handsome. However, it's his stunningly blue eyes that really do the trick as they seem to look at you and make you feel understood and cared about more than you'd ever felt before.

I look around to see if Damian found somewhere to hide. I'd not mind taking a step out of the limelight for a while. Damian is hiding in a corner by the glass doors leading out to the balcony we'd had our snowball fight on. Looks like a good place to hide once I shake the prince, which is easy enough when a delegate sees him and rushes to him immediately.

Damian gives me a warm smile as I approach, looking much the same as ever. "Good evening, my lady," he says pleasantly.

"What are you so pleased about?" I ask.

He shrugs. "Just enjoying the night before I tear my hair out tomorrow."

"Doing what?" I can enjoy the distraction.

"I'm going over to the theater to see how things are coming along, which is only one of many thousand other things on my to-do list." He sighs as if asking why he hates himself.

"Well, we could back out," I point out. Though that also means he knows I should be working on the delegation assignments I have. My delegation is next week. I'm doing my part, but I know there is likely a lot to do. Still, I'd have happily taken the distraction.

"Sure, and the war will be over next week," he says sarcastically.

"Still an option," I tease. Then sigh. How does he feel so good after eating all of that? I was sure he'd be as sick as me.

He smiles and shakes his head. "I'm afraid I don't have it in me to quit. But enough of that, you should be enjoying the night. Though you do look a bit green." He gives me a sympathetic smile.

I groan. "And you're not?"

Then someone comes to hide in our corner. I raise an eyebrow as Gavril slips in. "What? It's insane out there," he defends.

Damian chuckles. "'Tis their culture. I had a friend who was similar, but he preferred life rough and dirty."

"Those men wouldn't mind tossing it down though they agree with you," Gavril agrees, covering his mouth with a fist to hide a near burp.

"Don't let the ladies see that," I say dryly.

"I'm more scared of my mother," Gavril admits. I laugh.

Damian chuckles. "That is understandable," he says with a nod. "Her shriek would be heard clear across the ballroom."

"And one dead prince may ruin the proceedings," Gavril agrees. I roll my eyes.

"And just shy of your birthday too. A real shame that." Damian shakes his head in mock sadness.

"Oh, not you too." Gavril rolls his eyes. "It's all anyone who isn't participating in the talks wants to talk about." He means the other girls, I'm sure. I swallow. Maybe it would be better not to make a big deal out of it.

"Well, I can't exactly forget about it after the challenge you issued me." Damian gives him a playful glare.

"You could say no," Gavril points out. "I was joking. I still am not sure you'll do it."

"I have to do something. It's in my blood."

"I'm fine with it left alone." Gavril looks Damian over. "Are you part Alalusian or something?"

Damian laughs. "Oh no. I'd never eat that much in one sitting, even if it was my wife's cooking."

"How?" I ask. "Just avoided dinner?"

"Of course not. But I'm a servant. No one notices or cares if I don't clear the plate." Damian smiles.

"Of course," Gavril sighs. "I'm just trying not to be gross or rude. He's over here boasting how good it is to be staff."

"Sorry." Damian chuckles with a more apologetic smile. "Though you know, once upon a time, there were a few cultures that had a designated corner to vomit in, so guests could come back and keep eating because it was impolite to stop."

"That's worse." If I was emptying my stomach, I was leaving it empty.

"I would agree." Damian nods with a smile. "Can I offer you two a bucket?"

"No!" We say together.

Damian can help but laugh. "Sorry, that might have been a bit cheeky."

"You want to dance with all these excited ladies?" Gavril offers.

"I'm not as pretty as Cedrick." Damian smiles as he glances around Gavril's shoulder as if to spot his brother.

"He can't keep all twelve busy," Gavril points out. "Even when he's trying."

"Perhaps not. But my position makes few ladies want to say yes," Damian excuses. "But if you're insistent, I can give it a try."

"You really think they won't say yes?" Gavril chuckles.

"Not if they have a better option." Damian shrugs.

Gavril shakes his head. "Trust me, you could charm any of these ladies away from me."

"Happy married, thank you." Damian dips his head to him.

"So? What's wrong with stealing a dance?" Gavril says. "At least help out those who had to eat the whole cursed meal."

Damian sighs playfully as if it's a massive burden Gavril has placed on him then bows his head to him. "Very well." He then excuses himself and goes to join the dancing.

I can't help but laugh. "You think it's going to work?" I ask.

"Only partly," Gavril says, then looks at me. "He keeps them busy. You steal any opening."

"What?"

"If I promise to spin as little as possible, would you protect us both from our crazy visitors?" he asks me. That is likely the strangest "you want to dance" I'd ever heard, and I'm in theatre.

However, it sounds like a safe bet, so I nod uneasily. At least if we make ourselves sick, we can use the other one as the excuse. "Alright, just... careful on the spins," I agree.

"Trust me. I don't want to vomit any more than you do." Gavril grins. Which means we'd both love to empty our stomachs but know we can't afford to. I sigh and take his offered hand.

It is likely the calmest social dance I have ever done, but it does spare us from the others for a while. Gavril uses me as a shield a bit longer until he is able to sit and talk to his father for a while.

I try to escape, but in an almost déjà vu moment, Marquise Loretta comes over and offers me a gift of friendship: ironically, a hair comb to put in my hair as if I need help with the volume. At least it is not something too gaudy for my taste like the dresses these ladies wear.

After that, I decide it is time to slip away. I do not need to be thought of more as Gavril's favorite by him using me as a shield from the others. I already made a spectacle of myself in front of this delegation as well as the last, and I am more than ready to go to bed. Because shortly, it will be my turn.

Chapter 10

The next morning, my maids do all they can to ensure I sleep in since Damian is off at the theater. It does help though I have to rush to breakfast. I'm meeting with the other girls in my group to go over last-minute arrangements for our delegation with just a few days until they arrive.

We work all morning until lunch. I have a list of tasks I agreed to do, but they will have to wait until the day before or the day of. But I want to make sure all is right as well as making sure I have time to rehearse.

My mind is buzzing during lunch with all I have to do when a servant passes me a note. I look it over. It's in the prince's hand, asking for a date this afternoon. I frown. I'd hoped to catch up on my work this afternoon. I don't know if I want to waste it playing, but how often do I get a chance to go out with him? I do have to keep his trust and attention unless I want him doubting again.

I haven't sent a reply yet as I get up from my meal. Gavril must have figured I was debating because he comes out into the hall after me. "You didn't even see my signal," he play-pouts. "Did I offend you last night?" A hint of concern creases his brow.

"No, it's just my turn is up," I point out. "We have a lot to do."

"I thought you met with them this morning."

"I did but..." I have to make my schedule, review the etiquette, and ensure the flower arrangements are right when Damian has a second, so I need to make sure I can catch him at any second.

"But you are meeting again?" Gavril raises a brow.

"Well, no," I hedge.

"Then you can do with a break. You get all wound up, you'll be too tense. I'll come to your room to pick you up in..." he checks his wristwatch, "twenty minutes or so. I won't take your whole day unless you want me to," he assures me.

I'm not so sure, but he leaves before I can turn him down. I sigh. This new side of him is starting to get on my nerves. My maids look pleased with themselves when I reach my room. "We're ready for you, miss," Flur says.

"He warned you?" What in creation is he up to?

Flur nods. "Don't worry, miss. He's not going to eat you or anything."

At this point, I'd believe it. Vivian giggles, which is odd for her. "Come on, you'll like it," she promises. Well, I guess Vivian would know. I let them dress me in... it better not be fencing again. I'm not ready for that emotional ride. They have me slip into one of my dance suits.

I open my mouth to dare ask when there's a knock at the door. "Ready," Flur declares with a big smile.

I sigh as she goes to get the door, and Vivian makes sure my hair is secure. They really do seem excited.

For once, Gavril doesn't step in when Flur says I'm ready. He waits for me to be willing to come out. I feel a bit guilty. Yes, he was trying to talk me into it, but he was letting me say no even now. I sigh. I can give him a few hours. I am trying to do well in this event for him anyway, right?

I walk out and close the door behind me. I really hope he's not going for fencing again. His dress makes me think so: the kind of training clothes men normally use. My breath hitches, but I try to hide it. I have never seen Gavril in anything but his suits. His arms are exposed in short sleeves, and they are impressively strong looking. I know some dancers who are strong, but their arms do not look so good. He looks really good.

I control my breathing and force myself to look at his face while my mind replays the night he pulled me out of a ship's porthole. He'd done it like I weighed no more than Joy and set me in front of him as gracefully as a swan. I didn't realize his arms look as pretty as his strength felt. I try not to let my mind picture what the rest of him looks like.

"You look perfect." Gavril beams. "Ready?" He offers me his arm. He doesn't even look too bulky. I must really need a break if I can't keep my mind on track. I take his arm. He smiles more gently. "Thanks. I was sure you were about to change your mind."

"Why would I do that?" I ask as he leads me down the hall. "If I were going to say no, I'd do it with the full drama of slamming the door." Gavril laughs. "Okay, maybe not. That would be unnecessarily rude."

"It's okay. I slam doors a lot, mostly on Joy. She isn't ready to go everywhere with me, but she sure tries." He smiles at me. "Thanks again. She lives up to her name. I'm waiting for her to be ready before I let her wander about. I *really* want to see what happens when she meets Cuppy." I laugh. Cuppy is Ericka's little dog. He is cute, but a menace to society. "I don't know if she'll love the little dog or hate him. She gets along well with the cat, you know, Nippers. So, I can see her liking Cuppy and wanting to play. But she hates squirrels." I burst into laughter. "No seriously, she whimpers to chase them if I can't distract her. It's annoying and adorable. Most of the time they run off at her barking."

"I'd like to see that," I admit.

"When it warms up, perhaps we can go out and take her for a walk. She has to adjust to being outside sooner or later," Gavril says. "I know she misses you. She says your name really clearly." I flush a bit. "Don't worry, she's not pining. I think she likes me well enough." He smiles. He'd not been this normal with me in what felt like a lifetime. It's nice. "And she's doing better in most training. Though she has trouble attacking people. She'll get all scary and attack, but once she has you, she just licks your face off. I can't wait to try it."

"On who? A rebel?" I try to picture Jake breaking in and Joy jumping him like that. I have to stop walking with how hard I laugh. "You better hope that rebel has a good sense of humor." Father would not be as amused.

"Well, we tried it on Gentian, and it was hilarious." Gavril laughs. "He was *not* happy."

"He is a grump. Must be where Sage gets it," I say.

"I now have learned Sage is much more like his mother." Gavril smiles. "She's the one we'd want to meet."

"Maybe she'll show up for a wedding," I joke.

"You'll get to meet her then," Gavril agrees.

I really wish he wouldn't talk like that, but I also don't want to stop him. I search for a change of topic. "So where are we going?" I ask.

"We're here." We stop in front of the practice hall.

"You're kidding." Why do I not like the idea of having a date with him right next door to where the girls hang out?

"Nope. Only space I know for sure has the equipment we need."

"What equipment?" I frown as Gavril opens the door, and we step inside. He hasn't changed the room at all.

"Your tools," Gavril says. "I know you need to clear your head and dance always works."

"We could use the ballroom for that," I point out. And we'd danced just last night.

Gavril laughs. "No barre."

I laugh. "You're kidding." He's going to join me for a ballet lesson?

"No, I've been working on it. I even requested a routine be made up by your theater that we can learn," Gavril says as if he'd just ordered me flowers. "I saw what you did at Christmas, and it looked like a lot of fun. Cedrick seemed to enjoy it. I normally like dancing with you, so why not?"

"Well... alright," I can't help but smile. Maybe it's because Jake wouldn't dare try, but it's a funny thought to have my man dance ballet with me.

It actually is a lot of fun. Gavril clearly is not confident as he follows along through all the normal routines: plie, tendu, rond de jambe, grand jete, and the rest. When he feels he's doing it wrong, he'll exaggerate it for dramatic effect, reminding me a bit of Cedrick.

He then pulls out the surprise: a full routine for me to dance with him. He says it was choreographed by my mother, but since the accompanying song is about getting up the nerve to kiss a girl, I think Alsmeria may be the real choreographer. Despite that embarrassment, it is fun, even though we are far from perfect. I miss hitting my mark a few times, and poor Gavril struggles even more, but we're both laughing at least.

I back into him and almost knock him over when he is not ready for it a few times. "Your Majesty," I laugh. "You're going to hurt yourself if you don't pay attention."

"Highness," Gavril corrects me as he counts under his breath.

"What?"

"Majesty is for kings and queens on a throne. Highness is for princes and princesses," he reminds me. "Though, in some cultures, the crown prince or princess is addressed as 'Your Grace' as well."

I laugh. "I'll call you that when you start dancing gracefully again." He laughs too.

But Gavril is a quick study. I get the feeling he really is like me in that he feels better when he's moving and working through things. It really does feel wonderful.

"You are tireless." I laugh when I realize we've been at the routine over an hour. "You're going to be sore at this point."

"Not until I get it," Gavril insists with a grin.

"Or maybe you need to be happy keeping your hands to yourself," I tease.

"What? It's just a turn," he says innocently.

"Still." I smile back. "Enough for one day."

"Fine, only if we work on it later."

"Okay, but not later today, and not until my turn is over. You have any idea how much preparation something like this takes? And it's Japcharia. They don't like us, remember?"

"Would help if they'd stop trying to take over Merlake," Gavril comments as he goes over to take off his dance shoes.

"That talk isn't going to help," I say as I work on mine.

"Of course, I'd not say that to them. I'm just saying. Their kingdom was larger until they kept doing that." He smiles at me.

"I know. I've been reading all about it nonstop for weeks," I groan as I put my shoes away. "And now I get to read up on how not to offend them."

"You? Offend them? Not possible," Gavril jokes as he stands up after putting his regular shoes on.

"Hey, it's possible. I offend you all the time."

Gavril pauses as if to think. "Hmm, have you?"

"You're incorrigible." I sigh. "No wonder no one thinks you're ready to rule. You don't listen."

"I'm mostly sick of listening. Like you, I'd rather move than sit still." He smiles.

I smile back. That we do share. It's why we met out of bounds that night. I sigh heavily. If only it really was that simple as... I jump. Gavril is a lot closer than I realized he was.

"Sorry." He backs up. "I forgot. You don't like to act like we're dating."

I frown. "It's not that. It's just..."

"You don't want to be the favorite. How do you know I'm not just as bad with the others?" he asks.

"I don't want to know," I say with a hint of bitterness as I walk away from him to put my bag away.

"Sorry." Gavril clears his throat as he turns to look at me. "But if you don't want to be the favorite, you should at least let me treat you the same."

"I-I don't know, and honestly, not really thinking about it. I'm just trying to get through this next week without starting a national war."

"The others pulled it off without much trouble."

"The other two already liked us," I remind him.

Gavril ponders what to say a moment. "Yes, but that also means offending them could be worse. We lose an ally. If they still hate us after this, nothing lost, nothing gained."

"But if we get them to like us it's a lot gained, and if we talk them into a war without meaning to, it's a lot of loss."

"You really are high strung." Gavril frowns. "We're not going to send you back to your friends who are mad at you, you know."

That's not the problem! I hold in the retort. I look around for something else to do, but I can't find anything, so I just put my hands on my hips. "I know." It's about proving to myself I am a good choice for princess, proving I am his princess. I have to prove I'm good at this, or I shouldn't win. And I have to.

Gavril frowns. "Sorry. I didn't mean to hurt you. I thought that was why you're so tense about this."

I shake my head. How could I tell him all of it without making him angry? It is so easy to do. I don't want to lose him. I don't want to let our people down. I want to be good at this. I want it so badly. But I'm scared because I know I'm not a true princess. I'm a fraud, and I knew it when I came here.

"Hey, are you alright?" Gavril asks, leaning to try to see my face. I try not to meet his eyes. "What is it?" Gavril asks, coming closer. Carefully, he puts his hand on my arm. "It's alright. I'm not judging you. It's perfectly alright to be nervous. I am too. I'm only trying to help. I don't think I've ever seen you this tense."

"It's not you," I try not to snap but snap anyway.

Gavril's brow furrows. "So, what is it?"

"I just..." I take a deep breath and look up at the ceiling. "I want to do well, that's all. I came here to help my people, and now this is my first chance to do something real and prove I can do this. And I keep worrying that I'll get it wrong. And now I've put it off with other work, and it's so close, and I've done nothing for it. And now I have to do it in just a few days and..." And this test scares me more than I realize and being this close to feeling like he really is mine... It's just too much right now.

"Look, I was really teasing with the whole show thing. You don't have to—"

"It's not that," I insist. "The problem is I want to do it, and I'm scared of this delegation, so I wasn't working on it. Now... I can do it; I just don't have much time. I just have to review. Then I'll know I've got this and will feel better once I start."

Gavril smiles understandably. "You need to move." He pauses. "You need to feel sure of something." He's thinking about something, debating. I'm not sure I like that look.

"Kascia, I know you don't want to feel like you're winning, but—"

"Oh please, don't start that right now." I don't know why I say it.

"I'm not," Gavril promises patiently. That makes me stop dead. He'd not gotten angry? That's an improvement. "But being so tense might not help. You know what happens when you're too stiff when you try to dance?"

"Something gives," I repeat my mother's saying. "When you're too stiff, you fall."

"Exactly." Gavril smiles. "So though maybe you want me to take a break, I think you need to. What do you do apart from dance to let it out?" He smiles. "Want to take over the music room again?"

I sigh. "I really should get to work on the delegation."

"You're ready. You said so. What do you do with the girls all day?" he asks.

"Um... we play games." I shrug.

"Oh?" Gavril's face lights in interest. "Do you play Ostragie?"

"Yeah, my father had me play a lot." I shrug.

"You any good?"

"I guess."

"Hmm. All of you play?" Gavril asks.

"Well, the girls I hang out with do." I shrug again.

Gavril nods thoughtfully. "Okay, well maybe we can try that sometime. Or maybe chess."

"Never played," I admit.

"I can teach you. Why not do that now?"

"Gavril, I really should..."

"Calm down." He looks me over. "You have two more days to stress about it. You can change; I'll change, and we can meet up in the library."

I ponder it a moment. "But..."

"Okay, how about you change, and I'll come get you."

"Gavril."

"Deal." He doesn't offer his arm. He takes my hand. A jolt of electricity emanates from his touch. How stupid. I have been taking his hand, and he has even supported my waist for hours now. And this is what makes me feel excited? "Come on."

He brings me back to my room, and my maids dress me in a day dress. The prince didn't mention coming back. Maybe I can get some work done before... but instead of knocking, the stupid man cracks the door.

Joy comes bounding inside and jumps up on me in pure excitement. I laugh. "Joy, down."

I hear Gavril ask my maids if it's alright for him to come in before he walks through the door. "She needs training work. You can help me. We're going to walk the castle." He's holding a lead.

"Gavril."

"Come on, she'll be sad if you don't come now." He looks down at the puppy whose tail is wiggling madly.

"Fine," I agree.

Joy yips in excitement and rushes over to Gavril to let him put the lead on her collar. I smile as she tries to sit still, her tail wagging so hard that her whole-body shudders in excitement with each thump. She is so cute. But after only a minute of fumbling, Gavril finally gets the lead on. "Soon you shouldn't need it," he tells her as he stands up. Then he looks up at me. "Ready?"

I smile and nod. Gavril adjusts his shirt a bit as he secures Joy's lead to a clip on his belt loop. He'd opted for a casual white button up shirt with no waistcoat for now. I suppose it makes dealing with the dog easier as his nicer waistcoats might be a bit constricting.

As we walk, he tells me about Joy's training and how he wants to try the conservatory but is worried she'll dig. He lets Joy smell most everything to help her get used to it all. When I ask, he tells me it's her home too, so he doesn't want to force her to be on guard all the time.

Joy gets distracted by a suit of armor along a hallway. "He-wo." She makes her greeting sound.

"Joy, that's just a suit. There's no one in there," I laugh.

Joy looks at me as if I'm rude and says hello to the suit again. It doesn't reply. She gets annoyed and complains to Gavril. "It is just a suit, Joy. There is no one inside to say hello to. See?" He comes over and picks her up. He pushes up the visor to let her look inside.

Joy makes a surprised sniff sound. "Yeah, no one there," Gavril says and puts her down. "They all are empty. Our guards don't wear armor like that. I don't know if anyone has worn armor like that in years. Well, if they joust, I suppose."

"Does anyone do that anymore?" I ask.

"Not that I know of, at least not here," Gavril says. "Maybe in other countries. None of the ones I spoke to have mentioned it though."

We walk along quietly for a moment, watching Joy explore. She makes sounds like asking us questions, but neither of us have a clue what she is saying, so she just keeps sniffing, nosing, trying to check out the things around her.

We reach the ground floor, and Joy is very interested in the fine marble floor, sniffing at it and poking it with her paw and her nose as Gavril stands to let her explore before she walks on it.

Finally, she steps on the marble, her little claws making a slight sound against the floor. She makes a little huff when she realizes that her paws are making the sound. She then makes a lot of little clicks on purpose and tries to dig into the marble.

"No, Joy," Gavril says. But she doesn't listen right away, so he puts a hand in front of her nose, and she stops and looks up at him. "No," he says. "Don't dig."

She complains with her talking sounds but sits down obediently but with an heir of saying Gavril was no fun. She looks up at me. She huffs as if asking me if she can dig. "Sorry, but no digging," I say.

"O-wow," Joy says an almost perfect "oh no" and lies down as if she's been denied a treat. I laugh. She's so dramatic. She looks up with her innocent puppy eyes as if asking how we could be so cruel.

"You are being silly, Joy. It's not a big—" Gavril's cut off as we hear the alarm go off. It had been a while since they'd tried to get in. Confusion crosses Gavril's face, and he looks a bit behind me, I'm guessing at Sage.

"Come on, I know where the nearest safe room is," Gavril says calmly and starts to lead the way. Joy pants happily as we hurry along.

Gavril first leads me to the right, towards the reception room when we hear a grunt, and three rough-looking men come out of a door I'd never noticed before. Gavril stops, and Joy pants and says "he'row".

"You are the worst guard dog," Gavril tells her and pulls me back towards the back of the entrance hall. The three rebels had paused to see the dog but soon get their wits and follow us. Gavril runs to the door Damian led me through which led to the Covere room. Gavril takes me into that room.

He hurries me to the opposite side, rotates a bust on a pillar, and then opens a door to a cabinet which opens the door to a safe room.

He waits for me to get in. I give him a look. It's him, not me, the rebels want. Gavril looks into the safe room then pushes me on. I chuckle and get inside. Gavril pauses to turn the bust back to normal.

Joy, on the other hand, thinks this a great adventure because she barks in excitement and rushes into the room. The lead is not long enough to let her do that without yanking Gavril with her. I jump back to avoid him running into me as he falls into the room, and the door slides back into place with a heavy click.

I wish I could say I didn't laugh, but I do. It looked funny even though I wonder if it had hurt. It only gets funnier when Joy is ecstatic to have Gavril lying on the floor with her. She barks in delight and jumps onto him. She howls in happiness and starts licking at Gavril's ears while standing on his back.

"Joy, stop," Gavril tries to get her off.

Joy's reaction is unique. She barks, walks down his legs, finds his untucked shirt and pokes her nose into it then shoves her whole body up into his shirt until she is lying across his back with her nose sticking out of his collar. I can't help but laugh.

"Joy!" Gavril tries to get her out. I'm too busy laughing to help. Joy wiggles in more. "Joy, get out," Gavril orders, but Joy doesn't seem to know how to get out. She tries to walk forward, but she's caught in his shirt, and there's no way she's fitting out the neck hole. Instead, she almost pulls his shirt off over his head.

I stop dead. Joy is so tangled in his shirt that it is pulled up almost all the way to his neck. It is not how strong his back looks or how funny Joy looks in his shirt that makes me freeze. It was what is on his back.

I'd know those marks anywhere. I'd seen them on dozens of beggars, criminals, and even a few of my father's rebel workers. Gavril's back is covered in scars.

Chapter 11

I stand there in shock, staring at the scars as my mind spins. Where would the coddled, constantly guarded, pampered prince of Purerah get scars like that?

They're just like the ones I saw in town, only his look cleaner. There are at least six lashes. How old are they? Who would dare or manage to do something like this to him? The only possibility I can think of is his parents or perhaps his Custod guard, but no Custod would do that without a reason. His parents? No... but I'd been wrong about my father.

"Joy, stop it. Back up," Gavril orders sharply, making me jump as if he were yelling at me.

Joy noises her complaint, having trouble untangling herself. "You don't fit up my shirt, stupid dog. Back up," Gavril says. "Joy, back up!"

Joy whimpers a little then does as asked, her head popping free of his now well-twisted collar. She jumps down and whimpers some more and talks at Gavril, sounding worried.

Gavril jumps to his feet and frantically makes sure his shirt is down over his back. He then stands there, panting, still facing away from me. I keep silent as I realize we're alone in the room. Sage likely was too busy keeping the rebels back to get in before it closed. I don't know how I feel about being alone in a locked room with Gavril when he's this mad.

Joy whimpers again. "Shh, it's alright," I assure the puppy and bend down to stroke her. Her ears and tail are down. She looks up at Gavril in pure shame. "You're okay." And I hope he is too.

I keep stroking Joy as I debate what to say to gloss over the moment and pretend it didn't happen. "Sorry about that," Gavril says, his voice oddly even and measured as if making sure to hide what's under it. "I didn't mean to make a scene. It just shocked me." He's fixing his shirt and fiddling with his cuffs, but he still doesn't turn to look at me.

"It's alright," I say, trying to keep my voice even too, but I'm not as good at it today. I'm terrified he's going to snap at me any moment. "It would have frightened me too. I shouldn't have laughed."

He doesn't reply. He just keeps playing with his cuffs. I look down and keep stroking Joy, watching my hand run along her soft red fur. What could I say? How do I ask without being rude? How do I pretend I didn't see it? I wish I could unsee it. I wish I could return that privacy to him. But I know I can't. I'll be stressed about where they came from and if they are recent or if he got each one over time. And if I'm this stressed, Damian will get the truth out of me, and then what would he do?

"It's alright," Gavril finally speaks. I look up. "You don't have to pretend it didn't happen. Won't change anything." He sighs and lets his hands drop. "I knew I'd have to explain one day. I just didn't think it would be here." He pauses. "Or now."

"You don't have to explain anything," I say, looking at Joy again but not really seeing her. Gavril still has not turned around.

"I know," he says softly. "But you'll just wonder otherwise." He's silent once more.

"Wonder what? Why having your dog almost hang you on your own shirt was startling?" I try to lighten the mood.

"You saw them," he says harshly, almost accusingly.

I bow my head and bite my lips. I suppose there is no pretending. "Not really, just a small glimpse."

"Do you know what they are?" he asks in a low voice.

"Yes."

I hear his deep intake of breath. "What else do you know?"

"They're whip scars. I couldn't see how many. They ran along your whole back." I stop as I fight tears of fear and anger. I know how those hurt. I'd seen men pass out from the pain and heard the agonized screams. I try not to picture those screams as Gavril's. Try to block the image of him shaking in pain as he tries to keep conscious through the pain. I hold back the question I'm dying to ask.

"You know," he says almost conversationally, "you're the first to see them in years."

"What?" How is that possible?

"It's true. You're one of the very few who've seen them." He resumes "fixing" his cuffs, still not turning to me.

"How is that..." I frown in further confusion.

"I can use a changing screen as well as anyone," he replies. "And before you ask, no. Sage has not seen them. Nor has Godwin, and until today, I don't know if Joy has seen them. She has a habit of trying to wiggle into my nightshirt. I suppose that's why she thought my shirt was fun today."

"Who does know?" I ask as fear starts to creep into me. Was it hidden from Sage because it was his parents? I can't see the queen allowing her husband to do it, and she's too soft on her son.

"My parents. A few guards who were around when it happened," he says casually as if letting me know who'd been invited to a party. How is he so calm about this? "All of my staff who were with me when it happened are gone as far as I know. Maybe a few, but they no longer work for me directly. It's my own fault, of course. I don't like anyone to see them. I put on my own shirts. It's why I snap at my new servants who insist on dressing me."

There's an uneasy pause.

"And you've seen my temper. When they don't listen, I get shorter than I should. Having a friend has helped a lot. But I don't like people seeing them."

"I wouldn't want anyone to see them either," I admit. "I'm sorry I did."

He shrugs, still facing away from me. I'd give anything to be able to see his expression, but I don't dare move. I don't want to force him to face me if he's not ready yet. "It would have happened sooner or later. I knew I'd have to tell... the winner, one day. But I didn't expect it to be like this."

I swallow, still petting Joy who's keeping quiet, sensing the tension of the moment. So, it wasn't supposed to be me he told. I am not the one he'd expected or wanted to tell. I feel like I crossed unbidden onto sacred ground I never wanted to desecrate. He'd meant to tell someone he was much more intimate with, Forsythia or Zelda maybe.

"You still can have it that way," I say.

Gavril moves sharply. I look up, but I can't tell what he did as he still stands where he was, slightly turned to his right. I wait with bated breath. He hadn't meant to turn to hit something, did he?

"No," he says as if to himself, "you deserve an answer."

My heart races at the words. He actually feels I'd earned an answer. I'd proven I was something to him.

But he doesn't go on. I wait as long as I dare before I ask, hating myself for it. "Who did that to you?"

"I wish I knew."

My mouth drops open, and I stare at him. How could he not know?

When I don't speak, he finally turns to face me. His expression is oddly blank as he looks at me then at Joy then back again. "I don't know." More certainty is in his voice now as if he's paying more attention to his words. "I don't know his name or where he is today or much about him. But I know I can't forget him." Gavril's eyes drop, and I see the battle in his eyes as he debates how much he can trust me with.

"Did one of your guards do that?" It's the other thing that makes sense apart from his parents.

Gavril shakes his head slowly. "No, it's not their fault. Unless you count their failure to stop me." He shakes his head again and looks away, his eyes lost in the emptiness of the room. "The only injury a guard has given me was the fear he may actually kill me when he pinned me by the throat. It wasn't one of them."

"I-I don't understand." I swallow. "But I don't have to." This is personal. I have not told him my deepest secret. I have no right to ask his.

"You'll just wonder otherwise," he brushes off. "And I'll have your word you won't tell a soul, right?"

I nod, then realize he may not see it, so I look up to find him looking at me. I nod more firmly. "Yes." I won't even breathe a word to Damian.

Gavril nods his acceptance then looks at a spot over my shoulder as he thinks. I bite my lips. I would accept a no even now. Does he trust me? Is he debating if I am safe to tell?

"There's just one thing I'd like you to do if I tell you," he says slowly. I wait patiently, heart thudding in my throat in anticipation. "I have a lot of questions. You'll answer them, right?"

"Best I can," I reply quickly.

The hint of a smile flashes across his face. "I know this may seem a bit morbid, but I can only see their reflection and feel the top of one on my right shoulder. Are they... as bad as they look?"

I blink in surprise at his question. "I-I don't know. I didn't get a good look. Do you mean, do they look bad?"

"They look bad to me. They stand out so sharply and look..." he hesitates, making me more nervous. "Do they disgust you?"

I frown a little more. "No. They looked pretty clean from what I could tell. I only saw them for a moment, and Joy was in the way."

Gavril rubs his face anxiously. "Could... if you got a better look could you be sure?"

"Gavril, you don't have to show me," I insist. I don't want him to hurt more than he is.

"I know, but you already know, and I might as well find out," he says. "I'll tell you if you assure me it isn't as monstrous as it looks."

I heard the hidden "am I monstrous" in that question. "You're not a monster," I say firmly.

"You've not even looked." He smiles warmly.

"I don't have to. Those scars don't change who you are. You didn't change," I say stubbornly.

"Humor me," Gavril says. "I... would you feel them?"

"What?"

"Feel them. I hear scars are either rough or soft. The one on my shoulder is soft, but..."

"Would it help?" I want to. My morbid curiosity is peaked as well as just the chance to... be that close to him.

He nods one slow, sure nod. "Are you sure?" I check. He repeats the motion. I nod back more quickly, agreeing though my heart is pounding.

In one easy movement, he slips the shirt off from over his head while turning away from me, so I can see his back. I look at the scars, darker than his skin and slightly red even healed over.

He looks over his shoulder at me. "I won't bite," he promises. "And they won't bite you either. Here." He walks over to one of the beds that line the right side of the room — the first safe room I have seen that has beds — and sits down on the edge to make it easier for me to reach.

I force a smile and walk over carefully. I kneel on the bed behind him, holding my hand up as if to touch one but hesitate before I do. Should I really be doing this? If I do not win... I am not the one he should share this with.

"I-I..." I almost refuse but stop myself. He'd just tried to be open with me. I shouldn't turn that down. But it does not feel right or fair. I still have to hide my secret, and he is clearly giving me his biggest one.

"It's alright." He picks up his shirt. "I shouldn't have asked."

"No." I stop him, putting my hand on his. "It's just... it's not me," I say quietly.

"You're the only one here. You will not get into trouble for it," he promises me. "I won't make you. It's not a test. I should have known better. I just hoped..."

"No, it's not that," I say quickly. "You meant to have the winner do this, not me." My heart shatters at the idea another girl was slated for this moment.

"Please," he says gently, "I want you to."

I bite my lips. All I want is to do as he asks. I nod and flick my fingers a few times, hovering just over one of the scars before I dare run my fingertips along one of them from his shoulder to the bottom of his left rib cage. It feels deep and surprisingly soft to the touch.

"Well?" he asks after a moment. I'd gotten lost looking at my fingers against his skin as I took in how the feel of him makes my fingers tingle and my heart race.

"They're..." *perfect* "soft."

"Well, one worry taken care of," he jokes before he pauses. "Does it help?"

I shake my head a little. "How did this happen?" There are so many of them. They all look like they happened at the same time. There are at least six of them. They may be soft, but I worry they hurt when I touch them. How could his protective family let this happen?

The tension that runs through his body presses into my fingertips as his breathing picks up. I instinctively put my full hand to his back as if to soothe him. I'm not sure he notices.

"I was stupid and didn't listen. I questioned their protectiveness and tried to prove I was smarter." His body tenses again, so I rub his back, avoiding the scars best I can. His tension drops only slightly.

"I was fourteen, and my Custod guard at the time really annoyed me. I felt he and my parents were being overprotective. I wasn't a child anymore, and frankly, I was ready for them to realize it more than I even realized. I thought there was no harm in me going into town. I knew the rebels broke into the palace to come after me. I saw the bloodshed and knew the danger, but how dangerous would it be for me to go into town when they weren't looking or expecting me? They wouldn't hear of it.

"So, I decided to prove myself. I came up with a plan to show them I could not only get out just fine, but that I could do it without any harm to myself, so I could visit with the guard in the future." He drops his head.

"I was a foolish child. It was a rash plan. I knew the guard's rotation, and I could fit into the smaller guard uniforms. I was able to smuggle one into my room, used pillows to make it look like I was still safe in bed, changed into the uniform, and climbed down the wall."

I stop as he glances back at me for a brief moment. "That's how I knew how easy it would be for you to scale the wall. It's not that different from mine, and yours isn't over the ocean." He turns away again. "I suppose it worked in part. I got out," he says bitterly.

I swallow hard. "So, the city guard caught you?"

"No." He shakes his head. "No, I only wish it were so. I'd not have gotten hurt if so. All I'd have to do is tell them who I was and show my royal mark, and they'd not touch me. I'd also be able to name who did it. It was a rebel who found me that night."

My breath catches in horror. A rebel? It could have been someone I knew: Jake's father, perhaps or one of the dozens of other leaders I knew?

"Guards travel the city in pairs, you see. I didn't know that. So, when a rebel saw me wandering alone they thought they'd get lucky and be able to get information out of me about how to get into the castle. They thought I was just a guard."

Gavril stops again; his shoulders tense as if ready to spring into action. I bite my lip and wonder what I should do. I am scared to move my hand or move away from him or even try to see his face. What if I startled him? I do not want to feel what him striking me would be like. But how could I just sit here? Yet, it is all I can do.

He jolts under my touch, and instinctively, I put my other hand on his back as if to steady him which only feels even more stupid. I am likely making it worse, but fear keeps me from backing away. Fear and the feeling I have to do something, though I do not know what.

"I wasn't strong enough." His voice almost cracks. "I tried to get him off me, but I just couldn't push him off or away. He had no trouble keeping me down with just his foot as he—"

Gavril jerks under my touch again, and without thinking, I take his shoulders as if I expect him to start convulsing. I'm painfully aware of how close I am to him now: shirtless, exposed to me, and how warm and smooth his skin feels under my palms.

Gavril doesn't go on for a long time. He takes deep, measured breaths that make his shoulders rise into my hands. I bite my lips as I fight tears. I wish he didn't have to tell me. I wish I could make him forget. How scared he must have been. I can't even imagine. I'd never had anyone really hurt me, not physically. Father had given me a nasty hit in training now and then, but it was nothing to what that man had done to Gavril.

Hatred burns in my chest, stronger than anything I'd ever felt. I despise whoever had done this, and because I don't know who attacked Gavril, I feel hatred toward all the rebels I'd once trusted. They drove civilians from their homes for their cursed cause and hurt innocent children.

"I'm sorry," I whisper as a hot tear runs down my cheek.

It also explains so much. Why he did as the guard told him, why he accepts his parents' orders, why he's so strong now. He must have done all he could to prevent it from happening again. I had done the same when Jake ripped my heart out. Gavril is just more successful than me. My grip tightens on his shoulders.

It is like I pulled a trigger. Gavril snaps up. I flinch, thinking he's going to strike me, but instead he takes me into his arms and kisses me deeply: warm, hot, and steady. I take in a sharp breath, but the tension of the moment lulls me closer. My hand grips his shoulder again before running down his chest. He's so smooth, so strong. His expanding chest pressing against my hand excites me, sending tingles up my arms, down my shoulders, and across the rest of my body.

Gavril cradles my head with one hand while the other wraps around my back as he kisses me deeper and deeper, making my heart quiver and melt into a helpless puddle that invites him to dive right into it.

My right hand finds one of his scars, but I don't care. I fiddle with its unique texture as I focus on returning each kiss as he almost fights for more from me. This is better than the river with Jake.

He's too strong for me, and before either of us realize it, he's knocked me backwards, and I fall onto the short end of the bed. Still, he kisses me as if he had hardly noticed. The only hint he has registered the change is a sudden shudder that runs across his body under my hands. I sigh at the feeling as I relax at his command.

We both jump a mile as Joy leaps onto the bed, barking in delight at the game and licking our faces. Gavril pushes himself up in an impressive movement that shows not only is he strong, but he also has complete control of his body. Joy's tongue tickles, making me laugh as I sit up to try to get her off me, but she jumps right onto my chest to try to take me all to herself.

She turns to Gavril and talks at him as if daring him to try to take me from her. I can't help but laugh at her playfulness.

But Gavril doesn't rise to the game. In fact, he doesn't even respond to do more than glance at her before turning away and running a hand through his hair, leaving it there as he takes deep breaths.

After a moment, he turns back to me, mouth slightly open, studying me. I frown but give him space to think as I try to figure out what he's trying to say. He looks down a second before he turns away again, running his fingers through his hair.

Joy tilts her head in confusion too. I stroke her to calm her and get her to sit next to me instead of on me. "Gavril, what is it?" I ask.

He turns back to me, mouth open again. I see the struggle in his eyes so let him think it through. His eyes fall onto his shirt, and he picks it up quick as a flash and starts to put it on. His hands are shaking so badly he struggles with the buttons.

"I'm sorry," he says, a slightly formal tone coming to his voice.

"It's alright." I smile, getting up to help him with his shirt. He freezes. "Though how we went from you being tortured to that, I'll never know."

"Guess easier to do that than talk about it," he says.

My face falls a little as I pause at his collar button. His neck and jaw are still red from where Joy had yanked his shirt over them. I lower my hand and let them rest on his chest, debating how to say it. "Is it that bad?" Was it so bad that he'd take such an excuse to avoid it?

I watch his eyes drop to the floor. "Maybe. I suppose not. I'm sure others you know have been beaten much worse. He smacked me around a bit before he went to the whip. I don't know how many times. I had a hard time counting with how they fell across my back."

I frown as I see the pain return to his eyes. I embrace him, trying to help heal the hurt I see. "How did you ever get away?" I ask.

"He gave up eventually. I managed to get to my feet and stagger back to the palace. They don't worry so much about people getting out, so it is easier to sneak out than in, which was lucky for me. I was spotted, but once they were close, I collapsed. They recognized me and rushed me to my room and got the doctor." Gavril's eyes are far away, staring into emptiness he didn't see.

"My parents were scared out of their minds, most of all my mother. Father was furious and spent months trying to catch the rebel who did it, but I haven't seen the man since he left me there. Could have died in a raid or died trying to get into the place or escaped millions of miles away for all I know.

"It took a while, a few weeks or so, for me to get back on my feet. I begged my Custod guards to let me work out, even asked them to teach me defense, but apart from teaching me fencing, which my mother already objected to, they refused. That's when I started to work out by myself, using books as guides and training at night when they thought I was asleep. First time I did it, I was covered in dried sweat the next morning. My staff thought I was sick. I played along, so they didn't find out. It's why I bathe at night now, even though Sage lets me train all I want; it's just habit."

My eyes fall to his chest again as I think this over. We're quiet a long time. I wish I had something to say, but what is there to say?

"Anything else you want to know?" he asks after the silence drags on.

I shake my head. I wish I didn't know. I wish this hadn't happened. It feels like a lifetime ago since I'd agreed to this second half of a date. I should have stuck to the work I wanted to do and avoided this whole thing.

"I wish you didn't have to tell me," I apologize in a quiet voice.

"Why?" he asks in confusion.

"Because this wasn't meant for me." It was meant for his princess, the winner. The true princess he deserves, not the girl playing one. He shouldn't have had to give that up.

"Wasn't it?" he asks in a quiet tone that makes me love and hate him all the more.

I close my eyes and turn my face to the floor to hide how much that question hurts. No, I am not a true princess, but at least, I could maybe trick my way around the tests and win him anyway. I wouldn't cheat, but I could perhaps work around the tests if they were dumb enough.

But I hadn't earned this moment yet. Someone else might have, and I just stole it from them.

"What if I can't... I'm sorry." I'd give anything to take it all back. "You shouldn't have to tell me."

"Even if I have to later?" he asks me gently.

I fight more tears and bite my lips, not looking up. If he looks much closer, he will see through my disguise. He will know what a fake and a lie I am. One who does not deserve his trust with such an intimate secret. "You don't know that."

He pauses for a long time before replying. "Do you want to win?"

My head snaps up. He's not really asking again, is he? "What?"

"Do you want to win?" he repeats.

My mouth freezes open for a moment before I close it and swallow. "You're not offering to let me go again, are you?"

"No," he says firmly yet gently. "But after all, you finally know my secret, but you hate it when you're seen as the winner. You shied away from both delegations when they showed they favored you to win. You avoid any public displays of affection, and sometimes, avoid it even when we're alone as if you're terrified of being in the lead. I figured it was fear of the other girls, but I can't just assume anymore. So please, be honest. Do you want to win? I will not judge you either way."

I look at Joy who's now chewing on the blanket on the bed quite contentedly as I try to decide how best to answer honestly and without hurting him. "It's not that," I say. "Not wanting to win, I mean."

"Then what is it?" he asks with a hint of frustration in his voice.

"It's..." It's that I'm a fake. It's that I'm a former rebel who came to murder him. It's that my past is a lie, and I'm nothing but a fake. That little street rat from the musical and I are more alike than I ever thought. I'd never understood why he didn't tell his princess the truth from the start. Now I get it. "Complicated," I finish.

"We're used to complicated, Kascia. Does it also have to remain unsaid?" I hear the betrayal in his voice, and he's right. He just trusted me with something he shared with so few others. Something he never meant to give me. Couldn't I at least give him something?

"What if I don't win?" I give him the greatest of my fears, but not the most dangerous. "What happens to you and your heart then?"

"You're still worried about that?" Gavril frowns.

"How aren't you?" I snap. "Have you ever lost what you loved and wanted? Most of all when it wants you back?"

Gavril can't meet my eyes. I realize what a rude question that was. Of course, he hadn't. He hadn't been loved before.

"Sorry." I take a deep breath. "It's just... I did it once." And it tore me apart. Jake's words still sting and make me feel like no one, not even Gavril, could really love me. Gavril likes me because I am the most perfect princess in his mind. Once he knows the truth, and I am not key to his mission, I will be dropped once again. I have lost my ability to give my heart without question, and I do not want to do that to him when he has to sell his heart away to the winner no matter how he thinks or feels. "And it's hell. I don't want to do that to you. And I can't help it." I stop to fight tears.

"You don't want that to... to happen to me?" He's trying to look into my face, but I just can't look at him. "Kascia, please."

"Yes. Alright. I don't want that to happen to you. I know you have to date all of us. I know how this game works. It's just..." I fear I can't win. If I do, it's because their tests failed to weed me out. "What if I do?" I tremble at the pain inside me. If I lose, he'll hurt; I'll have lost him, and there's no going back to Jake. I had slaved away to love Jake only to succeed and be ruined for anyone else. It's different with Gavril. I am trying to quail my feelings, and they grow anyway.

"But what about you?" he asks, his eyes full of pain for me.

I don't need his pity. "I've already done it once. What's the difference?"

"Kascia, I'm not him," he says. No, he's not. He's much better. Even when I had to watch him kiss the others or be cute with them, he's been the best thing I've ever had. "I'm not going to—"

"End up with someone else?" I cut him off, glaring up at him. I hate how he acts like he can pick me, when the truth is he can't even pick his breakfast in the morning. "You said it yourself. You have to be neutral. You don't get to pick. And we all know it."

"So, who are you protecting? Me or you?" he challenges. "Are you afraid of losing or me losing?"

"Both." *What a lie.* It's him I'm protecting. I'll get hurt either way.

I jump as Gavril moves towards me in a swift, exact movement, but instead, he pulls me into an embrace. "Shh, just have some faith. You don't have to do this," he whispers to me.

Fresh tears break through. I wish I could. I want to feel like his and his alone. I want to feel like he's mine. Why is he being so stupid with himself when odds are not in my favor as I couldn't be further from a true princess?

"You're not being smart with yourself." I beg him to be.

"I know," he says tenderly, "and sadly, I don't really care. The truth is—"

I jump a mile as a loud click cuts the air, and I step away from Gavril.

The door to the safe room opens as Gavril swears under his breath. "What?" he demands as a shape comes to the doorway.

"Well fine, if you'd rather stay in there," Gentian's voice comes from the passage opening.

"I don't think you want to make that an option, Father," Sage snaps back.

"What are you talking about?" Gentian frowns. Or I think he does by his tone. I can still only see his outline, or is that Sage? I think it's Sage as he comes into better view.

"Look around the corner," Sage suggests.

"Oh," Gentian says.

I blink, and finally, they come into clearer view. Sage and Gentian enter the room. Joy barks a hello then barks her "weirdo" sound at the pair of them. It's the only thing she ever calls Sage. When Cedrick taught Joy to say everyone's name, she had called Sage "weirdo" and the laughter that ensued convinced the puppy that was Sage's name and refused to call him anything else.

"Come on." Gavril sighs, holding out his hand to me. "We better get you to your room to be counted with the rest. My parents will freak out if I don't check in. But I can at least take you to your room," he offers.

"A-alright." I'm still not sure I am quite confident yet. I move as if to take his hand, but I can't help but feel the glare on my skin. I assume it's Sage, but it might be his father or both. I can't bring myself to look.

Gavril's mood gets angry again before he takes my hand. I tense, expecting to be snapped at. He pulls me closer and says quietly to me. "If you don't like it, you can just pull back. It's not you that's the problem." It does make me to look. Gentian really is giving me a death glare.

Almost defensively, Gavril pulls me to the other side of him, away from the two guards, and back out the door. Joy follows, tail wagging excitedly. She complains at Gentian as he follows as if telling "weirdo-o" he can't come.

"She calls him weirdo two," Gavril explains as I look at Joy in confusion. I laugh at that.

"She's rude," Gentian says.

Sage sighs. "Sometimes, it's earned." He comes closer to Gavril and me. I want to pull back, but Gavril doesn't let me right away. I think he wants to make sure I know if I really want to let go I can, but he's also making sure these two men don't make me pull away just to please them.

We don't speak much until we reach my room. "I'll make sure they know you're alright," Gavril says. Then he sighs. "Would I..." he looks me over, "offend you if I checked in before you retire tonight?"

"No." I wouldn't be offended. I'm a little worried though. Sage leans on the wall, not looking at us. He's actually being more polite than I'd seen him in moments like this. Of course, he might be when I can't see him, but I don't think much about it. I like to pretend he's not there. "I'd not be offended."

"Alright. You're sure you're alright?" Gavril's studying my face still.

I manage a smile and nod. I'm processing a lot now. He manages a weak smile too before kissing my hand. He tenses again before letting go. Does he do that to everyone? I don't think he does.

I can see in his face, though not easy to read, he's keeping a lot inside. I can understand how he lost it for a moment when they cut in. Who knows if he'll get to say it now.

"I'll be taking watch." Sage glares at his father as he pushes himself off the wall. "You keep out of the way this time." Gentian rolls his eyes as he and Gavril leave.

I turn to go into my room when Gentian grabs my arm painfully hard and shoves me into the wall. "Ow," I snap. "Let go."

"What were you doing?" he demands.

"What you guards tell us to. We went into a safe room where the rebels didn't see us get in," I say. I am really not in the mood to deal with him. Why won't he just let go? He has no evidence I did anything wrong.

"You shouldn't still be here. I know what Sage found on you, and I know he's right. I don't know how you're even passing as more than an actress playing a princess, but I'll find out. Whatever you've done to charm them, I'm not falling for it. The others at least come from families with influence. What do you bring?"

"I don't answer to you." I am resisting the urge to do some very un-princess-like things to him right about now. I am not ready to deal with him. "Let go." I try to pull away, but he holds my arm tighter. "You have any idea what the royal family would do if they knew what you are doing right now?" I snap.

"Going to get your bewitched prince to help you?" Gentian asks.

This makes me so angry; I don't even realize I'm slapping him until I feel the hard sting against my hand. I am not upset at what it means for me. I am not controlling Gavril. No one does.

My slap does me no favors. He only holds me tighter. "Mark my words, unlike my son, I'm not just waiting for the evidence. I'm going to reveal you for what you are. I'll find whatever lie you're using, and your prince will be the first to know."

I'm too angry and upset to even reply. Many replies run through my head, but I am not thinking clearly enough to use any of them. That might be my saving grace though. The more I fight, the angrier this

Custod becomes. I fight with my own temper not to hit him again or worse.

"You're going to hang yourself on your own lies. And I'll be sure to make sure it happens," he snarls, his face so close to mine I feel his spit on my face. I shove him away, and he finally lets go.

"You may regret that," I reply with more calm than I feel. Did I just threaten him? Oh no, I think I did. What am I thinking?

I see the anger in Gentian's eyes. I stiffen my resolve. I'm too angry to fight, but I keep to what I said. I open my door and step inside before he can make another attempt. I slam the door to make sure he doesn't try. I think I do hear a satisfying grunt of pain.

I press my back to the door and take a few deep, shaking breaths, trying to get a hold of my emotions. *And that was supposed to clear my head?*

I don't care how undignified I look. I go to the balcony to cry out my mixed-up emotions: longing, hurt, anger, grief, and more.

I stay out there as long as I can before I have to go in. As I sit to let my maids work, Damian walks over and places a few chocolates in front of me. I smile and stand to hug him in thanks. Damian wraps his arms around me and hugs me while stroking the back of my head as if I were his own daughter. I accept it, hiding my face in his chest for a moment. I may not really know Damian well, but I know he does not lie to me.

I need to get my head right. No matter how I hate the mess I am in now, I am in it, and there is no going back. I have to keep this secret close to my chest as I have countless others and tuck it away in the back of my head as I deal with the more immediate threat: whatever the Japcharians throw at me.

That tension makes me pretty tense when Gavril finally does come to check like he asked. He can tell I'm too wound up for even him to calm me down, so he doesn't stay long. I have to be ready. Our people's lives may depend on it.

Chapter 12

I'm not sure how I survive the next few days. The quietness makes it hard not to stress about what will happen when they finally arrive. When the day itself dawns, I'm full of nervous jitters. Vivian keeps gently helping me pull my shoulders back as they start to creep up in my stress.

At least I can enjoy this latest masterpiece from my team. It's white with a floating thin skirt with a proper Japcharian jacket over it. Japcharian dresses normally have high collars with fabric buttons holding it down the center. The sleeves are long and white with an inner sleeve and an outer sleeve just three or four inches shorter than the first. The patterns on the jacket are gold with cherry blossom patterns. The skirt and jacket are decorated with golden and pale blue ocean wave designs. My maids put my hair in a stunning updo decorated into a golden headpiece with blossom designs matching my dress. They finish the look off with golden, low-heeled sandals and soft makeup that makes my eyes look a bit sharper than normal with deep red lipstick. It is a Japcharian style that is not my normal look, but it would make a good impression on them and help me look official.

We have to be ready by breakfast because they had arranged to have a small celebration for Gavril's birthday, though I still get the impression he would really rather just skip the whole thing. I don't understand why. I'm torn. I want to respect his wishes, but I also think he deserves something fun.

I am able to guess part of the reason once breakfast is over and they clear it away. The first thing I note is that Gavril does impressively well at hiding how much he'd rather do anything else. The only hint I see is the flash of irritation at what a big to-do Ericka makes of presenting her gift which is a pink "bonding blanket" for him to use with Joy.

"Cuppy loves chewing the little toy in it with ours." Ericka is beaming. The blanket has a plush squirrel on one side, a pink one.

"Might help her be better behaved at night," Gavril agrees, "Thank you, my albatross." Ericka beams in pleasure, and I don't miss her looking around to gloat at those of us who don't have nicknames. I look around to see if anyone else notices his flash of actual emotion. It looks like he got away with it. The nickname was not a compliment. Damian had explained to me that sailors use the term to mean "their burden to bear" as if to their grave. I am not envious of that name.

The rest of the gifts are similar in theme, all trying to stand out by being thoughtful, though I can't help but notice many went for the dog owner theme. *If you can't beat 'em, join 'um.*

Though Bella made a stunning waistcoat she clearly is terrified will not fit properly. I can tell Gavril likes it just because she made it. Bella also made a matching bandana for Joy to attach to her collar.

Azalea had a similar idea, getting a collection of harness covers that will help Joy look more official at events. The harnesses will grow with her as they are not strictly sewn and won't look big for her now.

Forsythia is creative in comparison though. She got Gavril an actual desk aquarium with several kinds of fish. One makes the queen jump by looking rather like an eel. I catch Gavril stopping a laugh. Guess Forsythia got to help decorate his office anyway.

I look around, realizing that the only gift left is mine. The other girls were eager to present their gifts, and I don't see anyone ever out-waiting Damian.

Finally, Damian steps forward and presents the small box to the prince. "I promise it won't wiggle this time," he jokes.

"That would be good. Too many pets and I'll lose myself in my own bedroom," Gavril jokes good-naturedly as he accepts the box.

He opens it to reveal the charming little music box with a monkey holding cymbals on top. He smiles as he lifts it out, but it is the same smile he has been using, and though I'm not able to prove it, I'm almost certain it's mostly a show.

The music box starts to play its song on its own, gently clapping. Gavril tilts his head at it, seemingly liking the music but not knowing what it's from. That's when he notices the papers at the bottom of the box. He picks up the papers and puts the box down.

His forehead pinches as he looks over what I recognize as a ticket. He clearly does not quite understand it. I suppose they are hard to read. I see him mouth "royal box" to himself as he translates the ticket. Then he notices the invitation.

His jaw drops. "You what?" He looks over at us. I giggle. He really hadn't thought we'd pull it off. And in the royal theater. I am suddenly filled with excitement for it to finally come true.

Damian grins and folds his arms smartly. "Well... you did challenge me. And I never do anything halfway."

"What is it?" Ericka asks curiously.

"Your Highness, would you mind reading the invitation aloud for them?" Damian requests.

Gavril huffs and reads out the invitation that gives the date, time, and place of the performance. I can hear his amusement. He's impressed we have pulled off the location. The other girls look just as shocked. Zelda looks, if anything, envious.

Damian grins widely then pulls something from his pocket. "And this is the advertisement which will appear in tomorrow's paper." He holds it in front of him and reads, "The Royal Theatre presents *The Phantom* with Lady Kascia Thorapple reprising her role as Miss Christine Daae for one night only. Tickets go on sale tonight at 4 pm sharp. Get them before they're gone and don't miss this once-in-a-lifetime opportunity.

"You are all invited, of course." Damian smiles at the rest of us as he puts the ad back in his pocket. "Your attendants will have your tickets in hand a week prior to the performance."

Zelda gives him a satisfied nod.

"This is... amazing." Gavril shakes his head. He clearly is saying "you win".

"I'm glad it pleases you." Damian smiles smartly with a bow of his head.

The rest of breakfast is fine for the rest of us but looks painful for Gavril. His mother keeps trying to ply him with all his "favorites" and going on about birthdays past, of course all when he was little. Some girls enjoy the embarrassing stories more than others. I can tell Gavril wishes it would stop.

The queen is making an overly large deal about it and fawning over Gavril more than usual. I can't blame him for not enjoying his birthdays if they're all like this. It's not like he gets to enjoy any of the things he likes and gets treated smaller than normal even with the king trying to remind the queen he's in the middle of a dating game.

But with that out of the way, Dahlia, Zelda, Jonquil, and I have to see to the preparations for the welcome party. Jonquil sees to the food being prepared in the kitchens; Dahlia checks the decorations, and Zelda handles the flower arrangements while I check on the staff arrangements for their arrival, seeing their suites are ready for the moment they arrive.

The last step is to let the queen know we are ready for her to review the preparations before the guests arrive. After a quick examination, she agrees we're ready with no corrections mentioned. I don't know if she'd corrected the other girls, so we just wait nervously for the news that the Japcharian delegation has arrived.

Zelda tries to comfort me as I pace the floor. "You pulled all our ideas together perfectly. You look in charge. You have nothing to worry about. You are a natural at this, even if you don't realize it."

"You want her to beat you?" Jonquil snaps in her anxiety.

Zelda glares at her. "Don't you want our team to do well?"

"They still are judging one-on-one," she points out.

"So, we can still support each other," Zelda says. "A princess builds her people. She builds those around her, not tear them down."

"Sometimes you have to break someone to build them properly," Dahlia says.

"Not in something like this." Zelda helps set my shoulders and apron properly. "We're a team. We build each other. They'll arrive soon. And I don't think this talk will impress them."

"We just need to stop them getting angry with us," Jonquil says to comfort all of us I think.

"Right." Zelda seems to realize that's the best way to calm most of us down. "It's not your job to make them adore us. We play hosts. We aren't in the table talks."

"We just have to work with them on talking points," Dahlia says.

"Not today. That's tomorrow," Zelda says.

Today, I just had to be nice and look pretty. I can do that. I also have to remember my curtsies. You deep-curtsy to royalty: king, queen, prince, and princess. Not quite to the floor but pretty low. Most of the people we will deal with will be half curtsy. Though a few of the lesser nobles would be very small with a head bow. They would likely all look the same. We'd have to guess.

A servant announces the delegation has arrived. We quickly get into place to greet them. There are six of them in total, a smaller delegation than the others. The lady in the lead is quite tall with long black hair allowed to mostly hang down her back. Her narrow eyes are elegantly painted and set against her pale skin, made paler by her makeup.

"We welcome your delegation." Zelda smiles warmly at them after she curtsies to them. They come in as a group.

The woman in the lead bows to us as ladies of lesser nobility. I refrain from frowning. Princess Zelda, at least, is a princess. She should have the full curtsy. They are already putting us down on the hierarchy.

I look over the whole delegation as they all copy the leading lady's curtsy level. There are two men and three women with her. I notice one of the girls is surprisingly young and stays close to the leader. She is beautiful with pale skin and bright green eyes shining through her dark makeup. She cannot be more than sixteen years old. She's a bit shy, letting the taller lady speak as she looks around. I think she finds the decorations and food comforting. At least she smiles a delicate smile. She reminds me of Lilly.

"I am Grand Duchess Kira," the head lady introduces herself, but unlike other delegations, she does not introduce any of the others. "It's an honor to be here after so many years." I hear the jab in the language and tone, reminding us of the long gap between visits.

I glance at the men as the other delegations had let the men lead. They are waiting for the grand duchess to dismiss them, looking around the room. They look nice in suits similar to our styles apart from their wrap style shirt that wraps up to their collars in the place of a waistcoat. One man has dark skin and coiled hair, typical of royal families, whereas the other is pale with dark hair. One of the ladies, an older woman, has the same dark features as the one with coils. I wonder if they're siblings.

When none of them speak, I smile welcomingly with a bob of a curtsy as is their custom. "Please, enjoy yourself. You have had a long journey, and we wish you to be comfortable before the work begins."

The young girl's eyes light up at my invitation, relaxing a little. The grand duchess just bows her head; the fancy golden headpiece she wears jangling gently. It makes her whole look more flowing as she turns to walk away, the red of her dress striking the room.

The younger girl follows her closely. The other ladies go to mingle with the other girls, going over to Lilly, Bella, and Azalea. The two men take different paths. The darker one goes to speak with the king and queen while the other goes over to the food. I can't help but smile.

I glance at the others in my team. Zelda's face is composed with a gentle smile, but she reads the attitude as well, if not better, than I do.

Dahlia's lips are pursed as if unhappy with the outcome. She looks around the room in one quick glance and goes over to join the lady speaking with Lilly, Bella, and Azalea.

The grand duchess has found Gavril and is talking to him with a friendly enough air, if not very formal.

I wonder if I should try to join in to entertain one of the others when I spot the younger girl slipping away from the grand duchess to get into the cheese dumplings we set out.

I smile and decide the best way to host is to see that even the littlest of the party is well taken care of. I walk over to be friendly, giving her a curtsy as I join her. "Hello." I smile as princess-like as I can. "I'm Lady Kascia. I'm happy to get to meet you one-on-one. May I ask your name?"

"Oh." She blinks her green eyes at me before she looks around in surprise. But then she smiles with a hint of gratitude before she looks back at me. "Tsikyria."

"Tsikyria," I repeat. "That's beautiful. Honor to meet you. I'm glad I'm not the only one who likes the deep-fried dumplings."

"Oh yes." She smiles brighter, more like the girl she is. "I like the Aleph cheese inside best, just as you have them." A little color enters her cheeks, but her smile is the same. "I don't get to enjoy them much at home; they like the white ones more. And I like those too." She nods at the star-shaped ones we have at the table as well.

"I prefer the yellow too."

Her smile grows, and more color comes to her face, making her eyes light up a little. It... seems familiar. "But the seared meat and vegetables are good too. Yours are drier than ours at home. I think I like it drier better. Then you don't need a dumpling scoop."

"That would help. I'm still learning to use them," I admit.

"Ah yes, I forgot you're not from a royal or courtly family. Where are you from in Purerah?" she asks, more proper in her tone with the question.

"I'm from Rosepla. I was the theater's prima actress."

"Oh, you must be very good to be the prima at the capitol theater," she giggles. I laugh too. I never made that connection before. "Is that how you got so far?"

"I have no idea."

"I'm glad I don't have to try." Her face falls, and she looks over at the grand duchess who's still talking to Gavril. I have never seen Gavril be so formal, even with the other delegates. He must know that's how to behave with the grand duchess. She doesn't look displeased at all with his conversation. There's a nervous look in Tsikyria's eyes.

"He's not bad," I defend.

"Of course, you think so. You are trying to marry him." Tsikyria forces a smile.

"That's not fair." I frown a little. "I've actually had lots of chances to change my mind." Even if I didn't really want them.

"Oh." She frowns as if in apology, and she looks down in thought. "I suppose that is true." She turns to me. "What is he like? Do you think he'd be a good husband?"

This sounds more like the grilling Damian would give me when I question what I want. "I'd not stick around if I didn't." I give the proper answer which isn't exactly untrue. "In honesty, he may not be perfect, but he is trying hard, even with all his struggles. It can't be easy not getting any say in your marriage."

"You are new to the royal world. That's normal for the crown heir," Tsikyria says.

"Yes, they are more arranged, but they get some kind of say even if the parents overrule it," I reply. "He has all of us in front of him, knowing he'll have to marry one of us but has no say in which one or even control over which of us he really likes. It can't be easy." Most of all, when they seem to never let him choose anything, let alone his life companion.

Tsikyria nods sadly. "I suppose that is true." She looks over at him again.

"You act like you were almost in the running." My brows pinch. "You don't have to worry about it. You're not in line."

She bites her lip. I frown. I'm missing something. I must be.

"What if all of you lost? What would they do then?" She looks more scared at the idea than I am.

"I don't know. They don't talk about it. They really do think at least one girl will win. But it's nothing to be afraid of. You look more nervous than me."

"Well… it's just…" She looks around.

"I can keep secrets if you want to tell me, but you hardly know me. I understand if you don't want to. I just don't like to see you so worked up."

"I heard how you defended little Lilly," she says quietly.

That takes me aback. "You… you know who I am?"

"Oh, I know who all of you are." She nods at Princess Zelda. "She was the first to arrive. She was here two weeks before they announced it. Prince Gavril had met Princess Rose and a few others before. According to your papers, you're a favorite along with Princess Zelda, Rose, and Isla."

I blink. She does know a lot. "How do you know that? You get our papers?"

"We get the papers, and we have contacts here," she says. "Perhaps I can tell you more later. But I know who you are. Dahlia is a favorite of your people, but not of any of your visitors thus far."

"Why do you care so much? If I may ask." I curtsy again.

She frowns. "Because my parents hope it fails."

"What?"

"It's complicated, but they have watched with the slight hope it opens a door for us," she says as her eyes dart about the room.

What kind of door would the Enthronement failing open for their people? And why would this girl be involved?

"What is he really like?" she asks me again.

I smile a bit. "Strong, even if he doesn't know it." Even his temper is strong. I hold in my chuckle. "He listens well." Perhaps too well sometimes. "And honestly, he takes after his father. He can be a bit of a goof if he wants to be."

"I can't see it." She's watching Gavril standing perfectly and nodding at Lady Kira with a worried frown back on her face.

I look up at them too. "I've never seen him so serious," I admit as I study the almost perfect posture, a polite nod of his head, and appropriate focus on the grand duchess' face. All a picturesque example of friendly formality. All he'd have to do is swap crowns with his father, and he'd look the part of king perfectly, better than his father at the moment. Even with the queen on his arm, the king doesn't compare. Gavril is beyond ready for this. Even more than I realized. He's perfect for this as if a prophecy had made him so.

"I didn't even know he could be so formal." I smile just a little.

"Really?" A bit of hope is in Tsikyria's voice.

"Well, on our first date, he made the best of us getting attacked by a broken sprinkler." It felt like a lifetime ago. "And he will take the chance to pick on his Custod guard when he can." I smile a little. "Like brothers."

"I can't imagine how much trouble I'd be in if I did that to my brothers." Tsikyria frowns deeper. The cultural divide is showing. "Even when I want to."

"Well, perhaps you'll understand what I mean in time. He isn't trying to be cruel, just to get him to lighten up. His guard can be serious in places where it's alright for him to relax, so he teases him to loosen him up," I explain. "He wants to look after him like he does everyone else."

"I see. Perhaps our cultures are more different than I was led to believe," Tsikyria muses. "Even if the food is so similar and so good."

I laugh. "See, Gavril would find that funny."

Tsikyria flushes. I frown. "Don't worry, that's a good thing."

She doesn't reply. She just takes another dumpling, still looking rather uneasy.

I fish for something to say. I can see now why she'd been so tense this whole time. "But you don't have to worry about that. I don't think we'll all fail. You won't have to deal with it."

The face she makes I understand all too well. Both options are terrifying to her. Why? "Are you here with your family?" I try to change the topic.

"No, my family is attending their duties at home while I forge relations here," she says, putting away the dumpling scoop she'd been using.

"So Grand Duchess Kira isn't your relative?"

"Distantly. As we're both in the court, I'd think there'd be some kind of connection if you go far enough back," Tsikyria says. "But she is attending me."

Attending!? Who could the grand duchess be attending? That indicated that the grand duchess is lower in station, but there are very few court positions that are higher than the grand duchess. How could that be? If Tsikyria was higher than the grand duchess, she should be running negotiations. And she can't be older than sixteen, easily the youngest of the group.

"You mean she's teaching you?" That would make more sense.

"In a way," Tsikyria hedges.

"So, she's running the negotiations on your royal family's behalf?"

"Until she isn't."

I open my mouth to ask when Tsikyria asks a question first. "What part do you play in this summit?"

"I'm part of your delegation's team," I explain. "I helped prepare the parties and will assist in running the scheduled meeting tomorrow. Princess Zelda, Lady Dahlia, and Lady Jonquil are part of the same team. If you need anything different in your rooms, let us know and we'll see to it."

"I shall," Tsikyria says with a ring in it that reminds me of Gavril dismissing his staff.

"Do you normally do this kind of work at home?" I try to lighten the mood.

"A bit."

"What do you do in your free time?"

"I... I like making dumplings," she says.

"Really?" Lilly had told me of a Japcharian-style dumpling she and her mother made. "Do you make Jynsada dumplings?" I ask.

Tsikyria's eyes light up. That is what I want. "I do. I like the flower designs best."

And she goes on to tell me all about the designs she makes and how they're done. I am fascinated. I have never managed to do that kind of work: look at my Christmas cookies.

We end up talking the rest of the party. The grand duchess comes over to call Tsikyria to settle into their rooms before dinner. I curtsy to them both as the delegation leaves. At least Tsikyria looks much happier leaving than she did when she came in.

As soon as they are gone, my team sets about organizing the staff for clean-up and discussing how we felt it went.

"The men are stuck up," Dahlia complains. "Hardly spoke to me when I tried."

"Remember, they're big on propriety. He shouldn't speak to you without another man with you," Jonquil says.

"Wasn't his friend enough?" Dahlia asks.

Zelda sighs. "No, as he also is a stranger to you. Did you listen at all to Lady Keva?"

Dahlia glares at her. "Of course, but I didn't think that wouldn't be enough. But they ate most of the food, so I think they enjoyed it."

"The grand duchess did seem standoffish, but I am starting to think she's not the one running it all," Zelda says. "When I spoke with her, she avoided talking with full authority, but I have no idea why. This is their full delegation. We're not waiting on anyone else. Do you think it was one of the men?"

"Maybe," Jonquil shrugs. "If so, they were keeping quiet to hide who. Maybe the couple?"

"Which are a couple?" Zelda asks.

"Vicereine Nan and Viceroy Ziam," Dahlia says.

"My Hyvia, that is their rank?" Zelda frowns. "The other groups were Counts and Countesses."

"None are related to the grand duchess?" A rather odd feeling was squirming in my stomach like an uneasy dance.

"Just the young girl," Jonquil says.

"No, she's not," I mumble.

"Oh?"

"I spoke with her. She said she's only distantly related to the grand duchess."

They all look at me. "Then why is she hanging so close to her?" Dahlia asks. I shrug.

"That is odd." Zelda frowns. "What was her name?"

"Tsikyria."

"Tsikyria," Zelda repeats with a frown. "Sounds familiar." But she doesn't go on.

"What is she like? Was she enjoying the food too?" Jonquil asks.

I nod. "We bonded over our shared love of the Aleph cheese dumplings."

"Perfect!" Jonquil beams as if it's the best news in the world. "This will be easy. They act formal, but the way they were pigging out, I don't see them being hard to handle. Bribe them with treats, and they'd do anything."

"Don't be so sure. This only just started, and honestly, the grand duchess is being rather disrespectful and cold. We have a long way to go yet," says Zelda sternly.

I have to agree and do my best to ignore the uncomfortable dance happening in my stomach. Something is not right. I just cannot place it.

Jonquil reminds us we have a lot of work to do to have the feast ready on time. We taste test everything (including wines) one last time before we're assured the kitchens have it well handled. The reception room is ready to socialize after if the delegation wants. I make sure to tell the staff to prepare extra Aleph cheese dumplings for dinner. If the girl likes them, I want to make her extra happy and feel important. Even if she is a no one to her group, she could be a special someone to us.

I review the course plan in my head as my maids help me prepare. *Sweet honey dumplings with more Aleph cheese dumplings, beat soup, spiced fish in dark sauce, fried fish with vegetable dumplings, snap pea salad, rice balls, cheesecake.* I repeat it to myself and nod, feeling confident in the choice.

My confidence is bolstered by the stunning design Damian made. It's not solely Japcharian. It's a stunning blend of our styles. The flowing skirt with a firm waist is tied back with an obvious ribbon. I love the soft pink that blends into the belt. The top is white with carefully done bishop sleeves that are semi-sheer. They put a gentle white and gold hair piece into my hair at the back, and to look more Japcharian, they try to straighten my hair.

It is pointless. My hair will not go straight even after they wash it and dry it straight. Even with their long, hard effort, it still has soft waves that dangerously twist into curls at the ends. It still looks really nice, but not exactly what they were going for. I assure them it makes a better blend of the two styles anyway. They do my make-up in the Japcharian style to make up for it, dark red lipstick and sharp eyeliner. I feel stunning and confident as there is no way I'll get overfull on this meal.

The meal came off perfectly, and it's my favorite yet. The blend of what I'm used to and unique dishes from Japcharia are exciting. Our visitors feel the same. Viscount Ziam and Count Baek lighten up and chat animatedly with the royal family and Princess Zelda as they are closest at the table. The grand duchess, countess, and vicereine remain demure, though Tsikyria is smiling and openly enjoying the meal.

The best part is her huge smile when we present another course of her favorite dumplings. Her smile may have made my year. She catches my eye once everyone is distracted with gratitude in her eyes. She knows I made the request for her.

The grand duchess is deep in conversation with the men of her delegation and the royal family, leaving Tsikyria on her own to enjoy the food. I ask her more about the food she likes to make at home. I even suggest if we could find time, if she and I weren't busy, for her to show me how it's done. I also suggest Lilly might enjoy helping her as her mother makes the dumplings too. Tsikyria can't stop smiling.

Though it might be seen as the smallest job anyone on my team can do, I am happiest entertaining and making friends with Tsikyria. The delegation doesn't want to move into the reception hall but happily takes a last cup of tea before bed. I make sure to use the chance to introduce Tsikyria to Lilly before we turn in for the night. I don't think Lilly has looked so happy in a long time.

I go to bed that night feeling like a million deep gems perfectly polished. I sleep easier than I have in a long time, feeling sure I have done a good job. It's just the agenda meeting left. The rest will be easy.

Chapter 13

We wait until after breakfast the next morning to dress for the agenda meeting, and once again, Damian pulls off a masterpiece. The dress makes me look regal and powerful. The red and gold fit the Japcharian style as well as our Purerahian styles. There's a gold band going down my left shoulder to under my right arm with red cherry blossoms decorating it. The same design, only with golden blossoms, decorates the pointed shoulders, and runs down my long sleeves, ending at the slit in the cuffs. The floating skirt is simple but powerful, almost floor length once I have my heels on. To mimic the Japcharian style, there is a gold and dark, marbled green latched belt that makes a strong middle, and the gold border around the high collar creates a point down the center.

They pull up my hair into a bun, using my fringe to shape my face as always, making the contrast high and powerful and soft at the same time. The makeup is more my normal style apart from the red lipstick. The final touch is a gold, almost phoenix-looking head piece that goes around my large bun. A few gold chains hang down the back of it with pearls at the ends. It mixes the two styles perfectly. It's hard to feel at all silly as we get the impressions of this dress. Mother will find that funny I'm sure.

We go down into the meeting room, the one Gavril had shown me near the royal offices, to make sure all is set. There's a long rectangle table with chairs on either side, so the two groups can sit across from one another to confer. Each spot has a notebook and pencil to make notes. The chairs are proper but also padded to make what might be a long discussion more comfortable. We have servants ready to serve tea and little cakes if needed. It looks like we're all set.

Zelda is working with the staff to make sure all the notebooks and other tools are laid neat and straight. Then we make sure each chair is perfectly spaced before we give each other a once over to make sure we're all stunning and presentable. I'm smiling, but Zelda still has a hint of worry fluttering between her brows.

The royal family enters with the Grand Duke. I fight not to give him a dirty look. He studies us before anything else, narrowing his eyes at us. Gavril and the king are in conversation while the queen looks nervous, muttering to Maryum, her attendant, who's with her. The king's attendant and Godwin enter after the others.

"They're on their way," Godwin announces as the king's attendant sits by the king.

I give myself one last brush off before the Japcharians enter. They're all dressed more formally than the day before.

The ladies all sport large golden headpieces, huge with many chains holding dangling gems. But the one that surprises me most is Tsikyria. She's wearing a floating style dress, much like the one I wore last night but on a much grander scale. Her skirt, sleeves, and even her train floats in each small movement or breeze that passes. Her hair is pulled up into a high bun but with a grand headpiece that, honestly, looks like a tall tiara with dark green emeralds, matching her kingdom's main color. Her dress does the same with dark purple accents.

Zelda takes a deep breath next to me. "I was right," she says it so quietly I think I'm the only one who can hear it. She hardly moves her lips. I hide my frown, withholding my question, and look over at the royal family.

They all stand to greet the guests. The king and Gavril look perfectly formal and composed, not unhappy to see our guests. The queen and Grand Duke, however, look a little green. But as I look at Gavril, I see the slight hint of unease in his eyes. Something's wrong. And I know I should understand, but it's not quite hitting me.

The delegation steps to their seats in an almost rehearsed precision. As is their style, they each bow or curtsy in their rank order, viceroy and vicereine, the count and countess, the grand duchess... then Tsikyria.

My heart leaps into my throat. Only one class in Japcharia is given that bow: the royal family. That's when my mind recalls a name I'd read in passing as we reviewed the basics of Japcharian court. King Di, Queen Jo, Princess Tsikyria, Prince Duri, Prince Enjie, and they recently had another daughter, Princess Yon. How could I have forgotten until this moment when it was shoved in my face!?

I'd been unknowingly entertaining the heir to the Japcharian throne all day yesterday.

I fight to stop the flush creeping into my cheeks. So much for doing the smallest part. It's common courtesy to let us know a member of the royal family would be coming, right? They'd hid her all day yesterday on purpose.

My heart stops as we all sit down, and I digest what that means. What she said about her parents hoping the Enthronement fails makes sense. That means her parents, the king and queen of Japcharia, hope it will fail. From her behavior, I'm sure that means they want her to marry Gavril.

How? The age gap is huge. She's only *just* old enough to be engaged. There is a bigger age gap between her and Gavril than Lilly and Gavril, and it's clear Gavril already feels that gap is too big.

But it also means this is the greatest chance at an alignment than we'd had in generations. She is their crown princess. That means unless she abdicates to her brother, the kingdoms would be combined. As she clearly does not seem to want to be with Gavril, I can only assume that's what they want. But why? They hate us.

I hide all this with the skills I'd mastered long ago in the theater as Zelda begins the meeting by greeting us all and thanking our guests for coming, most of all the princess and stating what an honor it is to have her.

The grand duchess scoots closer to the Princess, but Tsikyria pretends not to notice, keeping a dignified expression and bowing her head properly to Zelda in thanks. Zelda outlines the discussion the king and queen have given us then gives Jonquil the floor to present what our party wishes to go over during the summit.

Jonquil hesitates in nervousness, but we'd all reviewed it and knew it was coming. Dahlia's foot is tapping anxiously under the table. I can feel it. I hold out a hand to help her stop. She does but not without giving me a sharp glare. *Pardon me for helping.*

"Trade agreements, border security... war effort assistance," Jonquil finishes with a firmer voice than I expected.

We watch our visitors carefully. They give one another quick looks before turning back to us. The grand duchess gives the Princess a stern look. I know it. Lady Hydrengia uses it all the time. It means "don't react". Tsikyria doesn't.

The viscount then gives their list which is quite similar to ours but for the last topic: "immigration". I refrain from frowning in confusion. What could they mean by that? Were a lot of Purerahians fleeing the civil war by trying to move to Japcharia?

The meeting goes well, though tensely, as Dahlia suggests which of the three groups should take each topic and on what days. I present the groups. The king and Gavril will take group one, the queen group two, and the Grand Duke group three. The princess and grand duchess will be in group one, the viscounts with the queen, and the counts with the Grand Duke. Easy enough.

We take a break after spending over an hour getting through the materials. That's when I see the hint of nervousness on Tsikyria's face. But it's gone before her delegation retreats to the corner where a set of armchairs and sofas are arranged.

The grand duchess starts whispering urgently to the princess as they sit down. But their expressions tell me little. We can tell our last topic is not something they want to discuss by how the two men are looking at the list of topics and frowning irritatedly at the bottom.

"How are we going to keep them calm about that?" Dahlia demands of us quietly, hoping the royal family wasn't listening.

"We aren't. We just have to walk through and get them to agree to talk," Jonquil says.

"I would suggest a compromise. We can discuss their topic first at the second to last meeting then war effort resistance at the last. They will feel safe if they think they can run out the clock on it, so they might agree to discuss it," Zelda says. "We just have to hope the royal family can handle it that way."

"And if they don't?" Dahlia asks.

"We have to hold firm. I don't think the king and queen will like having to discuss their people literally running away from the war," Zelda says.

"Or..." I am *so* not in my comfort zone. "We merge them into the same meeting."

"What?" Zelda frowns.

"Their problem and ours are likely related. We'll find out as we plan the meeting, but we want to finally end the war. I'm almost certain their immigration problem is because innocent people are fleeing the war. We stop our people leaving; they help us solve the reason why they're leaving. It's a win-win, right?" I feel stupid saying it. It's not like it's that simple.

The others are quiet. "If that is the reason they are leaving, that is brilliant," Jonquil agrees begrudgingly.

"What if that's not why they are leaving?" Dahlia asks.

"Why else would they be leaving?" Zelda asks.

"Unless their people are coming here," I say.

"What nut comes here?" Jonquil asks a bit too loudly.

I try not to laugh as we all hush her. I can see grins on Dahlia's and Zelda's faces though. I'm not the only one holding in a laugh.

"Alright. How about that's the plan if that is why they are worried," I say.

"And if not, we'll try my idea," Zelda suggests.

"Alright, seems a fair way to cover the bases," Dahlia says.

"I think it's nuts," Jonquil says with a sigh, "but it's all we've got."

"I'll take it to the royal family." Dahlia swallows.

We break our huddle and watch nervously as Dahlia runs our ideas past the king and queen; Gavril is forced to stand a little behind them but is clearly watching and listening to her. I bite my lip, wondering if they'll go for it when I sense someone walking over to me.

I turn and am surprised to see the grand duchess. "The princess would like a word with you."

I fight to keep the color from rushing to my face, pressing my nervousness down in my chest. I nod a thank you and follow the grand duchess to the armchair where the nervous princess sits.

Jonquil and Zelda's eyes snap to me. Zelda's eyes are wide, and her mouth slightly open. Jonquil's face is twisted in disgust, perhaps envy?

I bring my attention to the princess and give her the low curtsy her people use, still pressing the nerves in my chest. "May I speak first?" I ask.

"Go on," she smiles, reminding me of the girl I'd all but played with the day before.

I try to remind myself this still is that girl who I had discussed needlepoint and dumplings shaped like puppies with. "I wanted to apologize if I was too informal or improper yesterday. I did not know your station, and I beg your pardon." And I mean every word.

"Oh, you weren't supposed to know. You are more than alright, Lady Kascia." Tsikyria waves it off and nods me to sit, so I do. She's much more relaxed now, not quite confident, but comfortable in her role. "And I wanted it like this. I wish to ask for your help."

"My help?" I barely stop myself from stuttering.

The princess nods at the grand duchess to leave. The grand duchess scowls but does as asked. Why does the princess want to speak to me alone?

Tsikyria turns back to me, and I do the same, giving her my full attention. "My parents disagreed with my thinking you'd be the best go-between on this topic, but from what I learned from you yesterday, I think I was right in my guess. It's about what I hinted at yesterday."

I nod. "Your parents hoped to marry you off to Prince Gavril."

"You are as clever as you are kind," she nods. My cheeks turn pink for sure this time. "Yes, that was their hope. Then the Enthronement began, and now their biggest hope is it fails."

"So you can unite the kingdoms," I guess.

Tsikyria nods. "Yes, that is indeed their hope."

"You'd end your kingdom to become Purerahians?" I frown. The princess nods again. "Why?"

Tsikyria looks around to be sure no one is listening. "Don't let on I told you," she whispers with urgency in her eyes. "But we know what it's like to have war ruin your nation."

My heart stops. With whom? Purysia didn't mention anything, and they are the only other kingdom bordering Japcharia that could war with them without our knowing about it. Unless it was by the northern sea.

"Our farmland has been ruined. We hardly scrape enough for our people to get by without solid trade with your nation, and honestly, your nation has little left to trade." She glances up to ensure privacy. "And we are most certain the high king will not permit you to just give us back the farmland considering what happened the last few times you did that."

War. From my studies, each time we'd tried such a deal, war followed within five years. If we offer land back, the high king will likely see the start of yet another war and step in. He may even ask for Custod help. He had done so to resolve similar problems with Englaria and Spearim. If he stepped in, their smaller nation would be at a disadvantage. The high king was known to favor the kingdom with more land, historically speaking.

"I can see the problem." I let out a worried sigh.

"My parents had intended to approach the Purerahian crown with the marriage arrangement if he remained single. They were convinced it was the hand of the Creator that was keeping him single for so long, so we could be engaged," the Princess goes on.

I know that feeling. At least I personally knew who my father wanted me to marry. "It's hard," I say through the lump in my throat. I'm not sure anyone in this room understands that better than I.

The princess and I meet eyes. It's clear we both know what the other is thinking. The princess politely doesn't ask, only smiling in the joy of being understood.

"But how can we help without that? The high king will not allow a kingdom to merge without a marriage. How could we help?"

Princess Tsikyria smiles a little. "Not just your people or nation, Lady Kascia. I mean you."

"Me?"

"Do not tell Kira I said that. They still think I'm wrong." She sighs. "But I'm sixteen. Of course, they think so."

"Try being older." I smile a little.

"I suppose kings and queens are like that to their heirs." She smiles. "But that is partly beside my point. I need your voice, Lady Kascia. None of the other girls have enough influence or care enough. Princess Zelda is her own nation's crown. Lady Dahlia is... too competitive."

She sighs. "Lady Jonquil, well, she may work, but she's got her own plans. That I am certain. And that leaves you."

"Does it have to be someone in our team?" I think of Lilly. She'd be perfect. Even Isla would be better.

"No," Tsikyria says, "I thought of a few. Isla seemed possible, but she is too shy. I tried to get both of you to notice, and when she caught my eye, she all but left the room. I know she's not assigned to us, but I can't run the risk that's the only reason why she was nervous. You took the invitation. Not her. Same with Lady Lilly."

"I think you believe I have more power than I do," I confess.

"My sources disagree," Princess Tsikyria smiles, "and from what I see, I do too. The immigration question isn't just about people moving back and forth. It's the request to have us unite with you. When that happens, will you help us prove we mean no threat?"

I swallow. "Your Highness, as much as I'd love to help, I'm not supposed to be in more meetings than this. We are proving we can be good hostesses and prove we don't ruin a summit. That's it. I don't really speak for the king and queen. That's why we help with the agenda."

"Even if I request you?"

I can just picture Dahlia's red face if that happens and the horror of the rest of them. The king and queen would really worry then. But... "Are your people really struggling?"

Princess Tsikyria gives me a sad smile. "We went through the streets and towns of your country to get here. Sadly, though we don't face war, we don't look too different from you."

I bite my lips. "I don't know if they'll let me. They may even worry more." What would Gentian do if he learned I am a favorite of a foreign nation to the point they want me in the room to discuss their most controversial topic? He'll assume conspiracy and make it his life's mission to get me thrown out. Sage will likely feel the same or think that the rebels want the Japcharian Potentates to take over. Oh no. That would make a lot of sense. He'd think me a Potentate rebel. But....

"It may even make it harder to win this, but... but if it might save your people, I'll try." I cannot let her people live the miserable, war-torn life of my people. "But perhaps if your kingdom has any aid to stop these rebellions, that can go a long way towards unity."

"Then I think we can discuss that." Princess Tsikyria beams. "I might get out of this mess single." I laugh. "Thank you, Lady Kascia, and if what you said about him before is true, then I hope he will have more power soon." She smiles. "And I hope you're with him." I flush red.

She raises her hand to give me permission to go. I stand up to do so. The royal family are talking in low voices to one another. Gavril looks... smug? The queen looks terrified while the king, I think, is trying to calm her down. Jonquil and Zelda are talking in low voices, and the rest of the Japcharian delegation is talking together, looking frustrated, so no one but the princess and I see or hear what happens next.

As I go to leave, Dahlia walks right up to us, looking from the princess to me and back a few times.

"What are you talking to her for?" Dahlia says, glaring at me, though she's speaking to the princess. "It's not like *she* has any authority to help you anyway."

I glare at her. I know she's trying to undermine me, so I can't show her up. Can it not be a competition for once?

I turn to the princess to apologize and freeze in horror.

Her eyes are shining, and she's fighting to keep her face composed. Oh no, she thinks Dahlia was telling *me* that the princess has no power. She's already petrified she's doing a bad job in her mission, and the grand duchess is judging her every move, and now she thinks one of the foreigners just called her powerless.

I open my mouth to apologize and explain, but Tsikyria stands up quickly and walks away. I watch her go, turning as I struggle to figure out what to do. The princess is still fighting to hide tears. She stands away from the rest of her delegation but close enough to hide from our diplomats.

The grand duchess looks at her, and by the anger that crosses her face, I know she's spotted the princess struggling not to cry.

I whirl around to Dahlia, shoulders square and tense in anger and frustration. Her competitiveness may have just cost us the whole negotiation! I hold my body in perfect posture to direct the anger without looking tense. "What did you just do, you idiot?" I hiss to prevent myself from yelling.

"What? It's true," Dahlia rebuts, her air challenging and a bit condescending, almost smirking in her expression as she tilts her head to look up at me. I'm reminded of many a snarking protagonist in a teen performance. "You don't have any authority. You haven't won this yet, and everyone needs to stop acting like you did just because you made him horny in the safe room."

I clench my fists to stop myself slapping her. "Dahlia," I struggle not to yell. "How dare you? She thinks you were talking to me. That you were saying *she* has no authority. She's a sixteen-year-old heir with adults around her judging her moves. You don't think she'll be offended? Do you have any idea what you've done?" Containing my anger is not easy. I feel my face reddening in the struggle.

I freeze when the grand duchess sweeps over to the royal family in one smooth, powerful movement. She says something curtly which makes the king frown, and his brows pinch in confusion before the grand duchess takes the princess's shoulders and marches her and the rest of their delegation out the door.

"What just happened?" Jonquil's voice is tense in fear.

Gavril frowns after them, his brows almost touching in his confusion, mouth slightly open in question. "We... just got a no-deal." He looks at us.

"What did you say?" the queen demands of me in a higher tone than necessary.

"I told you," the Grand Duke says.

That only makes more heat rise to my face. He told them what?

"What did she want, Kascia?" the king asks calmly.

"It wasn't me," I say firmly. "I didn't say anything to upset her. It was Dahlia trying to undermine me." Normally, I wouldn't point fingers like this, but I'm so beyond angry I'm not sugarcoating it. "The princess thought Dahlia was saying all those horrible things about her."

Dahlia huffs, "Oh please, don't put this on me. I came over because I saw the princess looked upset." She's mocking me. The tension in my shoulders is so tight it's starting to hurt.

"I-I'm sorry. What just happened?" Zelda asks, looking utterly confused.

"Ask her. She was talking to her when she got upset," Dahlia insists.

"What were you talking about, Lady Kascia?" The king's voice is even, calming.

But not even his gentle tone could take this anger from me. I'm angry at what Dahlia has done to the negotiations and what this means for our people and theirs. I'm angry she had the nerve to try to cut me off and demean me like that. It is low, back-biting, cowardice, and little more.

But even angry, I'm not sure what to say. "I..." How could I tell them? I promised the Princess I wouldn't say anything until she spoke to them. Besides what would Sage say if I was honest? I glance at him, but he's watching with the same cold expression he always wore. "About what she told me yesterday."

When the king just looks at me to go on, I know I must tell the truth. I take a deep breath through my nose. Being kicked out for this would be worse than anything because it's not only undeserved, but it is also Dahlia's fault and could mean more ruin for our country.

"As much as I know you don't want to hear this," I say in a measured voice, "I can't say without breaking the confidence the princess placed in me."

"What confidence?" the Grand Duke demands. "You are not an authority of Purerah." I hear the accusation in his voice. If this is what they call me a traitor for, I'm not sure I'll be able to hold in the anger anymore.

How dare they? When I have done so much to help them: this summit, this kingdom, the life I sold when I didn't have to. They can charge me with treason and kick me out for other reasons, but this lie is what condemns me? This stupid lie from a brat of a girl who has just proven how unfit for the crown she is.

But no. It's not her who's being called traitor, blamed, and suspected, but me who was able to befriend Japcharian royalty. The first time our people have done that in over a thousand years, I'd be willing to bet. And the injustice is boiling inside of me, wanting to boil over and wreak havoc like candied water overcooked.

"I told her that, but she still wanted to ask for my help. I don't dare disrespect her confidence in me, Your Majesty." I curtsy to the king.

"You mean you don't want to get kicked out," Jonquil mutters, her expression sour.

My mouth opens ever so slightly as I stare at her in shock. Jonquil? She was my friend. We'd laughed and complained about the "elite" girls all the time. We'd helped and supported each other. Her anger is different than having Dahlia mad at me. We'd been friends. I'd not done anything to sabotage or hurt her. She'd never shown signs of disliking me, and I'd never disliked her. But now she sides with Dahlia over me?

This is the straw that breaks me. Hot tears flood my eyes, but I keep control over them as I turn back to the king.

"Let her speak," Gavril quails Jonquil and Dahlia.

I fight not to look at anyone else, knowing if Zelda agrees with the other girls, I am going to lose my cool. I don't know what I'll do. I don't easily lose my temper, and I don't want to know.

"Oh, so now you're playing favorites, again," Dahlia complains. "It's always been her. It's not fair."

"That's enough," the king cuts her off. "This is not about that."

But it's Gavril's expression that catches my eye. His eyes are creased, hurt, angry, and shocked. I can tell he wants to snap, but he keeps his tongue. That suggestion hurt him. He wants me to happily play his favorite, but when others say it, he's shocked? He wants to favor me but without invoking the others' ire? He can't have it both ways. If he really wants me most, he'd say so.

I'm taking deep breaths to control the emotional outburst that is longing to leap from my chest.

"Dahlia insulted the princess, though by mistake. She is the reason she was about to cry, and the delegation left." I stand by that truth, and if they punish me, so be it, but I'll fight them for their stupidity and injustice. I thought I was wrong about them. Perhaps I am about to be proven wrong yet again. I'm not sure I'll survive it, but they'll pay for every ache this nightmare has cost me.

"She's the one who made them walk out. We saw her talking with them. She's the one who should be failed." Jonquil folds her arms in irritation, clearly indicating if I do not fail, it is only favoritism that keeps me in.

My arms and shoulders clench so hard as I fight not to slap her that they start to shake as if about to snap. She is so jealous, she'd throw me under the wheel the first chance she gets? She hates me more than Dahlia who'd belittled us and others so openly? I feel betrayed and humiliated. I knew we were competing, but with the girls who felt like friends, it was different. We defend each other. Not anymore.

"We don't know it was Lady Kascia anymore than we know it was Lady Dahlia," the king is still using that quailing tone. "Let's not be hasty."

"But then why was the Princess upset?" the queen demands.

"A far more important question is what traitorous secrets are you keeping for the enemy?" the Grand Duke turns on me.

"Who are you calling a traitor?!" I lose it. The whole room goes silent. "I've slaved and fought with all I have to support this kingdom every day! I came here to do the same, and all you've done is make it harder and rip who I was from me. I've gotten closer to making a bond with the Japcharians than any of you cursed royals have in hundreds of years. I threw away all I had at home for this kingdom. You do not get to call me a traitor when you've done nothing more than watch to see which girls you should sweet talk to get us to fight for you in court!"

The whole room is dead silent, staring at me. Normally, I'd be horrified and humiliated. Instead, I'm fuming.

I turn to the king and curtsy. "Forgive me if doing what's best for our people seems traitorous to you." I turn to go.

"Where do you think you're going?" The Grand Duke has the nerve to stop me.

I raise my hand to slap him. He cowers away, giving me the moment I need to control my anger and lower it.

"See? Is that how a princess acts?" Jonquil says to the royal family.

I round on her. "How could you! I trusted you!"

"Enough!" the king interrupts.

I stand erect and take a few deep breaths to get my tears under control. "Dahlia mocked the princess for talking to me as I have no authority. The princess thought Dahlia was telling me *the princess* has no authority. I would be upset too if it were me. Before I could apologize, she'd walked over to the grand duchess."

"Liar," Dahlia huffs. "You're so desperate."

"To end this war!" I scream at her. "You just want to win!"

"I said that's enough." The king stands between us.

I roll my eyes. He's smirking. He's enjoying the show, the little...

"Lady Dahlia, is this true?" The king raises a brow at her.

"Of course not," Dahlia says. "I looked over and saw the princess looked upset. I walked over to make sure all was well, and she stood up and walked away. I don't know what Kascia said to upset her."

"It wasn't me," I say through tight teeth.

The king looks between the two of us, a hint of uncertainty in his eyes. Of course, he has only my word against hers, and with my outburst and refusal to give away "enemy secrets", he'll be forced to pick me.

"We should speak to the delegation first before we make any hasty decisions. Tempers always run hot during these events," the king decides. "Once we all calm down, we can find the truth."

"But she won't even tell you," Jonquil objects.

"Oh sh—" Gavril stops himself and clears his throat. Was he about to tell her to shut up?

"But Your Majesty," Dahlia's confused and hurt tone is some of the worst acting I have ever heard, "I just walked over. I didn't do anything. Why accuse me?"

"Because I trust your word as much as Lady Kascia's. It's your word against hers, and that's not just," the king says firmly. "I'm not going to rule you out without cause, Lady Dahlia. I give Lady Kascia the same courtesy." He glances at Gavril, question in his eyes. He wants to ask Gavril his thoughts. He does know us better than the king does.

"But..." Dahlia's fake lip shake offends me. Her eyes fill with false hurt and confusion, looking between me and the king. "So, I'm getting in trouble for something I didn't do?"

"Get used to it," I mutter.

"Or she is." The king nods at me, trying to point out it's only fair.

"It's because she's the favorite!" Dahlia whines and pulls out fake tears, stomping her foot. The display is embarrassing.

"Out!" Gavril's voice freezes the whole room.

"What?" Dahlia's voice is filled with shock, shaking just a little.

"Gavril, you can't—" the queen begins.

"He's not used any of his eliminations yet, Your Majesty," Sage cuts her off. "He can. It was in the agreement."

Any? So it's true; he has a limited amount.

"But that's not fair!" Dahlia almost shrieks.

The king chuckles. "Let's remember he has to live with the winner for all eternity. He has the right to reject those he can't stand."

"But you keep saying it's not his choice!"

"He has a limited use of eliminations without reason or question," Sage snarls. "We wrote it into the agreement that you all signed. I wrote that section myself if you recall." He gives the queen a hard look. "He has every right within the agreed amount and time limit."

"We did agree, Dalilly," the king reminds the queen.

Dahlia rounds on me, her face red. "I hope they see through your traitorous lies and feel bad for their deadly mistake."

"You and I both know it wasn't me," I reply. "If you'd stop just playing to win with no regard to what it will do to our people or even your kingdom, you'd not have lost."

Even with how angry I am, I do not expect what Dahlia does. She screams and lunges at me, nails out like claws. I cry out in shock, grabbing her wrists to keep her from clawing at my eyes which she flails like a crazed cat, knocking me to the floor.

Someone yanks me up and Dahlia back. I'm panting more in shock than anything while Dahlia is panting like a furious animal.

Sage has a tight hold on Dahlia, and Gavril has a grip on my shoulders, holding me back, yet away from Dahlia as if defending me, putting himself between me and her whereas Sage holds Dahlia from behind.

"Oh, come on!" Jonquil cries this time. "Just look at him!"

Gavril quickly lets go of me as if ashamed. I brush my shoulder and step away. If he is not even willing to prove I'm the favorite, he doesn't get the benefits of it.

"Enough!" The king looks angry. "I think we just found out who was lying. I don't think the honest princess would attack the other girl."

"She got me thrown out for something I didn't do," Dahlia snaps.

"And even then, attacking her over it proved the point anyway," the queen replies.

"Your Majesties, let's remember who started the argument," the Grand Duke says. "I do not believe we should let this matter rest with that. We should—"

"We'll talk to the delegation and get to the bottom of this," the king quails him.

"Of course." The Grand Duke bows to him then looks at me with fear in his eyes. Of course, he doesn't want me. He's more aware of my faults than I am. I knew he was faking wanting me to win.

Dahlia is glaring at us all, tense with anger. She turns her eyes on me with murder in them. Gavril moves closer to me and is about to put his arm around my shoulder to pull me back. It only makes the rage flare in her eyes. Gavril pulls away as quickly as he instinctively went to defend me.

The queen notices her anger and stands erect. "That's enough, Lady Dahlia. You can go collect your things."

Sage slowly lets go of her. Dahlia turns to glare at him. I notice there's a scratch on her cheek that didn't come from me. Is it a cat scratch? Maybe it was hidden under her makeup that came off in the fight. Sage sees her to the door and has other guards take her to her room.

"In the meantime," the king sighs heavily, "we'll give the delegation a bit of time to calm down before we reach out. See to it their lunch is brought up." The king nods at the Grand Duke who bows. "We'll have the girls keep to their rooms as well to prevent any other mishaps happening with the delegation until we straighten this out." He nods at us ladies to go on to our rooms.

Jonquil and Zelda curtsy to him and quickly shuffle out the door. Gavril bows his head to them as they go. Zelda pauses at the door, turning to look at me in concern before she leaves.

"You as well, Lady Kascia. You are not in trouble," the king assures me. "And for the moment, your ability to keep secrets has only helped. I'll permit your confidence for the moment."

I take a deep breath as that hint of trust relieves so much of the resentment that had built inside me. I curtsy to him respectfully. "Thank you, Your Majesty. And forgive me, I didn't mean to lash out at you."

"I know." His eyes twinkle in mischief. I can't help but smile.

He turns to Gavril when a meow makes us jump as Nippers trots up to the king as if demanding to know why his lunch is late.

At the same moment, Damian enters the room as if he'd been summoned. "I can escort the lady to her room," he offers.

"Yes please," the queen nods to him in thanks. I curtsy to her in apology as well, and that makes her smile before I turn to go with Damian. He smiles gently and offers me his arm. I accept it.

Gavril nods to me as we leave, just like he did the others. I nod back properly, not daring to speak. I see the battle in his eyes. I'll let him make up his confused mind before I decide how to handle him.

Chapter 14

I don't speak as Damian escorts me to my room, dealing with the rapid churning of emotions inside of me. A new feeling has entered now everything is over: shame.

I didn't mean to lose my temper like that. I was so tired of being pushed around that I suppose I finally snapped. I'd worked hard to be flexible enough to not snap under the pressure. I'm lucky they didn't hold that against me. That is not how a princess behaves. The only comforting thought that makes me more bitter than anything is that if they eliminate me, at least I have a likely position as ambassador to Japcharia.

My maids are buzzing about my room, getting it ready to comfort me. Damian directs them to help me into a more comfortable dress, and they don't question it. Though their care is touching, I am not sure how much it helps. At the moment, I want to calm this painful fire in my chest and scream.

When my maids finish, they step back to see what I do. I take the opening to retreat to the balcony, ignoring the January cold. I let the soothing sound of the ocean wash over me, begging it to douse the fire inside of me. I do not want to let that fire rage on Damian or my maids who didn't do anything wrong, but this anger is fighting to burn or be put out. I want to let it rage, but there is not a safe way to do that. I'd regret it if I did.

Damian watches me from a corner, and I don't mind, just sitting on the rail as I often have, knees pulled up to my chest as I hug them to try to keep the flames inside.

After I don't know how long, Damian speaks. "I'm sorry for what happened," he says sympathetically. "If it were me, I'd have already punched something."

"The temptation is there," I admit, still looking out at the water as if that would calm me.

Damian waits a moment then offers, "So if you need to let it out, this is a safe place for you. You can scream and shout. I will listen to whatever you want to get off your chest and only speak if you want me to or when necessary."

"You don't deserve my anger," I glower.

"Perhaps not, but you do need to let it out, and I am happy to let you. Bottling it up will only hurt more. I've seen it many times. I knew many a great lady to try to push it down and pretend it isn't there. Just letting the anger pass, never speaking of it, even becoming angry when forced, but in the end, it could not heal until she let it out. So please, as I said, this is a safe place. Feel free to express yourself."

I don't know if I really want to deal with the consequences, but the offer is too tempting when all I want to do is let the flames jump out and burn whatever they wish on the way out of me. "How am I the traitor?" I demand. "Have I not proven trustworthy?" Then I groan and hug my knees tighter. I wish the balcony was bigger to allow pacing. "I know what I am. But that's not even what they're accusing me of."

The fire burns brighter as I relive the rest. "And how could she turn on me!? What did I ever do to her that she could turn on me like that? I trusted her!" Jonquil's betrayal is a pain that is going to last, because unlike Dahlia, she's still here. "She hated Dahlia more than the rest of us, but she'd rather see me thrown out? How could she? I'd never do that to her, never."

How could I work with her or any of the others when any of them could suddenly turn? What if it is Zelda tomorrow after what she saw today? What if Bella decided it was her or me, so she picked Ericka over me? How could I trust them?

"I didn't do anything. I didn't ask for her to like me. The princess had done her research before she even came and picked me. I didn't ask or sign up for this." I bite my lips. "I didn't do anything wrong, yet it all fell apart, and I'm powerless to fix it."

Damian watches me a moment with a careful look in his eyes. "Can't you fix it? The princess is, after all, just a person, and you have dealt with her like before."

"But it's not just her. It's the grand duchess and the rest of the team that will defend their young princess the way the queen defends Gavril," I point out. "For all the good I can do, I might as well be eliminated. Perhaps that would appease them." But it will not appease the princess. She'd be upset; I don't know if she'd be angry, but she'd certainly be unhappy.

"I highly doubt that," Damian says, giving me a bit of a look with a slight smile. "But there is a slight difference between the two. Gavril's issue with his mother is actually slightly worse because his mother currently outranks him as queen. Whereas Princess Tsikyria outranks the grand duchess, and therefore, if she gives her orders, the grand duchess must obey. And clearly, the grand duchess does not have full authority to act under the direction of the king and queen of Japcharia. Otherwise, it would have been her leading the negotiations with the Princess watching on simply to learn. But that isn't how it went, is it?

"Which means as much as the grand duchess may pressure her and try to influence her, the bottom line is that it is the Princess's decision what happens with her delegation next. Now, being very young, she may not understand or believe she has that power, but if she does, she will be the key to turning this fiasco around. I highly doubt she has lost trust in you. She may see it even more clearly now: you are her only friend here. Should she wish to speak with you, and I imagine she will, you will be the link between ending the week as friends or returning to heated enemies. At that point, the choice is yours. Do you become the bridge between her and your royal family, or do you turn your anger on them and widen the chasm?"

"If they let me." I'm still unsure that the Grand Duke won't scare the queen so badly I'll be dismissed any moment.

"If they don't, that is on their heads. But there are two members who are not afraid to listen to you. You opened the king's eyes to his son once. Do you believe you can do it again for a foreign princess?" Damian cocks a brow.

"No, I didn't." I shake my head.

Damian gives me a small smile. "Gavril was in the delegation meeting, was he not?"

"They'd do that anyway." I frown.

"Really? They'd let him be in an important meeting with foreign powers when they won't let him in on a budget meeting?" Damian gives me a questioning look.

"The delegations would ask questions," I point out. But I had seen them kick Gavril out of a meeting before. Maybe Damian has a point.

"And the delegations did. Gavril was not in the last two opening meetings for the previous delegations. Even when they asked, the queen and the Grand Duke tried to simply excuse it and prevent Gavril taking part, and normally, the king would have agreed with them. But you opened his eyes. So, when others started wondering the same, King Aster made the first executive decision he has ever made in favor of his son. Kascia, he has *never* done that before. Even when Sage argued for Prince Gavril's right to have a say in the Enthronement, the king took it on Sage's authority as a Custod, but Sage's arguments didn't change his mind. No matter what Sage argued, Gavril was still never allowed in meetings until you."

I blink in surprise. I sigh. I wish that could calm the fire though. "They still aren't... I'm not a traitor." But I am. Just not to them. Maybe I was. I don't even know anymore, but that's why it makes me so angry.

"No, you are not," Damian agrees firmly. "But sadly, even if your past was squeaky clean, I doubt you'd get the Grand Duke to say otherwise. He knows he can use the queen's fear to influence her. He will do whatever it takes to keep that power and keep Gavril off the throne if he can. Because if Gavril cannot take the throne for whatever reason, the Grand Duke gets it as next in line."

And what then? I can't imagine what havoc the Grand Duke would cause. He doesn't care about the people. He cares about power. He has made that clear. But then... father said the Merlin prophesied the kingdom would fall if Gavril married. But I just cannot accept that it's true. The Grand Duke was worse, certainly.

"That doesn't show much hope for me if he talks her into it as Gavril gets no say," I scowl. "So, he gets to make the choice because he can make them panic?"

"Not necessarily. He has already been reminded twice that he does not get a say in the Enthronement when he tried to get Gavril's favorites thrown out, but that won't stop him from trying again." Damian frowns.

I sigh heavily. "Why is this whole game 'damned if I do, damned if I don't?'" This has happened so many times I'm tired of it. "Either they don't throw me out and I have to figure out how to work with girls I can't trust anymore, or I get thrown to the wolves with nowhere to go."

Damian gives me a sympathetic smile. "I highly doubt you will be thrown out. The king can handle his wife, and he is on your side. And remember, he already trusts you. His life depends on your silence about his bad lungs, and you have kept your end. He'll find out the truth about what happened today and see you suffer no blame.

"I just want to impress upon you the danger of the Grand Duke. I don't trust him. He may have less power than he pretends to have, but he's no friend to Gavril, and unless he thinks he can manipulate you to control the prince, he won't be your friend either."

I bite my lips. "So, he doesn't really think I'm a traitor?"

Damian shakes his head. "The fact he said that likely means he sees you are powerful and will be good for Prince Gavril, which will be bad for him."

That certainly helps me feel better. No one thinks I'm withholding information to hurt them. But that still leaves... "So how do I work with a team I can't trust?" I fight hot tears that rise to my eyes as I hear Jonquil's attempts to have me thrown out in my head.

"By remembering that not everyone wants to stab you in the back. Those who are not looking for power will care much more about you as their friend than their own success. I'm afraid Jonquil simply revealed her true colours. Admittedly, I had suspected something was off about her for a long time, but I couldn't say for sure." Damian frowns.

"How do I know someone else won't snap next?" I ask. "I... thought we were friends."

He gives me another sad smile. "I know. And that hurts beyond measure. Believe me, I know. A man I trusted for many years did that to me once. We weren't the closest of friends, but I believed him to be a person of honor. His betrayal hurt deeper than I could fathom."

I frown. "So, truth is no one ever knows." And I likely am just going to find more of it.

"Not perfectly, no. Even the smartest people can miss things. But if you look for it, you'll know. In your heart, you'll know. You trust me, don't you?" I nod, but he also isn't competing with me. "Even when we were strangers you seemed to trust me. And I hope you know I would never *ever* do anything to hurt you," he promises with sincerity in his eyes.

"I know that, but it's not you I'll have to work with to finish hosting the delegates."

He smiles. "I suppose not. But I pray you will not lose faith and keep believing in the good in people. It will not be easy. And people will disappoint you, but can you do any less? You are going to get hurt sometimes. I wish I could say otherwise, but Kascia, remember, the people you are fighting for don't just include your friends, family, and the rebels in the streets. They include Dahlia, Ericka, Jonquil, and Forsythia as well as many others. Competitions such as these tend to bring out the worst in people, but you have to remember, if you want to win, they are a part of the people you are fighting for, and they have some good in them. It may be deep down in some cases," he says with a tease, "but it's there. When the strain is gone, you may see it again. Don't lose hope. And... a true princess is a woman of virtue. As we get closer to the end, I wager we will see more good than bad."

I bow my head. "Then why do I still feel angry and betrayed? I've had everyone turn on me at some point. My father was always a lie as well as all he taught me, Jake lied about his feelings for me, even my mother was forced to lie to me. Gavril's doubted and turned on me.

And now my friends. Will everyone turn on me sooner or later?" Can I survive that? I already feel I cannot take one more, let alone everyone. The Grand Duke was right. One by one, they will turn on me.

"I refuse to believe that will happen," Damian says firmly. "Yes, I said, these things *can* bring out the worst in people. Not that they will. Your friendships with Lilly, Bella, and Princess Zelda matter more to them than some rank in a competition. True friends will always stand by you, through thick and thin. If Cedrick has taught me anything, it's that."

"He's your brother," I remind him. That's different.

He smiles in understanding. "Yes, but he wasn't always. I was adopted by his family. We didn't grow up together. We met during a trying time in both of our lives, and it drew us together."

"What?" I'd never have guessed. "You are... well, were..." I can't digest what a deep bond of friendship that had to be.

Damian chuckles. "I know. We get that reaction a lot. But the point is that no matter what the other was going through, we had each other's back. Even when I thought he should hate me, or me him, we never stopped caring for one another. A true friend cares no matter where you come from or what you have or have not done. They desire your happiness, even if it might cost them their own. That's what it means to love someone."

"I don't know if I can trust that anyone here feels that way," I confess. This fiasco shook my trust in any of them. I'm so tired of being beat up by those I trust; I am not prepared to give anyone else a shot at me. And I'm scared to lash out again. I could have been eliminated if I wasn't lucky in what I chose to yell at the Grand Duke. I can't risk that again. Defending myself is dangerous, and I don't think I'm strong enough to take another blow.

"Then look a little deeper. In your heart, you'll know. You'll know just like you knew you could trust me even while I was telling you to break the rules to sneak out and meet with the rebel leaders." He smiles a little.

"But I didn't know!" I snap. "I got lucky with you. I trusted my father with all I was! I trusted Jake and Jonquil. I trusted what the rebels told me. And we all know how horribly wrong I was. I don't know! I have no idea. I'm wrong!" Am I wrong about the royal family too? I recall the man they'd killed just for protesting. And of course, the prophecy... if it is real. Which I still can't prove. That's one of the biggest questions I have when it comes to the royals.

"Are you though?" Damian asks calmly. "Kascia, I am sorry for what happened to you. But you can't blame yourself for believing when you had limited information. You didn't just 'get lucky' with me. You made a deliberate choice to trust me with your pain. I didn't force you to trust me. You had already determined that I was someone who would care about you because I didn't try to reshape you into something I wanted. I'm sorry about Jonquil. Really, I am, but she is a mere speck in the grand scheme of things. She trusts no one and judges things only by their usefulness to her. Do not let her betrayal turn you into her. Don't give up, Kascia. You still have friends in the palace both in and out of the competition, and I mean more than just me. Vivian and Flur. Lilly and Zelda. You are a star, and you inspire them with your light and your desire to make things better for your people. Don't let Jonquil or anyone else snuff it out with their darkness."

"But it's not just her." It's that within months those I trusted proved to be false, and even when I thought I learned, I didn't. I have no control of it. "Their betrayal taught me nothing. I..." I can't figure it out. Even now they turned on me, I don't know how I'd have figured it out before they did it. I don't see in Jonquil what Damian says is there.

Damian sighs through his nose. "Does Lilly want to win this competition?"

"No."

"So, what would she gain by betraying you?"

"I don't know."

"Nothing," he replies. "She wouldn't gain anything by betraying your trust. And honestly, anyone that is trying to get another girl thrown out without cause will look bad in the eyes of the king and queen. Jonquil had no reason to attack you. She wasn't privy to your conversation between the princess nor to the one with Dahlia, so her voice means nothing in that situation. Princess Zelda knew that. She didn't speak because she knew her word meant nothing in the way of proving who was telling the truth. If she spoke in favor of you, that's all it would be, and she knew that. If she wanted you to be thrown out, she could have easily let you take the fall when you killed the rebel leader in the safe room a few months back. She had every reason to keep her silence when the queen argued it wasn't ladylike to be a fighter as no one saw ill of it in her. Instead, she not only put her neck on the line, but she threw down the gauntlet in your defense. Do you really believe she would do any different now?"

"I don't know." Which is the problem.

"Then can you at least trust that I don't?" Damian looks at me. "I held my tongue about Jonquil because I wanted you to be right and didn't wish to spread doubt in your friendship. But if you ask it of me, I can be your eyes and ears when your back is turned."

I nod a little. "I trust you." But even when I do, I'll be wondering. I don't even know how to tell. I've been wrong too many times.

He smiles a little. "Then I will protect you. And for what it's worth, I am sorry," he says with eyes full of sympathy.

I force a smile thanks. "I guess it couldn't have gone any worse."

He steps up and hugs me. "I can imagine a few ways. I was... waiting by the door. I was anxious to hear how it was going. When I saw them leave and heard shouting, I... I can't tell you how many times I had to stop myself from barging in, knowing if I did, I might just make it worse. I wanted to do whatever I could to protect you."

"Clearly I need it." I'm not doing a good job on my own.

"I don't know about that." He smiles a little. "You seemed to manage fine without me."

"No, I didn't."

"Yes, you did. I didn't have to come into the room after all," he reminds me.

"Well," I force another smile, "I'm not so angry anymore."

Damian nods. "Would you like to stay out here or come inside?"

"I'll just stay here a bit."

He nods again. "Come in when you are ready."

I sit out there a while longer before I come inside about half an hour later. I try to calm down before dinner, but honestly, I just end up pacing the room as I try to figure out how to be alright no matter what happens because the truth is, once again, I had no defense or control.

There's a knock at the door after I don't know how long, making me jump. I immediately retreat to the washroom to avoid being seen (as if he could see me through the door).

"I'm indecent," I insist to my maids.

"What?" Vivian frowns.

"Miss?" Flur frowns too.

"Just... tell him I'm indecent." I am not up to dealing with him or anyone else. I just want to scream and hit things. I'm not speaking with him right now.

Flur shakes her head. "My lady, I'm not sure..."

"Flur, please."

Flur bites her lips uncertainty. I groan and look at Vivian to do as I ask.

Damian stands. "I'll talk to him," he says and goes to the door.

I bite my lip and wait to see what happens. I'm honestly not sure what Damian means by talking to him either. He didn't say he'd send him away, and with how my day has gone, I'd not at all be surprised if Damian didn't.

But when he is gone a while, I dare step out to see if I can hear what they are saying. Then the door handle turns. I tense, ready to run or strike back if I have to.

Gavril steps inside, not looking overly excited to be here either. That makes two of us. After last time, I should have known Damian would let him in. I really am horrible at judging.

I fold my arms and look away, wondering if maybe running the water to at least start a bath would have been a good idea. I don't know if he knows I don't want to see him, so I don't know what to say. So, I don't say anything, determined not to look at him.

Gavril sighs heavily, but I still don't look up. "The obligatory 'are you alright' seems far beyond stupid at this point."

"Obviously," I reply stiffly.

"I just…" he stops, but I still refuse to look up, "wanted to make sure you were alright. See if I could help."

"Did you?"

"What she did was wrong."

"Is it?"

"Yes."

I doubt he's covering all the "hers" who are frustrating me right now. Not that it matters as he cannot choose them or me or anything.

"Suppose you've gone and smoothed it all out." He is good at this after all. He'd made the other two delegations happy anyway.

"No, they won't even let me try," Gavril says. "I just spent the last two hours trying to talk my parents into letting me talk to them just to prove you were telling the truth."

"You don't believe me?" That gets me to look up, glowering at him.

"Of course I do," he snaps back. "That's exactly the kind of thing Dahlia would do to make herself look good and you bad. I am sure she said exactly what you said she did. Doesn't mean they buy it."

"Here to talk me into telling them to prove it then?" I challenge.

"No. You've made the right choice in keeping my father's secret. You've not done anything to hurt us. If telling us is a problem, then I trust you." Gavril glares back at me.

"So, I'm not a traitor?"

"I'd slap him for saying it if I could," he replies stubbornly. "I may not know everything, and don't forget I know you won't tell me everything, so I can't exactly deny I know there isn't anything to worry about. But you turned on your former friends for us. You don't deserve such abuse. The only people you've betrayed are our enemies."

"So, I am a traitor?" I snarl.

"That's not what I said," Gavril shoots back at me. Then he sighs and rubs his eyes as if wondering if he'd ever not be arguing. "I-I suppose if you want to twist it that way. My point is, you aren't betraying us or plotting some mad plan with the Japcharians. He's just trying to scare us."

"So, what do you want if you're not demanding answers?"

"I wanted to know that you're alright. What he said was wrong. What she did was wrong. And apparently Jonquil's words cut deeply, so I wanted to make sure you were alright and if I could help. Is that so wrong?"

"Well no." But I do not want to see him or anyone. I want to stop feeling angry and talking to them does not help. I turn my face away, folding my arms again.

"Just another brick wall." Gavril rubs his eyes again. He shakes his head. "I understand it's hard. From what they said, I figured you weren't alright, and honestly, I'm not either. So, I stupidly thought I could help, but apparently, the more I care, the more pointless it is to try."

I shake my head, frustrated. "It's not like that."

"You have no idea," he mutters.

"Having to explain to everyone why we're on lock down again?" That might explain his frustration.

"No, I just spent two hours trying to tell my parents and Grand Duke to try to talk it out, remember? I thought if I couldn't do that with the delegation, at least I could try with you, but maybe they were right and my talking from inexperience is foolish and dangerous."

"You're not foolish or dangerous," I say. He likely could smooth this thing over all on his own. "You don't need us to fix it."

Gavril rubs his eyes again. "That's not the point."

"Then what is?"

"I... I wanted to help. I'm sorry if it was stupid or selfish. I thought perhaps maybe as I understand how angry, stupid, and frustrated you feel, I could maybe help you at least feel understood. But if you don't want me or anything save what you lost back then—" he stops himself. "I'm sorry. I didn't mean that."

"But you did." I frown, looking back at the floor.

"I mean I'm sick of watching you hurt, and I'm even sicker of being the reason why you're hurting," he says. "Perhaps my first instinct to give you space was better. I didn't want to force myself on you because I want to, thought what you want matters more than making me feel successful at something, but then I got the stupid idea that maybe I could help both of us. But apparently, I can't help or fix anything, and this whole process is pointless because the one who can actually help me fix this can't stand me just like everyone else, so we're all doomed together no matter what I say. I'm sorry I bothered."

But what he said reminded me of what Damian said. *They desire for your happiness, even if it might cost them their own. That's what it means to love someone.*

I take a breath to say something, but I don't even know what as the thought washes over me like being hit by the incoming tide.

"Sorry I intruded." Gavril bows to me and turns to go.

"Gavril," I try to stop him, but he's already out the door and slams it behind him, making me jump and feel about as worthless as the sand being pummeled by that same tide.

I stand there, taking deep shaking breaths as I try to figure out what to do as my eyes fill with tears. Damian opens the door and holds it open as if offering me the chance to correct my mistake.

I look down as the tears fall from my eyes. I can't. I don't even know what to say. He's better off without me making things worse. I'd stupidly thrown my fears at him no matter how I tried not to. I don't know how to fix this. What's the point of chasing him only to make him endure it longer?

"I can't," I get out.

"Don't let him leave like that," Damian says with a commanding edge in his voice. "If you care about him at all, then go after him."

"I can't!" Fear and the crushing guilt make it seem like I'm glued to the spot, trapped by it. I shut my eyes and can't stop myself crying. I can't fix any of it.

Damian sighs as he closes his eyes and bows his head. "I'm sorry you think so."

I can hardly control my sobbing, let alone move. I want to, but I feel stuck in place, trapped by everything with no ability to control it. I have lost all confidence and control. I want to fall to my knees, move at all, but I can't. I just can't, frozen by the fear in my chest that paralyzes me.

I feel arms wrap around me, and someone rests their head on mine. "I'm sorry." Damian's voice sounds weak and filled with regret.

It gets me moving, and I find myself shaking and hugging him back, but now I can move, I want to try. But am I already too late? I pull back and look at the door, trembling in fear but unsure what to do. Do I bother? I don't even know where he'd go.

Damian had left the door open, so I can see into the hall. He looks slightly confused but also sad as I pull back. I hesitate another moment before I finally get my legs moving to at least try. But the second I'm in the hall, I feel confused again. I don't even know which way to go.

"What now?" Sage's voice causes me to turn to see him towards the end of the hall, rubbing his jaw.

Gavril frowns at me in confusion. I can't believe he's still there. I want to run to him, but fear stops me. Like he'd let me. I still remember how dangerous he can be when angry. I look down as if apologizing for trying. "I-I," I fight more tears but badly. "I didn't mean... I-I'm sorry."

"I already said—"

"I know," I dare, still not looking up. "I didn't mean to shut you out; I just... was confused and angry, and I don't have control anymore, and it's only getting worse. And I just wanted to not be scared or have to pretend another moment. I didn't want to hurt you. I didn't want to push you away for anything you did. I just—"

"I know I should have left you alone, and I'm sorry." Gavril just sounds annoyed.

"I'm not asking you to apologize." I can't even look into his face anymore. "You didn't fail. Tha-that's all."

"Looking at the state of you, I think I did. You don't have to fake it to make me feel better."

"But you did. You tried even if it hurt." I bite my lip to stop it shaking. "What I wanted mattered more."

"It should have, and I didn't. I talked myself into it. I'm sorry."

"That's not what I'm saying!" I look up at him, not really yelling at him, but just saying it louder as if he couldn't hear me. "You said you wanted to give me space even if it hurt you. No one has really done that for me... as much as I once thought they did. It... it helped, alright? That's all. I... I didn't want you to leave thinking it didn't. I-I'm sorry."

Gavril sighs tiredly and rubs his eyes again. How do I not exhaust him? How do I keep from making it worse? "Thank you, but it's not your fault."

"I don't mean that." I can't look at him again. "I'm sorry I can't help you feel better."

There's a long pause in which I can't look at him. I don't have a clue what he's doing. I start to fear he'd left, but I'm far too scared to look up. I can't find the courage to check, and I don't want to drop the hope that he is.

I jump as I hear a slap and look up in fear I'm about to be struck only to see Sage is holding Gavril's shoulder, stopping him coming closer to me. Is it to defend me? I take a step back, unsure what to do.

There's a terrifying moment where I'm braced for many things to happen, but what does happen I don't expect. Gavril turns and tries to brush Sage off, but Sage only holds tighter. Gavril takes a shot at Sage's face which he avoids, but it forces him to let go and step back.

I am about to let out a cry as Gavril steps over to me in one smooth step, unsure what he's about to do, but he doesn't hurt me. He just pulls me close, as if calming me, protecting me. I hold onto him and fight with all I have not to sob as I hide my face in his shirt.

We don't say anything. I just stand there shaking, wanting nothing more than to hide here. Gavril doesn't let go for a long time. It gives me enough time to settle my heart rate and calm down. At least I stop shaking and my breathing evens out as I hide there, unsure it was safe to fully relax, but at least I feel like I can even if my mind isn't as sure.

Gavril's hands tense for a moment, as if he does not want to let go, but we can't stand there forever. But neither of us wants to move and be forced back into the world we can't stand anymore.

"You'll be missed when dinner is brought up." Sage finally speaks.

I gasp at the rush of tension that runs through Gavril's body, but it's not directed at me. I can feel that. But that does get Gavril to pull back, not looking at me. I don't blame him. I'm scared to meet his gaze and be unable to look away.

"Gavril," Sage says.

"I heard you!" Gavril snaps back.

Tears fill my eyes. "I'm sorry," I whisper. What is Gavril about to go into for me?

Gavril just shakes his head but doesn't speak. He pulls away, and I feel like I have something ripped off my skin when I can't feel him there.

I can't bear to see how tense he is as he turns away to go back to his room as I know I have to return to mine. I want to follow or make it not hurt at least. But I'm powerless yet again.

I take a few shuddering breaths before I return back to my room.

Damian gives me a weak smile. "I'm sorry if I overstepped my bounds."

I shrug. What happened, happened. There's not much more to it.

"I know it doesn't mean much when I say I respect your wants then go against them like that. I just... don't want the bottled-up pain to eat you alive. I know what that's like, and as I haven't helped much, I had the vain hope he could. I'm sorry if it hurt you," Damian says, bowing his head humbly.

"It's not like you said you were sending him away."

"True. I don't make promises I can't or won't keep, but that doesn't mean I'm any less sorry. This is your safe space. And I can't help but feel I violated it, and for that, I am sorry." He frowns.

"It's alright." I'm sure he was trying to help.

"Is it though? Even as I was talking to him, I wondered if it was wise. I know you like to think I'm perfect or all knowing, but I'm not. I just want to ensure you are happy, not just for today, but tomorrow, and the next day. And every day after, long after I am gone. Sometimes, I find myself quite clueless and foolish. I'm sorry if my foolishness cost you your self-assurance, especially after I *just* said you can trust me." He gives me a weak smile.

I force a smile. "I know."

"I'm sorry I broke your trust so quickly," he says with his head bowed, looking quite ashamed of himself.

"You just meant to help." I force another smile, just trying not to think on it too much. It's not like he hadn't always shown he'd help.

"So do Gavril's parents." Damian frowns. "I'm sorry I made that mistake. I promise it won't happen again."

"I'm sure it won't." I doubt Gavril would dare come to my room again even if I'm not eliminated.

Damian gives me another weak smile. "I did want to congratulate you on putting the Grand Duke in his place earlier. It was... well done." He nods approvingly though his head remains in a bowed position.

"At least I did one thing well today then," I try to keep a brave face.

"You did more than that." He smiles a little more. "But... while you were in the hall, I had Flur and Vivian draw a bath."

I nod. "Good idea." Not much else I can do locked in here. Damian nods then gives a nod to my maids. They come over and help me get into the bath to relax for a while. It does help.

I try to settle to rest then sleep, but that's not easy for me even on good days. But Nippers shows up around the time they're making the tea and keeps me entertained by attacking every wrinkle in my bed sheets as if it had insulted his mother. The best part has to be his insane meows. It's like he is trying to cheer me up.

I have to keep him away from my teacup though as he oddly tries to stick his nose in it as if to drink it. I let him try a small sample by putting a bit on my finger and letting him lick it. The tea must work on cats too because when I settle to try to sleep, he falls asleep purring before I do. Perhaps it's his cuddles, but it's not long before I fall asleep too.

Chapter 15

I want nothing more than to check on Gavril the next morning and make sure he's alright, but I can't. I'm limited to my room no matter how my heart bleeds and longs to be there for him, only able to pray he's alright.

A guard says Princess Tsikyria is asking for me to meet her in her room. I swallow but nod. I can't deny the princess, but I'm petrified as my heart races in my chest. I pray over and over I don't make things worse.

Her room is an entire suite with many doors leading from it on both sides and a nice sitting area. The room was decorated with the red Japcharians are fond of with gold and green here and there, the Japcharian colors. Emblems of the phoenix, as shown in their national emblem, and paintings of the northern mountains also decorate the room. The view from the windows is not bad either, though it doesn't have a balcony. I can see the ocean and the stunning fruit gardens.

Princess Tsikyria smiles at me as I walk in. She's dressed in the flowing dress her people are known for though she wears a calmer light blue today and blue flowers that replace the fine tiara she'd worn yesterday. She looks relaxed and more pleasant, yet also more in control.

"I'm so glad you came," she says as she stands from the sofa to greet me. I curtsy the proper low curtsy for a princess. She returns it, at the same level. I feel hot spots on my neck where the grand duchess must be glaring at me.

Princess Tsikyria invites me to sit. "Leave us," she orders all the others as if asking for tea.

"Your Highness," the grand duchess says carefully.

"You may return to your rooms." The princess stands firm. The grand duchess bows her head to her; the headpiece she wears jangles as she retreats to one of the rooms, as do the rest of the delegation.

"First, I'm sorry about yesterday." The princess frowns and bows her head. "It was not supposed to escalate like that. I should have known better than to retreat into the childish desire to hide behind an adult. I'm afraid it's caused more ruin than I could have anticipated."

"No, Your Highness, it's I who should apologize. Lady Dahlia said it to get at me. She meant *I* had no power, not you. She was trying so hard to put me down it hurt you, and for that, I am truly sorry. Her phrasing was poor and never meant to degrade you or your authority, Your Highness."

"It's only natural in such a competition. Most of all when some girls will be more competitive than others." Tsikyria nods. "But really, that is beside the point."

"If it helps you feel any better, once the truth was found she was immediately dismissed."

"Yes, your king tried very hard to assure us of that." Tsikyria nods.

"He was here?"

"Yes, this morning just after breakfast. He assured us that she was dismissed and promised she did not speak for the royal family and that such an insult would not happen again. He invited us to sit down with just the royal family to plan the meetings for the rest of our stay. The grand duchess refused unless the rest of the girls were kept out of all dealings with us all together."

"But that was the only meeting we were supposed to be in," I point out. "As I'm sure he assured you."

"Yes, but I want you there," Tsikyria says resolutely. I fight to keep the tension in my chest from coming out my tight throat. "But the duchess refuses to deal unless there are no more dealings with you ladies of the Enthronement. She will not hear of it. She... how did she say it?" The princess pauses to think. "She does not wish to subject me to being a tool in testing more... 'common rabble who have no business handling my princess' nonsense.'"

Tsikyria frowns, looking down. I can only imagine how hard it is for her to be the one with authority, but no one listens to her.

A meow makes me start. Nippers had somehow gotten in. "Chisaoime! How did you get in?" The princess smiles as Nippers leaps lightly onto her lap. The princess beams as she strokes the cat from head to tail. Nippers lies down on her lap.

"Ch... haisoime?" I try to pronounce it.

The princess giggles. "It means 'little blue eyes'. Did you know blue eyes are rare on black cats?" she asks as she keeps stroking the overly pleased kitty. "I have two Siamese at home. One likes to play; the other likes to cuddle. This one does both." She tickles the cat under the chin. "Is he the queen's? I've wanted to ask."

"No, he's a talented stray." I smile at the silly cat. "I call him Nippers."

"Nippers, that's sweet. Is that your true name, Chisaoime?" she teases the cat.

"Would be if we could say it."

The princess giggles. Nippers' presence seems to calm her. "But as I was saying," she returns to the work while stroking Nippers, "she does not want to deal with the Chosen ladies at all, even to having them at meals. She finds my fraternizing with 'wannabes' insulting and degrading. She's wrong," she adds when she sees my face.

"After what Dahlia did, the duchess has every reason to be upset."

"No, she does not," the princess disagrees. "I'm sorry I went to her. It was a mistake." She sighs and keeps stroking the cat. Nippers is enjoying it far too much, closing his eyes with each stroke.

"Is that really the only way to resume talks?" I ask. "If you wish to speak to the king and queen, surely you can do so without her."

"They won't let me leave the room, let alone go to a meeting." Tsikyria frowns in despair.

"You sent a guard for me," I point out.

"Yes, with great effort, and honestly, I doubt I'll be successful again." The princess shakes her head.

"How did you do it?"

"Nippers, as you call him." She smiles.

"He is so weird." I give the cat a look.

"Mind if I keep him?" the princess jokes.

"If you can tame him, I wish you luck. No one has." I shake my head. Nippers' purr gets an odd sound to it as if he's chuckling.

"Well, I doubt the grand duchess will let that pass again," Tsikyria sighs.

"So how do we get them talking?" I ask.

"I fear the only way is to convince my delegation that the fact that the Enthronement is happening shouldn't be a factor in these talks," the princess says.

I sigh. "But it really doesn't. The only part we have left is preparing the leaving feast and party, nothing more. You have my word on that and the king and queen's."

"Lady Kascia," Tsikyria says with authority in her voice, but also a shiver of anxiety. "As much as the others pretend this mission isn't much, it's of vital importance. Without agreement, our people may not survive."

My face falls, and I bow my head. "Then I'm not who you need to speak to."

"You are because the royal family will never trust a girl from Japcharia waving the white flag after how many times our people have used that means to weaken your defenses," the princess says. "My parents know this better than even our own delegates. It's why they sent me. It's about the futures of both our peoples."

"Then why do you want me?" I ask. "I have nothing more to offer than Lady Dahlia or even Princess Zelda."

"Do you see so little?" the Princess asks. "It's you I need because the truth coming from anyone else will not be believed. The king will not believe me, most of all with my delegation not respecting me. The queen will look at me as too young and naive as she does most everyone. Your prince is trying so hard to prove he's ready, he'll be afraid to trust me against his parents' views. But if he can hear our cause championed by a source he believes, he'll fight for it. The king will believe it from you."

"No, he won't. Why would he? I am sorry to say, I've not exactly passed the guards' notice as 'safe'."

"I do not see that as an issue," the princess disagrees. "You are what your kingdom needs because what your people need — and mine — is change. None of your common girls left in the Enthronement are going to make that change. The princesses will not inspire your people to change. Your people do not respect them enough to accept them once they are in power. Only you have the fire to drive change without burning the kingdom.

"You came to help me because I looked shy, and being so young, you believed I had no real position in the delegation. You did the same for girls in your competition. Your people need someone who will do the same for them. If there is any way we can help you secure the throne, you name it, and it will be done."

"Princess Tsikyria, it's not like that." My cheeks were getting redder by the second. How does she know all of that?

"He likes you. It's why the gamer was so competitive," Princess Tsikyria says. "He likes you." She smiles and chuckles as I roll my eyes. "At least more than most. I didn't miss his worried glance at you as we left."

"Of course, he was worried because it looked like I just started a war."

She giggles. "It wasn't that kind of worried."

"Your Highness, it doesn't matter. He doesn't choose."

"He dismissed the girl yesterday."

"But he can't just dismiss all of us until the one he wants is left standing. His parents have ensured that."

"Are you sure? Perhaps the answer is waiting until the Enthronement is over," Tsikyria wonders. "How long do you think that will be?"

"No idea. They don't tell us what's coming unless we have to prepare for it like these meetings. Could be weeks, months." I don't dare say years, but it's possible.

"Hmm, so that won't do." The princess nods, still stroking Nippers. "Is there no way to perhaps speed up the process?"

"What are you suggesting?"

The princess studies me carefully as she continues to stroke the cat. "If it is true, as they say, that the king intends to hand over the kingdom to his son once this is over, you'll have a direct line to the king to tell him what I told you. Convince him we mean it."

I shake my head. "That only works if I win."

"True, so what do you need?"

"Your Highness, it's really not like that."

"Why not?" She smiles playfully at me. "He'd be thankful for it in the end. Perhaps that is the talk we need to have with them."

The idea makes me feel sick. What would the royal family do to me if a delegation lobbied for me to win? No one had done that. The delegates assume favorites and give them gifts to win affection, but nothing like what she's suggesting.

"Why would you even want me that badly?"

"Because you can make that change," the Princess insists.

"Then it's the prince you want to talk to," I insist back. "He's the one who'll turn it all around, not me. He handles all the delegations as if he's one of them. He listens to our complaints more than any other ruler has in generations. He's smart enough, brave enough, and humble enough to take the correction and make the changes others fear. He's the one who's going to save this kingdom, not me."

"Is he?" She's smiling at me.

"It's not like that."

The princess laughs at the expression on my face. "So, you think it's him I need to talk to?"

"He has the power to do something. I don't."

"And you believe he will?"

"If he knows, I'm certain he will."

"Hmm," the princess nods. "But he will not trust me. The past will make him worry, and the way my delegation has behaved will ensure that."

"He's far more trusting than you think."

"I see." The princess strokes Nippers more slowly, and his purring gets louder. She looks at him and nods as if agreeing with some unspoken statement then says, "Yes, that is true. Perhaps that is the best way."

"Your Highness?" I frown.

"Perhaps the Enthronement is more about you realizing that I'm right than the royal family." She gives me a teasing smile. "But if you trust the prince so much, then perhaps that is the answer. I refuse to return home without at least trying for the sake of my people. If I tell him the full truth, he'll help us?"

"Yes. If he has the power, he will." I nod confidently.

"Then this is what I propose. I will need to speak with him to make any arrangement, and there is no way I'll be able to get to him. I'll need help to arrange it. Speak to him for me; tell him what I told you, what my parents wanted and how we need his help. Tell him I'll explain everything to him and him alone. If you can do that, I can get both our nations the aid they need."

A sickly slithering makes my stomach tickle unpleasantly. "After our last conversation, I'm not sure I can talk the prince into anything."

"Only natural." The princess shrugs. "My parents have lovely fights before they come to the best choice, such as sending me here. I'm sure you'll work it out. You'll win this, and if you need help to do so, we'll be there."

It's as if her words drop a hard stone into my stomach with a painful clunk. That makes two princesses who have pledged their aid to me. "Can you really promise that? Your parents may not be so happy."

"If you get the prince or the king and queen to deal with us, yes, they will be happy. They will surely add their aid to your winning," she says seriously. "And I will be telling them that is the wisest course of action. Win or not, you get the royal family to listen, you'll have what support we can give. You aren't the only ones who want this war to end."

"If I don't win, all this is going to be for nothing," I point out. "Shouldn't you at least—"

"No. It won't be for nothing because so far, it hasn't happened, has it?" She smiles at me. "Speak to the Prince and get him to speak with me alone. Then, if you can, convince the king and queen to do the same. Have them push past my entourage if they must. Explain to them I am more than willing to deal, but we must get past my delegation first. If they can do that, I will discuss with them, and I doubt my delegation will hold fast to their end of the deal."

The king and queen sound easier. That I can do and perhaps even convince them to meet with her. "I'm not even allowed to leave my room. How do I make a proposal?"

"Servants send messages all the time," the princess laughs. "You can't even do that?"

I suppose that's true. I'm not allowed to do that to ask for a date, but I suppose this is not asking for a date. I hadn't even wondered if we are allowed to seek time with the king or queen.

"I thought so." She smiles. "You work on that, and I'll keep trying to talk my foolish delegation into getting over themselves. By this afternoon, perhaps we'll have at least one meeting planned."

I nod. "I'll try." I just don't feel safe making any promises.

"Good. I will try to soothe them over lunch to make the overture."

Tsikyria gives Nippers a final pat before putting him down. "Sorry kitty, but we need to get to work."

Nippers meows but not unhappily. He rubs himself against the princess's legs before trotting off toward the door. What is he going to do? Walk through it?

The princess turns back to me. "If you wouldn't mind seeing the cat out if he wishes?"

I chuckle. "Not at all." I stand and curtsy before going to see myself out. Nippers is waiting at the door, looking up at me with those blue eyes. "Don't you go saying 'I told you so'," I tell him, "or you can stay in here."

He meows at me, complaining now as I open the door. He runs down the hall, tail in the air, and out of sight. I shake my head as I go back to my room.

When I get there, I find Nippers sitting on Damian's workbench. Damian is scratching the cat under the chin as I close the door. He glances at me then smiles. "I take it all went well."

"I... I suppose so," I say. "Is..." I can't believe they've not taught us this. "Is there a proper way to ask to speak to royalty?"

"Not really. You can send a note or tell a messenger. Either works," Damian says.

I swallow. "Right." And in this case, I'd seek the king and queen. I go over to my writing desk, make the request, and ask Flur to deliver it. She curtsies more formally than she has in a while before taking the note and leaving.

"It's... not undermining the other girls, is it?" I ask Damian or even Vivian if she has an answer.

Damian chuckles. "No, it is not. You have every right to request an audience with the king and queen without seeking approval from anyone else."

"Even though we're supposed to do this as a team?" I question.

"Well, seeing as you are all confined to your rooms unless directed otherwise," Damian points out, "and half of that team fell apart yesterday, I think you're fine." He smiles encouragingly.

I nod. "Alright." I am starting to wish they'd teach us less about dealing with situations we have not seen and more about how to properly navigate our roles as ladies. "And you're sure that's... proper?"

Damian gives me a look. "Kascia, it's perfectly alright. If anything, Princess Zelda will just be glad someone did something to save the delegation. And if Jonquil has anything to say against it, I'll have her bite off her own tongue and have it boiled for you," he says with an absolute calm as if he were commenting on how the weather had changed before finishing it off with the kind of smile I'd come to expect from his brother.

Okay... that escalated quickly. I am not sure if he's... joking or not. I manage a smile and look away. I'm not sure what I just saw or heard, but at least I am now sure Damian is quite capable of doing exactly what he just said he'd do.

Nippers sounds like he's coughing up a hairball. At least he is doing it over the bin.

It isn't long before a servant arrives and brings me to see the queen and king. At first, I presume it will be a normal meeting room. But they have me climb up several staircases and towards the west side. We pass the music room Gavril and I used on the test date. I recall the girls saying it was close to the royal rooms. I almost freeze in place. Where are we going?

My feared answer turns out to be correct as the servant takes me to a well decorated door and opens it. "They await you in the main room." The servant bows to me.

I slowly step inside, nodding at the guards on either side. It's not too different from the last suite I entered. It has a foyer with several chairs that leads into the main reception room. The main room has a fireplace on the left, two sofas facing one another with two armchairs and a table between them on opposing sides. End tables stand at the two sides of each of the sofas as well.

The room is amazingly perfectly oval. The walls are all in a perfect curve, even with the round walls, there are doors. There's one just to the side of the fireplace on either side and two on the opposite wall. Then the view of the ocean is remarkable. It looks a lot like the view from the ballroom balcony.

"They'll join you in a moment, Miss." The servant bows to me then waves me to one of the sofas. I sit uneasily, reminding myself to sit properly and straighten out my skirt. I can't believe I'm here. I fight off wondering what it would be like to be on the other end of this meeting. I notice a little candy dish in the center of the main table. I can't help but smile. I feel like the king uses that to test how long visitors can resist it.

I'm wondering what kind of candy he puts in there, sweet or sour, when a door in front of me, to the right of the fireplace, opens. I stand at once as the king and queen enter. They look more casual than I'd ever seen them. The king isn't wearing a jacket or waistcoat, just a simple shirt. The Queen's day dress is not fit to her form and more relaxed, and they are either wearing slippers or dressing slippers.

"No need, no need. Sit down." The king waves a hand at me as if finding my formality a bit amusing. I sit down to hide my swallow.

"It sounds like you were able to get some news," the queen says as she sits in the armchair on the far side from me, but still on the same side of the room, so she could look out the windows on my right if she wanted. The king sits in the one nearer to me.

"Yes, Princess Tsikyria called me to her suite today," I say as properly as I can.

"Did she seem upset?" the king asks, pausing to cough harshly. The queen pats his arm. When he doesn't stop right away, she opens the drawer of the table between them and offers him... a sweet? I frown a bit. The king chuckles and shakes his head, taking her hand in his left before turning back to me.

It pulls me back to what I'd been saying. "No, Your Majesty. Actually," I sigh, trying to recall how informal these two have let me be with them before. No need to be afraid of offending them by not being proper. I'm just so nervous. Stage fright has nothing on this.

I then explain what the princess told me about her delegation trying to prevent her speaking with the royal family, but she's more than willing to forge alliances.

"Would that be a problem?" The queen frowns.

"The princess and we outrank the grand duchess. If the princess wants to, the grand duchess can't stop her," the king points out.

"What if the queen isn't happy we took advantage of her inexperienced daughter like that?" The queen frowns.

"She's not as helpless as you think," I state firmly. They turn to me. My cheeks turn red. "My apologies, Your Majesties, but Princess Tsikyria is young and unsure how to overrule those older than she, but she's not helpless. She isn't afraid to offend the grand duchess either by using your authority to help her. Her parents should be proud of her thoughtfulness and boldness."

The king smiles a little and nods to himself. "They should," he agrees, but his tone seems to imply he means more than just the king and queen of Japcharia. He turns to his wife. "What do we have to lose?"

"The respect of the king and queen of Japcharia," she says as if it's obvious.

"For respecting their daughter more than their grand duchess?" I question more harshly than I mean to.

The king chuckles. "She has a point, Dalilly."

"I know there isn't much time left, but that only puts her into a position to want to get down to the main work. If you listen to their needs, she'll listen to yours," I assure them.

"So why won't they deal?" the king asks. "Why aren't they listening to her exactly?"

"Pride. They are still offended that we made their princess feel worthless in front of our whole delegation."

"Why does she want to speak with you?" the king asks.

I bow my head a little. "As much as I know it's not true, she seems to think I have more say and authority than the other girls."

"Because of what Jonquil said?" The queen frowns.

"No, she spoke to her before that," the king reminds her. "Did she give you any indication why she thinks that?"

Actually, no. She seemed to know things she shouldn't. But I give a more diplomatic answer. "She seemed to avoid giving a direct answer, but I did become friendly with her before I knew she was the princess, and I introduced her to Lilly. The two got along like family."

"Alright. Well, I suppose it's not relevant," the king says, hiding a smile badly. I am not sure what that means, but it makes me nervous. It makes me more nervous as he and his wife exchange a special look. I don't know how to explain it, but it's like they communicate without words with that look no matter what they are trying to say. "What is it she wanted to speak to you about?"

"She asked me to speak to you on her behalf. She knows the tensions between our kingdoms and fears without a trustworthy source from your own people you won't believe her intent to treat peacefully with us."

"Even with it, I'm still unsure that they aren't trying to lower our expectations to trust them." The queen frowns.

"Hmm, is Kascia so easily taken in?" the king teases. "I don't know. I am a bit skeptical, but she is working hard to prove she means to negotiate honestly with us. She went out of her way to pick a Chosen girl she felt sure we'd trust. That makes me think that even if her delegation isn't as eager, she is."

"That leaves the same problem." The queen frowns.

"I'm not so sure. She is the princess with more power to sign any agreement." The king shakes his head. He calls his valet. "Could you see what our heir is up to?" he says playfully.

My heart launches into a high-speed run to get away but only reaches my throat. I'm not ready to deal with them all at once. I don't know how I'll be able to even look at Gavril.

"Do you have any further questions for me, Your Majesties?" I ask.

"You mentioned something about the princess hoping to get aid from us?" the queen asks, dashing my hopes of escape.

"Yes, she has hinted heavily at it." But that is a secret I am only free to share with Gavril. Why does she have to be so set on that? I wish I could tell them then just get out of there.

"Are you sure?" The king frowns. Now *this* he has trouble believing? Tsikyria did have a point.

"Yes. Even though her delegation wants to be more careful about it, the princess confided in me that her kingdom needs our help as much as we want theirs. She is certain that without someone to act as a trustworthy advocate on their side, they won't get the help or the trust from you they need. She asked me not to say exactly because she wants to tell you herself. But with how things spiraled out of control, she thought if I spoke to you, I could help you agree to talk again."

"We aren't the ones unwilling to talk." The queen gives me a sad smile.

"I know." I sigh. "And so does Princess Tsikyria. She apologizes that her delegation reacted so harshly. She understands no offense was meant. As I said, it's the grand duchess who is stubborn."

"Yes, unless we end the Enthronement or keep all the girls far from the talks, they won't negotiate." The king shakes his head.

"Can you blame her? With that incident and knowing the girls aren't exactly well trained or experienced." The queen frowns at the king. "We did worry this could happen." The king nods and glances at the door. He's waiting for Gavril.

I, however, do not want to wait. The king bursts into another coughing fit that only makes me more nervous.

I bow my head. "Is that all?"

"Yes, if you wish to go." The king nods, clearing his throat and refusing the sweet again.

"Thank you." I stand and curtsy hastily before I hurry out the door.

I don't avoid Gavril all together though. I'm almost to the staircase when he and Sage come up them.

Gavril pauses, frowning in confusion as he stops and watches me pass.

I still have to talk to him. I hesitate then quickly and rather sloppily give him that stupid signal he'd arranged forever ago before I hastily get out of there, not even sure he got the message. I half hope he didn't.

Chapter 16

My maids are beaming in pride when I get back. I ignore it to help my nerves and work on my script to distract myself, but it fails. Did Gavril get my signal? Do I need to try again?

I turn to Damian. "Damian. Do you know how to... write a signal?" I try to phrase it right. When he looks up, I try to explain how Gavril had come up with our signal to ask to speak without breaking the rules.

Damian smiles and tilts his head. "Would he understand it if it came from me?"

"Um... I think so. He said he didn't have it with anyone else and as you are my attendant, I think he can figure it out."

"Alright. Then I think it's time I check on Joy's training," he says and stands.

I smile. "Thank you."

"Of course, my lady." He smiles, bows to me then leaves.

I debate if there is any way out of this impending conversation for me. Perhaps there is if I can somehow just ignore yesterday or our drama, but how do we have a conversation about what the princess said without bringing all that up? I'm going to have to be ready, or I'm going to make a mess that could doom many to death. I have to keep my head on right. I must be the princess; Purerah's princess and the one Japcharia's people need as an ally.

I stare at my script without seeing it, trying to prepare myself when Damian returns with a small smile, almost a smirk, on his face. "Well, he got it."

I sigh. "Guess we wait to see if he shows up." I wouldn't be surprised or blame him if he didn't.

"Indeed." Damian nods and takes his seat then looks over at me. "Do you know what that sign means?"

"What?" I frown.

"The signal you and Gavril made. Is it from a sign language?" Damian asks.

"Uh, I don't know. I don't sign."

"Alright. I was simply curious." He smiles then goes back to work.

I sigh and try to keep myself busy. I'm so anxious and nervous yet... unswayable. I don't want to do this, but I couldn't talk myself out of it if I wanted to.

Rather than jumping when the knock finally comes, I let out a sigh of relief. We're finally getting it over with.

Flur answers the door. "Ah, glad to see you. Makes it normal," Gavril teases her, making her blush in pleasure as she lets him in.

I take a deep breath and stand properly to greet him, giving him the curtsy due a prince. I don't miss the look that flashes across his eyes at my formality. He returns a slight bow. "You wanted to talk?"

I nod, unsure what to say.

"Want out of this room?" The monster knows me too well. "Conservatory?" he suggests. I nod my agreement.

Gavril offers me his arm. I take it and glance at my maids who just smile their approval. But it's Damian's eyes I seek, unsure what I'm about to do and terrified of it. His nod doesn't communicate much as Gavril and I leave the room.

"Are you alright?" he asks me once we've left the hall.

"Fine," I nod curtly.

Gavril's arm tenses briefly. "I suppose under the circumstances that is all I can ask." I shut my eyes at the proper tone he uses. I deserve it. I started it, but it stings that our relationship has come to this.

"How have you been? It didn't seem to go well this morning."

"I wouldn't know. I believe Father went on his own to try to calm the delegation this morning." There's a stiffness in his tone that tells me he doesn't approve.

"He shouldn't have tried?" I ask.

"He should have, yesterday," he replies.

"Think it would have helped?"

"It would have given them less time to be stubborn in their feelings and make up reasons why we hadn't apologized," Gavril replies. "But she spoke with you?"

"She asked for me," I confirm as we reach the conservatory.

"Is that what you want to talk to me about? You could have talked with my parents. You were there when they asked for me." He gives me a sideways look, hiding a smile. He is not unaware I am afraid to talk.

"I thought it better if you all work out your strategy on your own. I'm not supposed to be there."

"Yet you asked for this meeting." He looks at me out of the corner of his eye as we keep walking. "I presume this is a meeting."

"Yes." Guilt floods my stomach like someone dumped a bucket of thick, heavy slime into it. Like admitting I am only after him for his power, not because he matters to me.

"So why not just tell me and them at once?" Gavril asks.

I take a deep breath. "Because there are some things she wanted me to tell only you." I look at my hand on his arm.

That makes Gavril pause and look at me with a strange expression. "She wanted you to tell only me? Why?"

"She... doesn't think the king and queen will believe it."

"What did she want you to tell me?" Gavril asks slowly.

"Why she was afraid of you. What her parents originally planned for this summit, and what they mean by negotiating immigration." I finally meet Gavril's face. "They planned to propose her marriage to you."

"What?"

"They wanted to unite the kingdoms in a way the high king could not object. Because their people need the support. The Japcharians are struggling to survive. They are desperate and thought uniting with Purerah as one kingdom would solve it."

"Why are they struggling?" Gavril asks.

"She hinted it was from the loss of farming land in a war of some kind. She just said her people knew the scars of war then said the farmland was ruined."

"Really?" His tone is disbelieving.

"Was she wrong to trust you?" I challenge.

"I'm sorry; it's just there's been no hint of war up there. It sounds... a little hard to buy," Gavril says. "I don't doubt they are in need if the princess is this desperate. I just have a hard time buying that as the reason."

"Why would she lie?"

"You said she hinted," Gavril points out. "She didn't say it directly, did she?"

I frown. "I suppose not."

Gavril nods. "And why tell me and not my parents? I understand not believing it, but it wouldn't be hard to prove it, would it not?"

"Because she believed you'd be more likely to believe that they meant no harm. That they were asking us for help and are in need." I meet Gavril's eyes again. "Was she wrong?"

"No, I believe it. I just question what help they really need and if we can help when we don't know the cause, and I find it odd she only wants to tell me," Gavril admits. "I'm not in power."

"Not yet, and your parents listen to you."

"They do not," Gavril chuckles.

"Your father asked for your opinion," I remind him.

"And he'll listen to maybe half of what I say." He smiles at me. "So, what is she hoping I'll do?"

"Get your parents to believe it and find another way for the kingdoms to unite without the high king stepping in."

Gavril nods slowly. "That would be tricky. I can see my parents selling, but as you seem aware, the high king has forbidden that. Is she expecting us to just drop the Enthronement and accept the proposal?"

"I'd imagine if you did, the princess would throw up."

Gavril laughs. "That would make two of us." I can't help but smile. "I'm not ready to give up this game yet." He looks down at me.

I shove down the rise of emotions and square my shoulders. "She wanted me to talk to you to get you to believe her story and speak with her in private. As I told your parents, they aren't willing to let her out to discuss anything with anyone, but if you went and asked for her, there's no way they could respectfully turn you away."

"They turned my father away," Gavril points out.

"For a full meeting. This would be a friendly chat."

"Like we're having now?" Gavril can't help but smile at me.

"This is friendly."

"Your tone isn't."

I roll my eyes, pretending I didn't hear the hint in his voice. "So, are you going to help or not?"

I expect him to question her honesty, my ability to read the princess's intentions, or even suggest I'm falling for a trap. What I do not expect is the way his face falls. He goes a bit pale.

I pull away instantly. "Oh please, you are going to do nothing?" I cannot believe it. I must be misreading him. This is not the prince I have come to know. But I'd misjudged Jonquil, my father, and countless others. Am I wrong again?

"It's... not that," Gavril says nervously.

My jaw drops. "You believe us, right? That her people need our help."

"Yes. I believe you and her," Gavril says, still with that nervous wince.

"But you won't help?"

"It's not a matter of won't," he hedges.

"Then what is it?" I fold my arms.

"I'm not in power, Kascia."

"You don't have to be. She can have a promise you'll help when you are. It won't be long now. We all know it. Once this game is over—"

"Will it?" Gavril demands. "They never said it, and they certainly are not hinting it."

"Even if you just promised her aid when you're in power, it would be a step in the right direction," I argue. "Can she have that?"

Gavril's hesitation makes the fire from the other day flare up again. "It's not like that." He reads my expression.

"Isn't it? It's not like you don't have the means."

"Well..."

"Gavril, I've lived here. I see what you live in. It may not seem like the best to you, but there are thousands of your own people who'd kill for half of what you have." Gavril raises his brows and tilts his head like he doubts it. I let out a huff of disgust. "You have no idea, do you?"

"No, Kascia, it's not that." Gavril shakes his head.

"Yes, it is. You can't even promise the aid when you are in control." I glare at him. Have I really misjudged him so badly? Do I really have no ability to understand people or how they really think? What if Father is right about the prophecy?

"Kascia, it's not that simple."

"Really? Explain to me how it isn't when you run a kingdom that takes in far more from its people than any other and brings in more in tourist trade than any other. Explain to me how you don't have enough to help those that are starving." I fold my arms, waiting for the answer. I still am haunted by the man I'd seen shot down on Restoration Day for protesting. I may try not to think about it, but things are still that bad. And I still don't know why they allow it. Unless they have endless acting energy and have been faking everything about them since the Enthronement began.

"I knew you of all the girls were going to have this problem," Gavril mutters as if to himself though he addresses me. "Kascia, I... I didn't say I wouldn't try. I just can't..."

"Won't."

"*Can't* promise anything," Gavril corrects me.

"Of course you can; you just won't. What else are you going to do with it?"

Gavril looks to the ceiling and sighs, rubbing his eyes like he had the other day. I hate it when he does that. It's like he's trying to use how tired he is as a weapon to make me feel guilty. What I hate more is it works.

"There are things you don't understand," Gavril finally says.

"Sure there are. Like what?"

"I..." Gavril stops and looks off to his right, shaking his head a little. "I can't tell you."

"Won't." I shake my head.

"No, I really can't." He looks at me with a dead serious look in his amber eyes as he meets mine.

"Of course, you can."

"No, I can't," Gavril says firmly. "It's in the rules."

"Sure it is. I thought you weren't what they told me you were. I thought I'd misjudged you. Was I wrong?"

"Of course not." Gavril looks at me in dismay. "Kascia, have I given you any reason not to trust me when I say I can't tell you?"

"You can help. I know you want to help your people, but is that all that matters? Don't people outside your kingdom matter?" I ask.

"It's not that." Gavril shakes his head, looking off into the distance again as if trying to gather his thoughts.

"Then what is it?"

"I can't tell you."

"Because you can't trust me?"

"Because I'm not ready to give up yet!" he snaps at me, making me stop. "I cannot tell you," he says slowly, towering over me. I glare back. "It's literally in the rules. I can't tell you."

I laugh; I can't help it. "The rules say you can't trust me?"

"Even if I told you what I could, you wouldn't understand without the details."

"Which you won't tell me?"

"Can't," Gavril insists.

"What's the worst that will happen? Really think I can think less of you?" The second I say it I regret it. I can't believe I said it.

Gavril shuts his eyes, taking a deep breath: the one I know well. He uses it every time he is restraining the reaction he wants to give. Ericka gets it out of him almost daily, and his mother is expert at it. He runs his fingers through his hair, eyes still shut as he gets a grip on his reaction.

"Apparently not," he finally speaks, tilting his head a little and opening his eyes to look at me. "But believe me or not, I'm not exactly thrilled at the idea of getting you eliminated."

"There's no way—"

"They would," Gavril says in deadly seriousness.

I shake my head a little. I just can't believe they'd eliminate me for him sharing something with me.

"I knew this fight was going to happen," he mutters to himself as he runs his fingers through his hair again. "I just hoped… whatever." He shakes himself. "Kascia, I have told you more than anyone else in this palace. You know things Sage doesn't know. You think I would hide it from you if I had a choice?"

"You always have a choice."

"Do I?"

"I didn't make you tell me then."

Gavril shakes his head once more and tilts his head back as he struggles to convince me. "This is different."

"How?" How could it be different than his best kept secret?

"Because it... you... it's not you," he struggles.

I look down. That stings. I know I shouldn't win.

Gavril's face falls. "Kascia?"

"You don't..." I sigh and look up to try to stop tears.

"I just meant it's not that I can't tell *you*. It's that I can't tell anyone." Gavril's watching me uneasily. "What did you—"

"Nothing," I cut him off.

Gavril turns his head a little, watching me from the side of his eye as if trying to figure out what I thought he meant. "It's not you I can't tell. It's anyone. No one is allowed to know what I can't tell you."

That makes alarm bells go off in my heart. I can almost hear my father desperately pointing out I'd been wrong, and there is something wrong with them. They won't even confess. Was I wrong and Father right? But then why couldn't I find evidence of the prophecy anywhere?

"So, you won't tell me?"

"I can't." Gavril's tone is rising in frustration. "I thought you understood how little power I actually have."

"I thought you had more than you gave yourself credit for," I argue back. "Maybe I was wrong."

Gavril shuts his eyes again. I'm getting good at that. Then he does something weird. He holds up a hand as if to stop me, but he doesn't look at me, and I wasn't moving.

"Do you have..." Gavril stops.

"Any idea?" I ask. "I can't if you won't confide in me. I know how much you take in, Gavril. You took a good chunk of it from *my* theater. I also know how far that money can go. You expect me to believe you don't have enough to at least give them aid if not make them part of the kingdom you exact the payments from?"

"I don't expect you to." Gavril shakes his head. "That's the point. I know you won't. I knew you'd have this struggle faster than the others. I don't expect it to just make sense to you. I just expect you to trust me when I say I can't tell you yet."

"Yet?" There is still hope.

"There's only one person I get to tell."

Of course, the blasted winner. I groan and roll my eyes to hold back the ache. Yet? He doesn't know I'd win. "Why?" I try instead.

"I told you; it's in the rules," Gavril says.

"That's not stopped you before."

"Stopped me from what? This isn't like any of those other times, Kascia. I honestly can't tell you. Do you want me to tell you and get you kicked out?"

"Maybe I do." If the secret is bad enough, I don't want any part of it.

Gavril groans in frustration and looks up again, taking another one of those measured breaths that makes his chest expand and my heart skip a beat as I watch.

"How could it be so bad? I challenge you with a question I asked once with no idea how deep of a question it was. How can you sit here knowing how you glut off the backs of your people? How do you do it knowing you could help people instead? Even just promising to help down the line?"

"I can't..." Gavril roars in frustration. "I cannot tell you. I know you won't understand. Please don't think I expect you to just understand and be alright with it. All I'm asking is that you trust me."

"Trust you?"

"You once asked me to believe you when I couldn't swallow that you didn't think me a spoiled prince. Is this any different?" Gavril challenges.

The stupid negotiator has a point there. I cannot tell him either without risking life and sanity. Is what he would risk in telling me as bad? I hate him for bringing it up.

"What did I say then? I couldn't buy it if you couldn't explain, so I chose not to think about it. I trust in time you can tell me. It's no different now," Gavril says carefully. "Are you telling me you can't give me the favor you asked me?"

"This is different."

"Is it?" Gavril asks.

"How isn't it?"

Gavril stops, looking at me in complete incomprehension. "Can you really not see how the same it really is?"

"My secret doesn't involve why I can't save a nation."

"For all I know, it does," Gavril points out. "Please, I don't ask you to understand yet. I just ask you to trust I'll tell you in time."

"If I win." Which I'm doubting more by the day.

"Yes."

"So, you don't think I will?"

"Kascia," Gavril sighs, "I can promise you won't if I tell you."

"Really?"

"Really."

"Why?"

"Because..." Gavril sighs and rubs his eyes again. "Look, I want to tell you. I really do."

"Then why won't you?"

"Is it really worth being eliminated over?" he asks me.

"Is it to you if you might lose me either way?"

Gavril shuts his eyes and clenches his jaw. "If you're going to be so obstinate about it!" he finally shouts at me. He hits a nearby tree with such force, I jump. "But it's more than just that. The moment I tell you and you are eliminated, and perhaps worse, you'll regret it. I know you would. Please, why can't you just trust me? What have I done to lose the faith you swore you had in me?"

"Because you say one thing and do another."

"Like what?"

"If I'm your favorite, why not act like it all the time instead of just when it gets you what you want?"

"Oh, please tell me this whole fight isn't really about that." Gavril shakes his head again, this time in a different kind of disbelief.

"No. It's that you say such things, but then treat me like anyone else. If you feel so sure, why not tell me?"

"I..." Gavril takes a deep breath. "Do you have any idea how hard it is to never be alone with you?" he says so quietly I hardly hear it.

I freeze though. Is that all that holds him back? Sage? That confuses me. I know Sage would love to see me thrown out, but that still doesn't make sense. But then the most important part of that statement gets through. Would he tell me if no one knew? If Sage wasn't around to tell anyone else or kick me out himself? He said it so quietly perhaps Sage hadn't even heard it.

"I have to be careful how I behave around my parents, and frankly, everyone in my life. Sadly, nowadays, even you." Gavril gives me a dirty look as if he is upset I'd taken that from him. Did he ever not have to play the game around me? I am a Chosen. He has to play it with everyone. "And you keep telling me you don't want to be the favorite."

"I don't want more false promises."

"Have I made those?"

No. Gavril hasn't promised me anything he hadn't followed through on. It's everyone else who has.

"Is it so much for you to prove your faith in me by accepting I have a reason to hesitate? I didn't even say I didn't want to help. I hesitated. If you have that faith in me, prove it."

It is the challenge. He likes me because I am the one he can trust and the one who has faith in him, not because of his position, but who he is, his character. He'd questioned if I really had that faith in him when I was embarrassed to lose to him in fencing. And now when my faith is tested, he sees it crumple like a house of cards. If I want his heart, I have to prove it.

"Why do I have to prove it when you don't?" I ask.

I stiffen in shock as Gavril crosses the distance between us in the blink of an eye and kisses me: deep, hard, intense. The shock it gives me only makes it that much more intoxicating as his intensity sucks me in.

"How do I prove it when you shove me away when I do?" Gavril snarls at me, making my heart race. He's so close, so tense, dangerous, but he doesn't frighten me this time. He excites me. My hands pressed to his chest are shaking at how strong he feels. His full breaths pressing against my palms and caressing my face.

"Prove it by not being what I thought you were," I say quietly back.

Gavril shuts his eyes with a slower, more gentle breath. He releases me. I hadn't realized how tightly he was holding me until he let go. "I can't promise it, Kascia. I will try. I'll talk to her, see what she can tell me. But that is not a promise I can keep. I don't give empty promises. Even if doing so... could get me the one thing I want."

"I don't understand."

"Can you trust me anyway?"

I look down. "I-I don't know."

Something changes in Gavril's face. "Do you trust anyone anymore?"

"I don't know," my voice breaks.

Gavril actually swears under his breath, angry. I can't hear what he mutters to himself as he pulls away from me, but I swear he just cursed someone and something about time?

Gavril turns away from me, his back to me now. He takes a few of those steadying breaths and runs his fingers through his hair again. Slowly, he stands upright then lowers his hand.

Finally, he turns his body back to me, but doesn't fully turn around. "What do you want?"

"What?"

"How do I prove it?"

"I... I told you."

"And what satisfies that?" he asks me. He's much more normal. No, normal isn't the word; he looks like he does in a meeting. "That is a very vague concept. How do I prove I'm not a brat?"

"O-oh," I blink. I don't know. "How did I make you believe I didn't think you were a brat anymore?"

"Hmm." Gavril nods slowly. "Alright. I'll not only satisfy the princess in reassuring her that she'll get the help she needs, but when this is over, we'll do better than that for our people first. How do I help outside my borders when my own people are in just as bad a shape?"

I try to keep my face from showing it, but that is an excellent point he hadn't even tried to use in our argument. How does he help them when he has to help those he has an obligation to first? Is it fair to judge his leadership by problems outside his jurisdiction?

"If I do that, you'll believe it?"

"Likely."

"Kascia." I look up at him. "Will you ever understand how well you've done?"

"What?"

Gavril shakes his head a little. "I just... nothing," he shakes his head again. "Would you like me to escort you back to your room?"

In his oddly changed mood, I'm unsure if I do. He reads my expression correctly and nods. "I'll have Sage send for a guard for you."

"I'm sorry." I didn't mean to throw so much at him, or maybe I did.

Gavril just gives me a weak smile and nods to have me follow him back to the main entrance. Gavril then goes one way, towards the Japcharian suite, while a guard comes to escort me the other way.

I don't look at the guard, hugging myself and looking at the floor. I'm almost to my room when I realized what a mistake it was not to let Gavril escort me back.

The guard grabs my arm and shoves me into the wall in a way I'm starting to find familiar. Gentian is snarling at me, uglier than ever. "What do you know that Sage doesn't?" he demands.

He was listening!? I'm so angry my reply is to slap him hard across the face, shove my heel as deep into his foot as it can get in one hard stomp, knee him in the face as he bends over in pain before I slip away from him, and with a hard side kick, force him away from me. "That I can do that!" I snap at him before stepping into my room and shutting the door hard behind me. I find the lock and turn it.

I take a few deep breaths, trying not to cry, angry and more confused than ever.

Damian is still at his workstation when I get back. "I take it did not go well," he says without looking up.

I swallow. "Not exactly," I say with more anger than I meant to.

Damian sighs and glances up at me with his eyes only. He doesn't speak, but I can almost hear him ask "do you want to talk about it?" just from the look in his eyes.

"I don't know if I can do this." If I'm this upset now, what happens if it gets worse?

"Do what exactly?" Damian asks, tilting his head, setting his work aside.

I look down. "If I can keep playing this game." Or even be queen with how I'm reacting now. Maybe it is easier when you have actual power.

He frowns. "Do you care for Gavril?"

I bite my lips and fight tears. I still can't deny it. "Yes." I'm mad at him. I feel like I hate him, but I don't want to see him hurt or fail.

"Then why give up fighting for him?" Damian asks.

I look down. "What if I am the wrong choice?" If I can't handle this drama, if I can't negotiate this, how can I help him? Anyone could fall for his charms. He needs more than that.

"And what makes you think you are?"

"I don't know. I don't know if I'm horrible or perfect or just a puppet of the tides."

"Well, you must have some reason. Why else would you flip flop so much? Kascia, I have seen you shine with confidence, boldness, and tenacity. You have excelled in every test and event. You have won the heart of the prince, his parents, your people, and that of foreign nobility," Damian says, exuding pride. "And yet, you consistently bog yourself down with doubt and despair. I can hardly understand it." He shakes his head. "So really, why do you continue to believe or even allow yourself to think that you are the wrong choice?"

He hit the heart of it. I notice my maids have stepped out. I couldn't have asked for better timing. I didn't even have to ask. "Because I have to lie to them."

"Well, no one is perfect. And there is the chance they won't throw you out if you tell them the whole truth. After all, you mean them no harm now, correct?" He meets my eyes.

I am able to meet them back. "Yes."

"Then that may be enough to release you from this horrible lie you carry."

"If it is so clear it should be me, why can't it just... seem easier to see?"

"I don't know. Sometimes I wonder if it's merely because you cannot see yourself that way."

I sigh. "Not when it seems like those I want to listen most don't hear me, and I know... I didn't come here for the right reason."

"What do you mean those you want to listen don't hear you?" Damian asks.

I sigh heavily. "I'm not sure Gavril is really listening."

"Oh? How so?" Damian tilts his head.

"I explained to him what the princess is after, and he clearly didn't think we could help."

"Perhaps he knows something you don't."

"Like what? It's not like we couldn't use the help too," I point out. "They can't provide for themselves. They've tried."

"And I'm not saying they haven't. But things are not always as they appear to be. I'm sure Gavril and his family will help where and how they can, but you must realize, Kascia, you do not have a full knowledge of what the royal family must deal with on a daily basis. Please, do not judge what you do not understand."

I frown. "I-I don't understand." How can Damian defend him not wanting to help?

"I know you don't. But can you trust him, even if you don't understand?"

I bow my head. Now Damian is asking me. "I don't know. I believe he can do it." I'm scared of the word faith now. "I can try." I have to try, or I won't survive here.

He smiles then comes over and hugs me. "Good. I promise the answer will come in time. And when it does, you'll be glad you did."

I give Damian a look after I pull back from the hug. "You know, don't you?"

"My brother works with them. Of course I know." He smiles a little.

I nod. So it is that I'm dangerous. Damian is not even a Purerahian and knows. "What do we do now?" I ask, feeling the little hope I gathered faltering once more.

But Damian pauses and looks at me carefully. "First, I want you to understand something. This matter is of extreme secrecy. The only reason I know is because my position in being here is... unique. The king and queen do not realize I know, but as I share everything with Cedrick, he also shares with me, under the condition I tell no one else. He, being an advisor to the king, had to know in order to best help them. It is, in fact, a large part of the reason my brother was called here. I'm not sure even Gentian knows, and he is a Custod. Though... a bad one at that," he says with a bit of a smile at the end.

"Are we sure?"

"Yes, I am sure he is a bad Custod." Damian nods with a grin. "But in all seriousness, there is no reason he would need to know, and the fewer that know, the better. There are even members of the court that are not privileged with this information as it is kept on an extremely strict need-to-know basis."

I look down and nod. I wish I knew what this meant for us going forward. But I suppose I'll never know. Not unless I can somehow win.

Damian puts his knuckle under my chin and lifts it, so I meet his eyes. "But someday, you'll understand," he promises with a gentle smile.

"Maybe." Not with the mess I am making of things. How long can I keep pushing Gavril like this before he snaps "out!" at me?

"I'm sure of it, if nothing else," he continues to assure me. "But, for now, it's best not to dwell on it. And to get your mind off it, how about I fetch your dinner?"

I nod. "Suppose that's a good idea."

While he's gone, there's another knock at the door. Flur answers and tells me it's the prince again, clearly asking if she should see him away.

"I don't have to come in," I hear him say.

I go to the door. He gives me a small smile. "From what I gather, you'll be stuck in here awhile, anxious. I had a thought," he offers me a box. I frown at it.

"It's an Imajoel," he explains. I'd heard of them. It's a device, rather like Zelda's tablet, but it can only play games that are put into it using small chips. "I don't have time to use it, and I thought you could use the distraction. Thought perhaps you'd like to borrow it. Unless you would rather not."

"No, it... might help." As I couldn't get much rehearsing done on my own, the games might help.

Gavril smiles and offers it to me. "You change your mind, one of my staff can pick the box up." The prince bows to me, a small smile on his face as he leaves.

I turn and see what he'd been smiling about. Vivian is looking at me in shock as if I have done something of unbelievable difficulty. "Did he just...?"

"What?"

"That is his?"

"I assume so as he just offered."

Flur is hiding a smile as Vivian stares at the box as if it were the Merlin's sword or a death blade. I carefully put the box on the table.

Damian returns with dinner, and he and my maids start setting it out for me. He asks what I have, and I tell him, realizing I don't have a clue how to use it. He then offers to have Cedrick come show me. We just finished eating when Cedrick turns up and helps me pick out a game I'd like to try and runs me through basic what he calls "gameplay". We play until Damian offers to get my tea, and I prepare for bed.

Damian warns me not to get caught up and play too late before leaving for the night. As he goes to leave, Nippers slips inside. "You missed Cedrick," I tease the cat.

"Indeed, he did. Seems as though he's decided you're his home for the night." Damian smiles.

"You pick a new home most nights, don't you?" I tease as I stroke the cat. He purrs and settles on the bed, letting me do the same.

Damian smiles gently. "Good night, my lady." He bows to me.

"Good night, Damian." I smile back. Nippers meows at him. Damian chuckles and pets the cat's head then leaves the room.

I settle into bed, holding the game in one hand and stroking the cat with the other, pausing only to sip at my tea. I have to admit, it's one of the coziest things I've ever enjoyed. The purring cat is nice. Though after a while, he starts to paw at my hand. "What?" I ask. "I finished the tea. You can't have it."

Nippers gives me a look as if asking why he'd want to eat dung. I laugh. He licks my hand. I giggle at the tickles. He then looks over at the clock. Oh, he's right. When did it get so late?

I save the game and put the device away in the box the Prince kept it in, sitting on the side table.

I yawn and settle into bed, the lights dimming. "Good night, Nippers." I stroke him. He purrs and settles beside me, letting me pet him until I drift off to sleep. The cat helps. I should get a pet to help me sleep. I ignore the other thought my mind has as I drift off.

Chapter 17

I spend the next morning rehearsing with Cedrick or Damian on scenes I have with them and discussing blocking and the like I'll need for when we finally are able to start rehearsals with the rest of the cast next week.

The meetings yesterday and this morning must have gone well because I'm informed that after lunch, I'll need to meet with the rest of my team to prepare the leaving feast and ball that night. I'm anxious about how they'll react. I haven't spoken to any of them since the meeting.

These anxious thoughts tumble through my mind as I enter the Ladies' Chamber. Zelda has already started. She looks up when I come in and squeals in happiness. She puts her tablet down on the table and rushes over to me to hug me tightly.

"Are you alright?" she asks the second she has me in her arms. She pulls back to look at my face. "I was so worried with how it all went. I thought you might just go mad."

"I'm fine. We just need to be ready." I turn to work.

"Hey, you sure you're alright?" Zelda asks with a frown.

"Why not?"

"It isn't like you to just want to jump in. I mean, you get to work, but you... are you okay?" Zelda is studying my face.

I look away, not liking the feeling. "I'm alright."

"Kascia, you don't think I think any less of you after what happened, do you?" Zelda asks nervously.

"Of course not." I put on a proper smile.

"You're too good at this. A princess knows when another princess is putting on the face, Kascia."

"But I'm not a princess," I blurt out before I can control it. "And they all resent me for doing well." I resist saying "you all".

"I hate to break it to you, but resentment from the court or even other royals is normal in our line of work." Zelda gives me a sad smile.

"But it's not mine yet. And I…" I sigh. "I never thought we'd turn on each other while girls like Ericka and Forsythia were still around."

"And you're terrified to find who turns on you next. Me, Bella, Lilly, Azalea," Zelda guesses.

"We all want to win."

Zelda hesitates. There it is again. She often mistakenly dropped hints she didn't want to win, but I know better than to ask.

"True, but only the truest of princesses will be faithful and kind until the end. Even if it were Dahlia she was trying to have eliminated, Jonquil's behavior would not have been tolerated in my home," says Zelda. "It did show how many girls are going to feel. That's how girls are when they get competitive. Only one girl comes out on top, and that's the girl who proves royalty. And hopefully, on top of that, she'll prove the best choice for your kingdom. I never would have tried to prove you did wrong to get you eliminated even if you had done wrong. Trying to get other girls eliminated won't help anyone."

"I know all of that. It's honestly because it's Jonquil. We… She was in our group, Zelda. She'd play games with us and was friendly with us. She was our friend. How could she act like we were enemies in the blink of an eye?"

"I never would have guessed she'd explode like that," Zelda says.

My head snaps up in shock. "Really?"

Zelda nods sadly. "I know a lot of the girls dislike those they see in the lead. It's not just you."

"It's not?" I feel relieved and tense.

"No. They don't like me for how many dates I get. No one ever forgave you for what happened in the safe room that one night." I blush as Zelda goes on. "Bella has been seen having non-arranged moments with the prince that look pretty chummy. And Azalea suddenly started getting a lot of attention, so they all assume she did something to please him. Oh, and of course after Forsythia's show, everyone is looking at her with contempt."

The list makes my stomach knot. Those are his favorites. The list I know he has. The list I want to avoid and yet I make myself sick worrying. At least Zelda is on it with me. Five girls. Five girls when there are fourteen left.

"But don't lose heart. Remember, if you are prejudiced towards someone for something they didn't do, the fault is on you. If you treat them with trust and respect and they break it, that's on them," Zelda advises me.

"But it still hurts."

"I know. But that's what your real friends and family are for. Kascia, as far as I'm concerned, you've proven yourself as worthy a princess as Rose, Amapola, Laurina, or I. Most of all, you've proved it in the way you've handled these events. Pardon me if my saying so makes you uncomfortable, but even if you don't win, if they don't give you a position befitting the kind of royal you are, my people will. I'm not even exaggerating. You are one of us, and we will not leave you alone. I promise."

"I don't think Rose or Amapola will agree."

"Hmm, well, perhaps when they are finally humble enough to admit a girl not born royal is a princess at heart even without a marriage, they will come around. I can promise that." Zelda smiles. "Meantime, you'll always have me and Lilly. Heaven knows that girl is far too sweet to turn on anyone even if they handed her over to the sharks. But let's get to work while we wait for the Baroness Jonquil." Zelda smiles.

I laugh, understanding her putting Jonquil down as the lowest nobility she feels she deserves.

We are just getting into a flow when Jonquil enters. "Sorry, I didn't mean to be last," she says as if we were back for any normal afternoon study session. "Guess I was knocked out of the flow."

"I suppose so," Zelda says with a tone that does not betray any other meaning. "I'm just finishing with the flowers if you want to inspect the place settings. I also thought you could take over Dahlia's tasks that we set for today."

"Of course, I'll handle whatever we need," Jonquil says brightly and sets to her work. She spots me and smiles as if nothing happened.

My heart clenches. I want to demand how she can act like nothing happened, but as she is pretending, I will too. That's what I tell myself all afternoon.

Our work goes smoothly, and before I know it, my maids are preparing me for the leaving feast. The dress is likely my favorite of this style yet. It's white with an amazing gold Japcharian design around the end of the flared skirt and making up the tall, Japcharian-style belt at the center. The high collar only goes halfway up my neck this time, which I like, and has a styled line going down to the belt. The floating sleeves are long and a lot like the dresses Princess Tsikyria wears.

They put my hair into a soft bun with a golden hair piece weaved into it to match the style. They use the sharper eye makeup of the style to help blend it all together. It's a lovely blend of our two cultures' styles once again.

Feeling powerful and confident in my outfit, I head down to the dining hall to greet guests. We inspect everything carefully before the queen comes and does the last check which she declares it 'ready' for our guests to arrive.

The delegation is surprisingly polite and warm when they arrive. The meetings must have gone well. The delegates are chatty and relaxed, all but the grand duchess who is still hovering protectively around the princess who is bubblier than I'd ever seen her: chatting pleasantly, beaming and waving at me as if we're old friends.

Princess Tsikyria has nothing but compliments for the dinner and insists on getting the recipe for some of our dumplings. All goes well, and I personally think it all looks lovely. Jonquil is more nervous and excuses herself early to make sure the ballroom is ready.

When the meal is finished, Zelda and I stand and invite our guests into the ballroom. The music and decorations are perfect. The music is a bit slower than we normally play, but that fits the styles of our guests. It must be perfectly fitting because they are happy to jump right into the dances.

Zelda inspects the tea table to be sure all is in order as I walk the perimeter. The Grand Duke asks the grand duchess to dance. She doesn't look overly pleased. I keep an eye on that as I check the rest of the room.

The princess is dancing with Gavril, her stunning red dress fluttering like a butterfly as they make their way around the line of dance.

As the prince starts to dance with the grand duchess, I look over at the Grand Duke to ensure he doesn't stir trouble with how displeased the grand duchess was to dance with him.

"How did it go?" a younger man, I presume the Grand Duke's attendant, asks him as they watch from the side.

"She didn't seem very interested in my thoughts on the topic," the Grand Duke says in a low growl. I step behind one of the pillars to avoid being seen. I shouldn't listen in, but now I'm curious. "If only they hadn't been so careless. It's because I wasn't there in the main meeting."

"They rely on you so much, they don't even realize they have to ask for you. That should be an honor," the attendant says sycophantically.

"Ah!" the Grand Duke complains, waving his hand in dismissal. "It's because they have their threesome they have grown accustomed to. I was dishonored in their forgetting the invitation. It's taken me out of the equation, and that, they will pay for."

"You were missed," the attendant tries again.

"If this is to be kept in proper order, we cannot have it happen again. You and your boys keep a sharp eye on the next round and make sure there is not one meeting that does not happen without me. If we have to bribe room attendants, so be it," the Grand Duke complains, taking a drink from the table, looking sour. "I am the Grand Duke. I am not just another courier seeking more power than he ought. I have been key in helping them get this far. They can't just cast me off because their rising star is finally catching their eyes."

"They do trust him with more than they should," the attendant agrees. "He only just started."

"And someone needs to keep that reigned in. We will have to ensure it does." The Grand Duke nods, taking a draft of his drink. "That unbridled temper of his will be our undoing."

"Is that so bad?" the attendant asks quietly.

The dark look the Grand Duke gives his attendant clearly says "not here, fool" before he speaks. "Of course, it is."

"When they see it, they'll know to recall him." The attendant shrugs. "Sometimes, the child has to touch the stove to learn."

"Yes, but when the child burns more than himself, the risk is not to be taken," the Grand Duke says. "And the way it looks it's going with the grand duchess, they may not learn in time."

"That's what you're for. You'll set it right." The attendant smiles. "Though the king and queen are free. Perhaps..."

The Grand Duke spots them too, downs the rest of his drink and makes a direct path for them.

I look around but seeing nothing else to keep me busy, I follow.

"Ah, good to see you," the king says brightly to the Grand Duke.

"I would hope so. I was starting to fear you'd forget me," the Grand Duke pouts playfully.

"We really are so sorry. Our staff were running wild, and we did not realize they had forgotten. It will not happen again," the queen assures him.

"So it's not that I'm no longer important?"

"Of course not," the queen insists.

The king looks away. I can't help but wonder what expression he's hiding.

"We're making sure that you are brought into the meetings," the queen goes on.

"I should hope so. To be suddenly so rudely dismissed was quite the insult."

"None meant." The queen smiles.

I would rather not listen to the Grand Duke getting apologies out of the queen, so I start on my rounds once more. But after what I just heard, I want him as far from this mess of a summit and the royal family as possible.

"Kascia!" I hear the princess's bright voice. She's sitting by the tea table, enjoying a cup and invites me to sit with her. I don't dare say no.

"You look stunning," she says. "You'd fit in with our courts in seconds. You're perfect for this."

"I do my best." I smile. "It is my test," I joke playfully.

"So, you can't enjoy the night?" Princess Tsikyria asks. "I can't allow that. You have to at least ask him for one dance. You can't waste that stunning dress by not dancing in it."

"What?"

"You don't ask the prince to dance?" She frowns.

"Uh, well, I suppose I can. If that isn't the same as asking for a date, which is against the rules. But normally, he asks."

"Oh." She blinks a little. "Is that normal here? It's the ladies who ask in Japcharia."

That explains a lot about the men's behavior. They are not to speak unaccompanied to the ladies they do not know and are not supposed to ask. Why didn't Lady Keva tell us that? That would be helpful to know. How did they miss something that big? "I suppose your ladies do show more power and confidence."

"Well, why not catch his eye, so he'll ask?"

I sigh. "Not exactly the time for it," I try to keep the talk diplomatic. Talking badly about the prince now may not be the best idea.

"Why not? It's supposed to be fun. He must like to dance with you best. You must be the best dancer here."

"I don't know if he likes to dance with me best. He's not said." I shrug. "And he's likely danced with us all about equally."

"Well, maybe he said it to me." She's taunting me. I can hear it in her delicate voice. I suppose she can forget this is still a summit event, so she feels safe to play and tease like friends do. But I have to keep up the act. It's getting annoying, and part of me wonders if she knows it. "You should ask him."

"I'm not supposed to. I might get into trouble."

"What if I ask for you?"

Oh, that's going to make things better. "I don't think he'd want to."

"Why not? He seems to be in a good enough mood." The princess frowns, watching as Gavril twirls the grand duchess in a dance. That man is brave to even try that one. Then again, with their culture, she likely asked him. That's an odd thought.

"It's... complicated."

"Did you not speak with him before? He seemed to understand. I was certain you'd spoken with him." She frowns.

"Well, I did. He just... didn't want to be helpful." I really wish I could avoid this conversation.

"What do you mean he didn't want to? He was perfectly helpful." The princess frowns deeper. "Did you really have to talk him into it?"

"You could say that." I really didn't want to go into the details with her.

Princess Tsikyria tilts her head, trying to understand. "Dating him must be really complicated." I laugh. "Because none of this makes any sense. You won if you had to coax him. He was as accommodating as he could be."

"There shouldn't be a 'could be'. Not with... stakes so high," I try to put it delicately.

"It's not like he's king. He can't hand over whatever he likes any more than I can." She smiles a little. "So, there's not really anything he could actually offer other than pleading our case. I think it helped. We won't know until it's all over, and we have the meetings."

"You don't know when it will be?" I frown a bit.

"Well... perhaps." She flushes.

"Do I want to know?" I ask.

"Maybe. But only if you ask him to dance." Princess Tsikyria looks like the teenage girl she is with that grin. I'd almost forgotten with how proper she behaves. She suddenly reminds me of Alsmeria, my best friend back at the theater.

"What?"

"I'll tell you how it went if you dance with him," she insists. "Give you a chance to get over whatever fights you had to use to get him to agree."

This isn't funny, but she's smiling and hiding her giggles. I could use some back up. I am not sure how to politely tell her to stop being a pest.

"Be a shame to waste such a nice dance dress," Princess Tsikyria keeps trying. "I'll ask his bodyguard if you ask him."

"I don't think he'd say yes," I say.

"I don't think he asked Princess Zelda." She smiles.

I do recall, now she says it, that I had seen them dancing once or twice. I suppose we are allowed to ask him. "I wouldn't make you do that."

"Alright, I'll stop if that isn't an incentive but go on. How often do you get to enjoy a party like this?"

"Honestly, this is about our fifth this month." The princess giggles in response. "Besides, he has to be fair to everyone."

"That means you too."

"Well, maybe if I see an opening." At the moment, he's still on the dance floor, and I'm not going to cut in.

"You'll see an opening." The princess smiles. "But on the topic, no matter what tension it's made, whatever you told him was helpful. Even Lady Kira lightened up a little. Perhaps that's why she even asked him to dance. It is seen as polite."

"I'm not sure I really made a difference. You could have told him yourself and gotten the same." I smile a little.

"I doubt that. I think soon you'll see." Oh no, what does she know that I don't? She looks smug again.

I open my mouth to ask what she's gloating over now when the song ends, and the dancers make their way off the floor. The princess is making sure I have an opening and actually calls Lady Kira over. Gavril, annoyingly, follows.

"I hope you enjoyed your dance. I wanted to ask a few quick questions about our departure tomorrow," the princess says to Lady Kira. She gives Gavril a brief glance. He returns it before looking back at me.

These little traitors are conspiring against me. Gavril gives me a slight bow. "I didn't get through everyone yet, but I guess you're already sick of that game," he says as I sigh heavily. "While you wait for Her Highness to finish?" he offers, hand outstretched.

They both cornered me. I can't say no without being incredibly rude. I sigh and accept his offered hand. Gavril helps me to stand and takes me onto the dance floor. I wish I could have asked for a faster song. The style has a painfully slow tempo. I try to focus on the dance.

For longer than I expect, Gavril lets me. But when we get into a sequence of more closed hold positions, he dares speak. "Am I really still in that much trouble?"

"I never said you were in trouble."

"You don't have to." Why is this dance so painfully slow? It's giving him way too much time to draw close to me and chat.

"What do you want?" I ask, hoping getting to the point will help get this over with.

"You look amazing."

I give him a look. Is that really what he wanted to say?

"Are you still accusing me of not being willing to help?" he asks innocently.

Please pick up, music.

"I never accused."

"Right, guess it's not an accusation in your mind if you're sure it's true."

I don't reply as we circle each other painfully slowly.

"Did the princess say I wasn't helpful?"

"No. She said you were very helpful and sang your praises."

"You've never danced so tense." Gavril runs a hand down my arm in the flow of the dance, but keeps his fingertips along my skin, making goosebumps rise along my body. "Relax, I'm not going to hurt you."

"Aren't you?"

"No." Gavril's amber eyes meet mine. "Have I yet?"

"Not on purpose," I say before I can think it through.

"Well, I suppose I could say that in reverse as well," he admits. "I'll give you that."

We are silent through the next refrain of steps, but Gavril doesn't let me stay silent long. "So, if she said I was helpful, why are you still so cold?"

"She couldn't tell you were reluctant. You played the part." I give him a sideways look.

"But which part am I playing? Prince or secret villain?" He returns the look.

I sigh. I haven't decided, but if he wants to play like that... "Well, not all princes are good guys. I refer you to the Ice Queen."

"Ouch." Gavril sighs. "Got put in with that bunch." He gives me a twirl. "Maybe it's just a diamond in the rough."

"Most don't go from looking good to then being trouble."

"You thought me a brat before you met me."

"So, I flip-flopped."

"Which as far as I know is unprecedented, so I'm good."

I shake my head. "It's not just another fairytale, Gavril. This is real."

"So why compare me to them? I'll forget that you said you may regret this if you'll do the same. I know I can't be open with you now, but how about we ignore what we can't share and save judgment until after we can? I know it might be... lopsided as I have a lot more to hide than you."

I had so much more to hide than him. But I hide in the dance He has sharp eyes; he'll spot my unease. "So, I have to trust you blindly?"

"Am I not trusting you blindly?"

"What am I hiding?"

"If I knew, then it wouldn't be blind trust, would it?"

He's right, but he shouldn't know he's right.

"You still won't tell me about Jake. You never really told me why you really came here, even if I have a few guesses. And your family situation is... odd, to say the least. Your father makes you fear going home while your mother is quite sweet and kind to us. Though I suppose she could be an amazing actress like you. I know I don't know everything about you. I trust you anyway. Can I not get the same benefit of the doubt?"

I sigh. "You could eliminate me like you did Dahlia."

"Too soon for that, or trust me, someone else would be gone," Gavril says.

I pause and look at him. He's serious, and he clearly doesn't mean me. Then who?

"Is it too much to ask that we just put those fears and questions on hold until it's time to let them out?" Gavril asks. "We've done it once.

I decided to ignore how I felt about that fencing match to move past it. I still struggle to believe it wasn't that you thought losing to me an insult, but you say it wasn't, so I chose not to think about it and move on so I can at least try to believe you. Can we not try that again?"

"How many times can we do that before we break?"

"As many as it takes if you want it to work. Don't you?"

Do I? Do I still want him? I want him to rule above anyone else. I want to help do that, or at least I did when I thought it my duty. Do I still want to? Or is this just the only path allowed to me, so I chase it?

"If I told you, would you still want it?" he asks quietly.

"I don't know. I don't know what you'd tell me."

"So, are you annoyed at what I can't share or that I can't share it?"

I have to think about that. The truth is I'm tired of being unsure. I'm tired of these games. I'm tired of wanting him then being broken when someone else got what I wanted. I have been betrayed so many times. I'm losing the thread of what I really feel or want in the madness.

"She said I was helpful. Do you think she's lying?" he asks me when I don't reply.

"I don't see any reason she would. Then again, she did corral me into dancing with you."

"She wasn't very subtle, huh?" Gavril sighs. "Well, I had to get you to talk to me somehow."

"It's not like I'd never talk to you again."

"But only when forced. Kascia, I swear, once you can't be eliminated, I'll explain everything. I promise. I'd tell you if it didn't mean your immediate elimination and then likely worse. I am not telling anyone else about this either. Just trust me until then. I'm doing the same for you. Why is that so hard?"

"Because having someone else break that trust might break me," I confess. Most of all his, the one I want to be real so badly it forms an ache in my chest that makes me feel ill.

"Do you want to trust me?"

Yes. I do. But I feel like even a hint of that trust being broken will shatter me. If Father is right about the prophecy... I'll lose it. I'll just lose it. He can't be. Our kingdom is doomed either way if its true.

"Kascia. I am not going to hurt you like they did."

"You don't control that." His parents do. This game does. I can't give him my full trust because it's not in his power.

"That was true when you did give me your trust. Can we not go back to that moment?"

"When did you think you had it?" I can't remember when I felt that confident in him.

Gavril thinks that over a moment. "Before we went fencing. Which, I'd like to point out, was after I knew about your questionable friends, so I was trusting you without all the answers."

"Why do you trust me?" I demand without meaning to. How could he do it? I wouldn't be able to if we were reversed as we clearly see.

"Because I trust my instinct more than my head."

I frown, not understanding.

A little smile plays at Gavril's lips. "Did you forget what it feels like?"

"What what feels like?"

The music comes to what I think is a stop. But instead of stopping, it picks up pace to a rather fun beat.

Gavril gives up on words and pulls me to the edge of the line of dance to pick up our steps with the music. I open my mouth to ask, but he pauses to put a finger to my lips to keep me quiet. I don't understand, but instinctively follow his lead into the dance.

The beat isn't stunningly fast, but it's strong with a long string of spinning elements that sends us into some impressive quick turns that melt into slow steps and brings us close together again.

It's like he has stripped the rest of the world away as we focus on nothing but the music and each other to keep in step with one another. Each unified step is like stepping on water, splashing a sudden light through my body, making me feel lighter than air, so lost and free in the night until he grounds me, joining me in this enchanted world: one where the words, drama, and politics do not matter.

A magical electricity makes my skin tingle, starting in my fingertips, then lifts me like I weigh nothing as we own the space that is ours and no one else's. We are dancing on air away from the problems, so we can see nothing but each other.

And though the words had failed us, this escape into the world of dance allows communication that is not possible with our limited words. I feel his longing. There is a nervousness in how he grips me, but a certainty once he does it is as if he fears I will pull away no matter how easily I fold into his hold. An uncertainty of outcome but a certainty of choice.

When the music finally comes to a stop, it's hard to return to reality with how close we are. I don't want to leave. I do not want to return to the confused world I have been forced into by my father and Jake. I want to live in this enchanted world only Gavril and I can make.

"Now do you remember?" Gavril's low whisper makes every hair on my body stand on end.

I bite my lip and close my eyes as all the warmth and magic washes over me like a warm ocean wave. I am afraid to speak and break the moment, so I only nod. I don't dare hope for more. We're in a crowded room. And though this world is our escape, it is not promised to me or him.

"I'm not giving up on you. Don't forget." Gavril plants a soft kiss on my forehead before he pulls back, taking my hand to escort me back to the edge of the room.

We're almost to the edge of the dance floor, where the princess is talking to the grand duchess, when Jonquil rushes over to me in a panic.

My heart shoots into my throat, wondering if she will scream at me for being the favorite again. But instead, she clasps my arm frantically and drags me over to see that the viscount is slobbering drunk. Jonquil is clueless on how to handle the very drunk Japcharian delegate but thought I'd know.

We'd just ignore drunks on the street, so I suggest having Gentian handle it. I do enjoy watching Gentian trying to handle the stumbling, giggling drunk out of the room. Gavril seems to enjoy it too. Sage is trying not to smile. Despite the drunkard, the party goes on for about another hour before the princess comes over to thank me for all my help. She thanks Zelda and Jonquil too but pulls me aside before leaving with the others.

"And don't forget my offer. I still mean it," she says stubbornly. "Anything I can do." She hands me a wooden stamp. "Anything you send marked with that will be for my eyes only. Feel free to reach out at any time." Then she smiles. "But then I'll see you at the next summit." She sounds so sure it will be me. I wish I could feel half as confident. We give each other a curtsy before she leaves.

Thankfully, that is the cue for the rest of us to go.

My maids prepare me for bed, and when all is set, I just lay in my bed, looking up at the ceiling thinking it was a miracle we made it this far. I am done. The event I'd prepped for so long is over. It may not have gone perfect, but it is over. I, for one, am going to savor some extra rest after this one.

Chapter 18

Damian is kind enough to give me time to breathe between my delegation and getting down to hard work on the performance. I'll start going in person and spending most of my afternoons at the theater in the new week. Then the following rest days will be the biggest adjustment. I wonder if Damian will get me out of princess lessons workday mornings to give us as much practice time as possible.

But for today, my maids insist on a mini spa day, encourage me to read or show them the screen games, or go to the Ladies' Chamber if I want. But I need a break from Jonquil, so I plan on hiding in my room. Though that idea doesn't go quite as planned.

Half an hour after lunch, Bella, Azalea, Lilly, and Isla ask if they can join me. My maids set up the little table we use to sit for meals when I eat in my room to let us all enjoy. Damian helps set up as well, looking rather amused.

"We've missed you," Bella insists, greeting me with a hug as Azalea examines my room. Lilly sits down without invitation. They settle in like we do this every day. It feels nice not to have to be formal around people.

"It does feel like a lifetime," I sigh tiredly as Flur leaves to bring in tea and biscuits.

"You did amazing though." Azalea smiles at me, a hint of longing in her eyes.

"You'll do well too," I assure her, knowing she and Isla have their delegation next.

"Yours was harder." Bella smiles. "But you did well. You're still here, right?"

"Yeah," I sigh heavily.

"Don't you want to be?" Azalea asks, a hint of horror in her voice. I give her a sideways glare. I really don't need more of that.

"That's not what I meant," Azalea says. "I just... you don't seem like one to give up is all. Was the delegation that bad?" Her eyes betray a hint of fear for her own delegation.

"No, it wasn't horrible." At least the delegates themselves weren't. "It was stressful. It was the only delegation to have a real problem," Isla says sympathetically.

"And an elimination," Lilly adds, oddly relaxed in her seat. She even tucks her legs under her comfortably.

"How did you get Dahlia kicked out?" Bella asks eagerly.

"I did not get her kicked out," I insist, shocked they'd even suggest it.

"Not according to the papers," Bella says in a singsong voice.

Oh no. "What is Dahlia telling them?" I groan.

"No idea." Bella shrugs. "But the paper said there was some kind of fight between your team that got her kicked out. Everyone is too scared to ask Zelda. And Jonquil isn't as open as you, so what did you all do?"

I sigh heavily and explain what happened between the princess, Dahlia, and me as honestly and shortly as I can.

"So, she didn't try to attack you?" Azalea frowns.

"Or scream at you for being the favorite so you get away with everything?" Bella asks.

"Who said that?" If it's in the paper, I'm just going to die. I'm going to crawl into the safe space under the bed and hide away from the world.

"It's just the rumor around the castle," Bella says. "The paper just said Dahlia was eliminated for fighting with her team and was going back to training before playing sparkleball again. The article was actually really nice about it, making it sound like it was a good thing and everyone was excited to have her back."

I sigh. At least that's not out in the world for people to discuss. "Well, after she was eliminated, she did blame me and attack me." I don't say Gavril kicked her out on his own before that. I don't want to get into it. "Which just solidified in their minds she isn't a true princess."

"So, she was saying she was kicked out for that mistake because you're a favorite?" Bella frowns.

I swallow. "Actually, no one else saw what happened, so they weren't sure if it was me or Dahlia who offended the princess. Dahlia insisted it was me. I wasn't sure how to prove it. But she threw a huge fit, and so... so they guessed it was her, and she insisted they sided with me because Gavril likes me more. It was mostly Jonquil complaining," I admit.

"That's why she won't talk to you," Azalea declares.

"She didn't," Lilly gasps.

I nod, not meeting their eyes. "She would rather see me go than Dahlia, I guess."

"Ouch." Bella frowns.

Azalea is more sympathetic. "I'm sorry. I don't know how I'd react if any of you did that to me. Just be glad you didn't cave in and slap her."

"Honestly, I was too hurt to do that. I'm just glad we got through the rest of it."

"Did you talk to her about it?" Isla asks with sympathy, creasing her brows.

I shake my head. "It just seemed better to agree to work together than to acknowledge it and go on. I doubt we'll really be friends again."

"But you have to at least understand why." Azalea sounds like my mom trying to stop girls in the troupe fighting. "In all honesty, you are more of a challenge to beat when it comes to winning the Enthronement."

"So, you turn on a friend for it?" I demand. "I wouldn't turn on you like that." I look at all of them. I want to ask, "You wouldn't me, right?", but I don't. How could I dare ask? They'd say no, but would that be true? We are friends, right? Sure, we each want to win, but we at least wouldn't tear each other down, right?

"But maybe it will be easier to forgive her if you understand," Isla suggests.

"I can forgive her and not let her hurt me again," I reply dismally. "As sad as it sounds, I still wouldn't try to get her kicked out. I just... I don't know if I can trust her again."

"Well, maybe as more girls leave it will get better," Bella says hopefully.

"We keep saying that, and it's not happening," Lilly squeaks.

We all go quiet.

"Must happen at the top ten," Bella jokes.

"Or this ends faster as the cat fights fail girls," I point out.

"And what's worse. It means more of the girls we actually like will start leaving," Bella sighs.

We all pause again.

Vivian comes over and offers us tea and cakes which is a great relief. I thank her with a smile. My servants are the best. I wish I could give them a pay raise. They really deserve it. It helps as we chat about what might happen if Joy met Cuppy.

We chat on this happier topic until Damian leaves, likely to help with Joy's training.

Bella watches to make sure he's gone. Her eyes land on his notebook on the desk he works at before glancing back at the door.

"Bella what?" Isla starts to ask, but Bella must have felt sure he was gone because without warning she bolts for the desk and snatches up the notebook.

"What are you doing?" Lilly asks curiously.

"I've been dying to see how he does it," Bella confesses. "Is he always here?" Bella asks me offhandedly as she flips through the pages.

"Most of the time. I don't think he has his own workspace. I know my maids work in here or their rooms," I say, watching her as she flips through all of the sketches.

"Why does he draw the cat?" she asks, frowning at one page.

"I think he doodles now and then when he's brainstorming. Nippers will nap in the window or on my bed sometimes. He likes Damian. I thought he owned Nippers for a while."

"Oh, this one was one of the best," Bella coos over one of the pieces then goes to my closet before pausing. "Sorry, is this too private?"

"Go on," I invite her.

Bella beams and opens it and finds the midnight blue dress covered in gemstones. "He did it perfectly." She sighs, looking at the finished dress from the concept art. "Oh my vene! Is this new?" She spots another design and drops the corner of the dress she was holding. "He's brilliant. This is stunning. I... the lines..." she looks up at me then smiles back at the sketch. "Oh, and this would spin so nicely on you too. He's... yep, he's captured the balance too. And that would contrast your eyes, and oh, it's lovely."

"We lost her," Azalea says, turning back to the rest of us. "She'll go on for hours if we let her."

"How do we stop it?" Lilly asks curiously as Bella goes on as if anyone is still listening. I try, but I can't listen to two conversations at once.

"Tell her Damian is coming back," Azalea shrugs.

"Where does he get your shoes? Does he get them from the same person who does your dance shoes?" Lilly asks curiously.

"No, he makes it all himself."

"Everything?" They all frown.

"Everything." Bella rushes over in excitement. "Look at these designs, shoes, even some of her hair pieces he's designed. I think these are the kind of notes blacksmiths make." She's in total geek mode. "I'd never heard of magic glass, but he has notes for everything from scratch. He gets total control. How old is he? It would take a lifetime to master all of this."

"I don't know. I just know he's much older than he looks," I admit to her. "Sorry."

"Why doesn't he just write a textbook?" Bella sighs as if in disappointment. "What I'd give to know how to cast a duplication spell." We all laugh.

"And he designs for you." Bella looks up at me.

"I hope so. I wouldn't want to look like Ericka," I joke, making us all laugh, even my maids.

"No wonder Ericka wants to steal him so badly. I just want him to teach me," Bella goes on. "Has he started work on the periwinkle one?" She looks up at me.

"I have no idea," I confess.

My maids shake their heads in apology. So they hadn't seen it yet either.

"I'd love to see one in progress," Bella sighs.

"Be careful. He'll think you're trying to steal his trade secrets," Lilly teases.

"No one tell him I found it." Bella suddenly looks nervous and holds the book, now closed, to her chest. "You won't breathe a word, right?"

"When would we?" Isla laughs.

Bella looks at me. "He might figure it out on his own, but I won't tell him," I promise. "But if he asks, I'm not going to lie."

"Alright," Bella sighs, looking a bit defeated as she opens it again. "He's so good at this." She has longing in her voice now.

"You are easily as good. Your dresses work perfectly," I assure her.

"But you'd never want my work over his. Not sure I'd ever be this good." Bella shakes her head.

"You'll be too busy being princess," Isla teases, making us all laugh.

"Oh, right. Guess." Bella closes the notebook again. She has the air of being done, but at the same time, she can't bring herself to put it down.

"If you're done, put it away before he notices," Azalea advises.

Bella sighs in disappointment and opens it again, flipping pages as she walks over to Damian's workbench, as if unsure what else to look at but not wanting to look away.

"Maybe for your birthday I need to hire an enchanter to steal you a copy," I tease as she finally closes the book and puts it down. "Meantime, when I go to the theater, I can ask my mother for some of our costume design books. Damian made notes in the ones for *The Phantom*. She'd be more than happy to get you a copy of it with his notes. She has a copier she works with."

"Really?" That cheers Bella up.

"Of course, maybe if this doesn't turn out, you can work for her. She always needs updated or new designs," I suggest.

That brightens Bella up at once, and we talk of happier things.

It's over an hour before Damian returns, and we've drunk most of the tea and had most of the biscuits before it's time for us to go about our afternoon. It was nice to detox with friends and feel at least a bit safer that they are still my friends. I'll have to relearn to trust again, but at least I can feel it happening.

But after another day of tea, games, and rest on the final rest day, it's back to work the next day. The main difference is Damian gets me right to the theater, not even going to breakfast as the meal starts about the time we start rehearsing.

It's the oddest feeling to be back and not just because of how everyone treats me like nobility, sometimes like I'm already a princess, but it's like an out of body experience to just be back as if castle life never happened. Thankfully, Damian being there grounds me and helps make that feeling not as intense.

It is amazing to see everyone and talk to them like things are normal. Of course they aren't and they all want to know about the palace, but it still feels more like home than I'd felt in such a long time.

Cedrick also is helping patch up the theater, which makes it look grander than I'd ever seen. Mother keeps trying to say he doesn't have to, but I can tell it means the world to her. No one has ever complained about the derelict state of the theater as it looks the same as most of the city if not better, but seeing the seats' being patched up to look like new and the fading paint brightened is a magic all its own.

Coming back for dinner does put the whole new world I live in back into perspective. I didn't realize how much I'd miss seeing Gavril until I get a surprise bubble of happiness when I see him at dinner.

The next morning, we all anxiously await the latest delegation. Dragia is one of the most aggressive nations in the world, and after Princess Zinna was so quickly dismissed from the Enthronement early on, they will look for any excuse to attack us.

The reception room is decorated very differently than it has ever been. The girls read the style of their delegation well. The colors are darker than normal, and any dragon themed art is set out. With how popular such artwork is, I'm surprised the palace has so few.

When the delegation arrives, I have to hide my stunned reaction. This is the largest delegation by far, and it's not even close to equal proportions of male to female; it's vastly more male. They introduce themselves as if they all are nobles, but I don't buy that for a second. Most look like warriors, not even guards, like important members of the army. Unless the kingdom is at war or discussing war, it is not the practice to bring military officials to such summits, ever. And no other delegation brought them.

Damian's choice of outfit suddenly makes more sense. Though most of the girls are dressed in sharper styles to appease the delegation, I'd have given my look the name of warrior style. It's white with a golden armor style corset that lines under the bust down past my waist into a sharp point. The fabric has white, sharp looking flower designs that go down the skirt and over my chest. The sharp V-neck helps with the more Dragian look, connecting almost to the corset itself. But the sleeves I like best. From my shoulder down to my below waist and hands is a golden scale design almost like dragon scales themselves. Then a more sheer version of the white and gold fabric hangs down in a wide cuffed sleeve. They pulled back my hair at the top to give it a pulled back volume but left the rest down to float around my back and shoulders, making a commanding look. My chosen crest sits on my chest to help with the look of the lines. It's fun to dress up a little fiery.

The room is full of the long, straight, dark-colored skirts of the other chosen girls. Even Ericka is in a darker pink, but none quite achieve the same warrior look. I also am standing out more than normal. Damian likes me to not quite match the others, but my white and gold certainly make me catch the eye first. I notice Gavril hiding a smile as he looks us over. The only person who seems to not have tried to make their dress match is Princess Laurina.

When the full delegation enters the room, Sage tenses tighter than a piano wire. He's counting and making notes on each of the visitors faster than I could ever process. Godwin stiffens too, and a man I'd never seen before, who looks a lot like Godwin, mutters what must be a swear to himself and glances at Gavril who does not return the look.

But the royal family and the girls in charge of this delegation: Princess Laurina, Kamala, Azalea and Isla, don't show a hint of their fear as they greet the group. I notice Princess Laurina is scanning the delegation, but thankfully, Princess Zinna didn't try to show up for this delegation.

The men dress like Sage, mostly black and dark brown with protective leather vests, vambraces, and hair smoothed back. The biggest difference is their preference for tunics over suits. The ladies are more elegantly dressed in smooth dresses: close to the body, lithe, reminding me of snakes, mostly black with hints of other darker, muted colors and hints of fire red and orange. Their hair is mostly like mine: pulled back from the fringe to the back of their heads, but otherwise left to float around. The lead delegate is a huge man with arms that make Gentian look normal.

The Chosen girls do their best to try to help them relax and enjoy the reception, but there is not a single delegate (or the ones who might be bodyguards) who are not looking around at everything as if appraising it.

I feel too nervous to try to snack on anything. Azalea is fighting the hardest to defuse the tension in the room. She tries to talk to the lead delegates, Duke Cadmus and Duchess Aine, but they rudely ignore her and start to walk the room. Azalea then tries the next highest in rank, one of the two viceroy couples, and they talk with her, but from how they keep looking around, I can't help but feel they're distracting her.

There was tension with the Japcharians, but it was nothing like this. I'm sure if anyone drew a weapon, Sage would have had a knife in their neck before any of the rest of us could even blink.

I try to help by going over to the table to find something I felt alright stomaching, but I'm not a fan of most finger food meats. I find some of our meat dumplings and dare to have those. It lets me look around the room. I can't help but notice two men examining the walls as if looking for safe room triggers. I check to see if anyone else is acting this way. The duke is standing nearby, looking over the long table by the windows.

"The work is exquisite, isn't it?" I try to distract him.

He looks over at me and smiles. Unlike most people, his smile does not light his features. On the contrary, they darken, making his already dark hair and brows overall less friendly in appearance. I wish I hadn't addressed him. It is like looking down the snout of a black dragon.

"It is lovely, even if it is worn and out of date," he agrees, striding over to me with more confidence than I am comfortable with. I hold my ground, even if my instinct is to back away and move into a defensive stance.

"Out of date is an opinion, but I never noticed the castle work is worn."

"It could do with a good touch up and polishing," he says. He looks me over in a way that makes me shudder and wish the sharp V neck wasn't so low, and it is not even showing anything. "I bet I can guess within five guesses who you are."

"Not all five born princesses are still here," I remind him.

"Hmm, you know none of them were even my guess," he complains playfully.

He's fishing. I'm not sure what he's fishing for, but it makes me even more nervous. I should have kept my mouth shut. I also don't like that he's clearly enjoying Damian's handiwork in a way I don't think anyone has. I clench my fists to stop myself from doing something stupid.

"What gives me away?" I ask, trying to play along to make sure not to make him angry.

"You don't look petrified."

I frown. "Excuse me?"

"Knowing Princess Laurina greeted us, you must be one of the other top ten," he muses. "So that leaves... pardon, I am terrible at your softer names: Lady Jonquil, Bella, Forsythia, Kamala, or Kascia."

I don't want to tell him he's right. But I can't exactly politely do so. "Well, I'm in your guesses."

"I normally would have guessed Lady Dahlia, but we all know that ended well," he smirks.

"All but one girl has to go sooner or later. As you must be aware, this competition isn't easy," I say, pointing out their own princess didn't get far without insulting them.

"That is true." He is still studying me like that. I'm not dealing with his eyeballing anymore.

"Well, I should see if the others need my help." I give him a short curtsy before getting away to anywhere he is not, even if I can feel his eyes still on me.

I try to avoid talking to any of the other men. I pretend to join into a small knot of girls speaking with two of the Dragian ladies. But I swear I can still feel his eyes on me.

I jump at a hand on my other shoulder and turn. "Is he bothering you?" Oh no, Gavril noticed.

"Not anymore," I assure him.

Gavril studies my face then turns and nods to someone. I look over, and to my horror, I see Sage moving behind the man who is watching me. Is he keeping tabs on him? I open my mouth to protest, but Gavril shakes his head slightly. I push my mouth to one side. I don't need him to baby me. I can handle myself.

But then I notice the king and queen are already looking over at him in nervousness. Gentian is walking the room, clearly on guard now. I also notice an even odder guard. Is Nippers pacing the room as if watching too? He jumps up on a decorative ledge and curls up, watching the proceedings as if he's going to pounce. Is the Dragian duke eyeing other girls too?

"Do me a favor," Gavril says so only I can hear. "Make sure none of the girls go anywhere alone, alright?"

"Gavril, I'm sure—"

"I said any of you." He gives me a look, glances at the delegate who's watching our exchange. "And please don't get mad at me for this."

I draw my brows together and open my mouth to ask what he means, but he walks over to Zelda where she's talking to a couple from the Dragian delegation. To my surprise, he actually puts an arm around her as if it were completely normal. Once she's looking at him, he moves his arm around her waist and starts talking to the couple standing across from him.

I would assume that means they are closer than I thought, but what he said before only confuses me more. I watch, trying to understand what is going on. The couple they are talking to eventually move on, and Gavril whispers something to Zelda who nods firmly and then says something back. Gavril's eyes go to the long food table before nodding.

To my surprise, he then goes around doing the same thing to the other girls. He even gives Ericka a kiss on the cheek. I want to vomit at that, but whatever he's doing, it's more than just being openly flirtatious with us. I almost find it hard to be fully jealous knowing he's up to something.

When it's time to prepare for dinner, Gavril sets Damian to escort me back before I even realize it's time to go. Damian smiles kindly and bows to me then offers his arm as he glances at his brother who is actually in the room this time. That is odd. I'd never seen him in one of these receptions.

He nods at Damian. Then he looks at Sage, and they meet eyes. Cedrick nods over at Zelda. Sage nods and glides over to her. Is Cedrick giving Sage directions? Even more, is Sage accepting them? Cedrick then looks at Gentian and nods as if assuring him he is in the right spot.

But that's all I see before Damian escorts me from the room. I frown a bit. It must be worse than I thought. I just don't know why Custods are taking directions from a military advisor unless... but no. Damian shows no signs of being a Custod, and if Cedrick were, so would Damian. I bite my lips and glance at Damian.

"Walk swiftly," he says to me quietly as we turn a corner, though I notice he glances back as if checking we aren't being followed.

"What is going on?" I ask. "What are they planning?" But I do walk more quickly.

"We'll talk more in your room," Damian says. "The walls have ears here."

I nod my understanding, and we go as quickly as we can without running to reach to my room. Damian leads me to the door but doesn't go in yet, giving my Custod guard a meaningful look. She notices and nods firmly. "Would you mind checking the room?" Damian asks.

Lila, my security lead, nods again and steps into my room without question. I wait, folding my arms in anxiety. She checks everywhere, even checking the safe space below my bed and the washroom before she steps out and nods an all-clear to Damian.

I noticed he'd unsnapped something at his belt to make it easier to reach his weapon.

"Thank you." Damian nods to her then takes me into the room and closes the door behind him.

"You don't think they are going to attack, do you?" I ask quickly.

"Not necessarily. More like kidnap," he says calmly as he nods to Flur and Vivian to help me change, so I can relax.

"What?" I frown. "Why?" My maids set to work right away. I let them but don't take my eyes off Damian.

"Logic would say in an attack of petty revenge," Damian says. "Dragons are known for that, so why not the people who associate themselves with them?"

"You think that's what they're really here for?" That would explain the large guard.

"I've been doing a little more than thinking," he says. "The man you spoke to, what did he say to you?"

"Not much. He mostly just leered. But he said he could likely guess who I was by my lack of fear of him, and he assumed right I wasn't a born princess and had a list of guesses."

Damian nods. "I doubt they'll go for a born princess. From what I overheard others say to some of the other Chosen, they are looking for Gavril's favorite."

My blood goes icy. "So, they're going to do what to us exactly?"

"I can't say. Take you for sure. After that, who knows? It could have even been Princess Zinna's idea. The prince refused her, so she'll take the one he likes the most," Damian says thinkingly then frowns and arches a brow at me. "Who was on his list?"

"Me, Kamala, Jonquil, Bella, and Forsythia."

Damian nods. "I'll let the royal family know. But you didn't tell him your name, did you?"

"No."

Damian nods. "Good. And I doubt their princess remembers any of you well enough to give them physical descriptions, but it sounds like she gave them what she could."

"It sounded more like he knew from the fact I didn't cower at him. So how do we handle that without... well, driving them out and giving them the excuse they want?"

"We don't give them the hints they need. And you're not to go alone anywhere," Damian says, almost commanding. "Cedrick will speak with the king and queen to make arrangements for a tighter guard, and you'll have to stay in groups. It'll be harder to take one that way. It'll be tricky, but if everyone works together, we can get through this week without incident." He looks to Vivian and Flur. He means them as well. "Sadly, it will mean we'll have to work out other arrangements for rehearsals until they leave." He sounds stressed at the idea, but safety comes first. I'll have to work extra hard to make up for it.

"So, we're confined to our rooms again?"

Damian pauses then slowly tilts his head. "Not if they're smart."

"Why?" I ask. "Because we're isolated?"

"And easier to get to," he nods. "Remember, they're looking for a favorite, and they have a rough idea of how the day pans out because Zinna was here. If you are all locked in your rooms, they'll realize we are onto them and may become more aggressive. The result could be disastrous, being they try to make their move quickly and get out. We could lose more than one girl in the process and have another war on our hands."

I let out a heavy sigh. "So, we just have to not fight among ourselves as we use each other as protection." This is going to get complicated fast.

"Exactly," Damian smiles sympathetically, "but the Ladies' Chamber is the safest place for all of you to be. They won't dare attack an entire room full of people, and I'll be there as much as I can to help to guard you."

"I guess with rebel attacks that won't make them suspicious," I say as Flur finishes with my hair.

"Well, and I'm not officially a guard, which can divert suspicion as well," Damian points out.

I nod. "I suppose that helps." We only have a few hours before the dinner will start. The poor girls running this delegation are really having a hard time.

"Indeed. But while they are discussing that, I'm afraid you're stuck in here 'til dinner." Damian half frowns for me.

"Thankfully that's only a few hours." I smile. "I can keep busy that long."

"Good." He returns it. "Then we can get you ready for dinner, and I can escort you there."

I nod my agreement. This dress is unique. It has short sleeves and comes to a loose turtleneck. Damian keeps the armor theme, and similar to the last one, it has an amazing silver design and a floating skirt that has a slit up to my knee. It has quite a powerful look to it as I walk, and it floats about. I like the dark blue that has just a hint of green to it. They pull my hair back for this one and add earrings to finish off the look.

We're taking the impressions to send to my mother when there is a knock at the door. I drop my arms from my playfully scandalous pose as Flur gets the door.

"Hello Flur, is she free for a moment?"

Flur nods and steps aside.

Gavril steps into the room, looking more serious than I'd seen him in a long time. He brushes his hair back and looks at me with a weak smile. "You look better without armor," he jokes.

I give him a look. This isn't funny.

"Sorry," he sighs tiredly. "You're right. This isn't exactly a formal visit." He glances at Damian before looking back at me. He looks me over. "Can't hide a weapon in that, can you?"

"Gavril," I tell him off.

"What?"

I pause as I realize he's serious. "The rules say we aren't to be armed," I remind him.

"In this case, I'm not sure any of us would mind," Gavril mutters to himself then sighs. "I don't have much time. I have to review security with the other girls too. And I presume this will work for you, Sir Damian, but if you need more information, I will spare you a minute." But he doesn't wait for Damian to answer but turns back to me. "I'm sure you notice the tension."

"And him trying to guess who I was."

"What?" Gavril's face falls. "What exactly did he say?"

I forgot Gavril wouldn't know, so I tell him about the duke's joke and his "top five" picks for who I am. Gavril clearly takes note and nods. "I guess we know who they are already eyeing. They are clearly planning something. So let me repeat, you are not to be on your own."

"You make it sound like I do that all the time," I border on complaining, trying to tease and lighten the mood.

"Not now, please," Gavril pleads a bit.

I pause at the intensity in his voice, like he's putting his heart on the line. I bow my head, feeling bad he feels he had to jump right to that level of emotion. I suppose we have not managed a safe, normal conversation in a long time.

I look up as he pinches the bridge of his nose. He does that a lot these days. "Please, I just have to get through it all. Your arrangement is different than the others as you are the only girl left on your floor." It sounds like he deeply regrets that, not that he can control it. "But in the morning, you don't go down to breakfast without Damian or your Custod guard. You then go with the others to the Lady's Chamber and stay there until escorted to meals. We can't have you in your rooms because—"

"They will know something is up." I smile a little. "I get it. It's fine." He pauses then looks at Damian as if asking if he already told me the plan.

Damian smiles and gives him a shrug. "Cedrick's my brother. I know how he thinks."

"It wasn't his plan." Gavril frowns. "It was mine." I blink. They listened to Gavril for once? There is hope on the horizon.

"Oh." Damian blinks then smiles, pleasantly surprised. "Then you and Cedrick must think alike."

"Maybe if you knew that you'd have won the game." Gavril gives Damian a slight smile then turns back to me. "Then you know exactly why. Please don't test the limits."

"Why do you think I will?" I tease.

"Because with your behavior lately and my luck, you'll be the only one who tries something," Gavril replies.

The irritation in his tone offends me. "Excuse me?"

Gavril sighs. "You've not exactly been behaving as nicely as you normally do. And with my luck, you're going to be pegged as the one they want. If too many of the other girls catch on, they may just set you up for it. So, for the love of Phoenix, please just behave."

He does not have to be this harsh with me. I fold my arms and raise a brow. "I didn't say I wouldn't." But he has a point. Jonquil would be happy to see them take me away.

"No, but you haven't been very clear lately either, so I'm just... begging you to behave. It's just a few more days, and it isn't your delegation. We're almost to the end of this." A strange look comes into his eye. Is it sad? Hopeful? "Just... hold out that long and behave, please."

"Alright," I assure him. "I don't plan on misbehaving."

"Plan on being too good if that's what it takes," Gavril insists.

There's a scratch at the door. Gavril sighs. "I have to check in with the guard. Just do what Damian tells you, please."

"Okay, okay. I got it." His repetitive reprimands are really starting to get on my nerves.

Gavril sighs and nods his thanks to me then to Damian before leaving. I notice he uses his foot to keep something out. I hear mad sniffing. Why is Joy at the door? Damian has a sad look on his face as he watches Gavril slip out.

"I've never seen him look so tired," Vivian says sadly.

"What?" Flur frowns.

"You didn't notice?"

"They hide it well," Flur shrugs.

Damian sighs heavily. "True, but I agree, Vivian. I see it too," he says then turns to tidy up his workbench.

I swallow. It has been a hard few weeks for all of us, but Gavril isn't on a team. He's had to be on point for all of the delegations plus the disaster of last week and now this nightmare. He's powerless, and that would make the stress worse.

When I arrive at dinner, the delegation is there already, taking up the full long table the royal family sat at. The girls who are part of the delegation are closer to that table, but unlike the past delegations, they aren't sitting at the table. Likely to protect them.

The talk is quieter with this group than the others. Perhaps it's the tension.

Gavril tries not to look at any of us, and if he does, he goes out of his way to wink or smile as if flirting no matter who it is. But that makes me wonder if that might even be too much. I don't notice him looking at me or Zelda which could be a problem if they notice who he's avoiding looking at.

I try to focus on the food. These long, seven course meals are getting exhausting. This one is particularly meat heavy. The first course is meat cake, like a crab cake, but not made with crab, I think. We then have a chicken dumpling soup, salmon, and the main course is a lamb chop with lots of potatoes and parsley coating all of it. I notice the delegation seems to enjoy theirs as they eat around the bone.

That's when I see Gavril glance at me, giving me a wink, then look at Cedrick. I didn't even realize he was along the wall like a guard. He nods, but his eyes are on the head delegate. I watch for a moment and see that Cedrick is looking to see what he's noticing and cuing Gavril if he needs to give a hint or distract him by flirting with someone else. What a complicated dinner. Poor Gavril is likely hardly noticing what he's eating, if he is eating at all.

We move on to a... well, a meat waffle for lack of a better term. I smile to spot Gavril slipping Joy one. There's a cheese platter which I enjoy more than most of the rest of the meal. The dessert is unique. It's a white roll topped with a sweet kind of gravy, like a sweet coconut cream.

I'm impressed by the king and queen being able to hold a decent conversation with the delegates without showing their nerves. The king most of all. Though I notice he's drinking a lot of water, more than normal.

Gavril is the one who announces the official end to the meal, which allows the Chosen girls to be picked up by guards. The delegation is surprisingly quick to head up to their rooms for the night. As we're escorted out, I can't help but notice the sudden coughing sounds. Was the king holding that in the whole time? I just hope he's alright because if the Dragians get any hint of his illness, this will become ten times worse. Why did we invite them? I pray we can just make it through this without anyone getting hurt.

Chapter 19

Damian had written to my mother to let her know we'll have to wait to do more work in the theater until after the delegation leaves. I worry that will make my mother panic that I'm not safe, but there's not much I can do about it.

The only signs of things being different is breakfast. Gavril looks as tired as the day before, if not more so. I have to eat slowly, so we all leave at the same time. When I do, I notice Cedrick is on watch again, but he's not alone. Joy is sitting quietly under Gavril's chair again. I'd never seen her be so quiet. How have Cedrick and Damian trained her to be such a good guard dog so fast?

Joy sees me, and her tail wags a little, but she doesn't make a sound or move otherwise. I smile at her to tell her she's a good dog before I go to the Ladies' Chamber. We try to play games, but even those games are halfhearted as all our minds are on what's going on outside. I keep looking over at where Azalea and Isla normally sit, wondering if they're doing alright.

As we're talking nervously, a sudden noise starts in the hallway. It sounds like a lot of feet stamping and shouting though none of us can quite hear what's being said.

We all go tense, but from the sounds, I can tell it's not fighting. At least not the physical kind. It's more like an argument. I think I can hear someone complaining as well, but I'm not sure.

"Not again," Lilly mutters.

"What?" I ask her quietly.

"It sounded kind of like that when the Japcharians got up," Lilly says quietly to me. "They have to pass this room to their suites."

My face falls. "You don't think they..." But something else stops me. The voices had died away, but... do I hear that coughing again?

"It's not even lunch yet. How much could they have upset them already?" Bella tries to be bright.

"It can't be hard," Jonquil says. I glance at Damian to see his reaction. He'd be able to tell better than us.

He sighs and moves to the door, sticks his head out into the hall then pulls back and closes the door with another sigh. "I'd say negotiations are over."

"Well done, girls. Guess whoever wins gets to deal with a second war," Forsythia complains.

"Not for sure," I try to be positive. "We turned the Japcharians around."

"They weren't planning on attacking," Forsythia says.

Damian smiles reassuringly at me. "With luck and skill, it won't come to that."

I nod. So it isn't that critical yet. I realize this is worse than it was for our team because all I can do is sit and wait for news. I don't know why, but the idea that all this stress is going to make the king have another attack makes me more nervous than anything.

However, we don't get an update until an hour or so before dinner, telling us not to worry and dinner will be held normally. I was sure they'd confine us. I wonder if the delegation is even still here.

At dinner, the seating arrangements are adjusted —a lot. There are only two tables now: the head table where the royal family and delegation are sitting and the candidate's table. The Chosen girls now only take up one table. There are only twelve of us left. I do the quick math. Two. Half of the girls failed this time. What did they do?

Azalea is on my left again, looking at her plate and trying not to meet anyone's eyes. I look around to be sure no one is watching us.

"Are you alright?" I ask Azalea quietly. She nods quickly but doesn't speak. "What happened?" I ask gently. "Hey, mine went badly too, remember?" I do my best to comfort her.

"I'm not supposed to talk about it."

I frown. "Is it still considered an active test?"

"Kind of." Azalea looks down the table at Isla, now the only member of her team left. "It's just the farewell left. Prince Gavril went with his guard into their suite, and it sounds like he got them to agree to come back to the table tomorrow without us."

"Gavril did?" I wish I could hide the impressed tone in my voice. But does that mean the king was unable to even try?

Azalea nods. "The queen was not happy about it, but he seemed tired of taking a sideline. He assured us we didn't have to meet with them again, just prepare the farewell party. I can't wait for this to be over. They had a few Custods guard us. I'm surprised they didn't send the prince's dog with us with how they were all behaving." I smile, sure Joy wouldn't have liked that one bit. "They said they'll let us know tomorrow how they want us to deal with the smaller team." She finishes uneasily. "I just can't wait for it to be done. Part of me wishes I failed just to get out of it."

"You're better than that," I assure her.

Dinner passes quietly otherwise. Isla is as tight-lipped about what happened as Azalea. We're escorted to our rooms. When I get to mine, I'm warned not to prepare for bed just yet, as I will likely have someone check in on me.

Thankfully, they don't make me wait long. I feared I'd have hours to wait. I thought it would be Gentian, or maybe a Custod guard or even Sage, but instead, Gavril steps into the room.

"Sorry to make you wait." He smiles at me. His smile looks so tired it makes my heart ache. I'd never seen him look so tired. His gait is altered, slower, and his shoulders are more rounded, as if weighed down.

A happy panting follows him into the room. Joy follows and sits at his feet properly. She looks up at him to make sure she is supposed to still be a guard before looking down. She sees me and almost stands up but pulls herself back down with a whimper of desire. Her poor little tail wags madly as she fights the desire to run up and say hello.

She looks up at Gavril again as if for permission. Gavril pauses then looks down at her, pausing longer than I would expect before he smiles. "At ease," he tells her.

Joy barks a "thank you" and rushes over to me, talking in her joy and making sounds that are similar to "I love you" as she jumps up to try to lick my face. I laugh and bend down to reach her easier and pet her as she dances in happiness. I laugh at how excited she is.

When I look up, I see Gavril watching with exhausted and envious eyes as if wishing he could steal some of that energy from the dog before looking up at me. "She is more fun."

That stings more than I think he meant it to. It is not that he is not fun when he wants to be.

"She's a puppy." I ignore the sting. "They're always full of energy and fun. It's why they're called puppies, right?" I scratch Joy's ears, "Always happy and hyper." I wish I knew what to say. Why is every interaction with Gavril so difficult?

He lets out a heavy sigh. "That they are. I wish what I had to say was as fun as the dog."

I look up in worry. I am not being eliminated now, am I?

"Not that bad," Gavril assures me. "It has to do with this delegation. I know you're busy preparing for next week, and heaven knows, dealing with drama with the other girls, but the team for this delegation is two girls short."

"I noticed." I stand up and fold my arms. "Did it go that badly? Or can't you tell me?"

A flash of irritation crosses Gavril's face for a brief moment before he shakes his head. "No, well yes, it did go that badly, but if you accept what I ask of you, I can tell you."

"What do you need?" I ask anxiously.

"We need a fourth girl to help run the last part of this delegation's visit," Gavril says. "I was able to calm them down to negotiate, but we need the last part to go as smoothly as possible to ensure they do not overturn it at the last moment or give them an opening or excuse to hurt anyone. Zelda just agreed to help lead as the princess on that team. I know you just finished your test with Japcharia, and it was hard, but we need the best on this."

Why do I feel a hit of smugness having him say I am one of the best options? I repress my smile.

"And if you say yes, do me one other favor." He looks over at Damian. His expression saying, "don't shoot the messenger". I giggle. "Keep him off me." Gavril's tone is more lighthearted at the joke.

"It's not like I can leave," I confess, "not with security."

A hint of guilt creases Gavril's eyes. "I'm sorry about that."

I shrug. "Not your fault."

"Hmm." He leaves it at that.

"But if it helps ensure everyone is safe, I'll be happy to help," I say. I swallow. "What did the girls do to make them so angry?"

Gavril sighs and looks around as if deciding if he should ask to take a seat or not. It's almost a signal to Damian. He brings out two chairs and the table we used for meals with the normal elegance and efficacy I'd come to expect and still admire from him.

I smile and accept Damian's offer, patting Joy before going to sit at the table and looking at Gavril invite him to do the same.

He really does look exhausted. The shadows under his eyes look worse from here, and there are bags starting to form with impressive carrying capacity. I suppose he's not used to so much work, but at the same time, I imagine he's got more stamina than that. It must be going really badly. It has been a rough few weeks he's had to navigate. Not to mention two more girls were just eliminated, ones perhaps he cared for as much as me.

"Thank you, Damian." Gavril nods at him before taking a seat. The way he lets himself relax into the chair makes me want to go over and rub his shoulders like I used to massage Jake's after a long raid. He looks like he could use the positive touch and support, even if I'm not very good at massages.

"But of course, Your Highness." Damian smiles and bows his head to the prince with his hands clasped behind him. He then looks to my maids and nods to them.

To my surprise, they bring over some tea and a plate of cookies. Gavril smiles and nods his thanks. I repress a smile. He looks like he could use a sugar rush. I am happy to take the tea and thank my maids, making sure Gavril at least has one of the cookies. If I know my maids, they will have gotten his favorite. I also notice Gavril adds more sugar than normal to his tea. I keep silent to let him have some tea and a bite before going on.

"Thank you," he says after a moment.

I frown. "For what?"

"I don't think I've had a truly quiet moment since this morning, if then." He gives me a slight smile.

"Need some coffee?" I tease.

"I don't like coffee. All the cream and sugar in the world don't help." Gavril shrugs. "Father does sometimes, but personally, I don't like it."

"Oh." Why is that a surprise to me? It was too expensive and Custod tradition didn't endorse it, worried about their warriors becoming dependent upon it or too hyper as it was said the Merlin was overexcited when he had the stuff. "It must be madness." I refer to his day.

"Well, we have a new staff member to break in, a delegation who wants to kidnap and or harm my girls. I'm the only one the delegation will really deal with because of my ability to understand their ways, and I have to find a compromise on a practice I find distasteful. All that will make for a rather long day," Gavril admits.

"Compromise?" I then look away. "I'm sorry. I know you can't tell me."

Gavril sighs in frustration this time. "It's fine." His tone has a bite to it that makes me want to stiffen or recoil. I do neither. "But you have more urgent things to ask about." Gavril rubs his eyes for a moment.

"I guess."

"Well, unless you don't care to know what mess the girls made for you before going out." Gavril gives me a sideways look.

"Oh, of course, forgive me." I'm slipping in the hint of formality Gavril is holding. I don't know if it's because of how we've been with one another lately or because of the nature of his visit.

"Well, at first, all was fine. The Dragians were trying to stir trouble. They thought if they could tear me down, things would be easier and they demanded to know why I thought so little of them, their people, and of course, their princess. This escalated, and Princess Laurina called Princess Zinna a slut."

I cover my mouth. It is a horrible thing to say, but at the same time, it must have been hilarious to see their reactions.

"I suppose it was funny in hindsight," Gavril chuckles. "Well, then Kamala decided she had to put in her thoughts, as she does, which also insulted Zinna, and this gave the delegation the excuse they needed to walk out of there offended. I tried to talk my father into going after them, as last time we waited it did not go well. I lost that argument."

"Then how did..." I begin.

"I... went after them on my own while father was... otherwise occupied," Gavril put it delicately.

I recall the coughing I thought I heard. "He had an attack?" I ask quietly.

Gavril smiles at my deduction and nods shortly. "He and Mother were otherwise occupied," he confirms. "So, I went down and ironed out what we could discuss and how to proceed for the rest of the summit, which they agreed to as long as the girls were no longer in planning meetings, which of course, was the plan anyway."

"Risky to let us have so much power in your meetings." I smile weakly.

"Well, that was a large part of the point of doing these meetings all at once," Gavril says. The formality is starting to kill me.

"Your mother must have been livid. Has she eaten you yet?"

"No, but as I was successful, I'm hopeful she'll let it drop." His formal language is not improving. I try to think of a way around it. "Father may have more of an earful for me though. He told me not to go, and I did it anyway. I'm likely banned from similar meetings ever again."

"Even though it worked? I'm impressed you did it on your own. I..." Is it wrong to admit I am rather proud of him for finally ignoring their orders? I know how being talked down to bothers him. I do not want to make that mistake.

"Well, as we have to be careful not to make his attacks larger, and since we have a few days left to go, I might get away with it. Or I may just have to deal with it later." Gavril shrugs.

"So, while he takes it easy, you're running the court?" I ask hopefully. That would be a great step for them finally letting him do his job.

"Not exactly," Gavril says delicately. "I'm just helping where the slack is dropping."

"So everywhere."

Gavril chuckles as he sips his tea. "Maybe."

"Just maybe?" I can't help but smile.

"Well, I pick up all the slack on my own." He takes a bite of a cookie.

"No, Zelda and I will help. Again, until I'm able to safely leave for rehearsals, I'm not doing much otherwise. I am happy to help."

"You always are." Gavril sighs heavily as he puts down his now empty cup.

Joy, who has settled next to him like a good guard dog, looks up at him as if worried. She looks over at Damian who just nods to her. Joy comes over and rests her head on Gavril's lap.

Gavril strokes her without really thinking about it. I can tell Joy likes that, but she makes no noise, glancing at Damian as if to make sure that's good. I look away to pay attention to Gavril instead of the odd interaction between the dog and my attendant.

"You're keeping a guard at your door, right?" Gavril asks suddenly.

"What? Oh, of course. I do every night. Even before," I assure him, confused by the question.

"It's just a few more days." he says, still stroking Joy gently. "I can't imagine all of it will be too crazy." He goes quiet again, still stroking Joy without paying attention. "And Damian is escorting you when you're not with the other girls?"

"Yes." I finally catch on. "I'm keeping the rules just like you asked." Why does he keep insisting?

"Good. Just a few more days." He nods again. Then he lets out a sigh. "But I should let you rest." He pops the rest of the cookie in his mouth.

"No, it's fine. I am not the one with a dozen meetings tomorrow," I assure him. "If you want to stay," I hint, hoping he'd just take a moment longer. He'd hardly been here five minutes.

Joy agrees with me because she sets her head even more on Gavril's lap and even puts a paw on his foot as if to keep him still.

"No, I really should get back to it."

"To what? It's late." I frown. Alright, it is not that late. It is only about eight in the evening. "You can't have more meetings tonight."

"No, but I do have to prepare for them," Gavril replies curtly.

"What do you have to do to prepare?" I ask. "Doesn't your staff do that?"

"Yes, but I also need to have them get the information I need," Gavril explains.

"Ah yes, them. I noticed a new one at the welcome yesterday," I hint.

Gavril nods, stroking Joy again. *Ah!* It is working. I give the dog a slight smile. She sees it and pants for just a moment as if to say she is happy too.

"Reinold. He's actually Godwin's brother. Apparently, they both applied to be my valet, and with me being a more active part of the delegations, Father's valet decided I needed a court liaison to help with these meetings. Then he'll help with matters of court after the summit is over."

"That's good, isn't it? Means that you'll be in on more meetings," I try to cheer him up.

"I hope so." Gavril nods, still not quite focusing as he speaks. "But I have to find out what trade to bribe the Dragians with in order to keep things as calm as possible. And they are eager to begin old practices which they prize mostly highly as part of their visit."

"Old practices?" I frown. "Is that the distasteful thing?"

"Not my favorite topic to study." Gavril shakes his head. "They used to come to our coasts to hunt big game."

"Big game?" What could you hunt in Purerah that they couldn't find elsewhere? It's not like we have better bucks or wolves or frankly anything worth hunting that I know of.

"Fish," Gavril says shortly. "They prize themselves as big sport hunters, and we've banned most large fish hunting in more recent times. All large shark hunting as well as whale hunting are banned during the season they are here. In fact, it's rather a funny story. We banned it from May to November and give free hunting the rest of the year." Gavril smirks. "Joke is on the hunters; the whales aren't here in the colder months with their migrations. Well, Dragia wants the right to come and hunt again."

"And so, you're going to have to give it to them?" I frown.

Gavril rubs his eyes tiredly. "I'll have to find a compromise of some sort. So that's what I'll be doing all night. Making trade proposals and trying to find the least distasteful way to let them make sport of some of our most unique and spectacular creatures." He scowls at the idea.

I look down. "Sorry, that has to come down to you. I know how... well, you like the ocean." That was the dumbest way to say it. He's passionate about studying ocean creatures. Letting the Dragians kill them for nothing but pride is not going to be easy for him to swallow.

"Well, it was permitted once, and we did manage to keep it from harming the wildlife." Gavril shakes his head. "I just have to figure out how."

"Still can't be fun."

"No. No, it isn't." Gavril drops his head back. "And it's just to please their desire to be brutish dragons. Dragons used to hunt sharks, but that was because it was really the only fish large enough to satisfy them. For Dragians, it makes them feel powerful to have killed the strongest thing in the ocean and put its corpse up on the wall."

I make a face. I don't know if I like that idea. "How?"

"You can taxidermy parts of it. It's a strange magic."

"But wouldn't they have to kill it just right, so the body doesn't look bad?" I frown.

"Well yes and no. They do have to keep the injuries small, at least cosmetically speaking." Gavril explains. "It's harder with sharks than with whales. For whalers, if you want them just for sport, the trick is to drown them."

"Drown them! They live in water."

"They do. So, it's not easy." Gavril shakes his head. "It can take hours if not all day, depending on the whale they're going after. They shoot nets at them with weights that keep them attached to the ship and pull them down. They also try to exhaust them by giving them hope they can swim away and only drag the ship for miles. It's helpful in exhausting them, so they drown faster."

That's sick. You had to make it die painfully? Couldn't do it quickly?

"But if you can afford—" Gavril stops suddenly. "The right work ers..." he says slowly.

"Gavril?" I frown.

"I think you just solved the problem." Gavril stands up suddenly. Joy barks in complaint. "Oh hush, Reinold isn't even here." I laugh.

"I'm sorry," Gavril addresses me, "I didn't mean to..." he sighs tiredly.

"Do you want help?" I offer.

"What?"

"Well, if I solved it, mind telling me what I did?" I ask playfully.

Gavril chuckles. "There are enchanters who do their freezing charms and can heal the wounds to make the taxidermy look better, but they are pricey. There are only two people in all of Purerah who can do it. That's the answer. Make it limited and too expensive. The animals cannot be taken out of the country until they are properly handled, and that keeps the business in the kingdom, and that on top of how expensive the license to kill one whale or shark a year could keep the numbers low enough, yet give them what they want."

"And you could ban that drowning hunting method?"

"That could work."

We go on like this for at least a half an hour, bouncing ideas off one another about how to regulate the limits and hunt times when Gavril spots the time and leaps up. "I-I don't know what I'm still doing here. I'm sorry. I-I don't know how my staff isn't pounding down the door." He runs his fingers through his hair and looks around for Joy, who is sitting at his feet looking at him as if wondering why he stopped.

Gavril nods when he spots her as if noting he had her before looking around as if for his jacket, which he'd never taken off. I wait for him to figure it out, but he actually doesn't notice right away. I frown at how long it takes him to realize he's wearing it.

"Gavril, are you sure you're alright?" I ask. How tired is he?

"Hmm? Fine." He adjusts his jacket. "Thank you, I..." he pauses, swallowing. "I shouldn't have taken your time. Mind if I...?" He indicates my messy notes I'd taken as we spoke.

"Uh... if you can read them," I admit but pull back to let him take them.

He picks them up, scans them then looks back at me, struggling for words. I see the debate in his eyes. "You are keeping the guard at your—"

"Yes, I told you," I assure him tiredly.

"Of course, I know. I just..." Gavril takes a deep breath. He looks as if he'd lost two hours of sleep in the last few minutes. "I didn't mean to take your time. For tomorrow, Damian will escort you to the designated area for you to help prepare for the party. The Lady's Chamber needs to protect the other girls. I-I should have told you that half an hour ago." He runs his fingers through his hair once more.

He starts as if remembering something and turns to Damian. "They'll let you know where that will be in the morning once they have arranged it." Gavril is starting to sound unsure again, formal, like he had when he first arrived. The fact he kept looking around as if trying to keep track of something he keeps forgetting is starting to freak me out.

Damian nods. "You need to get some rest."

Gavril nods. "Wh-when I get a moment," he tries to assure Damian, but his tone sounds more like he's just taking it in while his mind is reeling over all he has to do. I think his breathing is even starting to pick up. "Just..." Gavril looks back at me. "Be careful, right?"

"I told you I would." I know he doesn't trust me, but this is starting to feel like how his mother bothers him.

"I know, I just..." Gavril stops again, looking up at the ceiling. I wonder what he's thinking when he does that. "Please, just... be careful."

"I just said I would." Now he's really starting to worry me.

"Just don't ditch him, alright?" Gavril says, nodding at Damian.

"I'm not going to," I say, the irritation coming to the surface. "I didn't mean anything like that. I told you I would. You don't have to hound me."

"Sorry, and thanks, just..." Gavril sighs. "I suppose I'll see you tomorrow then." He nods jerkily, bows to me hastily, and turns to leave before I even realize he's finally leaving.

I stand and open my mouth to say something, but he's already gone. My shoulders drop. I hadn't wanted to leave it like that. I feel like I hurt him again, but I don't know how. I just wish I could have said something. And going after him might just break the promise about being careful I just made.

Damian sighs as if frustrated. "Go after him," he says with a slight nod to the door.

"What? But... I just promised—"

"That man needs a hug at the least. Go after him," Damian urges.

"But..."

"Go!" Damian cuts me off, pointing to the door.

I jump a bit. If my guard is telling me, it must be okay. I go out the door. Gavril hadn't gotten too far. I run up to him and take his arm. He turns around, but before he can tell me off for running out, I give him the hug Damian suggested, hugging his chest best I can.

At first, I think he's surprised as he pauses a moment. But then he embraces me back tightly, as if I am the one thing holding him to life. He rests his head on mine as if covering me protectively. I smile slightly, enjoying that feeling and settling into it. I want to do more to comfort him, but I don't know what else to do.

I can feel how desperate he is in his grip, how tired he is with how his fingers clasp me. There's a tiredness to his breathing, but as we stand there, a relaxed quality settles into it as well. Tension I feel throughout his whole body slowly starts to fade.

With a tired sigh, he finally pulls back but can't meet my gaze. "Just... please, stay out of trouble," he begs me.

I smile weakly and nod my promise, unsure what else to say or do. I want to do more. But what can I do?

Then like he did in my room; he lets go and is nearly gone with little warning.

"Gavril." I take his hand this time.

He stops and looks at me, a hint of confusion creasing his eyes.

I meet his amazing amber eyes, trying to figure out what to say to make it alright. To forget the tension and the drama that has formed between us enough to just get him through whatever this struggle is.

I step close to buy myself time. He moves closer too, watching me with an expression I'm not sure I've seen on anyone before: tender, longing, warm. It's like his energy is a magnet pulling me in, luring me to be closer to support him.

I struggle for words and can't find them. I am only able to bring myself to move ever closer to him as he watches me, waiting for me to speak. We're so close I can feel the tension. In theater, we call this the kiss-or-kill zone. If two characters get this close, we expect them to kiss or attack with intent to kill.

His eyes flicker to my lips as I instinctively do the same at the thought. I am just about to close my eyes to let him kiss me when he presses his lips to my forehead. I close my eyes at the tender touch. It speaks far more about how he feels about me than him taking the kiss I'd offered him.

But it's over in a blink, and Gavril vanishes up the hall before I can even register he isn't in front of me.

"Gavril," I almost whisper his name. It's pointless anyway. Do I give chase again?

"It's alright. Let him go." Damian's voice comes from behind me.

I swallow and nod, turning to look at Damian.

"He does have other things to attend to before this night is done, but now, he's a little stronger, knowing that someone cares," Damian says gently. He's standing, arms folded as he leans against the wall.

"He's really not alright, is he?" I ask, still worried.

"No, he isn't. But so is every king without his queen to help and support him," Damian says. "Until that moment just now, he felt he had no support at all."

I look down. "I didn't do anything."

"No, my dear girl, you made a world of difference." Damian smiles softly. "In that simple act, you did more than you could ever know. But come on. We should get back into your room." He nods to the door.

I nod and let Damian take me back. I feel lost on what to do. I don't even know if he wants me after our fight, and I don't blame him. I'm still not sure what I feel anymore. I want the job. I want to help him, but... I just don't understand what he's thinking. And I want to trust him. I want to know how to trust him.

Damian closes the door behind me and looks at me. "You don't understand why he keeps asking you to stay out of trouble, do you?"

"He's worried I won't." I shrug.

"No, he's simply worried for you. Because regardless of if you accept it or not, he does love you. And if something were to happen to you, he doesn't know what he'll do. You're not just the favorite; you're the one he cares about above all others. He'd lose his mind if he lost you. He's barely holding it together as it is," Damian says frankly.

I swallow. "I guess I just keep feeling unsure, that's true." I know he cares, but more than the others?

"Well, you don't exactly make it easy for him to show it. How many times have you snapped at him or told him off for showing you too much affection? Even in private settings no one else can see," Damian points out. "Perhaps, you've made him unsure how or when to show you that he cares or if he even should, and he doesn't want to be snapped at again. You keep sending him mixed signals, and we're guys. We don't understand how women think or why. He can only do his best by interpreting the signals you've given him."

I shut my eyes. I know. I know I shouldn't want to be a favorite. No one should be. It not only protects us now, but it also protects him. But I can't help it. And it seems like he's struggling too. "I just don't know what to do anymore."

I'm scared to trust him. I'm unsure of my own ability to know anymore. I question my feelings for him then there's a moment like this... and I don't know how I can doubt. But then Forsythia's giggles as he tickles her comes to mind. What had happened to what we'd had when I felt so sure before the Harvest attack?

"You can start by not fighting it. He clearly has. His heart has already chosen for him, and he knows it. Denying it won't make it not true. And it won't make it hurt any less if you are eliminated. In fact, it'll likely hurt more because you have wasted the time you had with him. So, you nor he will have memories to cherish. It'll just be a bitter sting like a poison that will eat you both until death. Trust me, neither of you want that."

"But... if it's true, I can't lose." I can't let that happen. "And... I want to win, but..." but then I don't want to. Then I remember I don't have any other option but to win. I have nowhere else to go.

"But what? If you can't lose, then don't. Besides, imagine if you did win and your whole relationship leading up to it is this horrible hesitant denial. You think that's going to just go away because you won? It'll be easier, sure, but then your uncertain feelings will carry over. I know they will. You'll fret and worry about whether it was right of you to win or if he likes someone else and on and on." Damian sighs with a shake of his head. "You are setting yourself up for failure, whether in this contest or in the life after. Please, stop doing that to yourself and to him. You're here. Alright. You can't change that. The past is past. Please, stop building a life of uncertainty. If you love him, start by changing your attitude about yourself, so you can win with confidence. You do love him, don't you?"

I swallow. I don't know. I flip flop so rapidly. One moment, I can trust him. The next, I question all I believe about him. I recall how enwrapped I was by him and how he's able to make the world disappear for moments. But is that enough to build a life off of when one false move and I'm out? How do I put faith in something that could disappear in seconds?

Damian's shoulders fall slightly, and he sighs. "Do you not?" He glances up to meet my eyes.

"I-I care about him." But do I love him, or is he just my only option?

"But you aren't sure if it is more?" Damian checks.

"I don't know if I even know what that means anymore." Did I ever? Sometimes, it's magic; other times, we're just yelling at each other.

"Love is putting someone's happiness before your own. To trust and respect them, no matter what happens or what is said," Damian says. "Being that as it is, I ask you to think hard about this. Do you love him?"

Have I been good enough to put what he wants first? I don't know if I've managed that. But even when I can't stand him, I can't say I don't respect him. "I don't know." I can only say yes to half of it.

Damian nods slowly. "When you love someone, they make you want to be a better person. My Emily did that for me. I was in a dark place until I met her. I doubt I'd be who I am today without her. So consider how you feel around Gavril. How does he make you feel about yourself and who you want to be?"

I look down. "I wish I was the princess they wanted." Even if I know I'm not enough.

"And you can be. What you did tonight with Gavril proved you are exactly what they need. What *he* needs," Damian says as he lifts my chin gently.

"What did I do?"

He chuckles. "A better question might be, 'what didn't you do?' You broke down his formal wall and got him to relax. You listened to his frustrations, *and* you even spent half an hour helping him work out his problem. Just watching the two of you work was magical."

"That's what anyone would do."

"No, Kascia, they wouldn't. You really think that Ericka or Forsythia would have cared? Sure, they'd pretend, but they'd have used his exhaustion to press their advantage as they have done in the past. Florence, Jonquil, and others have done the same. And two of the remaining princesses' homelands are landlocked, so they don't have experience with sea animals. Princess Amapola lives on the opposite coast, sure, but she doesn't listen well. None of the girls do what you do, Kascia. None. I believe he's told you that many times."

I am not sure I want to admit I have a hard time believing that. "I didn't add much, just asked questions about what he knew. They could all have done it."

Damian takes a deep breath as if he is calming himself down. "How can you be so open-minded, and yet, so amazingly thick headed?" he says, watching the floor.

I laugh a little. "I don't know. I don't know much anymore." I start playing with my fingers, missing my ring that I used to wear. But I'd thrown it at my father. "I forgot how to be sure."

"Isla is too timid. Florence, too scared. Lilly is both. Azalea is not grounded enough. Bella comes close, but she gets nervous when the prince starts to be open with her. Jonquil is hard and abrasive. Forsythia is frankly a whore." He shakes his head. "She plays compassionate for the prince, but their conversations aren't very deep. Ericka is too self-centered; she has her own version of the prince in her head. Amapola lacks understanding. Rose is too stiff and traditional. And Zelda, well... they have fun, but their relationship is... different from others."

"She could have done it." *She should win.*

"As Sage described it, they are playful and combative with each other. So, I doubt it. She likely would have told him he needed to sleep before she beat him fencing or something of that nature," Damian says.

"He likely should have slept. I should have told him to." I swallow. "She'd be good."

Damian rolls his eyes. "But she still wouldn't have given him help with his problem and just because you tell him to, doesn't need he will," he points out. "It isn't like she can ensure he gets sleep."

"Guess she just..." The words get stuck in my throat. I swallow. "I want to go home." I want to be sure of something again. It feels like a lifetime since I was sure of anything. But worse was all of those things were a lie. I bite my lips to hold back the pain in my heart.

Damian frowns. "Do you really mean that?"

I shake my head. "The home I thought I had wasn't real. It's not possible to go back." I miss feeling safe. I miss knowing my own heart. I'm fighting tears.

Damian sighs as he comes forward and hugs me. "Oh Kascia."

I return it, hiding in his hug. "Is the problem that I'm scared to love what I might not keep?"

"Perhaps, but I have found it is better to have loved and lost than to never love at all. And you were confident in your feelings once. Do you remember? After Ro was taken, you were willing to do what it took to win to have the chance to stop the rebels and find her. I still believe you can win, but you can't keep switching between confidence and denial. You must choose. If you don't think you can win or that you should win, you might as well ask to leave," Damian says firmly. "No amount of denial or restraint will save either of you from how you feel. Accept that if you lose, it is going to hurt, no matter what. But if you want to win, you must find it in yourself to pass every test. Because I believe you can, but that doesn't matter if you don't."

"But I have no choice. If I don't win... even if I shouldn't. I... I-I don't know what to do." I shake my head against Damian's shirt.

Damian holds me a moment longer then lets out a sigh and pulls back. "Come on. You should probably prepare for bed."

I nod. He has a point. Tomorrow is going to be busy. I have a delegation to prepare for, rehearsals to try to keep up on, and as always, this tangled mess of emotions that is my heart.

When I finally settle to bed, I notice the bed is oddly warm, like someone used magic to keep it that way. It makes the bed feel even softer and more comfortable than normal, like a soothing, enfolding embrace that swaddles me protectively. I don't know how they did it, but I'm grateful. The warm fire crackling in the background helps too, so even through the wild tossing of my mind and heart, I'm able to sleep.

I meet with the other girls to plan the feast and party the next morning. The feast is easy, but the party after is not going to be. It would be too easy for a delegate to lure one of the girls away during the dance.

I think of a better idea. Rather than a party, we could do a banquet performance as is often done in Dragia. The problem is, between all of us, we'd still need Damian's help to pull it off. But to my surprise he agrees, and even more, the day of, he has brand-new performing dresses for me.

"When did you make this?" I demand as I look over the stunning red dress Damian had made for the tambourine piece.

"I don't sleep," he says dryly.

"I could have used the one mother sent," I object, but I admire the real gold along the neckline and how sharp and floaty the skirt is. This is so much nicer than mine though they look so alike.

"I like things done properly," Damian says.

I roll my eyes. No kidding.

The show itself goes well. The king and queen are nervous about the idea at first, but it goes perfectly. I do the tambourine song from *The Hunchback* which requires three male backups. Damian had said he'd take care of it, so the live performance is the first time I hear the backup. I recognize Cedrick and Damian easily, but the third takes me a moment. When it ends, I realize it was Gavril. How Damian got

Gavril to agree I'll never know. I had to push really hard to get him to sing with me when I realized he did sing. And even then, I'd not gotten him to do it once since then.

The delegation gets rather drunk, but they clearly enjoy the show as they whoop and whistle at us. When it's over, they shuffle off to bed in a good mood.

We're feeling pretty successful as Damian leads a group of us to our rooms when an alarm goes off. An attack now? Is it the rebels or the Dragians? I pray to the Maker it's not both!

Damian snaps into action, whipping out his cane sword to guard us as he leads us into a safe room off the hall.

I'm surprised there are any nearby. I invite Damian to follow us in, not stepping in until he does. He oddly hesitates, panting a little, before finally meeting my eye. He's debating leaving to help whatever the fight is, but he seems strangely out of breath. As he looks away then back at me, he seems to have made his decision and steps inside with me before closing the door behind him, still catching his breath.

"Has he been armed this whole time?" Ericka sounds offended.

"Does it matter?" I snap. Ericka huffs at me and turns to Forsythia to keep complaining.

The other girls are still too freaked out to notice much, so I focus on Damian. "You're not hurt, are you?"

"I'll be fine," he says as he slides to a seat on the floor, looking exhausted, but at least his breath is evening out.

"You sure?" I kneel next to him. I ignore the other girls flipping out. He gives me a crooked smile as he meets my eye. "I've been through worse. I'll be fine."

I frown. "You sure? You're not hurt?" He wasn't this tired a moment ago.

"Just winded," he excuses.

I give him a look, raising a brow and tilting my head a bit. Does he really think I'll believe that?

He sighs. "You're right. I'd not buy that either." He manages a smile.

I return it. "What happened?"

"It's kind of hard to explain," he says, resting his head against the wall. "Just that... I'm not that great with magic, and I might have used too much energy."

"Oh." I smile. "So, you literally do magic."

"Small amounts of it, yes. Nothing grand." His smile is bright, but his eyes still droop. "I tire myself out if I try anything much more than that."

I nod. "Can... I help?"

"Not really. It'll come back over time... after I've rested." He sighs. "It would help if you ladies tried to remain calm, though," he says to the other girls.

I nod and stand up. Ericka is still kind of freaking out. "How have we had him armed and not known?"

"Seems unfair." Forsythia sounds more annoyed than angry though.

"Shh. Remember, they can still hear us," I remind them.

They look at me. "Of course, you know. You armed too, Highness?" Forsythia mocks. She'd been so quiet before. I knew she could be harsh too, but I guess without Dahlia, she feels she could have more wiggle room.

I shake my head. "Of course not." I ignore her insult. "And we only have the one guard."

"And we're stuck with the one they most want to kidnap," Ericka complains, but it is in a quieter tone.

"What?" Isla frowns.

"Are you deaf?" Azalea says. "We need to be quiet."

We hear some noises outside. We all go quiet. I look at Damian to make sure he's alright, listening intently. Are they rebels, Dragians, or both?

Damian seems like he might be listening too, but it could be he's just tired. I stay beside him, ignoring the other girls' attitude. He notices I shiver a little in the cold room with my thin costume.

He puts the end of the cape he wore for his part of the show across my shoulders. We sit in silence a while. I watch as he closes his eyes and eventually falls asleep.

I don't know how long we wait before Cedrick shows up, amused by Damian's state. He wakes Damian up, who's oddly young-looking in the face, childish as he remains mostly asleep, making sure Cedrick looks after me.

"Overdid it, uh?" Cedrick smiles in amusement. "I'll take care of her and you." Cedrick has me wait while other guards take the other girls to their rooms, and he takes Damian to his.

He's all smiles when he returns for me. "Feeling better now it's down to twelve?" he teases me.

"I suppose." I still was wrapping my head around being in the last twelve girls.

Cedrick smiles a little. "As long as he learns to choose, I guess it will be worth it."

The way he says it, it's like he's declaring the Enthronement will be a success if he does. "Wait, what?"

But he walks me into my room, kisses my hand, and is gone with a nod to the Custod guard as he arrives before I can get more out of him.

But... he has answers. I felt them, and he was about to share them. I go to see if I can catch him, but as mysteriously as his brother can, he's gone. Those two are so creepily different and yet so creepily alike.

Chapter 20

The delegation is gone, and we're all safe the next morning by sheer luck alone it feels. And though I get to sleep in a little, it's soon that I'm whisked away to the theater to start rehearsals in earnest.

I am excused from princess lessons to rehearse, but at dinner, the prince has an announcement. Celeste Day, a traditionally romantic holiday, is quickly coming up. The girls have been talking about it. Florence seems to hope it will help boost her chances. I am wondering how it will work. With twelve of us left, I'm not sure everyone is going to manage to get a turn.

Gavril has thought of this too. "Because I'm one man and there are twelve of you, I decided we'll make it a bit of a game to see who will get some of my time that day. We'll do a bit of a tournament. We'll have each of you try to beat me at a game of Osterie. Whoever wins their game against me gets a date that day. And if you want, I can have someone who plays often help you practice." He gives us a smile. "That fair?"

With the king and queen watching, I doubt any of the girls left would have the guts to say no. I have seen pretty much all the girls play at some point with the endless hours we'd spent in the Ladies' Chamber. I wonder how good the prince is at the game. I'm not brilliant, but I'm not dreadful either. But I have no doubt Damian is good at the game, and he can help me prepare. I can at least have a good shot at a date that day.

"Good thing we play often," Lilly tries to be bright.

"That's going to be a nightmare. Is he really good? I've never heard him mention the game," Ericka says with a sigh. "Has anyone?" We all shake our heads.

I can't help but worry how good. Could I even win? Do I want to? I bite my lips. To win and get the chance to have him fair and square, no right to complain during the ball, at least? That sounds magical. But can I beat him? I'm not a master at the game.

But preparing for my game will have to wait. I still have a show to do this week. The anxious excitement is really starting to grow, and I'm not sure I love what I do more than I do in that week. Damian is brilliant in his role as a director and as the Phantom himself.

Though it's intense and busy with so much to practice, improve, and set up before the end of the week, I'm happy at my work. But I am more stressed about hurrying to be ready for dinner when I return to the palace than I am about the show.

I'm hurrying to my room to dress for dinner when I run into someone. Joy pants in happiness and says hello before huffing her sound that means my name. The man with her is the man I'd seen with Gavril during the delegations, the newest member of his staff is my guess. At first, I think its Godwin, but then I notice this man has less freckles. Plus, he doesn't look at all pleased to have Joy or to have her chatting at me.

"Hello Joy." I smile at her. She sits, tail still wagging in delight as she says my name again.

"Pardon, I didn't hear you coming," the man says. "I don't think we've properly met, Lady Kascia. I'm Reinold."

"Reinold," I repeat his name to be sure I have it. "You assisted the prince with the delegations, correct?"

He nods. He really looks like Godwin. They have the same hair and eyes. "Yes, I'm his court liaison." He has a smoother voice than his twin though.

I smile a little. "So now there's nothing for you to do, you get to walk the dog?"

Reinold looks down at Joy with a slight twinge of disgust on his face. "Sometimes."

Joy barks, making Reinold jump. I look at Joy in surprise. "I don't think I've ever heard you bark." She makes cute little sounds and small barks perhaps, but that is a proper dog bark.

"Oh, she barks at me all the time," Reinold complains as Joy runs around as happy as she ever does. Reinold tries to stop her from tangling him in her lead, but he fails, so there are two rounds of the lead around his legs. He sighs exhaustedly.

I frown and look at Joy, wondering why she'd bark at Reinold. She doesn't seem to dislike him from what I can tell. Joy pants up at me in delight and talks at me as if explaining it. I think she's expressing that it's fun. Then she barks at him again, and he jumps once more.

"You know, it would help if you didn't jump," I suggest.

"Oh yes, my lady, I know, but I can't help it." He gives Joy a look. The nervousness in his eyes hasn't gone away. I thought it was running into me. Perhaps it has much more to do with the dog than I realize.

"Don't like dogs?"

"I'm far better with people than animals. I'm not much of a fan, no," Reinold confesses, still looking at Joy in exasperation with a hint of nervousness.

"So why do they have you walk her?" I frown.

"They're nuts," Reinold replies as he carefully tries to untangled himself from the lead.

Joy barks in complaint, making Reinold jump.

"Joy, be nice." I bend down to her level, stroking her and scratching her ear to help Reinold get free. Then I recall I have to hurry to be ready for dinner. "Sorry to have to run; I'm surely already late for dinner."

"Of course, my lady." Reinold gives me a small bow.

Joy complains as I hurry up the hallway, but Reinold ignores it. "You don't talk," he insists to her. "You're a dog." Joy just barks back at him. I love that little dog, but I don't have much time to think about her or Reinold as my maids quickly prepare me ready for dinner. Afterward, Damian plays Ostragie with me — as he does every night this week — to give me the best chance of winning a date on the holiday.

I don't expect to see Reinold anytime soon, but the next day, he shows up at the theater to make sure I got my invitation for my game with Gavril. He doesn't look too pleased but confesses his options were either bringing the invitation to me or taking Joy for a run. I chuckle and thank him, though he causes quite a stir among my single castmates. Reinold is right; he is better with people. He might look like Godwin, but he behaves far more like a gentleman, and it is attractive. His proper bows and smiles get Alsmeria fluttering again. I have to apologize for her excitement.

"Yes, excitable, isn't she?" Reinold smiles in amusement.

"That would be the word," I admit.

He just tips his invisible hat to me. "Well, it takes all kinds. You can thank them for their kindness for me, but I better get back, so I don't arrive so late I get the task of putting the puppy to bed."

Getting back into rehearsals is tricky after that. The girls keep giggling about Reinold long after he's gone, which irritates Damian. "Ladies, please, let's start from the top, and pay attention. There is no worse disaster than a distracted rehearsal," he reminds us. Mother beams to hear him use the quote she's so fond of.

But that isn't the only interruption we get. Fabian likes to come by from time to time to get the inside scoop, which doesn't please Damian at all. He looks more like the dark and angry phantom than ever as he glares Fabian down.

"What is it this time?" Damian asks, folding his arms in annoyance.

"What? Just trying to get a behind the scenes to drum up publicity." Fabian defends as many girls giggle to see the two at it again.

"There will be no interactions with the press until after the performance. And Lady Kascia's time is extremely limited. You can only speak to her if you receive permission from the king and queen. You know that." Damian arches a brow at the reporter.

"In the palace, yes." Fabian puts on that grin he often uses.

"And in the theatre, I am king. Now stop distracting my rehearsal and get out," Damian says in an almost musical firmness.

"Please." Fabian tries puppy dog eyes that makes many of the cast members giggle. Damian's brow stiffens to a hard glare. Fabian doesn't let up though, perhaps thinking to try to outlast Damian. Damian was saying he didn't have time after all.

Damian then glances off to the side at his brother. I hear a bark and look over to see Joy, to my surprise, coming over to Fabian, clearly after Fabian's shoes.

"Hey!" Fabian laughs.

"Joy," Damian looks down at the dog. She looks up at him, panting happily. "Sic' him," Damian says if it's a command and nods at Fabian.

Fabian cries out more playfully than seriously as Joy takes the order and jumps up to tackle him down, still too cute to really seem scary, but he does take the hint and leaves while half the cast is laughing.

Joy calls "oh-row" and looks sad her plaything is gone. I didn't even know they'd brought Joy to give Reinold a break.

Damian frowns at her. "No, you're supposed to scare him off. That's the point," he tells the dog. "That's a good girl."

Joy complains though that she wanted to chase him more before he got away, or so I think. The rest of my cast is still laughing.

Damian sighs and looks at Cedrick. "We need to work on that."

"What? She wants to chase things. It just means she'd chase an attacker out of a building. Throw her a ball." Cedrick tries to reason.

"Fair, but would you mind taking her back?" Damian asks.

"Not at all. We'll get a chase toy there." Cedrick grins and clicks his tongue to get Joy to join him, attaches her lead, then jogs away. Joy happily runs along with him.

Damian then takes a breath and turns to us. "The rest of you, let's start at the start at the top of the play-within-a-play." It shakes them all back into the moment, and we hurry into place.

But it's not long before it's show day. I'm not sure I've ever seen Damian this stressed, and yet, so certain at the same time. His brother does a good job handling it, teasing him to get him to relax — though sometimes perhaps pushing that a bit too far — or helping get things on track when they are slacking.

The flutter of activity before the start of the show is as familiar to me as the singing of birds in the morning or the rustle of bed sheets when one awakes. It is familiar, comforting, and exciting. It's fun to put on the stage makeup the way I always have, having our one makeup artist come around and make sure the makeup is done properly, letting the costume department dress me which feels even more normal now I need help to change most of the time. And it is magical to see myself in the mirror morphing into the character I love playing more than any other.

The rest of the cast is anxiously trying to peek out at the crowd, wanting to see when the royal family arrives.

"More time sitting around means more time for someone to try to get to them while they're busy." Cedrick makes us all jump. "Stop peeking," he teases the cast. "Trust me, you'll hear when they arrive. The audience will react."

It's less than five minutes to curtain when the sound comes Cedrick promised we'd hear, the increased muttering and movement of the crowd, some calling and even cheering. The girls all rush to the corner where they can try to peek out. How are professionals so anxious? I roll my eyes, though I am dying to see.

We all get ready as the stage manager calls us into position. It's only another minute before Mother walks out to a full house of applause which I haven't heard in so long. She runs through the normal introduction of the show with reminders about audience etiquette before she gives the final welcome and applause fills the theater once more as she disappears and the curtains part for the opening scene.

The rest of the night is all magic. The gasps and cries of shock or delight at the lighting of the grand chandelier, the magic of being whisked away in my opening song, the dark energy as Damian draws me into the phantom's lair, the screams of fright at Damian's impressive feats vanishing, his voice echoing around the theater. The whole performance is one of the best I have been in, each magical moment building off the last. I don't think there is a person who does not at least jump if not scream when the chandelier comes crashing down at the end of the first act.

I thought Damian would be in a mood or at least irritated at small imperfections he sees that I never do, like he did in rehearsals, but on the contrary, I think he's as swept up in the magic as I am and having more fun than I think I have ever seen him have.

In the second act, I think I get too wrapped up in my last large solo, but I have never felt so close to the piece before, wishing I had my father back but in a very different way. I had never noticed how alike Christine and I really are. We both thought the man we'd grown up with and loved was the best for us, only to be wrong, and yet, were willing to give anything to have him back. My father had played my phantom more than on stage, and that makes the piece pierce me to the very heart.

When Damian's haunting whispers call to me at the beginning of the next song, I feel the longing for him to be as true as I thought, but my anger at the truth that none of those names, wandering child, pitiful one, lost, helpless, none are the true name. I am my own night angel. I don't need that imposter.

Cedrick's voice cutting into our back and forth helps lure me back into the show as he talks Christine out of trusting the Phantom. And part of me wishes I was the one fighting him away, fueling the energy of the show. It makes it that much better and when I have a break backstage, I can't help but smile. This is a show I — and no one in the audience — will forget.

Not an eye is dry in the theater at the closing scene as the Phantom releases us and somehow Damian does the most impressive vanishing trick to leave the stage. One I still do not understand. Alsmeria's gasp of shock may have been real as she draws back the cloth to reveal only black smoke where Damian had once been. I don't recall him doing that in rehearsals.

The applause at the end is deafening. When Damian and I come out for the final bows, Cedrick winces at the sound as the crowd goes wild. I curtsy with Damian presenting me, clearly wanting me to take as much attention as possible. I look up at where I know the royal box is. It has never been filled before. They're too far for me to see clearly, but they're all on their feet as they applaud us. I notice there's someone with Gavril, but it's hard to tell who for sure. I think it's Zelda. I suppose it would be expected he'd bring a date.

I thought it would ruin my mood, but it doesn't. I smile and blow a kiss in their direction. We have a hard time getting off the stage politely with how intense the applause is as we do our final group bow. We have to bow several times before we're finally able to hide behind the curtain line, so it can drop.

I have no idea how late it is when I finally leave the theater. We had a great time celebrating the rousing success. Mother gives me a box of props and costume pieces that Damian insists are mine with a proud smile: the edelweiss crystal flowers that had gone into my hair, the earrings that went with it, the mask from the masquerade scene, things like that. It reminds me this is likely my very last show of my life. I'm thankful the truth of that didn't hit me earlier, ruining the night.

Damian even makes the night special for one other person. Layla, the little girl who I'd seen at plenty of my shows and who came to the live public interview last fall, is brought backstage where Damian gives her a tour and has me show her around. She is tired from the late night but so excited I am not sure her poor mother will ever get her to sleep.

There are also people waiting outside waiting for autographs or impressions, more than I have ever seen, but with Damian there, I am not worried about what kind of security threat it could be. I take and sign dozens of things. A few people give me gifts which I give straight to the guard to inspect. But it is a good half an hour at the very least before Damian and I climb into the carriage that will take us back to the palace.

"You were magnificent." Damian beams at me proudly. "I doubt the original Christine could have done better."

I smile. "You're the one who pulled it off."

"Without you, I couldn't have. Thank you. Doing this with me means more than you realize," he says with that soft but proud smile of his.

"What do you mean?" I smile. "I'm the one who got the best gift. Well, other than perhaps Gavril who got his first show to be the best ever done in that theater."

Damian laughs. "True. I'm sure he thoroughly enjoyed his chance to be outside the palace walls for once."

"I'm sure he did." But I'm still studying Damian, wondering what he means.

"And not a single incident. That should make the queen happy, or at least, prove that Joy is doing her job." He smiles.

I chuckle. "Well, sounds like all is well. The guard didn't freak out. So, I presume they're all safe." I study Damian again. "What does all this mean to you? Did you do this before?"

Damian smiles warmly with the hint of being caught and bows his head as he thinks for a moment. "I suppose I should have known you'd catch on to that. But yes, I have. It was… a long time ago."

"So why does this show mean so much?" I ask. "It was one of the few I could get you to sing along to without realizing it."

He huffs out a chuckle. "I suppose that is true. As I believe I once told you, it is one of my favorites, if not my favorite. It's one of the few plays that speaks to my heart because I truly understand the characters, their passions, their dreams. As if… there's a part of me in them. If that makes any sense at all."

I nod. "It makes sense. I understand that feeling. That's… often how I feel." I rub my arms uneasily.

Damian meets my eyes with a smile. "I suppose that is why I love the theatre. Cedrick and I were in many shows together, as was his wife. They made the perfect pair in any show." He smiles to himself. "And

I was happy to design and build everything for any play we did. But once she was gone, Cedrick went into a dark place, and a lot of things weren't that important anymore," he says with a sigh.

I look down. "Must be why you're good at everything. You did everything in the theater." I want to ask more, but I also don't want to make him share more if it hurts.

He meets my eyes again with a sad smile. "It was my life. One I thought was long dead, but you helped me relive it tonight. And I thank you for that."

"As sad as it sounds, me too." I force a smile. "I doubt I'll ever get to do that again."

"Perhaps not. But I feel you have so much ahead of you." He smiles with that proud shine in his eyes. "But for what it's worth, you're welcome. I'm glad I could give you that."

I hug myself. "I have no idea what is ahead." And I'm not sure I ever will until it's happening.

"Hard to be certain." Damian nods. "But you aren't out of the competition, and you do have the Ostragie match tomorrow which could be promising."

"Right," I swallow. "Well, if you're as good at teaching games as you are theater, I'll have a good time tomorrow either way."

"True, but I believe you stand more of a chance against him than you think." He smiles.

"I hope so. I've never heard of him playing before."

Damian chuckles. "I have. A few weeks ago, I actually played against him. And I must admit, he is rather good. No one has bested him yet. Even I had to forfeit after an hour of playing to get back to work."

My face falls. "What? He beat you?" I'm in trouble.

"We were decently matched, but yes. I had to call it quits which does count as a loss." Damian nods.

I swallow. "I'm not sure anyone can beat him if you couldn't." Maybe Zelda would get lucky. Gavril might have been too careful in his way of keeping the number down.

"I doubt that. Zelda may be able to sneak out a win, but I've seen her play you. She's good, but not that good," Damian says. "And I said that I forfeited, not that I don't know how to beat him." He grins.

"Then why didn't you?"

"Because the amount of time it would have taken would have been ages," he chuckles. "But there is a way to beat him faster, but not by me. You, Kascia, stand a much better chance because you can distract him in ways I can't. In Ostragie, only half of the game is on the board," he reminds me. "And if I am being fair, I feel you know him in ways that can help interpret his thinking and will be able to find his strategy better than anyone else."

"In what way?" I'm not sure I'm following.

"I've taught you the various strategies, but you'll have to read him to know which he is using. Meanwhile, you distract him, so he doesn't figure out yours."

"How do I do both? And why does that work for me and not you?"

Damian gives me an amused smile. "Because Kascia, you're a woman."

I bite my lip. "I'm not sure it's that easy." Gavril doesn't seem that easy to distract with a pretty outfit.

"It might be. You'll have to talk to him. Get his mind on you, not what you are doing," he says. "And with any luck, he'll be tired. I noticed yours is in the evening, so you'll likely be last. I presume he wanted to make sure you got your rest after tonight, but that means you'll be fresh, meanwhile he'll have been playing all day, which can be to your advantage. However, as that isn't a guarantee, we won't place our bets on that card. But talking to him should help. When is the last time you two have really talked?"

I had to think. "At the leaving ball for the Japcharians, I think."

"Then you have things to talk about."

I nod. "Just hopefully nothing that distracts me. This is the man who intimidated Dragia."

"True. But he likes you much more than them." Damian smiles.

I smile but then it slides a little. "I hope so."

He chuckles. "Trust me. You'll do fine. But you are psyching yourself out. If you fear you will lose, then you've already lost."

He has a point. "It's how much he likes me I wonder."

"Do you want him to like you?" He arches a brow.

I nod. "I think so, most of the time."

Damian sighs and looks at the roof of the carriage. "He needs to take you out more."

"What?" I frown.

He looks back at me. "Frankly, I don't think that man understands the point of courting. If he did, I doubt you'd be so unsure. At least, not as much or as often."

"Not like he has much experience." I sigh. "Then again, neither have I." I'd been with Jake, and that is it.

"True." Damian nods. "But as for tomorrow, I have every confidence in you. Don't allow him to get inside your head. You must be confident, but not cocky. I've taught you the deeper strategy of the game, but you have to believe you can win."

I take a deep breath and nod. "Well, let's at least hope it's fun."

Damian smiles warmly. "Of that, I have no doubt."

We reach the palace walls, and the normal security check is run before we ride to the castle gate. The castle is quiet, like the night we slipped out to meet with the rebel groups. I nod my thanks to Damian as he helps me step out of the carriage, and the staff ride to the stables to relieve the horses.

My maids compliment me as they help me prepare for bed, but I dismiss them as soon as I can. They leave the tea for me and say they'll see me in the morning. I slip into a dressing gown to finish getting ready for bed. Damian finishes preparing the tea and clearing up his workstation for the rest days ahead.

I just finish tying off my braid when there was a knock at the door. I frown and glance over at Damian, wondering if this is something planned. But he doesn't give me a clue if it is or not but goes to check the door. I make sure my dressing gown is properly tied and covering me as Damian answers the door.

"Ah, hello Damian." Gavril's voice makes my heart skip then pick up. "I hope I haven't come too late. If she's already in bed, I can just…"

"It's alright," I call to Damian. Though if he stayed much later and I would have turned him away. I'm not sure why he came, but I must know.

Damian bows his head to me and steps aside to let Gavril walk into the room. I stand up, brushing my hair behind my ear even though I'd already tied it into the braid.

Gavril smiles at me with a look in his eyes I can't quite read. "Sorry if I am bothering you later than you'd like. But with security, there wasn't a chance of a snowball in summer that the guard would have let me try to speak to you at the theater. I wanted to… well," he chuckles a bit. "You were stunning."

"And you had to come say that tonight?" I tease, unsure how else to react.

"With how badly I did the last time I tried to tell you how beautiful you were, yes." Gavril's amber eyes meet mine. My breath hitches. "I've never seen or felt anything like it before. If you told me it was magic you cast, I'd have believed it. You took me to another world tonight, and I had to thank you and admit it. I couldn't stand to have made the same mistake that night when you first showed that magic to us."

"You really think that's the real me? The one on stage?" I try to tease to test his reaction.

"In some ways, yes, not that you are that helpless. But sometimes, I do wonder if you're that confused."

Curse him for being perfectly correct. I put on a smile though. "Well, thank you, Your Highness. I'm glad my gift was a hit."

"You have proven the best at knowing what I'd like best," Gavril agrees, coming closer. I don't stop him, but I'm unsure if that is a good idea. "And even before that, you have always been the best at being what I needed, even if I didn't know it."

"I'm not sure I even knew it." I look up into his face again.

Gavril smiles a little. "That just makes it all the more impressive." He's even closer now. It's getting harder to breathe calmly. It has been a long day. "Thank you," he says after a long moment. "It really was one of the best nights of my life."

"Not the best?" I tease. I really need to stop deflecting. It's like a reflex I can't control.

"So hard to tell when all of the best you gave me."

I didn't realize my breath could catch twice in one conversation. He's so close, but I still feel that wall, like I'm not allowed to touch him. "No matter what happens, at least I know we had this," Gavril says and looks down at my hands. I think he'd take them if I let him, but with how I'm holding the dressing gown as if making sure I'm covered, it would be awkward if not rude. "I suppose it sounds silly and pointless, but I just had to come and say thank you. Let you know what it meant."

I smile and meet his eyes again. "You're welcome." And I understand he means for more than just tonight.

Gavril's eyes look into mine, from one to the other as if trying to decide something. "Kascia, I know it's been..." A sound cuts into the silence of the night making him stop. He lets out a frustrated sigh and glances over his shoulder. It must have been Sage. He's likely reminding the prince it's late. "It's been a wild ride." But his tone tells me that's not what he'd been planning to say. The tone is completely different than it had been before. What had he wanted to say?

"Well, we all knew the Enthronement would be." I accept the odd apology, or I think that is what he's trying to do.

Gavril hesitates before he brushes my cheek with the back of his fingers. I close my eyes at the touch, inviting it. It reminds me of the lover's song I'd performed just that night, and I daydream of him being the other half of the duet. He'd been too shy when we'd taken over the music room to try it.

"Ever wish we could go back to when it wasn't as twisted?" he asks.

"Daily," I confess.

He smiles, still studying my eyes. "Thank you for giving me even more of your time. I should let you get to bed. I'm sure it's been a long day. I had to let you know how wonderful it was. How... amazing you — it was. You're a treasure on that stage. I..." he looks down, "am sorry it could be your last." With how my father planned it all, it was, but I couldn't tell him that. "And know if it's not, even if I have to gag and hogtie my mother and guard, I'd not miss it for the world."

I chuckle at the idea. "Doubt it will be an issue."

"I pray not." Gavril's eyes are locked on mine again, and the old electricity that has felt muffled for so long returns. Gavril moves closer, his hand sliding across my cheek into my hair, but then he pulls back. I cannot hear it, but I know Sage is why. "Good night, Asteria."

How did he make my breath catch three times? It makes it too hard to reply, making me miss the chance before he takes my hand to kiss it, bowing to me before leaving as quickly as he often does. And I'm not sure I'd ever longed for him or anyone to come back in my life.

Chapter 21

They are kind enough to let me rest the next morning. I'm nervous for our game but hopeful that I can scrape a win and some time alone with the prince. It feels like so long since we've had a proper date. I'm scared it will melt into another fight or worse.

My match is set for just before dinner. However, his other games must have run late because, on my way back from looking for more evidence of the prophecy in the library, Godwin finds me and asks if I'd mind playing over dinner. I don't mind at all, hoping that will help distract him more like Damian had suggested.

The outfit choice is lovely. It's an off-the-shoulder piece with a nice flowing skirt. The top is like the night sky, the bottom like the rippling sea, all shimmering with stars. They do natural loose curls in my hair and put my chosen necklace on to help with the shape around my shoulders. I let out a sigh as they do my makeup only a little fancier than normal, trying to draw attention to my eyes.

"Distracting?" I ask Damian, letting him look me over.

"To him, indeed." He smiles.

Reinold comes to let me know the prince is ready for me. The suite is quite a few floors up and when the door is opened for me, the first thing I hear is "Joy no!" I laugh as Joy stops mid-run to get to me. "Don't jump," Gavril orders.

I have to walk around a corner to see the room. It's nice. There's a large window looking over a balcony over the ocean. There are two sofas facing each other across a center table. On the side facing me are two armchairs across from a table that has the Osterie board painted onto it.

The room is light and airy. There's a smoldering fire keeping the room warm. The room's colors are an ocean green that border on blue but helps bring a kind of calming air to the room. It's like a living room in how it seems built for relaxing, though it does have the social/meeting circle of sofas and armchairs most rooms in the palace have.

Gavril smiles and bows to me. "Thank you for your patience." He looks over my dress. "Of course, Damian went for something different. You look much more comfortable." Joy whimpers. "Oh alright, you can say hi," he tells her.

She "talks" in delight and runs over to leap up at me. I smile and stroke her head and rub her side. "You must love all the girls you get to enjoy," I say to her.

"She doesn't love all of them," Gavril admits, "but she doesn't seem to hate anyone. She wouldn't be as excited for them though. I will be nice and not tell you which."

"As long as it's not me." I smile as I stand up.

"Joy, at attention," Gavril tells her. She runs over and sits beside Gavril's chair. I smile. He waves for me to take a seat. He settles into his chair and snaps. A few servants come over and set up a side table for each of us and lay all our dinner on top, rather than bringing course by course per normal the noodles, vegetables, and dumplings. I nod a thanks to them. Gavril does the same before he dismisses them.

"Oh, and Joy," Gavril says, looking down at her. She looks up. "Be good and you can have some." Her tail wags happily.

"She has to just sit there?" I frown.

"Well, she's been good all day, but I can't have her just run around."

"Can..." I bite my lips, "she sit with me?"

"After you eat. Don't want her begging for scraps." Gavril chuckles. There's an odd clicking at the window.

"Joy, no," Gavril says, but it's too late. She turns to the window, barks, and runs over to the window. Gavril sighs, "And she hates the squirrels." I laugh. "Joy, Joy, come here."

Joy makes worried noises and looks back at the window, tail stiff in anticipation. "Joy," Gavril sighs, "come on. You can't have it, and it's not hurting anyone." She whines a bit more. "Joy," Gavril says. "Joy, come here. It's fine. It won't hurt anyone."

Joy barks at the window. She stands up and puts her paw up on the window, tail wagging before going still. She whimpers and sits down again, her tail wagging then going still again. She repeats this a few times, barking on and off.

"Joy, Joy, come here," Gavril tries again, but it's no good. He sighs and moves as if to stand.

"Joy!" I call. "Joy, girl, look." But she doesn't listen at me either. "Joy!"

She turns to look at me. "It's okay," I say. "Come here." She turns back to the window and barks again.

"Joy." Gavril gets up.

I try one more time. "Joy, girl, we're safe. Come here." Joy turns to us. "It's okay," I soothe. Gavril pauses to watch. "It won't hurt us. Come over and sit with us. We have biscuits," I tempt her.

Joy whimpers and looks back at the window.

"Joy, come guard Kascia," Gavril says suddenly.

Joy leaps to her feet, turns, jumps over any obstacle in her way, then bolts right for me. She sits down next to me and looks up at me as if making sure I'm alright.

"Good girl, no let the squirrel get in." Gavril smiles and sits back down.

"I can't believe that worked," I say.

"Me either." Gavril is still smiling. "First trick that works. I have had to deal with her acting like that for hours before." He sighs. "But feel free to eat. Mind if I eat a bit before we start?"

"Oh, no, but I think I'm going to go ahead and get started setting up."

"Sure," he says and sets up the divider, so he can't see where I put my pieces. I start to set up while Gavril slips in some food before he starts on his pieces. He doesn't make me wait long. He's halfway done by the time I'm finished. Damian helped me come up with the arrangement. I hope it works.

Once we're both done, he takes the divider down, but now I have to work on the second part: distraction. I'm more nervous about that than anything else. I suppose it's because I know Damian is right. This is the best way.

"Feeling alright after playing all day?"

"Yeah, I took a break for lunch, but I didn't want it to go too late. I had plans for tonight, but some games went long," Gavril chuckles.

"Any winners?" I raise my brows in question as I take my turn, leaning over the board a little as Flur had suggested. She said it would be more distracting, and with Damian's outfit, she's likely right.

Gavril gives me a teasing smile. "Someone has to win, Kascia."

"You know what I mean." I smile as he makes his move.

"I know." He waves off as he sits back. "What do you think?" He studies my face carefully.

"I think..." I say, leaning forward as I move my next piece, "you're scared to tell me."

"Scared?" He laughs. "Scared of what?"

"Of what I'll do." I smile.

Gavril chuckles and shakes his head. "Not so much, no. What is the worst you could do?"

"Do you want to know?"

"If you're going to be this mysterious about it, yes." He makes another move on the board, confident as he leans back.

I'm lost on what else to talk about. How do I distract him without distracting myself? I take my turn a bit more hesitantly. He's still watching me with that hint of a smile, almost a smirk, on his face. I see the calculation in his eyes. How is he so alert at playing the game after so long?

"Who's on guard today?" I settle on as I finally make my move. "Sage or Daddy?"

Gavril chuckles, arms folded, relaxed yet firm as he watches me. "It depends on the hour. 'Daddy' is night watch most of the time. Sage is hanging around. Oh, then of course, Joy." He smiles at her, patiently sitting by my chair. Then he rolls his eyes. "They'd be mad that I told you that."

"Why? I'm not a threat," I say, bending over to move my scout into place to start testing which of the two places Damian suggested Gavril's flag might be.

Gavril rolls his eyes again. "Not if you ask them. Besides, they'd freak out if I told anyone that. It's not just you. Apart from maybe Joy." He looks over at where she's sitting next to me. It lets me sneak a bite of food.

I get a new idea. "How did you get the Dragians to come back to the table?"

"I assured them their princess was still a true princess even if she left first and a lot of speaking their language." He notices the question in my expression and goes on. "Yelling. They do a lot of yelling. I was as aggressive with them as they were with me, and they respected that. It wasn't fun, but I got through it. I had no voice the next day."

"Really?"

"Really, I had to sign to my staff, who don't sign by the way." He makes his move. To my annoyance, Gavril doesn't even hesitate. He's too confident. He must know exactly what I'm doing. I have to throw him off somehow.

"Were you disappointed when she left?"

"I pretended as much to them, but no. Between us, I'd rather not have my face sucked off."

I chuckle and move my next piece. We exchange this kind of casual talk for a while, but nothing I try really distracts him.

I try to keep my mind on the game as we exchange turns back and forth. He does manage to cut his way into my ranks, but he's not gotten close to anything valuable yet. My hope is to distract him, so he falls for a spy attack, and I can swap in my better pieces to track down his flag.

I try to talk about his father's health, the other delegations, how his father is planning to let him into some meetings, anything to get his mind off the game, but it does the opposite. He battles one of my pieces. I'm sure I have him with my eight, but he just smirks, calls it, and I toss it aside. I am worried he knows exactly where he's going. How does he know? He's really good.

In a flash, I figure it out. This talk doesn't distract him because that is why he's good at this. This game, along with chess, is a strategy training tool. When he's frustrated about not being able to do something, he gets good at something else. He can't help the real war, so he masters this instead.

I smile a little. "Well, I hope he does let you into those meetings. He has no idea what a good asset he's wasting."

"He's starting to, or so I hope. But now the delegations are over, and we enjoyed the show, I'm sure the new normal will start." He sighs. I can tell that means along with the next test.

"Not long now."

"Not long now." He nods, looking up at me with just his eyes.

"But I like how schooled you are," I say, trying to lean extra hard into my next move. "You're a great dancer. You play well. You have almost memorized star charts. You're really good at this game, or so I'm told. You are good at a lot of things. Even Joy thinks so." I smile down at the dog. She looks up with a wagging tail.

I clap to let her up onto my lap. She gets up in one try. She's getting so big. I smile and stroke her. I had finished eating, so I'm not worried she'll try to take my food. Gavril chuckles and makes his move.

"Don't believe me?" I pout.

"Well, when everyone says it but doesn't act like it, gets harder to buy." Gavril smiles at me apologetically.

"Like with the fencing?" I feel like a total jerk bringing it up, but it does make Gavril miss my next move.

The look Gavril gives me makes me drop it right away. I had gone too far. Joy tilts her head then barks at him.

"Reinold has ruined you," Gavril says to her.

"She's a dog, they bark." Reinold startles me by speaking. I didn't realize he hadn't left the room when he brought me in.

"She didn't bark at us like that until you came in acting all scared of her." To my disappointment, Reinold's interruption does not make him any less sharp in his moves.

As I watch him, I get a memory of Damian making the same move. He'd been showing me a type of defense known as a Mercutian defense. If I'm right.... I glance at where that means his flag is. It also means there's one way to get to it.

But would Gavril use that? I thought he was good at this game. Mercurian defense is a basic strategy used by inexperienced people because the only way to counter it is to use a spy swap and a diffuser.

"Sorry I mentioned it," I try to use that to distract him again. "I really didn't mean it like that."

Gavril's jaw tenses like he does when he's thinking something over. "Kascia, it isn't that I don't believe you." He pauses again to think over his words. "It's that I realized not even you can be perfectly open with me. No one can be until this is over. You must be 'perfect' in everyone's eyes just to get by. And I didn't and still don't want to put that on anyone. So, if I can avoid a flaw that will get you into trouble, I do. That pride might give my parents the excuse they need if it comes to it. It's not worth that to me." He moves a piece.

"Then what is?" I ask, looking up at him.

He smiles and meets my eyes. "Find out."

I freeze and look at the board. Is he... does it count if he knows what I'm doing and loses on purpose? Is he losing on purpose? Or is he sending a message? He is really... strange when he wants to be. He seems so childish like his parents think, but then he has these veiled messages and meanings I can't follow. Like how his nicknames for the girls have deeper meanings than was on the surface. He has the communication skills needed to freak out any delegation he wants.

"You can't throw the match on purpose."

"Am I though?" Gavril smiles again.

Damian is right; he is tricky. He is trying to get into my head. It makes a rush of emotions flood me. I find it quite attractive. I could throw the game and kiss him right now. It also makes me feel sorrier for him. He knows how to play the game. Why won't anyone trust him to?

It also annoys me. The little brat thinks he's got me pegged. It comes down to me reading this correctly. If I do, I think I'll win this. If not, I'll just have to keep fighting for it.

If his goal is to win, my idea is foolish. But if I understood what he'd said correctly, that's not his goal. What is his goal? He did say someone had to win. That means using an easy defense would ensure at least one girl won. But can I say for sure no one would expect Gavril to play such a simple plan?

If he is trying to win, using the spy swap I'd been planning would spell the end of the match for me. But if he's trying to throw the match, it's a stronger piece I can take out with either my biggest piece or my spy. Do I know him well enough to know which he's going for? Is Gavril going to play easy because he wants me that night, or is he going to throw himself into this and try to win all the matches?

I smile a little and take my mid-power piece and use it to take the one he moved. "Three," he says. I smile and take it off the board. Gavril smiles too. I smirk in confidence. I think I just won the match. He doesn't know where my flag is, but now I'm certain I know where his is.

"Yeah, I think you are," I say. "So, am I the favorite or not?"

"Am I allowed to tell you that?"

I give him a flirtatious smile as I bend closer as if in confidence. "No one wrote that rule down. Is Sage going to get mad if you do?"

"Should I care?" Gavril replies.

I move a piece before I sit up. "Well, you won't stand up to your parents."

"Unwillingness and accepting I have to try other ways are not the same," Gavril says as he sends a piece after mine.

"Oh, I see." I keep the pieces moving as rapidly as I can, so he doesn't have time to read my play. "So, you won't admit you're too chicken."

"Too sore," Gavril disagrees. "And I do try sometimes. I did literally walk out as my mother yelled at me not to go to the Dragian's suite."

"What did your father do?" I am glad Gavril is falling for the rapid movement.

"He told me 'no' then laughed once I left. I think he might be close to caving in, but we'll have to wait and see. So far, we just have been trying to recover after the craziest month we've had in a long time." Gavril moves a piece then looks at me as if in a challenge.

I move my piece into his ranks. I really hope I'm reading him right. "That is a good thing to do. But he has to start training you sooner or later."

"I hope sooner." Gavril takes the bait.

I smile. "Nope. Taken out."

Gavril falters. "Oh... I did read that wrong."

I smirk. "Yup, spy."

Gavril shakes his head and lets me pick up my piece and then puts up the shield, so I can swap out my spy with any piece I like. I take the divider down and put my new piece in as he puts his back in the pile. "I'm impressed. No one has managed to get that past me today. First spy swap I've seen today. Rather advanced tactics."

"Not even Zelda tried it?"

"She tried it. She failed," Gavril says. My heart skips. So, she lost? Would I be the only one to win if I pull it off? That makes excitement gush into my body. I might scrap the win.

"That's pretty gutsy."

Gavril nods. "Most played intense strategy." He's watching me. I think he's hoping to see me pull this off, but I can't be sure. What if he's as proud of his game skill as I was of my Custod fencing skill?

"How do you know I'm not?" I ask as I move another piece into his ranks.

"I'm finding out." Gavril grins. "But I don't think you're playing strategy." He puts a piece closer to my new piece.

"What am I playing then?"

"Me."

I put my diffuser onto a piece. "Bomb." He nods. He knows I have a diffuser. I can hear it in his tone. I take the piece out. Gavril then takes out my piece, so I use the scout I snuck in to get the piece that was behind the bomb.

Gavril gives me one of my favorite smiles before he meets my eyes. "Do I have to say it?"

"So, who do I have to share you with?" I smirk.

"No one. You're the only one to win." My smile matches his.

Chapter 22

I can hardly contain my excitement when I get back to my room. I try to behave as I close my bedroom door, biting my lip as I press my back to it. I can't stop the smile. I can't believe I did it. That I won a whole night. It can't come soon enough. I finally pull away from the door. I suppose it's now time for bed, but honestly, I can't imagine getting some sleep. I'm too excited. I notice my maids are gone. They must have gone to fetch my nightly tea.

"I take it, it went well," Damian says as he glances over at me.

I nod, still biting my lip. "We did it!" It was his training after all. "I won!" I can't believe it.

He smiles with happy pride in his eyes. "Congratulations, my lady." He bows his head to me.

I smile again. "I'm the only one who did."

"That's exciting." He smiles. "It'll just be you and him the whole day then."

I nod. Then pause. "Did you say day?"

"I did." He nods then sits back and arches a brow. "Is that a problem?"

"You mean... it's not just the ball?" I can hardly believe it.

"Well, he was allotting his time so as many girls who won had time with him on that day, and since there were no other winners, which would mean all his time goes to you," Damian explains. "Starting after breakfast the day of."

I cover my mouth to try to hide my reaction. Maybe it's nuts, but I actually am more excited than anything. Perhaps I should be worried about the other girls, but I won this fair and square. I fight to keep the feelings from exploding. I could just sing!

Damian takes a moment to watch me before asking, "How do you feel?"

I take a deep breath. "I don't know." Excited, elated, nervous, giddy, all of them?

"Is it good or bad?"

I bite my lip to hold in the giggle. "If it was that bad, I wouldn't have fought to win."

He chuckles. "I'm glad to hear you say it."

I can't stop the smile. I can't believe I did it. That I won the whole day. It can't come soon enough. I finally pull away from the door.

I can't shake my upbeat mood even into the next day. It's as if having earned the day fair and square made me feel not as bad being... for lack of a better term, into Gavril. I'd never found him distracting during meetings before today. Lilly giggles at me and asks what's got me in a good mood. I guess they didn't announce who won, and I am not going to say it. The girls can find out when it happens.

It doesn't help that the girls are mostly bubbling over about the show still. Isla most of all, saying it was even better than the first time. "The whole crew and updated cast were the best I've ever seen." Bella is almost as excited, declaring it the most beautiful thing she'd ever seen. She and others insist they cried several times.

I wonder how long this giddy bubble is going to last as we go back to lessons a few days later. I can hardly pay attention; my mind keeps floating off into daydreams about winning and about Flur's wedding tonight. Because of the show, she refused to hold the wedding over the rest days, but we insisted she take this following week off. I'm happier than I think I've ever been in the palace.

It is a small affair, though it's clear Damian (having more information about it than me) worked hard to make it special anyway. He had insisted on doing it no matter how much Flur said she'd be fine with something else. But the dress is, of course, perfect: a simple yet elegant A line with long sleeves that come to a point and a square neckline that outlines Flur perfectly with her long blonde hair flowing down her back with a white rose tiara attached to her veil, finer than she'd had without Damian for sure. Her sweet blush makes her all the more beautiful.

Karrigan's suit likely was done by Damian too with how perfectly they fit. Vivian also had brought her organizational skills and talent to the events too. The simple ceremony is held in the sanctuary that has a direct connection to the palace. I'm sure Damian had to talk the guards into letting me come. The other surprise is it isn't just another worker who runs the ceremony. Cedrick handles it with more poise and propriety than I'd ever seen from him. Flur seems to enjoy that, even if she's a bit embarrassed we're all making such a fuss. But if anyone deserved the fuss we're giving it, Flur does.

They look so happy, even with how small it all is. Karrigan can't stop smiling, and the flush on Flur's cheeks keeps growing. I'm not sure a bigger affair would have suited them. A few of her friends on staff are there, but clearly, I'm the highest ranked there, but I don't mind one bit. The first dance is simple and sweet, and watching Karrigan try to get Flur over her shyness by teasing her with the cake is also a sweet moment.

We see them off for their small honeymoon with hugs and rose petals before going to dinner. My dress is easily good enough for dinner, so I go straight there. I don't think anything could break my mood... until something changes.

The evening after the wedding, I notice Gavril is distracted. He is talking with his parents in a low voice, looking distractedly at his food or off towards the windows. He also is clearly trying to avoid looking at someone, but I can't tell who. Is there someone else he had a good time with today? I fight not to let my giddy bubble deflate.

The real reason is almost worse. On my way to my room, a servant stops me to warn me I'll have a visitor before bed, so I ought not to retire too early. That makes the knot in my stomach tighten. What would Gavril have to take me aside to speak about so formally? He is the only one who would need to talk to me so late.

I don't feel much better when I notice another one of the mysterious notes I get now and then. This one says:

Don't worry. I'm still fine. Good job with your assignments. Keep it up.

I'd feel better if I knew who they were from. I don't know the handwriting.

After what feels like forever, though it isn't long, there's a knock at the door. I nod at Vivian to let him in. But it's not Gavril.

I pause as Lilly comes into the room. When Vivian shuts the door behind her, Lilly bites her lip as if holding in tears before she runs at me and gives me a tight hug.

I frown. "Lilly?" I hug her protectively. "What's wrong?" She isn't allowed to be making visits any more than I am, so why is she here, and even more, why did a servant announce it?

She smiles as if in amusement as she pulls back to wipe her eyes. A different kind of dread fills my stomach. "Lilly, you didn't..."

"Fail? No. I didn't fail anything, but..." She looks down, clasping her hands in front of her properly, twisting her hands on opposite sides as she does. "I told him."

My stomach drops. "You told him you don't want to win?"

"Yes," she nods meekly, "over our game."

My brows furrow. "But that was days ago."

"I know. I told him I was scared to leave because of my father. He didn't have to dismiss me."

Anger rises in me. He didn't have to send her away, but he was anyway, and he took time to decide it? I never would have thought Gavril to be so cold. Lilly only had to hold on a bit longer to get into the top ten.

"Oh no, it's not like that," Lilly quickly corrects me at the expression on my face. "No, it's a good thing. But I have to explain." She looks down at her twisted hands. "I have to apologize to you."

"To me?" I frown.

"I made the whole thing with the Japcharians harder, and I didn't even know it."

I take a deep breath. "Here, we can sit," I invite her to the table and chairs Damian and Vivian pull out for meals or when visitors (normally Gavril) come to my room.

She smiles and nods a thank you as she accepts a seat, setting her hands delicately on her lap. She smiles warmly at me, more confident than I think I've ever seen her.

"Are you alright?" Her rapid change of mood frightens me. "What happened?"

"After the Japcharian delegation left, the princess left me a note, and my mother wrote me not long after, so excited for me. I am so sorry. I am the reason they were learning about us, about you." She goes a bit pink. "I wrote my mother in confidence about what was happening. My mother is the princess's fourth cousin apparently. I had no idea. She was telling Princess Tsikyria about what was happening. It's how she knew so much about you; I didn't mean to make her or anyone single you out."

That explains so much. "It's alright. At least it wasn't that they had a spy or anything." I smile.

"Yes," Lilly giggles. "But I told the prince all of this over our match. I told him everything: that I wanted to go home but feared how I'd be rejected."

"But if you made it to the top." I frown. "So why is he sending you away now?"

"Because I already have a connection to the Japcharian government." She looks up at me. "And besides princess, what more honorable position can I get than the main Japcharian ambassador?"

My jaw drops. "Gavril was able to guarantee that assignment?"

She smiles and nods. "It took him a few days, but yes, he did. Because of how they're feeling right now, I won't be able to start until the Enthronement is over."

"Then why not stay?"

"It's part of the reasoning in letting me go. They need the girl over Japcharia ready for their summit. I can't say when it will be, but it's soon, and the more time to prepare, the better. I'll be learning more of their culture and etiquette and educating myself on how to best serve as the ambassador so when the day comes, I'll be ready.

"And besides that, there's enough drama going on without a girl who isn't even going to try for him. It's better for everyone that way. Even if it means missing so much here for a time, and you." Lilly forces a smile. "But when it comes to ending this all, it's better for you."

"Me?"

"He can have more time for the one he really wants."

"Would you stop it? It's not about that right now." I frown.

Lilly smiles. "It always is. They want it to look like I failed; they didn't want me to tell anyone, but I begged the prince to allow it, and I think he only just convinced his parents over dinner to let me. I didn't want you to worry why he eliminated me."

I nod, heart sinking. I got along with other girls, but Lilly is the one I really joined the social circles for. She'd been like a little sister to me. Defending her from the other girls gave me a place in that social dynamic. Without it, what did I do?

"Guess I'll make better friends with my maids," I joke.

Lilly frowns. "Not everyone is worth hiding from. What about Bella and Azalea?"

I shrug, and honestly, I don't really want to talk about that when I don't know when I'll see her again. "Either way, I'll miss you."

"You're not angry with me?" Lilly asks tentatively.

"No," I smile, "of course not. I'm not angry at all; I just... I-I'll miss you."

"I know. Me too." Lilly manages a watery smile as tears come to her eyes. "It's the only reason part of me doesn't want to go, but I can't stay forever."

I nod. "It's alright. It is the best choice for you. And I'm happy for you. I just wasn't expecting to have to say goodbye so soon." I really had subconsciously told myself she'd at least stick around until the top ten. With her leaving, it brings us down to eleven girls. One away from that coveted number. "You're sure your father won't be upset?"

"Maybe a little, but the fact I will have about the highest position possible without winning will certainly bring him around. Mother is already so excited. She called her mother down to help me learn their ways. Father can't complain, and with such a position, whatever husband comes around will certainly be the kind he's asking."

"And you'll like him too." I try to make it sound less like just another bonus to make her father happy.

Lilly shrugs. "Maybe. I'm not really thinking about it. After all this with Gavril, I'm not sure I really want to play that game yet. Just look at you two. Giddy then glaring at each other then just plain sad."

I can't help but laugh.

"And as harsh as it sounds, those ones seem more real. I do want to marry one day, but I don't think I'm ready for that drama or commitment." She smiles widely at me. "And it gives you more reason to win, right? Then I'll still get to work for you, and it also means for sure I'll get to come to the wedding, right?"

"Why do you think I need more reasons?"

Lilly blushes. "Well... you're not exactly always sure."

It's my turn to flush. She's not exactly wrong. "Still, doesn't mean you need to give me more reasons."

"If that were the only reason, I'd not bother, but that just is a bit of a bonus with all this." Lilly smiles again. "And right now, you don't seem to need one. I'm sure he was teasing you yesterday, and you've been so happy. Did he finally kiss you not in public?"

I bite my lip, holding in the laugh. "No, I beat him."

"You won the game?" Lilly brightens. "Do you know who else won?"

She's not in the Enthronement anymore; I think I can tell her. "No one. He said I was the only one."

Lilly giggles. "You get the whole day." I nod. "See? It's not all bad, and with me gone, that's only ten more girls you have to prove you're more of a princess than." That makes it sound much more frightening. I don't think I can prove more of a princess than Zelda or Princess Rose. "See? You make that face." Lilly frowns. "You seem so sure then you make that face, and it's like all the reasons to believe it disappear. Why?"

I wish I could tell her. "Thank you for at least telling me," I deflect instead. "I don't know what I'd do if I thought you'd suddenly failed. Can... I write you about it?" I ask.

"Of course. No rules say you can't." Lilly smiles. "Though I don't know if anyone has. But you're free to write me as much as you like."

"I'd like that." I manage another weak smile. I can't believe this is really happening. I knew it had to sooner or later, but I just can't take in that it's real. I really thought Lilly would last longer. "I'm sure you could win this, if you wanted to."

"Not when there is only one position at the top. I couldn't ever outshine you," Lilly says.

I bow my head. "Yes, you could."

"Not to him." Lilly smiles. "He really does favor you; you know."

I bow my head. "I'm not so sure. It's not like I get a lot of dates."

"Most girls get one date a week, except?" Lilly prods.

"For me."

"Because he already knows how he feels about you. Stop worrying. I'll send you daily reminders if I have to." Lilly smiles. I smile too. She'd grown a lot from the girl who was scared of Dahlia's bullying. She is ready to move on from here.

"You're going to do amazing with the Japcharians," I say. "Even if you weren't related to them." Lilly giggles. "Just..." I shouldn't tell her. It might stress her, and I promised only to tell Gavril because the princess asked me to. "Don't expect it to be easy."

"I know. They were a hard delegation. I expect their actual court will be worse," Lilly agrees. "But I'm ready to try a new challenge and to use what I learned in all my lessons here."

I nod. "Well..." If this was it, this was it. "When do you leave?"

"In the morning. Most of the time, they slip us out first thing before breakfast, so none of the other girls see."

They'll notice Lilly's empty spot in the morning. Oh no, that means I move to the top side of the table with the born princesses. I try not to think of Jonquil's glare. And I'll be further from the head table, making distracting myself harder.

"Well, make sure to say bye to Nippers," I joke. "He'll get mad."

Lilly laughs. "I will." She gives me a watery smile before getting up to hug me. I hug her tightly. I can't believe I might not see her again. If I lose... there is little to no chance I'd see her again. "I'll write you as soon as I settle in," she promises.

"I'll write back as soon as I get it," I vow. "Stay safe."

"Don't worry; we get our own guard as ambassadors. I don't need you all the time." Lilly giggles, hugging me tighter before we let go. "But... thank you."

"I'll miss it," I say honestly.

"If you can't win for yourself, try for me," Lilly says.

I take a deep breath. I hope adding another person to that list helps get it through my head. "I'll try my best," I promise.

Lilly gives me one more hug before we have to go to bed. "I'll talk to you soon. It's not forever," she tries to assure me. I nod. I'm going to have to fight to believe that. Why is it so hard?

"I'll talk to you soon," I promise too before the guard gives us a look, saying it is time to go. I nod and give Lilly a tearful smile. She's fighting tears harder than I am. She waves as the guard sees her back to her room. I wave back but have to look away before she turns the corner, and I start to cry. It is like I am losing my only sure ally in all of this. But it had to happen sooner or later, and at least I have something to look forward to.

Damian leaves his workstation and pulls me into a hug. I smile a little as I return it. "Who do I trust now?" I ask. Jonquil's betrayal really stings right now. It is like her actions made it, so I cannot trust anyone who wants to win.

"Those with good intentions, who are in it for something more than themselves, and even some that are not. It is no sin to want to marry a prince. What girl wouldn't?" Damian smiles a little. "So don't be afraid. Many of the remaining girls are good people at heart, and you can trust them because they care about you. Kascia, you are not as limited in friends as you might think.

"But I do understand your fear. Your friend, Jonquil, betrayed your trust, and that hurts," he says sympathetically. "But her kind is rare in this competition. She appears fair on the outside, but I fear she has... more selfish and harmful reasons for her presence here. I am sorry you were hurt by her, but I would not let her example poison your trust with your other friends. I highly doubt any of them would do the same as she did."

I bite my lips. "I just don't know how much more I can take until this is over." I just wish it would end.

"I know. It hurts to lose a friend," he says, his eyes shining. "But those you truly love and who truly love you are not gone forever. And for those who don't love you back..." he sighs, "all I can say is the hurting does pass, and the wounds do heal in time."

I nod and hug him again. He knows this pain even more than me. He holds me tight. "It hurts to say goodbye, but the Merlin showed us that no goodbye is final, and all wrongs will be made right in the end. And there is hope in that," he says softly.

I smile a bit. That is true. I nod. "I just wish I... I just want to know how it ends."

He smiles. "We all do sometimes. But once we get there, we find it was worth the wait of not knowing."

I'll have to hold to that. I sigh in a kind of relief as my mind just accepts it finally happened. One of my friends has left. It will be the first of many. It's mostly my friends left after all. This pain is going to become more common, and I'm going to have to get used to it.

Chapter 23

The next morning is uncomfortable. At least they only took Lilly's place away and didn't move me to the other side of the table. That leaves me closer to the high table. Still, Forsythia and Florence are freaking out Lilly is gone. "What test did she fail?" Florence keeps asking over and over. The other girls look worried too. Zelda asks if I'm okay. I smile and nod. At least someone cares.

Ericka is almost giddy. I really hate her.

One more girl before the top ten. Florence is terrified it will be her, and her fear seems self-fulfilling to me.

Gavril is trying to meet my eyes, and I finally look at him as everyone settles into breakfast. He gives me a weak smile, clearly checking if I'm alright. I give him a formal nod to avoid attention, but yes, I'm alright.

Just before the first girl is done eating, the king makes a strange announcement. "The royal family will not be in the palace tomorrow," he says. The girls start whispering to one another instantly, but the king ignores it. "We're going to help prepare some of the coastal fields for planting. The farmers asked for some extra help. If you'd like, you ladies can join us. In fact, we'd love to have you. Inform your attendants if you wish to join us, so the guards can prepare for it. I just wanted to make sure you all know you're invited."

With no extra explanation, the king sits back down. I blink. Was there ever such an obvious test? I look around. Most girls look relieved. Florence whispers something to Isla. Isla frowns and shakes her head. I still can't hear what Florence is saying. I frown and look down the table at the others. Zelda just smiles at me. I don't think any of us are falling for it. I sigh. Well, at least we'll all be safe for now. Unless Florence loses her head completely.

I spend more time in the library trying to find evidence of the prophecy Father spoke of. I'd lost a lot of time being busy with the delegations and the show, but no matter how intently I look, I still haven't found anything.

When I reach my room, I'm still trying to get over how obvious of a test this activity was. After all, like Queen Esther, a true princess is happy to serve.

Damian is a bit tense as he bends over his work. He doesn't say anything, but I can almost feel the annoyance coming off him. I frown. "Damian?" I ask carefully. "Are you okay?"

"Just peachy," he says, his voice dripping with annoyed sarcasm.

"What's wrong?" I ask.

Damian lets out a frustrated sigh and sits back, still not looking at me. "I'm not really supposed to talk about it."

I giggle. "Is this about the test?" We all know it's a test.

Damian finally looks at me. "I can't confirm that."

"Okay, so what's wrong with... it?" I leave it vague.

"The simple declaration, that's what," he huffs. "Are they bloody idiots? I mean, really?"

I nod. "Well... they always announce activities like that."

"But they didn't have to. It isn't like it's a requirement," Damian says.

"Well, how would you do it? I was wondering the same," I admit.

"Simple. You have a servant, or perhaps each ladies' maids or attendant mention it and ask for their help."

I nod. "That would work. They tell you anyway," I agree. "But either way, it sounds like a nice way to spend the day." I bite my lip. Why am I excited at the idea of seeing Gavril working? Then I realize why and blush and try not to look at anyone.

Damian tilts his head and arches a brow. "What?"

"Nothing." I try to be good about it.

Damian gives me that knowing smile of his. "Nothing is *ever* nothing."

I laugh. "Nothing important." Or should I share?

I search for a distraction. "So, I'm guessing Sage will have a harder time hiding. The security will be a nightmare. Maybe we'll see Zelda's gargoyle guard for once." But the joke brings a question to mind. "Why doesn't Gavril have a gargoyle guard? How did Sage get the job when he's normally an assassin?"

"He wanted to get married, but the Head Custod believed he needed to show he was committed first. So, if he wanted approval to marry, he had to accept and serve six months here with Gavril," Damian explains.

"Oh." I feel like that time is up, but perhaps he just wants to see the job through the Enthronement. That makes sense. I don't see Sage ditching without the mission being "done". "Gavril mentioned him being engaged."

"Yes, he was." Damian nods.

I nod. It seems odd he said "was", but I'm not sure I want to dwell on the matter much. But then I realize it. "Oh, so that's why his father is here."

Damian nods. "That's why. You see, Sage's time should have been done in September. He stayed on of his own choice, but his fiancée was not pleased. She gave him an ultimatum, and still, he chose to stay. His family became worried and told him to come home. When he still remained here, his father decided to come to 'solve' whatever Sage felt he needed to accomplish, so his son would go home."

I blink. "What? Ultimatum?" That doesn't mean.... Does it? "So, they're all trying to get him to go home." So why does he want to stay?

"No, his fiancée moved on. As I heard it, when he didn't come home after his six months, she struck up a serious relationship elsewhere," Damian says plainly.

"What?" That fast? I couldn't believe that. I couldn't have done it. "Just like that?"

"Yes." Damian smiles a little. "Frankly, I think it saved him from a woman who wasn't committed."

"And they sent him here to prove he was committed." I manage a small smile. It does make me wonder where his mother is then. If his father is worried enough to come after him, where's his mother? Then again, for all I know she's gone.

"Indeed. So, his father is worried why Sage is ruining his life as he sees it," Damian says. "Which is why his father is going a bit mad. Sage tells me he isn't normally like this."

"They can't just unassign him?" I ask. "I thought Custods had to follow orders."

"They could. But obviously, they haven't. I think the Head is just happy someone is finally happy serving here."

I smile a bit. "I suppose that's true. I just... if he loved her, why?" I can't imagine doing that.

"That, I can only offer my own speculation on," Damian admits. "But I think he honestly cares for Gavril and sees he is the only one who will fight for him to have the ability to choose. If you'll remember during the conversation when Dahlia failed, Sage mentioned it was he who fought for Gavril's right to dismiss any girl at any time with or without reason. And it was he who wrote it into the rules of the contest."

I nod a bit. That makes sense. "Still, giving up the woman you wanted to be with. He took this miserable job he's not even trained for to be with her."

"Love can work in strange ways. We think of love between lovers or between parents and children, but love forms unlikely friends and binds them together in such a way that cannot be broken by any sword or circumstance. The Merlin loved his brother in such a way. He would do anything to ensure his happiness. And the brother in turn would do the same, no matter the odds or the cost. I believe Gavril and Sage have formed a similar bond. So, Sage asked his lover to wait a little while longer to help his brother," Damian says poetically.

I smile a little. "I guess when you put it like that, it's more like how could she not wait for him?" Or come here, but I guess if she was flighty enough to be off with someone else already, she'd be too much of a coward to come here.

Damian smiles. "I would agree."

I think it over for a moment. "And why leave now if there's nothing at home waiting for him?" Why would his father think Sage is nuts for not wanting to come home now? I know I wouldn't.

Damian shrugs. "Perhaps he doesn't see that Sage has changed. He only is reminded of the boy who didn't want to come here. And now the girl he was staying here for is gone, he doesn't understand why Sage stays in a place he hates."

"Guess he doesn't listen to Sage any better than he listens to us." I smile. He hadn't bothered me since I dug my heel into his foot.

"No, I doubt not." Damian smiles. "Though... there could be one other reason Sage stays."

"He needs more of a reason?" I ask.

"No, but it provides a deeper understanding of what may be happening here," Damian says. "Granted, I have no conclusive evidence on this end. It is pure speculation, but if it has happened, it would certainly strengthen my argument that Sage and Gavril share a strong bond."

"If... what happened?" I ask, now worried.

"Well... are you familiar with how Custods can swear themselves to an individual or group?" Damian asks.

I nod. A Custod can swear on their magic to someone to ensure an oath is upheld. If they fail, they lose their will to the person they swore to. I bite my lip as Damian pauses. He can't be saying what I think he is, can he?

"If Sage had sworn himself to Gavril in any way, his magic would focus him here until his promise is fulfilled," he says after a moment of silence.

"He can't have... can he?" Sage didn't seem like his personality and mind was gone like in the stories.

"It's very possible. And Custods have been known to do it before. As it undoubtedly was a willing promise, so there'd be no evidence of it unless Sage fails to keep his word," he explains.

I swallow and nod. "Why?" I have to ask. I would be terrified to bind myself to anyone that way. Even a mistake could doom me.

"To gain Gavril's trust," Damian says simply. "Of course, Gavril could release him from it at any point as well, promise fulfilled or not. But I believe if it *did* happen, Sage would have done it to show Gavril his level of commitment, in which case, Gavril would have to know Sage had done it, or it would have meant nothing, and the point would be missed."

I bite my lip. "I hope not." I don't like the idea of Sage trapped here. I doubt Gavril likes it any more than I do.

"Again, this is just speculation. The only way to know is to ask them," Damian says.

I chuckle. "Would you dare ask?" I tease.

Damian thinks a moment, tilting his head to the side then straightens up and smiles. "Yes."

I roll my eyes. Of course, he would. "I'm not going there." He smiles and shrugs and turns back to his work.

As he turns, Vivian comes over to help me get ready for my afternoon training. Thankfully, my music distracts me pleasantly. But I can't help but think about it every time I see Sage guarding Gavril around the castle, at meals, or whenever I see them in passing. They were like brothers. Was it just that connection? I'm not sure I wanted to know, but I can't help but wonder about him and honestly his sanity if his family is hounding him to leave and he's still here. If his mother is still alive, at least she isn't here. I am not sure how anyone would say no to a woman who was better at being the dark assassin Sage was. I just better hope we'd never get that far. I feel like she'd uncover my secrets in a heartbeat.

The day of the "not test", my staff dresses me in one of my favorite outfits yet, not for how it looked, but because it is just so comfortable. They put me in work leggings, tall sturdy boots, a short-sleeved base shirt with a well-fitted waistcoat that's the Purerahian blue I love so much, decorated with gold vine designs. I wear a dark golden-brown jacket to finish off the look. Vivian braids my hair nicely, so it's stylish but also out of the way for the work we're doing. I wonder if I should have a heavier coat, but as we'll be working, I'm sure I'll warm up in no time. I have leather gloves in one of the pockets of my jacket just in case. I'm really looking forward to the event.

We join the others in the entrance hall to arrange safe transport for all the girls. They planned this so last minute, I doubt any rebels uncovered our plan. It's nice to be outside. I take up a carriage with Zelda, Bella, and Azalea.

Bella makes it a point to sit next to me. When Azalea and Zelda are chattering about the views out the window, she turns to me. "Are you alright?" she asks quietly.

"What?" I turn to her. I hadn't expected her to speak to me at all. I'd be lost in the view of the city from a distance.

"Lilly was your best friend here. I'm sure it's hard with her gone." Bella frowns. "I just wanted to make sure you're okay."

I smile, grateful. "Thanks, but I'm fine." My heart sinks. What if she is fishing for information to use against me? How do I know who means their care and who does not?

"Really?" Bella gives me a disbelieving look that makes me laugh. "Just because we're both invested in this game doesn't mean we have to be rude. You were really shaken up after what Jonquil did. I just don't want to see you get lonely before you have to."

"It happens sooner or later. Either you win and are alone or shoved back to your old life."

Bella frowns deeper. "Kascia, really, are you okay?" She puts a hand on my shoulder. I look back at her, wondering the best way to act my way out of this. But the honest look of concern in her eyes is hard to shake. "I can't pretend I don't want to win, but I don't want that to be at the expense of girls like you. You've been kind to all of us, even when some of us were horrible to you. I still can't believe you gave Ericka advice on being herself the first day."

I laugh at the memory.

"You didn't do anything to Jonquil either after she was so bluntly rude to you when you didn't deserve it. Dahlia did. Jonquil had no reason to side with her other than that most of the girls think they have to take you out to win," Bella goes on. "I can't imagine how lonely this must make you. I just want you to know you don't have to be alone. I want whoever wins to know they have friends in the other girls. You'll likely have to work with them, after all, right?"

"Right."

"If it were me, I'd want you close to help." Bella blushes as red as her shirt. I can't help but laugh. "What? You're good at this. That's the real reason they're all scared of you."

"It's because I have the only public kiss," I disagree.

"That may have started it, but that's not why." Bella gives me another disbelieving look that makes me laugh. "You impressed the dignitaries, and apparently, the court is even whispering about it being you."

"They hardly know us." Other than the creepy Grand Duke.

"Which is why they whisper. They're just like the foreigners. They want the next princess to like them. And from what I'm hearing, you're on that list."

"Why are you listening?"

"You don't know?" Bella smiles. "I'll at least be in the top ten." I laugh at her cockiness. "I want them to like me too. I'm not able to really work with them yet, but I can listen. I'm surprised you don't know that already."

"I haven't really thought about what happens after." Any direction other than winning scares me. Thinking and hoping to win, only to have those dreams smashed again is not a trial I can take a second time.

"I'm only trying to say I want to help. It doesn't do me any good to treat you badly. Any true lady knows that. Doesn't that fact comfort you enough to trust someone?" It's hard not to believe the genuine concern and sadness in her eyes. "Don't you want a friend?"

I can't lie and simply nod.

"Then why can't we be friends, during and after what happens? Wasn't it you who said we should be friends, so we can help each other in whatever position this throws us into?" I think that was something I said. "So be princess or ambassador or courtier or even go home to your old job, we can still support each other. I hope you'll believe that." Bella frowns. "It's sad to see you close up more. You were pretty fun at games."

I laugh. She smiles and starts talking more causally, trying to help me feel comfortable with her again. She's good at it, but part of me is still unsure, but I'd rather trust than be guarded.

The carriage pulls up to surprisingly green fields rolling towards some sharp hills on one side and sloping down to the coast on the other. There's a manmade levee to protect the farm. It's beautiful.

Several farm workers are already about their day. "They're cute." Bella takes my arm, clearly trying to cheer me up. For some reason, it makes my heart glow. I try not to tear up. She gasps. "Do you think the prince will be wearing something like that?"

The farm hands wear rough looking shirts with short sleeves or longer sleeves rolled up and buttoned into place. They aren't tucked into their sturdy-looking work pants which are mostly a dark blue variation. The colors of the shirts varied from an off-white to many lighter colored patterns that are intended to match their dark pants. I can imagine their wives are the ones who try to get that to work.

"Could be anything," I manage to reply as she looks around.

"Come on, ladies," a man who looks like he must be the lead farmer today calls to us.

"Wow, that's a lot of flowers." Ericka points out one area of the trees that are covered in pink flowers. "I wonder what they are."

"Peaches." Zelda smiles.

"Really?" I frown.

"Really. They flower early, and this season has so far been good," Zelda says.

"Oh no," Forsythia sighs.

I look over to see two familiar faces. Fabian and Adam are walking around the fields. Adam, the impressionist both Fabian and the palace like to hire for public impressions, is already taking impressions while Fabian takes notes.

"Do they have to make it a show?" Zelda sighs.

The press must be getting anxious not getting anything from us in over a month. They had the Christmas special and nothing since. Christmas feels like a lifetime ago.

"We could do another round of interviews," Forsythia complains, "instead of them watching us during a test."

"Shh," Florence hisses.

Perhaps the two members of the press were the real test. Florence is looking at them with a determined look on her face. Maybe she has the same thought as me as she boldly goes to greet them.

"Well, are you ready, my pigeons?" Gavril's voice carries on the morning air. It had been a while since I'd heard him address us by our group nickname. He walks over to us with a smile. There's already dirt on his arms. He's wearing a short sleeve shirt, as Bella hoped, showing off the trim features he has worked hard for. He has tucked his white and blue shirt into his dark blue work pants, but he let the pants hang over his boots unlike some of the other workers.

I'm not the only one admiring his arms as he joins us. I glance around, and I'm pretty sure everyone is enjoying the eye candy of Gavril in work clothes, apart from maybe Princess Rose.

"I'm ready," Bella says, but her tone makes me think she doesn't mean about getting to work. Azalea hits her other arm with a giggle.

Gavril frowns in confusion. Poor innocent prince has no idea what we're distracted by. "Well, there's plenty to do," he says after looking us over in confusion. "We'll let you pick your assignments from the list or be assigned. What would you rather, my ladies?"

No one dares pick their own, perhaps worried it might cause them to be failed. I don't have a clue what would be most fun, so I have no opinion.

Gavril goes over the list and starts breaking us up into groups. I can tell he's trying to keep those girls who get along together. He sends Jonquil far away from me. He sets Zelda, Bella, and I to help with thinning the flowers of the peach trees.

This is a lot of work, but it's not hard. We have to carefully help remove some of the dozens of blossoms on the tree to give the fruit enough space to grow to proper size for sweet-tasting peaches.

"Lady of the Peaches!" Bella declares before she dumps her small basket of thinned flowers over my head.

"Hey!" I laugh.

A few minutes later, Bella does the same to Zelda which encourages us to dump ours on her head. Our laughter and teasing amuse the dozens of farm hands also working on the thinning.

"They are lovely flowers. Maybe we can make a collar of them for Joy," Bella suggests when we get back to work on our trees.

"Doubt they'll last that long," I point out.

"Could make it for the day. She's over there in the field working the soil with the prince." Bella points over to one of the fields below us. I look down to see her unmistakable red and white fur against the dark earth that Gavril and the king are working on tilling. Joy is rolling around in it and digging at random.

"She'd roll them off in the dirt," I point out. "Don't know if the flowers are good for the soil."

"Hmm. Well, it was a thought." Bella shrugs. "I suppose the pink may not go well with her red/brown fur." She smiles at me. "But it works to make your eyes stand out." She throws a few more at me. I laugh.

After a few hours, they have us trade out jobs. A new group comes to help with the thinning, and we go over to the apple orchard to help prune the trees.

"We're wondering if you more nimble ladies could try to get to the top," the worker says.

"Sure." And before anyone can object, I've swung up into the trees. Father thought tree climbing both fun and a good way to strengthen my body for Custod work. I could get to the top ones easily enough.

"They have ladders!" Zelda laughs at me.

"Kascia!" Bella laughs.

The farmer, chuckling, tells us what to look for and hands me the needed tools. I climb to the top of one tree. The others watch in amusement.

"The top branches are where it's the worst," the farmer directs me. "Careful, they get weak up there."

"Are you sure we should let her climb?" Zelda frowns.

"What's the worst that could happen?" I tease.

"A fall," Bella says instantly.

"Or she could get stuck like a cat," Zelda suggests. We all laugh.

Once I'm at the top, I start clipping off the branches like the farmer directed. Zelda opts to stay down lower as we go. "Most girls use the ladders, so we have trouble getting the inner branches," the leader says.

"Leave it to these girls to do something different." Gavril joins us. He's taking off his gloves as he watches us. "Oh, we finished with the plowing portion," he tells the farmer. "Where do you want us next?"

"Looks like the king is still at it," the farmer says. Gavril sighs. I hold in a giggle.

"Maybe he is, or he's just playing it up," Gavril says. "But what else would you like us to handle?"

"Well, you want to see about hauling these piles off?" the farmer says. "Unless you can't..." He stops as Gavril picks them up, no problem and puts them into the wagon that was waiting.

Bella stops working to watch him for a moment. I giggle harder. It makes the tree shake and draws Gavril's attention. "Uh, Mr. Triticum, I think you have a songbird in your tree." We all giggle, and I sing a few prettier notes from the bluebird in *Sleeping Beauty*.

"What are you all doing?" Reinold and Godwin join us. Godwin leans on the wagon Gavril just put a load into.

"There's a songbird in the tree," Bella says to him.

"Hmm, the problem I think will be getting her down. She climbed right up there and hasn't gotten down yet." Mr. Triticum smiles. "Hard worker, that one."

"A bit wild if you ask me," Reinold says.

"Perhaps," Godwin chuckles, giving his brother a sideways look that I can't read.

"Or she just likes being allowed to climb a tree." Gavril is still watching me. I bite my lip. I can play that game too.

"How do you get a songbird down?" Zelda teases.

"Shoot it." Sage mutters, clearly annoyed. Zelda rolls her eyes and hits his arm with the stick she'd picked up from the ground.

Gavril gives him a look too. "Why don't you go get it down?"

"No thank you. I will enjoy its song," Sage says dryly. I keep up the game, singing the notes. Sage gets the reference and gives me a look.

It's fun to tease Sage out here in the safety of the real world and the trees. It's even more fun to tease Gavril too. Maybe I'm being too confident. The sight of Gavril looking casual and dirty from working isn't helping. I think that's why Zelda is a bit giddy too.

"Is that the test? See who can get Kascia down?" Bella jokes.

"How would that test a true princess?" Gavril asks.

"I guess it's more like getting a fair princess down from her tower or glass hill, or in this case, her magic tree." Zelda smiles. Bella doesn't seem to appreciate the joke, frowning slightly.

"Oh, so it's me we're testing now," Gavril teases.

"I think you'd be too heavy to reach her," Mr. Triticum chuckles.

"Well, if you say it like that." Gavril grins, quite ready to take the challenge. I adore that smile. He got that mischievous smile from his father.

I sigh dramatically, "I don't think the pampered little prince could reach me." Zelda laughs.

The challenge lights in Gavril's eyes. It's so like his father. I giggle and make my way to try to climb further away. "Hey, that's not fair. She can keep running," Gavril jokes.

"There are easier ways," Bella hints.

"Like what?" Gavril gives her a smile that makes me a bit envious.

"Well, she'll get hungry," Bella teases. "Does she like berries or fruits?"

"Chocolate." Gavril looks back at me. I see the flash of disappointment in Bella's eyes.

Guilt creeps into my stomach, but it shouldn't. She just wants to win just like me. It's not like Gavril's only girl is in the tree. He could play that game with her. I do respect that she chose not to say it so bluntly though. Unlike Jonquil who would just tell him to forget me.

"I am without a bow or a horse that can climb glass," Gavril muses. "And her hair is not that long, and she doesn't want to come down."

"How do you attract a songbird?" Zelda smiles. "Some Hyvian birds will come to you if you play or sing music they like."

Gavril turns pink. I grin. He is not going to do that in front of everyone. I'd pay to see him dare though. He's far too shy.

"I feed the birds to keep them away," Mr. Triticum chuckles. "I doubt ladies are so easily swayed."

"Some are." Gavril smiles over to where Joy is having far too much fun rolling in the dirt. Gentian was put in charge of her and is not happy about it.

Sage follows his eyes and chuckles. Zelda's eyes light up. "You may not have a horse, but you do have a faithful sidekick."

Gavril's eyes light up. He whistles. Joy lifts her head, ears straight up. She's so cute. She bounds over and jumps up, getting dirt on Gavril's pants. He ignores it. "Find it," Gavril says as an order. Joy sits, tail wagging in delight. "Find Kascia."

Joy's ears go up in delight once again. She stands and looks around, sniffing all the girls. Mr. Triticum gets a lot of sniffing around his boots. But then she looks up and sees me. She makes two huff sounds I assume are "found it" and then howls up at me excitedly. I don't come down. She whimpers and looks at Gavril then back at me and barks.

Gavril laughs. "Oh no, did squirrels get her?" he hints.

I glare at him as poor Joy loses her little mind. She barks, yips, "talks" and does some worried zoomies before coming to the bottom of the tree to bark at the "squirrels" that must be holding me up here.

"Gavril!" The poor thing is so worried.

"Well, you better come down and show you're fine then." Gavril grins.

"You are impossible," I say.

"She is. She doesn't like squirrels," Gavril says.

I huff and glare at him. He really is such a little... I'll use Damian's word, twit. Little teasing, conniving, tricky, little prince. He doesn't have to drive his sweet dog mad over this. I sigh and start making my way down. Then, I get a better idea. I hope my skills hold from doing such tricks on stage. I try to hang off one arm to scoop the dog up and take her with me instead.

Gavril's too quick. He catches me around the waist and pulls me down before I can get away. Joy barks, tail wagging in happiness to see me "safe". We're both laughing as he pulls me away. He sneaks a kiss on my cheek before he lets go. "I got my songbird!" he declares.

"And the poor dog is appeased." Zelda pets Joy before pulling back with a face. "You are dirty," she informs Joy.

Joy doesn't care. She yips in happiness and tries to lick my face. I laugh. "Yes, yes, you both saved me from the squirrels," I assure her. Joy makes her "I love you" sound, flopping and rolling around at my feet in delight.

"She really likes you." Gavril smiles.

"She did pick her," Bella points out.

"True," Gavril agrees. He holds in a bit of an extra grin. I narrow my eyes a little as I watch him. What is he up to?

"Well, I think you all handled the trees perfectly. Hopefully they'll be right and ready for the spring growth and fall harvest." The farmer smiles. "Ready to try some other tasks?"

"Perhaps we can divert Father from plowing the fields we already finished," Gavril suggests.

"I would think helping trim hedges and inspect fencing would be a good way to keep him busy as well as yourselves," Mr. Triticum suggests.

That's when I notice Fabian still hanging around. Adam isn't too far, taking impressions of girls as they work, the land we're working on, and whatever else he seems to think would be helpful. Fabian is still taking notes. I wonder if Florence made the good impression she hoped for.

I expect Fabian to walk over to us, but instead he just hangs around. Zelda notices too as we start on the first hedge. "He was talking to other girls. I felt sure he'd try to talk to us." She frowns. "What do you think he's up to?"

"I don't know. He does seem willing to do whatever it takes for a crazy story." I watch him nervously too.

"Oops." I look over to see Bella tripping over a large root. Gavril catches her though, making her giggle and blush. I can't help but notice Adam getting an impression. I sigh. I can't be mad at her. She wants to win too, but it doesn't make this any easier.

"Maybe we should keep you with my father instead of where the roots come after you," Gavril teases her warmly.

"I can handle some plants," she defends herself.

"Alright, just don't hurt yourself," he says. "You don't have allergies or anything, do you?" Bella tries to hide it, but I see annoyance in her eyes. She's a bit offended at the hint. "Could make it a bit harder to be alert while working out here," Gavril explains, probably thinking she's just embarrassed. "You're not exactly clumsy," he grins and says quietly, "not like Florence." We all laugh.

"I'll be more careful," Bella assures Gavril with a grateful smile. The adoration in her eyes forces me to turn away. I hear a grunt from Zelda though, clearly not approving of whatever followed next. I don't know if I want to know.

"If you're done flirting, I could use a hand over here," the king calls us over.

"Oh, sorry." Gavril vaults the fence to join his father on the other side.

"Oh wow." Bella sighs.

"What?" Zelda laughs.

She gives Zelda look like she's crazy. "You knew he could do that?"

"Look at his arms. How could he not?" Zelda replies logically. She smiles a bit though as Sage follows Gavril the same way.

I hold in my own laugh. It didn't surprise me at all. Gavril can vault a fence, no problem with how he all but threw himself over the piano to get to me. I let my mind relive the fun moment for a while until I'm distracted by a branch hitting my foot.

"Sorry," Bella says, grabbing it as if that makes it better. "I should be watching where I'm trimming." She is smiling at Gavril still.

"Keep your goo-goo eyes on the plants, so they don't land on me," I tease. "Or you can trim this spot on your own."

"It's hard to pay attention with the view." She giggles. "Don't you think?" She raises her brows, clearly trying to get me into the excitement with her. It reminds me of Alsmeria. But in all honesty, her desire to get me excited mostly confuses me.

"Yes, yes, he's very cute, but not enough to risk a finger over," Zelda chides Bella.

"I would agree," Damian says, coming over. He's clearly been working as dust has settled in his hair, and there is dirt under his fingernails. But he has not really dressed for farm work. He's still wearing his usual white button up shirt and slacks, though he exchanged his formal shoes for work boots, and his sleeves are pushed up to the elbows. He's also wearing a plain work vest. He moves over to Bella and holds out his hand. "Here. You can keep staring, but I'd rather you not have those shears while you do."

Bella giggles back and replies as she hands them over, but I don't hear what she says. My eyes are locked on Damian's forearms. Like Gavril, Damian always wears a suit, so I have never seen them before. At least not up close or in good light. It's not that his forearms are strong, though they look it. It's the marks on them. His wrists have scars on them, deeper on one side versus the other. And along his arms at random places are scars like the ones that cover Gavril's back.

I close my mouth which had opened slightly as I yank myself together. Now is not the time to draw attention to the scars, no matter how they happened. I remind myself to conceal and transform, to shove the feeling away and put on the performance.

I return to reality as Zelda says, "Mr. Damian, do you ever not wear formal dress?"

Damian chuckles. "No, I'm told I was born in it," he says as he takes the shears and starts trimming.

"I guess you are always planning formal attire." Zelda smiles.

She returns to her work, and Damian catches my eye. He knows what I saw. He gives me a soft smile almost like he is concerned for me. I can't help but raise a brow. He's the one with marks on his arms, not me.

Damian sighs and leans into my ear. "Later."

I don't have long to struggle before a new distraction comes over. Fabian and Adam, who are still taking impressions, join us. I clear my throat to warn the others.

"See? Kascia agrees," Bella is saying but then she sees what I'm really clearing my throat about. "Oh, hello Mr. Fabian. It's nice to see you. Come to see how bad we are at trimming?"

"Oh no, you're all just fine. Just observing, don't mind me." Fabian smiles his large toothy grin.

"Here," Damian says, offering the shears back to Bella. "Can you get that far side?"

Bella glances at the sheers, then at us, clearly wanting to be closer to us instead to keep chatting, but then she glances at Fabian. She understands that Damian is giving her an excuse, and she takes it.

Zelda shakes her head and returns to her work as Bella giggles at us as she leaves. I spot Gavril laughing at his father as he tries to lift more than he can manage, helping repair one of the fences. The queen is doing some weeding with Princess Rose, Isla, and Jonquil.

I turn back to trimming when I notice Fabian trying to sneak closer. Damian rolls down his sleeves, a good idea around Fabian, and gives me a look, asking if I want his help to keep the flea off me.

I give him a small smile and shake my head. As much as I'd like to keep Fabian off, he might read into it.

"You do lovely work," Fabian comments.

"I'm cutting in a straight line. How is that lovely work?" I ask.

"You look lovely doing it." Fabian grins. I roll my eyes. "With so many sticks, perhaps the new royal pup should be over here," he suggests, looking over at Joy who's running around Gavril's feet as they work on the fence.

But it's not hard to handle Fabian's questions about Joy, the delegation visits, the show, and the like. It is not as hard or dangerous as I thought. Zelda has finished her section and asks if I'm done. I am, enough to get away by joining Bella further away. Fabian isn't deflected right away. Instead, he joins us and asks the other girls similar questions.

Gavril joins us not too long after, and by Fabian's reaction, I know he's still not supposed to speak with the prince. And he likely doesn't want to risk being banned from all of us, so he leaves with a friendly wave of thanks.

With Fabian gone, my worry turns to the king. "Your father needs to stop trying to keep up with you," I say playfully, but I mean it in more than that.

Gavril nods his agreement. "Think you ladies can keep him distracted for me on the hedges? I think he really is trying to keep up with me."

We all laugh. "Who could keep up with you?" Bella says then flushes, realizing what she'd said. Zelda laughs harder than I do. Gavril takes a second longer to catch up.

"Guess that's what this contest is about," he tries to lighten poor Bella's embarrassment. Then he looks at me. "Think you can talk him into it? If I suggest it, he'll declare I'm trying to cheat."

"He really is trying to keep up?" Bella frowns. "Isn't he like—"

"Shh, don't speak their ages aloud," Zelda says playfully, pretending to cover Bella's mouth, making us all laugh.

"I can help." The king does seem to like me. Though if I were Gavril, I'd have gone for Zelda who I know is his favorite to win.

"Thanks. He's starting to wheeze," Gavril confides when the others can't hear. "Try to keep the others from noticing if you can."

I nod, and he sneaks a kiss on my cheek in thanks under the pretense of getting one of the flower petals out of my hair. I give him a look which he ignores.

Thankfully, it doesn't take much to talk the king into it, and soon he's making all three of us laugh as we work on the hedge. His breath does go back to normal, thankfully. He keeps himself out of trouble to make sure he's stable. I see to it that he comes along with us to each of our assignments, and I pick them, so it's easy on him.

He and Bella have a bit too much fun when we return to thinning the flowers. And it gets worse when he tries to dump the weeds we work on over her head later. I spot Adam getting impressions which leaves me open as the king dumps weeds over me next. The resulting embarrassing impressions of me trying to tell the king off must be worth something to someone.

As we're making the rounds to different assignments, my eyes fall on a group of serving men gathering up the debris from trimming the trees and plants. It is grueling work; most are sweating as the sun rises.

There's one in particular that catches my eye, and at first, I can't think of why. But then, in one flash of recollection, I realize where I know him from. My mouth drops open. It's the crier, the man who'd climbed onto the fountain on Restoration Day and been shot down.

I was sure he'd been killed with how he fell. I knew the guards caught the body, but it didn't occur to me that he could have survived. But not only is he alive, but he is doing some hard labor. He wasn't that badly hurt.

His eyes meet mine, and the glare of hatred he gives me startles me. I stumble back a little.

"Oh careful," the king chuckles. I quickly hide my expression and look away from the man before the king can notice. Does the crier recognize me from that day? Or does he hate me because I'm a Chosen who wants the throne?

I'd been haunted by that moment, wondering how the royal family would allow or even want their guards to silence any who disagree with them. It had bothered me and added to my many doubts. Now I find out not only is he not dead, but they have at least treated him well enough to be able to handle some of the heavy work on this farm.

I'm struggling to reconcile all the pain and confusion it had caused me with the truth of what really happened. It doesn't help, I cannot get how he'd glared at me out of my head.

Thankfully, my acting talents are useful off the stage as well as on. None of the girls know me well enough to think anything is wrong. Closest is the king who thinks I am annoyed Fabian and Adam keep popping in and out and teasing me that I have the least to fear. If only we knew how wrong he was.

Chapter 24

As I predicted, no one failed the test. I can't help but notice the worry lines trying to hide on the queen's brow as she looks over the unchanged breakfast table the next day. But there are more in those worry lines than any of us know.

It isn't until after lessons when Jonquil lets out a squeak as she scans the front page of her morning paper that we get any hint as to what is really going on.

"What is it now?"" Rose asks tiredly.

"Nothing," Jonquil says quickly, too quickly.

It must be Fabian's article. I ask her if I can see the article. She pulls it away. "It's my paper. We don't play this game," she reminds me stiffly. But there's a worried or perhaps a concerned look in her eyes as she meets my gaze. She holds the paper, so the front-page article is out of view.

"I do." Zelda neatly slips the paper out of her hand and pulls it up. She reads the title and lets out a bit of a yelp too. "How?" is all she says.

"What?" I try to look, but Jonquil snatches the paper back.

"Nothing, I mean... we'll just get our own copies," Zelda corrects herself. I frown.

"Please do," Jonquil says stiffly. "This one is mine." She stands up with a snap and walks over to a far corner to sit away from us, so we can't see the paper.

What in creation is so bad? The event didn't go badly. What could make Jonquil and even Zelda say "nothing" to me like that?

Florence is as tense as a curtain rod. She takes a deep breath and marches over to Jonquil to try to get the paper from her. She has been stiff since Lilly left. Anxious might be too kind of a word. She vibrates with stress.

The ensuing argument distracts the other girls, leaving me the opening to turn to Zelda. "What did it say?"

She hesitates only a moment before replying, "Favorite Gets Rivals Eliminated."

My stomach drops. "What?"

"I don't know. I didn't get to read it. Looks like no one has." She nods at the fight as Azalea breaks it up. "I'm sure we can get copies quickly enough."

And I know right where to go for mine. I go right up to my room to see if Damian has read it yet. But he's not there. Vivian tells me he had business to attend to that morning. I hope it isn't about the story.

I pick up the paper, sit at the edge of my bed and look over the article. My heart drops.

The front page is mostly taken up with an impression of me when Gavril scooped me out of the tree. Did it have to be that impression? I quickly read the article:

> The unbiased nature of the Enthronement is now in question. Sources from within the place are claiming that the more recent eliminations were not due to failure to pass a princess test, but for crossing the wrong Chosen girl.

> Throughout the Enthronement, many lovely young ladies have failed to pass the royal family's princess tests. Only one lucky Chosen girl will be named winner and marry the prince. It has often been stated by palace officials that only failure to pass the test or show themselves not a true princess would result in being eliminated and sent home.

But that may no longer be the case. Our insider claims the last several eliminations were not due to failure to prove oneself a princess or breaking Enthronement rules, but through pure biases. Our insider claims that if a girl does anything to challenge the prince's current favorite Chosen to win, it's only a matter of time before she is eliminated.

This, coupled with recent rumors of infighting among the Chosen girls, has led many to wonder what kind of internal politics are rife within the Enthronement tests. The number of girls left is down to only eleven girls. Could the smaller numbers be causing extra stress and tension between the would-be princesses?

Upon attempts to investigate further by speaking directly to those recently eliminated, we were told they were under legal obligation not to comment. Though one of the more recent eliminates appeared quite irritated at her requirement not to speak out.

There has been no comment or explanation from palace officials about these accusations, but there have been no others alleging the Enthronement may not be as honest and integral as we all would expect from such an important and historic royal event. One can only hope these rumors are no more than girl drama and not a sign that our next queen may have become so through dishonest means.

I almost drop the paper in horror. The article may not have named names, but did it matter when they put an impression that's as big as the article itself, if not larger, of the prince holding me and laughing?

This is far worse than being thought the favorite by the other girls. This is worse than their being angry or jealous. Now whoever won, me or not, would have the people distrust that she got there fairly. Any girl who ascended to the throne would be assumed to have been the prince's favorite and mistrusted by her people. Whoever started this caused themselves harm as much as me if they hope to win.

My hands start shaking; I quickly put the paper down to stop the horrible rustling sound of the paper shaking. Was it Dahlia who'd leaked this twisted version of the story? It is the only thing that makes sense. But Lilly was eliminated most recently, and she wasn't allowed to tell anyone why. And she'd have no reason to want to turn on me like this, does she?

I fight not to dwell on that thought. No. She hadn't wanted to win. She wouldn't turn on me. She wouldn't. I have to believe that. I have to know I was right about someone, anyone. I take a deep breath and try to think of something else, but all thoughts are horrible.

What will the king and queen do to handle this? Will this insinuation get me eliminated? Would that even fix the problem? The impression makes it look like I'm the favorite, but the people could take that as it was, just speculation.

I'm losing the fight to control my breathing. I close my eyes and take deep breaths. Vivian is at a loss on what to do. Have they already read the article? I stand to clear my head and put the paper on the desk. They can read it if they want.

I can't hide from the others forever. By the time I go down to lunch, I'm sure every single one of them will have read the article. I stand upright and nod at Vivian. I need to be early or on time, but no matter what, I cannot be late.

Vivian is almost finished getting me ready when Damian enters the room and meets my eyes. "How are you doing?"

"Think I'm ready." I manage a smile.

"Good." He smiles a little. "I'm sure you had a rude awakening this morning." He frowns.

"Only after lessons were over."

Damian nods. "But you're ready?"

"I have to face the girls sometime. I can't hide."

"True." He nods again in agreement. "Just remember, your true friends will stand by you."

"What do I do?" Is there anything I can do?

Damian gives me an uneasy smile. "Frankly, my dear, there is no easy piece of advice I can give."

I nod. There's nothing I can really do but face it. It will be easier as princess to handle this because I won't be dealing with a horde of people questioning my authority, the biggest doubter being myself.

I walk down to lunch, doing my best to hold everything inside and put that energy into putting on the show. I think it works. I arrive at my normal time and sit and eat as normal. I glance up at the royal table, and they are conversing in low voices. It looks like Gavril is doing the most talking, but what he's saying, I can't be sure.

Rather than do my normal dance practicing, I go right to the Ladies' Chamber. That will show I'm not hiding and am confident in my place, even if I'm anything but.

I don't feel much like talking to Bella or even Zelda. I take my favorite seat by the window and hearth and pick up a book as if that's what I have been planning all day.

I only start to take in reactions as I sit up with the book I have been reading in hand. They're all looking at me. I'm glad I am able to hide my glance at them. A queen is graceful under pressure. There's no reason to acknowledge the accusations in several faces.

The expressions they give me speak volumes. Some are hoping to see me explode, and others look sad for me. Princess Rose, Princess Amapola, and Isla don't seem to be the leakers. I could have guessed that without help. Princess Zelda and Bella are clear too. I was with them the whole time. I'd have seen them step aside with Fabian, and they never did.

It might have been Jonquil. She knew all about what happened with Dahlia, and she certainly had proven she'd do whatever was required to get me out of her way. Florence had gone right up to him before we even started, but wouldn't that have made her obvious to us? Is she that foolish?

I process all of this with only a brief glance as I tuck my legs to one side of the cushion, so I face the ocean side. I'm not going to let them get me to react. A queen doesn't owe them a reaction. If that's what I want to be, I need to start now. That's when the brick drops into my stomach. Will the king or queen come after me? I almost forgot to worry about how Gavril will react.

I'm jarred from this thought as Zelda sits across from me without hesitation. I look at her and notice the other girls have gone back to their games, chats, and even nail painting in the back with Ericka. "Did you see it?" she asks.

I put on the right face and nod. "I saw it."

"Well?" Zelda's eyes are full of an anxiety I'd not seen before.

"We know it's not true."

"Of course, but... this will come back to get you. You're not worried?" Zelda asks.

"Why worry when I can't do anything?" I reply. Or that's what I keep telling myself.

"I suppose." Though her tone tells me she is worried. She tries to guess who it was, but she has as little to go on as me. To try to look normal, we pull out a card game.

Bella appears as if summoned by magic. "Mind if I join?" She tries to cover up but slips onto the sofa with Zelda, her back to the others and frowns. "Are you okay?" I shrug. Bella frowns and does something I don't think any other girl would dare do. She tries to make me meet her eyes by taking my face like Gavril does to stop me looking away. "Honestly, are you alright?"

"Bella, stop it," Zelda chuckles in amusement. "You're acting like my little sister when I dump a boy."

"I'm fine." I keep the line, even if I don't believe a word of it myself.

"Are you really?"

"I can choose to be fine or worry until something happens. I think being fine feels better."

Bella smiles. "Good choice," she agrees and sits back. "Do you have an extra pack, or should I get one?" she asks Zelda. Zelda only has the two card packs, so Bella grabs another one.

She lets us play the game for a bit before she grills me again. Zelda giggles with a knowing smile in her eyes I can't understand.

"You want help beating up Fabian?"

I laugh. "No."

"Sure? I heard a rumor he's related to Godwin. Maybe he'll help us," Bella suggests.

"Are you going to talk him into it?" Zelda jokes.

"I have my ways," Bella tosses her hair dramatically, making us all laugh.

"I just want to last the night," I admit as I play my first monster.

Bella frowns. "You think they'll eliminate you?"

"What good can I be if I win, and they think I did it by cheating?" I ask dully. "They need a girl the people like, or this war will never e-end." I am surprised how my voice catches. I want to be the answer to helping my people. The idea I won't, win or not, takes more from me than I realized.

Dinner is uncomfortable. Princess Rose and Amapola talk among themselves. Azalea seems afraid to speak to me, and they are my only chances for conversation over dinner with Zelda and Bella so far down the table.

The king stands and draws our attention. "Thank you all for your patience. It's been a crazy time." He smiles at us. I look away and fiddle with my food. "And we were thinking it's about time we tried to bring a little pleasantry to the people."

Probably to distract them from all this mess. I still can't look up at him and keep fiddling with my food, listening but not able to do more than turn my head towards them.

"We were thinking we could throw a festival of some kind," the king goes on. "And as you lovely ladies are all learning to help run, plan, and manage events as princesses do, we thought we'd ask you to come up with some fun, unique ideas for festival themes and activities. We will give you all a week to prepare then you will present your ideas and whichever one we like best, we'll put on later in the month. What do you ladies think?"

Test. But I don't say it. I don't say anything. The more outspoken girls answer enough for those who keep quiet. Forsythia declares it "brilliant" and says she's excited. Ericka agrees with a happy little high-pitched noise that would drive Joy and Cuppy crazy. Bella's and Florence's excited voices can be heard too throughout the din.

"Excellent." The king smiles. "Then we'll set time aside in a week and hear what amazing ideas you come up with."

The king sits back down, and out of the corner of my eye, I notice he rubs his eyes tiredly.

I dare look at Azalea to see if she'd want to discuss it. My heart sinks as she's turned to talk to Bella across the table instead. I fight not to slump back in my seat and wish I could just disappear.

Is this going to be the new normal for a while until either someone else is eliminated or something else happens? I try to remind myself that the other girls' opinions don't really matter. They'll all be leaving sooner or later.

That doesn't make me feel much better. I realize how lonely it will be once they are gone. I suppose it makes my options with Gavril much freer, but it's not like we'll have all day. I wonder what one-on-one etiquette lessons are going to be like. That doesn't cheer me up either.

Though I am starved for conversation at dinner, I find getting back to my room doesn't make me chattier after a dinner of those lonely thoughts.

I can hold out hope I can have at least my mother here if I win. But would it make that much of a difference? She'd go to work at the theater every day, and I doubt I'd be allowed to go with her.

Realizing there's nothing I can do in my room to cheer up, I'm ready to start getting ready for bed when there's a knock at the door. I let out a heavy sigh. This is it. I'm about to be eliminated. I know it.

"Should I?" Vivian asks tentatively.

"I doubt you couldn't."

I take a deep breath and prepare to pretend to be brave to whatever poor staff member they send to eliminate me and freeze instead. I didn't expect Gavril. Are they really cruel enough to make him do it? It takes all my willpower not to cry.

Gavril gives me a weak, encouraging smile. "This is going to sound stupid but are you alright?" he asks gently. "You didn't look too... well, you hid it well, but you seemed down to me at dinner." He takes a deep breath. "Did the girls ask you about Lilly?"

"No." I fight not to let my pain out on him. "Do you have to do this?" It leaks out slightly in my tone, breaking in through little cracks.

"What?"

"I just..." I look up with just my eyes, trying to keep them dry. This is why they thought me the favorite before. I get moments like this. He is not here to eliminate me after all. He's here because he saw my struggle and is worried about me. Normally, that would make me feel worth more than a million gems, but right now... *Don't snap at him. It's not his fault.* I try to tell myself.

When I don't go on, Gavril forces a brave smile. "I thought this might help."

I look down as he holds out a small box I recognize as a treat box, the kind that holds the things I am not supposed to have. The kind of things Jake knew got me into exactly the mood he wanted.

The tearful laugh breaks out before I cover my mouth. I look up again to stop the tears. This is why I'm getting into trouble with the other girls to the point they're using the press as a weapon. It feels wonderful, yet awful at once.

"If you feel that guilty, I'll split it with you," the tease in his voice is a million times better than the one Jake used with the same tease.

I adore and hate Gavril so much right now.

"Hey. It's just me. I told you once it was alright to scream at me, even if I don't like it. That still stands," he offers, raising a brow.

"Would you stop it?"

"What?"

"It's just... this." I frown.

"What part of 'this'?"

Why is he being so bloody patient?

"This is why I'm the target," I say. "It's... things like this. I mean... I know. I know. I just..." I sigh frustratedly. "I'm not sure I'm ready for this right now. I'm already..." I shouldn't unload on him. I already have made a mess.

"Already... frustrated? Angry? Defensive?" Gavril fishes.

I half want to laugh at his tone as he tries to finish the sentence for me. "A mess."

The tears finally come. Gavril doesn't judge though. He just watches me with surprising patience, even for him. "I don't know who I can trust anymore." It starts tumbling out of me before I can control it. It doesn't help that I don't know if I want to or not.

"I'm scared of what this will do. I thought you were someone coming to tell me I have to go home. The girls will hardly look at me, let alone talk to me, even those who did before. The one person I felt safe to talk to because I knew she didn't want to win is gone, and I don't know who I can trust that is left. Some try, but what if... they want to win too? I was so wrong to trust Jonquil. What if I'm wrong again? For all I know, she's the one spreading these stories, or with how they all see me, it could be any of them.

"And now they're all debating who will be the top girl once this article has me thrown out, even girls I trusted, i-if I even trusted them. I wish this stupid game was over, but then what about when it is? Where will I be? Even if I win... I'm alone and then what? I want them gone, and yet... I'll be fine but... a-alone. I knew that, but it just strikes so differently after no one even looked at me at dinner. And now I somehow have to get a clear enough head to plan this presentation, or I'll l-lose for good. I wish they were gone, but..." I pause to get a handle on my own rushing feelings and thoughts. "I thought I was just about over all of that. That I was alright with being on top, but..."

"But now you want and need them, but are scared to lose them?" Gavril asks. "And thinking differently will only make it worse?" I can hear by his tone he is including himself in "them". He's not wrong.

"It's not your fault. It's not fair," I sigh. "And it's not like we can even talk it out because there are still ten other girls out there you're dating as seriously as me, making this one complicated mess. To make it worse, for all I know, your parents have already dismissed me mentally but are keeping their word to protect me, keeping me here until they know how to keep me safe. Which is far worse than anything else when I just..." I stop myself again. I can't say that.

"I want to feel safe in my position, if it's even a position. It's not like you're free to call or really treat me like a favorite or the favorite or whatever. It's part of the rules." I hug myself. "And it's not like you need my problems on top of it when no one can fix them."

Gavril chuckles good naturedly. I give him a look. "I know they're small and stupid compared to your problems, but they are problems."

"My dear Asteria, it's not you I'm laughing at. It's the fact you think there are bigger concerns I have right now. My biggest concerns are you. The delegations are gone. I'm back to the dull routine you all have. I just don't deal with Keva and Miss Hydie." His face falls as he realizes what he said, and I laugh before I can control it. Did he just call Lady Hydrengia "Hydie"? "Please don't tell her I told you that," Gavril begs with a small laugh. "I couldn't pronounce it as a boy, so she let me call her that and never asked me to stop. Please don't let that get around. I forgot."

I am never going to get her being "Miss Hydie" out of my head. I can do with the laugh. It helps relieve some of the tension. I hug myself again. "At least if I'm in this alone, I can think of that in my head when I have lessons." I try to perk up.

Gavril's face falls a little. "You really don't think you'd be happy here alone, do you?" He puts the box down on the bench at the end of my bed before walking closer to me.

I look down, rubbing my arms. "I don't know. I'd not even thought about it. I was so nervous about how I'd feel as they left, I avoided it. I knew I'd have to someday but worrying about something I could do nothing about didn't seem helpful, and I had lots to distract me until it happened." I study the perfectly clean marble floors. My maids are amazing.

"But you want to win?" he asks.

I nod. "I just didn't calculate that into the cost until now. Dinner was... painful. Azalea wouldn't even look at me. I told myself it didn't matter, that they'd be gone soon anyway, but—"

"But that doesn't feel great either." He gives me a sad smile. "No matter who it is, I am sorry for whoever has to live in this cage with me. It can be lonely." Gavril pauses again. "But do you want to win, or..." He doesn't finish the question. I see a decision made in his eyes, but I don't have a clue what. "Do you just not want to lose?"

I'm not sure what he's asking. I already told him I want to win. "I want to win," I repeat, wondering if that answers his question.

Gavril nods to himself but doesn't go on whatever train of thought he'd been on. "I know it's not easy here in this position. It's not like you're used to this like I am. To me, having... the winner," he says carefully, "helps me not be so alone. To the winner, it isn't like that."

I shake my head. "Even with family here with me, they'd not give up the theater. But with security, there's no way…"

To my surprise, Gavril cuts me off as he takes a quick step towards me and scoops me into a hug before I even know what he's doing. I accept it before I even mentally have taken in what he did. "You… you don't have to do it, you know," he says. "If you don't want my life, if you want yours back, you can have it." I can hear he's keeping something back in his voice, but what, I don't know.

But it doesn't matter. He's wrong. There is no going back to my old life.

"I'm not going to force any of you to stay in this place if they don't want to. Even if I want them to. You know that, right?" Gavril pulls back enough to study my face.

"I do. I'm not asking. I don't want to. But they will keep that life. I just won't be able to," I snort. "I need to stop saying 'just'."

Gavril chuckles. "Just when Lady Keva can point it out."

I manage a wimpy smile. "I never thought of what day-to-day life would be like if I won. It is lonely without the girls, isn't it?" Something about him saying it and understanding it helps calm me down.

Gavril nods. "You have no idea. Most servants are too scared to be buddies, and Sage is the only friendly guard I've had."

"I got the better maids," I taunt.

"And attendant."

I laugh a little then let my head rest on his chest a moment. "I just… want the game to be over."

Gavril smiles and brushes some of my hair back, making me look up at him. "Me too." Oh, please don't give me those eyes. I want to, but… I let my head rest on his chest again. Will we ever be able to be just us? Is that freedom ever going to be there? He has to date all of us. Why can't he choose?

"I can't say exact numbers, but there aren't many tests left," Gavril says. "Soon it will be over."

Not many left? But there are eleven of us. "How, when the last test didn't eliminate anyone?"

Gavril laughs. "I knew it wouldn't. It was so transparent. My parents couldn't figure out any way for it to be less obvious and make sure all the girls received some warning at the same time. But if we find out who told the story to the press, maybe it will get one out at least."

"Good luck. It could be anyone," I sigh tiredly.

Gavril frowns a little. "I should let you go to bed and enjoy your chocolate."

My heart sinks. I was annoyed he came, but now I don't want him to go. If only this stupid game would end, he wouldn't have to. We'd be close. No one would object if he just let me hide in him to get some sleep. Perhaps I'm not the favorite they all think I am.

"Do you want me to…" Gavril stops himself. Is he going to offer to stay? He'd be in so much trouble if he did. He wouldn't do that, would he? "I wish I could do more," he sighs, his shoulders dropping a little.

The odd dynamic between us has been so complicated lately, but in this moment, it feels so simple. Like the drama does not matter or that it is part of the reason that this moment happened.

"I'd ask if you need anything, but honestly, your attendant would be better at getting it than me." There's a hint of pain to his voice.

Not unless Damian could end this game. Because as much as I hate it, I can't have what I want yet. I know he has to go.

"But whatever the press says has nothing to do with this, alright? They don't pick winners," Gavril says.

"Your parents do." I sigh.

Gavril doesn't say anything. He just strokes my hair again. "Just a bit longer."

"Is it though?"

"If the Japcharians are to be appeased," Gavril jokes. He sighs frustratedly. "I wish I could just… give you a countdown."

"Why?"

"It helps," Gavril assures me. So, he's been doing a mental countdown. He'll be happy no matter who it is. My heart aches. I want to win. But it also means facing more of this pain. "I wish I could give you any way to count it down. I am certainly not allowed. Will 'soon' be enough?"

I sigh and shut my eyes. It has to be. I can't have anything else.

"It's just a few more days until the ball. You can count that," Gavril suggests nervously.

I smile. Yes. There is that. No one is allowed to say I get it because I'm a favorite. I got it because I won fair and square. The one day that isn't allowed to penetrate the bubble. That gives me something. I miss Gavril's big smile when he sees my immediate reaction.

"Then maybe I can find other smaller counts for you," he teases warmly.

"Like what?"

"Maybe if you count the stars, you can find out." He lets go and steps back, kissing my hand. "If you need the morning, send me a note, and I'll pretend to have taken you out. Girls can't complain then. You haven't had a date in ages."

"Compared to who?"

Gavril doesn't reply. He just smiles. "So, if you need a lie in, let me know. Actually, I shouldn't tell you, but I'm sure your maid is listening," he says the last bit louder. His tone is teasing though, so Vivian feels free to giggle. Gavril chuckles. "Sleep well," he pauses, "my Asteria."

I nod. "And you, Your Highness." I recall to curtsy. But I question his name for me. He'd used it three times now: twice today and once after the performance. What does it mean?

I feel his hand tense in mine again before he releases me. He goes to the door then pauses. "If you're feeling lonely in the night, have a servant let me know." He then slips out the door.

I flush. He isn't... Now I want to see what he'd do. I shouldn't. We could get in trouble.

Damian lets out a tense breath as if he's not been breathing this whole time. I force a smile for him to assure him it is fine. I am holding in my emotions though. I feel empty again. I really wish he didn't have to go. I hug myself, glad the robe gives me something.

Damian gives me a little smile then offers to fetch my tea. I nod my thanks. I really couldn't have better servants. He bows to me then leaves to fetch it. I sigh and let Vivian help me finish getting ready for bed. They ask if I need anything else. I shake my head to let them get to bed. I bite my lips though. It is starting to feel like this room is too large for just for me.

When Damian returns with the tea, he pours it and prepares it before offering me the cup. I thank him and take it, sitting in my bed and sipping slowly and enjoying the little cakes Gavril brought. After allowing me to sit quietly, Damian asks if I want to take Gavril up on his offer. I giggle. "Not sure what he's going to do." But if Damian is offering. "I wouldn't mind," I admit.

Damian bows his head to me. "I'll be back," he says and leaves.

I smile a bit and sip my tea. It really is going to be a long night feeling like this. After several long minutes, Damian returns, stopping just inside the door and looks back at someone. "Go on," he says. "You can go to her."

I frown a bit. What is Damian... but then there's a clattering sound and a zooming blur of red and white races into the room, into the air, then on the bed. I laugh as I realize it's Joy as she licks at my face, tail wagging. She says hello, licks at my tea which I pull away from her before I finish it.

Damian smiles and takes the cup from me then looks at Joy. "If you're going to stay, you have to settle down."

Joy yawns and "talks" back. But I have no idea what she says as she goes to the other side of my large bed.

He chuckles at her then looks at me. "I think you have yourself a bed buddy for the night."

I smile as I pet the dog. "Thanks Damian." Though I know the thanks only goes partly to him.

He smiles and nods to me. "I'll let you go to sleep. Good night, my lady," he says with a bow.

"Good night, Damian." I let the lights go out as he leaves, and I lie down.

Joy settles down once the lights are off. She yawns and lies next to me long ways. I smile. "That's a good girl."

Joy huffs a "yeah". I smile again as I keep stroking her, more to soothe myself than her. I smile a bit sadly. "You're never lonely, are you?" I say. "He keeps you company."

With a little pant, Joy gives my face a tiny lick. I giggle. Then she makes some talking sounds, but I don't understand any of it. She nuzzles into me. "From your familiarity with the bed, I presume he lets you sleep with him." I sigh. "Lucky dog." She just looks up at me with those big puppy eyes.

"You'll keep us company, right?" Then I sigh. "If I can win this. You think I can do this?"

Joy sighs and puts her head comfortably on me as I keep stroking her.

"You'd know if he wants me to. Not that you can tell me."

Joy raises her head and makes more talking noises at me. I chuckle and stroke her head. She lies back down.

"Not that you would if you could." I manage a smile. It's getting harder as the empty pain and heartache in my chest struggles to escape. "I'm sure you'd like me to. You like me because I picked you." I swallow as tears come. "And I want this so bad, but can I do it? Can I trick their tests? Can I escape the girls sabotaging me?"

Tears come to my eyes faster than I can stop them. I wish Gavril would come back and let me hide them in his shirt. "I'm a real fool, Joy. I..." I don't want to say it out loud, but maybe saying the word will help. "I love him. And I think he wants me to win. I can't be assumed a favorite for nothing, right?"

Joy copies my "I love you" and lies her head back down. I smile slightly. I forgot she doesn't really understand, but neither does Nippers, though he seems to.

"Thanks, Joy." I stroke her fur gently, eyes staring into nothing. "I just don't know if I can win when I..." I take a deep breath as I settle into Joy. "What am I supposed to do? I have no other path to take if I lose, Joy. I want to, but if he knew... what would he do?" I shudder at how he shut down after he only feared I was nothing but the rebel he'd assumed. What would he do if he knew?

Joy is comforting though. She huffs and watches me, listening as intently as Alsmeria ever had.

"And it hurts to feel like he's out of reach, even more when I do think he'd... reach back." I shut my eyes, feeling the tears, and resting my face in the dog's fur. She likes that and nuzzles closer.

It's going to be hard to get through this, and even harder to adjust to being alone. But I wouldn't be. He'd be there. It's not like I just get to live in the castle like this full time. I'll move into... I think Gavril said the princess would have her own suite. That would be just more empty space. "Maybe I can just get a boy puppy to keep me company and be your buddy," I joke.

Joy lifts her head and talks at me as if saying that is the best idea ever. I laugh and hug her. She lies still to let me. It does help me not feel so alone, but the tears still escape which really is a bit of a relief because letting it out while feeling the comfort eventually gets me to sleep.

Chapter 25

When I wake in the morning, it's to the smell of fresh flowers. I open my eyes to spot a fresh vase of them resting on my end table, wafting their scent through the room. I move to get up and feel Joy pressed against my side. I look over to see she's lying on her back, her body twisted in a strange arc with her paws in the air like some kind of raptor.

"Joy, are you broken?" I ask as she flops herself back to normal with a large puppy yawn.

She denies it with her odd doggie talk and jumps sleepily off the bed to find Vivian to let her out so she can do her business. I stretch sleepily, finding it hard to get up after crying so much. My eyes are puffy and red or at least they feel it on top of being tired.

Vivian does a wonderful job soothing them with the treatments they use. That's when I spot the paper awaiting me on the end of my desk. I swallow hard, afraid of what I'll find. I take a deep breath before I dare reach over to it once I'm ready for the day, dread filling my stomach.

The article doesn't have a picture this time, just the bold heading: "The Palace Speaks Out."

Oh... the king and queen had responded? But as I read the article, it doesn't seem like that's what happened. The source is just "a palace official". He'd say the king or queen or at least indicate an "insider in the royal family" if it were one of them, I'm sure.

The article states the truth behind how most eliminations work, stating emphatically that all the eliminations had been approved by the king and queen without any influence from the girls. Fabian even gives a detailed report about how Dahlia had been fairly and humiliatingly eliminated three different ways: by the test, by the prince for poor conduct, and by the king and queen for attacking another Chosen, though who she attacked wasn't named. But it's the closing that really catches my eye.

There are many who are involved in the Enthronement and its process, but according to the palace insider, only one opinion matters here. And it is not that of the prince.

So, the question then remains, whose opinion is it that matters most? The official inferred we should perhaps check in with the stray cat that is known to wander the palace if we want answers. If this was said in jest, it — just like the truth of the most important competition in our nation's history — remains to be seen.

"What?" The word pops out before I can control it. What did it just say? I'm numb as I try to take in what this all means. Who is the one person? And what does Nippers have to do with it? Was that a joke? Or is Nippers' not a stray, and it is the cat's true owner that is the answer? Will this article be enough to protect me?

I don't have a lot of time to think about it. I have to get down to breakfast before anyone suspects something is wrong. "Are you sure you don't want your treat?" Vivian tries to perk me up.

"What?"

"The prince left it for you last night along with those this morning." Vivian is gently smiling at the flowers that are on the nightstand.

I look over at them, having thought it was something my maid tried to help cheer me up. They are beautiful: a mix of pink and blue island roses in budding stages, almost ready to bloom. I smile a little, touched. Apart from his attempts to cheer me up before, the prince had never really given me anything. I wish I had more time to admire them, but I have to hurry down to breakfast.

No one is behaving differently than yesterday, so my guess no one else had gotten a paper early appears correct. Our lessons help us prepare our festival ideas.

It does leave the question of what sort of festival I am going to plan. If Gavril's actions last night prove anything, it is that he at least is hoping I will do my best to get through this. The king said "unique". What can I do that is unique?

Most of the girls come up with their ideas after an hour or so and spend the rest of the lesson time working on it. I feel at a loss. The only idea that feels unique that I like is something like the feast of fools in the play I'd done before I came here. A day where the royals could feel what it's like to be normal and a day the people could feel like royalty. But how would I convince the royal family that is a good idea?

My heart tightens more as lessons finish, and Jonquil goes right for her paper. Her little start of surprise as she rushes to her normal spot on the sofa does not seem odd to anyone else, but I watch to see her reaction as well as to see if anyone else notices something off. Jonquil reads the front page then, without reaction, reads some articles on the inside. I frown. Did she skip a few pages to go right to the middle? Is she looking for an exact article? I should have looked over my paper more closely. What did she notice I missed?

As Jonquil reads her article, Ericka notices the huge headline, taking up the lack of a picture. "What?" She goes to grab it.

Jonquil, used to this, pulls it back with a dry sigh. "Why can't you all get your own?" she asks. Ericka gives her a look that could melt steel, but she doesn't bother otherwise. The only thing she can do to rattle Jonquil is drop her monster dog Cuppy on her lap.

"What is it?" Forsythia asks in a bored tone. "Someone else outdoing your best dressed maiden of the year or something?"

Ericka gives her an annoyed look. Cuppy even growls at her, but Forsythia just pets him, and he's used to her, so he quiets down. I still can't wait for Joy to get a hold of that mutt. "No, it says the palace responded to yesterday's article."

That gets all the girls on their feet. I quickly do the same to pretend I do not know just in case that makes me look less guilty of the accusations.

"Let me see it," Princess Rose demands of Jonquil.

"When I'm done. You don't get what you want just because you're born high princess," Jonquil says, getting up to leave with her paper. "You know how to get your own." She walks out to enjoy her paper in peace.

Zelda frowns and looks at me, the question in her eyes. I smile and nod. I don't mind letting my copy go around. She smiles a thanks, and we go up to my room to retrieve it. "I'm so glad someone doesn't see me as just another girl to beat," she says as we enter my room.

I laugh. "We have to find the release somewhere," I reply, trying not to think of how sad I'll be if I win and she leaves. But she would have to. If she doesn't marry Gavril, she's still the crown princess of Hyvil.

I pick up the paper and hand it to her. "And you can let others use it around the Ladies' Chamber. I'm not going to use it." Though I am curious what Jonquil was reading.

Zelda shrugs as she looks it over. Her mouth falls open as her eyes scan the page. It's a small part in her lips at first, but by the time she's done, her lips are fully parted in a confused O shape. She looks up at me. "A palace insider? Who would that be?"

"Whoever the king and queen sent." I shrug. "I know nothing about it."

"Oh, well then." Zelda frowns. "Who is... the one person who...? I was sure it was just the queen and king."

"No idea. Your guess is better than mine. You've been here longer. Did you meet anyone else when you came?"

"No, not that could possibly be the one person they're talking about." She pauses. "You named Nippers, right?" I nod. "He doesn't have an owner?"

I nod my confirmation. We return to the Ladies' Chamber and ask the others we trust, but no one else has any ideas. I can't help but try to ask Damian what he thinks when I see him after my daily exercises.

"You mean yesterday's article?" Damian arches a brow.

"The one from this morning." I give him a look. Damian is always on top of it. I doubt he's not seen it.

"Oh," Damian frowns. "I'm not sure I have an opinion. It simply looks like the royal family decided to address the rumors with the truth, but whoever they sent decided to have their own fun with the press."

I swallow. "And the one person whose opinion matters?" I dare ask.

He gives me a gentle smile. "You really believe there is one person that matters more in this competition?"

"Would they dare tell the paper that if not? It was in direct quotes."

Damian sighs and nods. "True." He pauses for a moment. "I will admit, the king and queen do seem to be seeking the approval of someone outside themselves. Even though I do not believe they should be looking outside the bounds of their own family."

"So why would anyone else matter and who? They seemed to think Nippers had something to do with it. Is he not a stray?"

"As far as I'm aware he isn't owned by anyone." Damian shakes his head. "If he were, I'd turn him over to them." He smiles a little.

I giggle. "See if even they could control him." I sigh. "It's all the girls can talk about." I take a seat. "I wish that person would make a choice." I would love to have this over.

"Not before you plan us a festival," Vivian tries to cheer me up.

"Right," I sigh, sitting at my desk. "Not that I know how to make my idea work."

"What's your idea?" Vivian asks, pausing and watching me with genuine interest that makes me smile slightly.

I force a shy smile and look over at Damian. "I was trying to think what felt unique. What a festival should be like, you know?" I frown. "And not have... incidents."

Damian cocks a brow. "Like?"

"Like..." I hedge, "public demonstrations?"

He nods slowly. "Like the last Restoration Day?"

"Yeah, I'm guessing you know what I'm talking about."

"If you were referring to the man who was shot off the fountain, then yes," he confirms with a nod.

I shudder as the man's glare during the service test flashes into my mind. I try to force it away, but it lingers at the back of my mind.

"You alright?" Damian asks, watching me carefully.

"Fine," I try to brush it off, unsure how to even address the topic.

"You sure? You shuddered."

I bite my lips. "Just never thought I'd see him again."

Damian pauses a moment. "On the service day?" he questions, looking back at me. I nod. "Did he say anything to you?"

"No." Just glared at me.

"What happened?"

"I couldn't place how I knew him at first, but he glared at me when he saw I was looking."

"I understand. I doubt it was personal. He was glaring at all the Chosen," Damian assures me.

"It was just a shock. I realized who he was then he just glared at me like that."

"Sorry he was being rude," Damian says with a soft smile. "But his outcry is what makes you nervous about planning a festival, right?"

I nod. "Rather not cause more harm."

"Well, in that case, don't give them a reason to do it," he says simply. He goes on to explain that as long as the people felt included rather than separated, there is little fear of such an outburst.

I explain my hope to do a kind of 'opposites day' where the people would understand how it felt to be royal (good and bad) and the nobility would feel what it was like to be the people (again the good and bad). Damian seems to like the idea and has a few suggestions.

There are more common folk than noble, so the focus would need to be on helping the larger group feel royal. So that's where I begin. I look into providing finer things for them to dress in: simple yet elegant dresses with flowers or other cheaply made crowns or tiaras. I also investigate providing the finer foods that are associated with royal life, but it is not all fun. If the people understand that, it will help with the struggle to bridge that gap. Royal lessons, games and challenges that simulate the hard choices that royals make every day could provide that and give me plenty of activities to plan.

In no time, I'm wrapped up in the fun of planning. I set a list of all that would need to be provided. I look over the budget and realize I only have extremely rough numbers and reach out to the local shopkeepers to not only check the normal prices but see if I can get deals on buying in bulk. That is what we would have done in the theater. And before I know it, I've got dozens of notes and plans scribbled on papers, notes, and boards across my desk. My desk has never looked so used.

I am so caught up in the fun of it all, the days fly by. I work on arrangements to let everyone have a nice bath to be clean like royalty, delicious food to get, royal-styled clothes, donations; Damian even offers to make things. I can't believe how fun this is to plan. Whether they choose it or not, I'm having a great time, forgetting the other girls are still nervous to speak to me. Even if they don't pick mine, at least I had fun, and I can keep these plans in a drawer for when I need it if I win.

It is just a few days left until the ball, and I'm enjoying this test more than any other. Damian even finds a good name for it "The Rags to Riches Festival". I love it!

I have spent so much time in my room enjoying planning, I figure I should take a break and join the girls in the Ladies' Chamber. Maybe I can get Zelda to play a game.

Zelda is happy to play, and even Bella comes over. At least these two don't feel like I'm a plague.

We're playing for a while when Ericka marches over, her rat dog under her arms, Forsythia standing beside her, arms folded, and both sets of eyes narrow at me. "Enjoying all your fan mail?" Ericka demands.

"What fan mail?" I frown. I haven't seen any fan mail.

"Those cartloads of letters you're getting," Ericka says. "Even negative press helps you. How do you do it? Who are you bribing?" The harshness in her voice makes me jump and Cuppy yip.

"I honestly don't know what you're talking about." I glare back. "The only person who writes me is my mother. I don't have my own money, and my budget is accounted for. I couldn't bribe someone even if I wanted to."

"Oh please," Ericka scoffs, "you're getting more letters than the king."

I blink, even more confused. I'd been keeping an eye on the mail for Lilly's first letter, so I'd have her address. But all I'd gotten was... "Oh!" It clicks. I give Ericka a look. "Those are not cartloads. And it isn't fan mail. It's replies to my inquiries with the shopkeepers about my festival idea. I've been asking price estimates and even seeing about getting discounts *if* they picked mine." My cheeks go pink. "I suppose I did get carried away."

"Is that how you think you'll win?" Ericka sneers at me. "By acting like you already won?"

"I said it may not happen, and I was looking for estimates," I insist. "I did not promise anything. You're welcome to do the same. I'm sure they'd love to hear from you on your idea."

"I looked up the prices in catalogs. I didn't think about bargaining for better prices," Zelda laughs. "I suppose that happens when you're used to having money. Clever." I shrug.

"Budget isn't everything," Ericka huffs. "A true princess and lady is one who plans and organizes well. Budgeting is only one small part, most of all for a princess. Look how well festivals in the capitol go. I plan those."

"Then you have nothing to fear from this test," I reply coolly. "Don't worry about me. I got overexcited is all. Perhaps the royal family won't like it just like you didn't."

"What are you planning?" Zelda asks, but she's cut off.

"You can't just act like you already have the slot. Unless you do." Ericka folds her arms, holding Cuppy still. "You are getting all the special treatments."

"I am not." I frown. "Like what? It's not like I get him all to myself."

"They gave you the best attendant."

"Luck of the draw. I had one that was pretty bad before," I remind her.

"You're still the only one he's kissed in public."

"I didn't ask for that. And that doesn't mean anything in who wins. He doesn't choose, remember?"

"It's still not fair," Ericka says. "All the delegations liked you best."

"And that has nothing to do with me. They make their own choices," I defend.

"I know we all think of her as the favorite, but let's be fair. They haven't actually given her any kind of privileges we haven't had," Zelda says.

"Haven't they?"

"Things may have happened that look like they are in her favor, but that doesn't mean they gave her chances we haven't had." Zelda stands firm.

"Even the press knows something is up. That 'make up' article isn't going to fix anything," Forsythia says.

"Then you have nothing to worry about because I'll be eliminated," I remind them.

"How about you worry about your chances instead of worrying about others?" Bella suggests. "Maybe then you'd not feel so scared. Do you want to win because everyone else loses or because you are the best?"

The glare that both girls give Bella is impressive, but Bella's solid stare down back is just as impressive. I smile. Perhaps she is better for the crown than I'd ever thought.

"We'll figure out how you're doing it then you'll be sorry," Forsythia says to me.

"Enjoy," I retort and turn back to the game. Bella and Zelda do the same, and that easily dismisses the other two.

"They really should focus on doing well instead of pulling others down. I thought it would get better, not worse, as more girls left." Bella frowns.

"It gets worse before it gets better. Give it time. If these tests work, their kind will be long gone before the end." Zelda glares after them.

"Just pray they're good at it," I say, but I only half mean it. If they're good, they'll weed out the rebel plant like me in no time.

Chapter 26

But I have something else I get to enjoy in the meantime. The ball is only two days away. Flur is in a good mood now she's back. I think getting married was good for her nerves. She seems calmer. Adding to all the fun, I receive another letter from Mother which doesn't tell me anything that interesting, but it is nice to hear from her now and again no matter how much or how little she has to say.

I am reminded about my search for prophecy evidence which I've been trying to squeeze in, but with all that has been happening, it has been hard to find time. But do I want to bother looking?

I go to the library mostly out of habit. It is quiet. As often happens, I am the only one there. The only sound is the soft ticking of the clock and crackle of the fire used to keep the room warm. I stand there, listening to that silence as I think about the question that only comes when I step into the room.

I'd come out of habit. This is what I do when I have a quiet moment. But is this really needed? My mind goes to what ran through my mind when performing *The Phantom*. My father had been mine for so long. He called me "the lost wandering child" ever since I came to the palace, but I am not lost. I made a choice.

I look around the library. I'd hoped to have my choice proven by the information here. But I'd spent how much time in here looking for proof to back up my faith? I'd looked for what really started this war if it wasn't the selfishness of the royals. I'd looked to see the truth of my father's claims in the prophecy, the rebels being the ones fighting for justice, all of it. But I hadn't found evidence to prove him wrong nor had I found any to prove him right.

And in that moment, I knew I wasn't going to.

I can't prove it any more than Christine could prove the Phantom wasn't her dead father. Yet here I am for the dozenth time hunting for evidence that likely isn't possible. Evidence that might not even change what I know. What am I really looking for?

Proof. I want proof not of what I already know because I want to my father to legitimize my choice. I want it for me. I convinced myself it was because I want to be able to defend it to the rebels, but it is my way of holding to the vain hope I can change anyone's mind. That I can finally feel certain of something.

But just like Christine, I have evidence. I have Father's actions. I have no paper or witness to tell me that my father was wrong and used me. I had his deeds. Like the Phantom had killed and twisted her view of the world to draw her to him, so had my father. It might not pass in court, and it was perhaps perspective, but I already have the proof.

I also have Gavril's action to compare him to. I don't have anything that proves Gavril is the king we need. I wouldn't ever find anything in history or the news that could do that. But I see he cares about me, even trusting me against evidence that proves he shouldn't. He chose to trust what he knows. Why can't I do the same?

I came here to try to turn my faith into evidence because I was so scared to have faith. I'm still terrified of it, but if I keep fearing it, I'll never be able to rely on it. I'll keep flip-flopping and risking that I'll go back to that web of darkness and lies.

I have to face the fact there is nothing in this library that can turn my faith to certainty. I'll always question the sources when Father challenges them. I could find the prophecy in black and white and still wonder if it had been modified or made up by those who recorded it. I'll feel sure until Father points out the flaws. I'll feel sure until Gavril makes me question his faith in me.

I keep saying I want this but then look for a back door in case I am wrong. Not if someone else is wrong. I am scared I don't know enough because I have relied on others to tell me what right and wrong is my whole life. Now I have to do it alone. I have to make the choice.

I take a deep breath. Could I just choose to live with my choice? If it was just me perhaps, but it wasn't just me. It is my people's lives. It is the Custod duty I don't have but choose again and again, even after I realized it was a choice. Now I have to choose something for myself.

Am I going to keep going back to the appealing past that had been a safe and comforting lie? Or am I going to turn away from that piece of my heart and choose the true light I had found outside of that twisted web? This isn't about finding the truth. It is about being able to prove to my heart I hadn't made a huge mistake. That I am not bad just because my father said I was.

Raul or Phantom? It is a harder choice than even Jake or Gavril. That had been a simple choice. Jake had wounded me deeply. Gavril offered hope. But between my demon and lover when the demon is questioned if he is friend and father or taskmaster and phantom. Do I choose to trust? Can I make that choice and not waver?

I have to try. I can't let my father or anyone else choose for me or control me. Even when I want to, the truth is I have to make the choice to stop looking for back doors or escape routes. I have already denied myself those. It is win this game or choose to go blind in my father's dark webs. I know that. There is no making it safe to go back by finding that my choice is wrong.

I have to accept I am either right or will have to suffer the consequences of being wrong. I have to stop trying to avoid them or finding an escape. I have to choose to stand by my resolve. It is like I filled in my test sheet, but refused to hand it in, looking over the questions trying to find an answer sheet to prove I got them right before handing it in. I have to either change the answers or submit the test.

I stiffen my resolve. I have to make the leap or be pushed. And I'm done being pushed around. I'd decided that at Christmas. If the girls aren't going to push me around, my father shouldn't get to either.

I turn around and leave the library, closing the door behind me perhaps more firmly than I meant to. I am submitting the test. I chose my side. So, what do I do now?

I prepare to be right. I prepare to win.

Chapter 27

With the ball being the next day, my maids really set to work getting me ready. They whisk me off to the spa and do the works: mask, bath, manicure, pedicure. They even do some kind of mask for my hair and a body wrap.

They make sure I'm perfectly plucked and clean and spotless for the following day. I half wish I could just go right to bed from it because I feel so relaxed, but I should at least have some kind of dinner.

Azalea notices something different though. "You dressed up for something?" She frowns.

I shake my head. "No." I realized my maids hadn't even put full makeup on me after the spa treatment. Instead, they applied some kind of tinted cream to help "prep my skin" as Flur explained. I'm sure I look different without makeup. I don't know if the girls have seen me without it. Has Gavril? I've never thought about it.

"Hm." Azalea is studying me, trying to figure it out. My hair might still be damp as it soaked in whatever my maids put into it. They'd braided it then tucked it into itself to make a nice looking but simple kind of bun. But my dress is normal. So, I guess I don't look too different without the daily makeup. Perhaps that's just how Damian likes it. I hold in a smirk. They really are good at their jobs.

Princess Rose had noticed too and is whispering to Princess Amapola. I wouldn't have noticed they were talking about me if it weren't for Princess Amapola glances in my direction. Princess Rose is doing the same. The look of disapproval in Princess Rose's eyes tells me she may have figured it out. Princess Amapola is holding in her reaction better. But even she has a slightly haughty look. I'd not thought about it, but do they disapprove of a non-born princess winning this?

That night, my maids put some more "overnight" beauty treatments on me before bed. Their pampering that afternoon was a blast, but this last-minute touch up is making me nervous. Is being this perfectly done up going to be required?

I don't know what my maids did, but I sleep better than I normally do, waking up pleasantly sleepy that gently fades into wakefulness as I yawn. When my normal braid doesn't fall down my shoulder, I remember what day it is and smile.

The dress they put me in is cute. There's a skirt that flutters just past my knees with a lovely twirl to it. The top has cap sleeves with a small jacket, more like a sleevelet that has a button that clasps across my lower neck to make a cute warmer variation. They apply natural makeup, using browns and natural reds to make my blue eyes pop. My hair sports the typical stylized bun they use often with an added headband to give it volume and show off my curls. The shoes look perfectly royal but are clearly designed to walk in.

My maids are adding the final touches when Damian joins us. "What do you think?" Flur asks him with a smile, watching me as I spin and fan out the skirt to admire how it looks in the mirror.

Damian watches me a moment with a soft smile and a finger laid aside his chin before he steps forward and adds my Chosen necklace. I smile. It adds a lovely effect. "Think this will do?"

He chuckles. "More than that. You look perfect." He smiles.

I beam. "Guess that's what matters," I joke.

He rolls his eyes and gives me a smile then lays a hand gently against my cheek and looks into my eyes with earnest. "Enjoy the day."

I smile back. "I'll do my best," I promise. "See you before the ball, I suppose."

He nods. "I'll see you then, my lady." He bows to me.

I curtsy back and hurry down to breakfast with a happy kind of rolling skip down the steps. I pause before I step into the dining hall, catching my breath and reminding myself not to look too happy yet. I don't want the girl drama ruining my day. I put a hand to my chest, shut my eyes and take a deep, delighted breath before I flutter to my seat.

It takes all my self-control to not look at the prince or his parents. I'm afraid my delight will bubble out if I do. My act works, and no one notices anything until I finish my meal and look up at Gavril for a cue on where to go.

He's smiling wider than even I have all morning. He nods at me to meet him in the entrance hall. I smile and get up with more happy fluttering and walk out.

Gavril doesn't take long to follow. I can hear the girls whispering when I'm hardly out the door. It's Ericka's dramatic gasp that cuts the air that makes me smirk. "She got first?" Ericka's tone is flabbergasted. "So, who gets tonight?"

I can't hold in the smirk even if I wanted to. Gavril joins me in the middle of the entrance hall and takes my hand to kiss it; his smile makes my heart flutter. If he yanked me in for a kiss, even in front of everyone, I'd accept it. I half wish he would because just hoping makes my fingertips fill with electricity at his touch.

"Are you ready, my lady?" he asks me, his eyes meeting mine and more energy fills the room.

I beam and nod, not moving my eyes from his. "I've been looking forward to it."

"Good." His smile somehow grows. "We better get to our first activity."

I raise a brow in question, but he doesn't answer, leading me to the stairs where a grumpy looking Gentian, holding a gleeful Joy, meets us, waiting.

Joy talks happily and tries to jump up to say hello to me. I smile and stroke her.

"I don't know who's more excited: her, me, or you." Gavril smiles his crooked smile at me.

"Excited for what exactly?" I ask playfully, struggling not to be starry-eyed.

"You'll see," Gavril offers his arm again, and I accept it.

Gavril doesn't cross the main hall. He guides me to the front doors where Cedrick opens the doors for us. I bite my lip to attempt to control the smile, but it's just not possible.

"What does she think she's doing?"

"There's no way they get away with this."

It sounds like Ericka and Forsythia gossiping, but at a glance, all the girls, apart from Zelda and Isla, have rushed to the dining room door to see where Gavril takes me.

To my surprise, I'm not embarrassed or annoyed with them. Instead, the smug feeling from before returns. I did win fair and square.

Once we're down the castle steps and the doors close behind us, Joy lets out a bark of delight and races to sniff everything and anything in sight. Gavril gives her an impressive amount of slack to explore.

It doesn't take long for Joy to start digging. Nippers leaps out of some rose bushes and puts his paw into the hole, distracting Joy. The cat gives the dog such a scolding look, I have to laugh. Joy sits down, panting in happiness to see the cat and licks him. The cat does not look as happy as he licks his paw to rub on his face.

After a lick or two, Nippers stands and jumps up onto one of the beautiful sandstone walls, meows at Joy, then races off, encouraging Joy to chase him. I laugh as Gavril lets out more slack to give the dog room to chase the cat until Nippers pounces on the puppy's back, and they start to wrestle.

"Imagine if that was Cuppy," I say dryly. Gavril and I both laugh.

As we laugh, Gavril slips his warm hand into mine, and my heart lifts even more and patters like a happy bird. I get to take his arm all the time, but taking his hand feels more intimate. I look down at his dark skin against mine. It feels so solid, warm, strong, sure, mine. I wish it could be like this more often.

Gavril has a soft smile on his face as he looks away from our hands and watches the two pets play. Then he looks at me and chuckles warmly at my expression. "What?" His tone makes my heartbeat faster.

I don't know how to put the happiness of this moment into words. Though the day isn't cold, it isn't exactly warm either with the weak winter light, but I feel as warm as if the sun were beaming right on me.

Gavril chuckles again when I don't reply. "That bad?"

"No," I smile softly, "it's not bad."

His smile brightens as I mentally add it to my collection. He can't stop smiling at me even as he whistles for Joy. She jumps to her feet and runs to us in her floppy, puppy way.

Nippers licks his paw to clean his head a few times before he jumps back onto the wall. Joy sees him and stands as if to chase him, but Nippers walks just out of range and walks on the path as if showing Joy the proper way to enjoy a walk.

Gavril and I laugh. I hold Gavril's hand tighter and take in this happy moment. I have had so few, I want to keep this one forever, just permission to be ourselves together. We are not even speaking, and I am as happy as a bird in flight.

Gavril whistles at Joy to try to stop her from eating a bee. "You will be very sick if you do that," Gavril tells her after her fifth run after a bee. "They have a venom that will make you hurt."

Joy whimpers and talks back.

"It will," Gavril assures.

Joy argues.

"I'm telling you; you eat a bee, you will regret it," Gavril insists. "And you'll spend the rest of the day with your vet."

"Oh wo," Joy howls to the sky and lies down to try to look pitiful.

"Then don't eat the bees," Gavril laughs.

For a while, only the sound of Joy's playing and the melody of the garden fill the air. I swear Gavril is drumming to the beat of it with his free hand. The trees are starting to grow their first buds, and a few are full of pink or white blossoms of some kind.

"I wish we could do this more often," I sigh after a pleasant silence. "Will that ever open up?"

"Maybe when it's over. So, soon." Gavril smiles and kisses the back of my hand again. He's so affectionate with me in a way he's not been before, as if it is as natural as breathing. It makes my heart flutter. "The hope being that once I'm married, my parents will finally accept I'm an adult, so I can choose to take a risk. Perhaps even without a guard breathing down our necks." His eyes meet mine, making my heart lift. "I couldn't have asked for better weather. I thought we might get a February rain."

"It feels like it's not rained in ages. We got plenty of snow, but no rain," I sigh.

"You like rain," Gavril observes. "It's just water."

"You don't know what you're talking about." I smile. "It's beautiful. It makes the world smell amazing; the sound is calming yet exhilarating. I love to play and dance in it: most of all, I love summer rains when it feels too warm to rain. Twirling in the puddles is the best, the feel and sound of the water..." I trail off.

"You make it sound so romantic. It's just warm snow."

"You'll just have to trust me until you experience it for yourself," I say confidently.

"I've played in the snow. Joy loved it too much." Gavril gives her a stink eye. "I had a struggle getting her to come back in."

I laugh. "When?"

"Christmas night. My toes were freezing, but no matter what I did, she refused to come in. I pretended I was going to leave her out there, and she didn't care. I was so worried someone would hear us and get mad at me for being on the balcony."

"So many rules," I sigh dramatically.

"Well, today we can ignore most of them." He squeezes my hand, sending another wave of exhilarating warmth through my body.

We continue our walk, laughing and keeping Joy out of trouble where we can. Nippers pops up now and then, walking on the garden walls, trying to catch bugs, or meowing at Joy to get her to behave. It adds a nice bit of color to the walk.

I close my eyes for a moment just to enjoy his hand there. I can hardly believe this is real. It's almost too perfect. It takes us a pleasant hour of laughing and joking before we finally reach the path that leads down to the beach. Not because it's far, but because we take our time, pausing to enjoy the flowers, stop Joy from digging, and pat Nippers when he sits near us.

When we reach the beach, Gavril offers to take my shoes, but instead, we leave them on the grassy side of the road and walk it barefoot together, still holding hands.

"Your feet are tiny." Gavril laughs at my small footprints next to his. "I heard rumors but good Ph—" Gavril stops himself with a chuckle, "blazes, those are small. Are those yours or a child's?"

I flush a little. "I know, little dancer feet."

"My little Cinderella feet." Gavril smiles, and his amber eyes meet mine. My breath catches at the intensity of his look.

I'm sure he's about to kiss me, but a bark makes us both jump and turn to see Joy, stiff at the sight of a huge flock of seabirds on the beach. She squeaks with desire to chase them.

Gavril chuckles. "Should I let her?" His eyes sparkle with mischief.

"If you can get her back after."

Gavril lets out more slack on the lead, an impressive amount. I had no idea the lead held that much. "That should be enough." He then looks at Joy and drops the slack, so she will feel the tension drop. "Go ahead, Joy."

The second she hears those words and feels the tension drop, she leaps into action, barking and pelting across the sand in an impressive zip over the golden grains. The birds shriek to the sky and take off in a rush of wings away from us, most flying out over the ocean, but a few go to hide on the large balcony that juts out from the castle.

Once each and every bird has been scattered, Joy walks back to us, panting in her victory, telling us of her conquest in her 'talk speak' between her heavy panting. "Yes, you beat the birds, good Joy," Gavril says with a soft laugh.

"So, it's just us?" I frown, realizing I can't see Sage anywhere and can't imagine how he'd hide out here in the bright sunlight.

"Oh, the guard is about," Gavril hedges.

I open my mouth to ask when Nippers meows as if in protest. I look to my left to see him gingerly stepping across the sand, shaking out his paw each time he lifts it. "What are you doing?" I laugh at the cat. "It's just a big litter box." Nippers gives me such a cat glare I can't help but laugh as he leaps onto a rock and starts to lick the sand off himself.

"Maybe sand is thinner." Gavril shrugs it off.

"Is it deep enough to swim in your bay?" I ask, watching the waves gently roll to the shore.

"Yes. I've never done it, but it is. Well, once," he corrects himself. "Before this all started. I brought Zelda out here."

"You did?"

Gavril nods. "Yes, maybe she told you, but she came first and had a few weeks here before the contest got underway. She fell for a mimic octopus, and it tried to drag her in."

I gasp in shock. Those octopi are known to drag people to their watery deaths. "What happened?"

"I... dove in after her and got it to let go."

"But you can't swim."

"Hence her shock."

I giggle. Gavril smiles. "My reaction was literally 'don't tell Mom'." I laugh. "Seems like a lifetime ago." He sighs heavily.

"Ready for it to be over?"

"More than you know." He meets my eyes again. "Or maybe you do." His eyes drop for a moment.

I wait tensely, my hand still in his, waiting for what he is about to offer me.

"Most of all on days like this." His eyes go to my hand, and he starts to fiddle with my fingers, like Jake used to. Electricity runs through my body at each of his little touches. In a rush of desire, Gavril pulls my hand to his lips and kisses the back of my fingers.

I close my eyes at the rush it sent through me. The wind brushes across my skin and brushes my hair as Gavril suddenly moves closer and kisses me deeply. I sigh as I relax into his kiss, the warmth of his kiss and the cool of the wind making a unique shiver run through my body as I wrap my arms around his neck.

He pulls back just enough for our lips to part, but he keeps his forehead pressed to mine, holding me close, his hands on my waist. His breath of desire makes me smile as more pure energy fills my heart.

In a slight jerk, he presses his lips to mine again and again. A tremor of bliss shudders up my spine as I run my fingers through his hair while my other hand squeezes his arm tightly.

He kisses me again, and again, and each relaxes and excites me more than the last. I could stay locked with him like this even as the wind tries to cool us and break us apart. There's a scratching at my leg, but I ignore it as I let Gavril soak up all I have.

Finally, and yet all too soon, Gavril pulls back, eyes still closed as he softly laughs at himself. "Sorry," he whispers as he runs the back of his fingers over my cheek. I shut my eyes, not at all caring if it was wrong and hoping if I stayed quiet, we could keep going.

Howling pops our bubble like the snap of a balloon bursting. We look down at a very confused Joy, whose tail is wagging while she looks up at us.

"You'll understand when you're older," Gavril tells her.

I laugh so hard I hold onto Gavril to keep myself up. Gavril smiles and hugs me, holding me tightly. I can't see it, but I can feel his happy smile. I shut my eyes and wonder if I can pretend to fall asleep, so he will never let go.

But I know that won't work. I sigh and pull away, unsure what to say after that.

Gavril clearly feels the same because he clears his throat. "Well, shall we press on?"

"To what?"

"On the walk, we can cross the beach to the other side."

I frown and look at the water. "You don't want to stay?"

"And do what?" Gavril studies my face in amused curiosity.

"Do what? You love the ocean," I laugh. "I'm sure you know lots of things."

"What do you suggest?"

"Anything." I cast my mind about. "We could just play in the surf if we're not safe to swim."

"What?"

"You know. You get as close to the waves as you can without getting wet."

"I haven't done that since I was a kid."

"It's more fun as an adult," I promise.

Gavril smiles. "Alright."

I smile back and lead him by the hand to give it a try, and I have to admit it's much more fun with the added challenge that Gavril refuses to let go of my hand unless he is holding on to me in other ways. It leaves us laughing and tripping over ourselves and each other. Though it means the waves win as often as we do, we manage to keep mostly dry. We're only soaked below our knees, which is good for me as it keeps my dress dry. Joy chases the waves along with us, barking at them and squeaking in terror as she runs from larger waves, making Gavril and I laugh.

The best part of this game has to be how Gavril keeps catching me around the waist to keep me from getting too far, resulting in our getting splashed many times. We had to have been at it for hours because we wear out even Joy who goes over to a soft spot of sand and flops down to take a break and let the sun dry her off.

"Maybe a break is a good idea. Should be about lunch," Gavril suggests. Have we been at this that long? It does not feel like it. But from the position of the sun, he's right. It's getting close at least.

My heart sinks a little. I may get him the rest of the day, but lunch also means the dining hall and the other girls. I take his hand, and we walk across the sand and pick up our shoes. We opt to walk through the grass to try to get the sand off our feet as we didn't think to bring anything to clean it off.

But when we reach the top of the slope that levels out to the main gardens, Gavril doesn't lead me left to the castle doors. He pulls my hand to the right, and we walk over to where several of the white and pink flowered trees are growing on a slight hill, giving us a splendid view of the ocean spreading out before us.

But the best part is what's under the trees. My mouth falls open. There's a blanket laid out between the trees and the garden wall. Resting on it is a basket with lunch waiting.

"Much better out here, don't you think?" Gavril asks me.

"Gavril, it's perfect," I declare, heart flooding with fresh happiness. He didn't want to give up a second either. I don't know if I want to turn to him and kiss him in thanks or rush over to start the romantic picnic first.

Gavril has brought a lot of my favorites, and we laugh as we try to eat some rather liquid-y clams from their shells.

When we're finished, he puts the basket out of Joy's reach and sits next to me again on the blanket with a satisfied sigh. He looks out over the view, the wind teasing his hair. I smile, studying his face as he relaxes.

I love the gentle happiness in his eyes as he pauses to take in the quiet moment, one arm resting on his knee while he lets his other leg stretch out in front of him. It is a bit odd to see him like that, so... well, normal. No pressure from his parents, other girls, or his position. I watch the wind tease his hair a moment as he enjoys the soft breeze.

He makes me jump when he suddenly falls back onto the blanket, crossing one ankle over the other and putting his hands behind his head as he looks up at the sky. I look up too.

Gavril comments on how many names we have for things, like clouds. I lie beside him, so he can point them out to me. I had no idea clouds had so many different names. He holds my hand as we lie there.

It's really relaxing here in the sun: not too harsh with the breeze, the sound of the ocean, and the warmth of his hand in mine. I think we're both enjoying the quiet moment as we digest our lunch. After a while, we stop trying to discuss the proper names of the clouds and start giving them names by the shapes they look like.

Joy wanders over and lies between us, huffing as if telling us we're being naughty. "Sorry, do you need pets?" Gavril strokes her head. "Just don't get fluff all over us. Damian will not want to de-fluff Kascia."

Joy pulls her head up and tells Gavril off with her funny talking sounds. At least she didn't bark, but it still makes me laugh. She then spots something and goes stiff. She'd seen a squirrel, and it takes Gavril a while to calm her down.

"Guess she's right. About time we moved on."

"Oh?" I frown, not sure I want to go back inside yet.

Gavril looks at me in surprise. "You want to go back to the beach?"

"Sure. I'm sure there's lots to see. That can't be the whole beach."

"Well, there are the tide pools."

My eyes light up. I'm sure Gavril knows every inch of it. "Really?"

"You... want to see them?" Gavril looks at me still with that surprised expression but with a hint of something else. Hope perhaps?

"Why wouldn't I?"

"Most of the girls hate the idea. Well, not Zelda, but she's up for anything that lets her take impressions and notes with her tablet."

We both laugh.

"I think I can help you get a good view of them though." He gives me that slight smile that makes my heart race every time.

We walk down the beach again to the area under the ballroom balcony. It's rather cold down here with the shade and wind blowing.

It's a careful walk out onto the slippery wet stones. I'm glad I'm good with my feet, tiptoeing around to try not to step on anything. Gavril keeps hold of my hand to help us both balance in a kind of careful dance across the stones. He then helps me bend down over a large section filled with water.

"Wow." I'd have not noticed if he didn't draw my attention to it. This pond is filled with green, almost glowing, plant-like creatures.

"Tide pools are funny that way. Unless you pay attention, it's easy to miss something." Gavril smiles at me. I like that smile. It's one of my favorites: slightly playful, tender, but also excited. "And my mother used to hate me doing this, but..." He gently prods one of them, and it closes, looking as dull and brown as the stone. I gasp. He laughs. "They all will do that but wait a moment."

I watch, fascinated as eventually it slowly, very slowly opens back up.

I smile and dare try it myself with a slightly larger one. I can't help but giggle in delight as that one closes up. Gavril laughs, enjoying my fascination. I'd lived near these things my whole life and had no idea they were here.

Joy sniffs around the rocks, but she's not much interested in us. Gavril locates a grotto filled with barnacles and mussels, and as I soon learn, much more. Gavril points out some more shelled animals with various kinds of shells. I never would have guessed they were animals.

With that gentle light in his eyes he gets when he's explaining things, Gavril tells me how the creatures hold tight to the rocks during the harsh changing of the tides. He points out anemones in various colors, most of them green, and explains how they are waiting to catch unsuspecting prey that may swim by: crabs, fish, snails or whatever else it can catch.

He then finds some urchins in various colors, crabs running around in the kelp. As he leads me deeper, we see some fish swimming with more crabs scuttling around. Gavril points out some sea stars that don't look like the kind of sea stars I expected to see.

Gavril has such sharp eyes for the details. He sees the big things that distract me as well as spotting the little things like the scuttling crabs I almost miss. I would have missed most of these animals, even the ones with bright colors if he didn't draw my attention to them.

I find myself watching his face more than the animals he's pointing out to me, like when he showed me how a ship's sails and rudder work. There's a soft smile about his lips, a keenness and a light shining in his eyes that enchants me. He even finds some well-hidden hermit crabs.

But his most impressive find makes his face light up as if he were really the little boy his mother thinks he is. "Look at this." He gently pulls me over.

I smile, watching him before my eyes go to what he has found.

He's pointing between two rocks, but it's so dark, it takes a moment for my eyes to adjust. In the gap is a bright pink sea star with its arms wrapped around a clam shell.

I keep my eyes on the animals, but my mind is on how close Gavril is to me, his warmth in my hand, and how I feel his energy and warmth so close.

I jump slightly when with a sudden pop, the sea star gets the clam shell open. "Wow," I breathe in amazement. Gavril laughs, beaming at my awe and looks back at the starfish. "So, what will it do now? Open it more and shove the clam in its mouth?"

"No," Gavril shakes his head, "it will put its... well, tongue is the kindest way to say it, into the shell and digest the insides before it pulls the tongue back. You know, it took that sea star hours to open that. We're quite lucky we saw that moment."

"You're really good at this."

Gavril smiles. "You just have to slow down and pay attention."

"I'm clearly not good at it."

"You'll learn." Gavril runs his hand along my arm again as he slowly stands up. He opens his mouth to say something when we both jump as a wave hits a rock near us with surprising force, spraying us both with salt water.

"Been here too long," Gavril laughs. "We'll smell of seaweed for hours."

"Damian will not enjoy getting that smell out," I laugh.

"I think that will be your maids' job, not his." Gavril helps me up, taking both my hands in his. "But we should let them get a leg up on it. It's getting late." The sun is going down. I shiver a bit now I'm wet and in the shadow of the balcony.

Gavril helps me tiptoe our way out of the tide pools. It's nice to let my feet settle into the soft sand. Joy yawns and stands up. I think she took a nap in the sand. "The seagulls will have very soft nests this year because of you," Gavril informs the dog as we walk up the beach.

Joy huffs a "no" at Gavril as we walk, insisting it is "my fluff".

"Then stop shedding it," Gavril teases. Then Joy spots more seabirds and goes to chase them away from her fluff. Gavril chuckles.

I realize this part of the day is almost over. I can't help but hold Gavril's hand a bit tighter. I don't want it to end. I could skip through those tide pools with him all day. I don't think I have felt so safe and relaxed in months. Gavril squeezes back but keeps his face neutral as we have to lure Joy back up to the main castle grounds. I take a deep breath of the flowers and grass.

"It's likely about time to get ready for dinner," says Gavril.

"Is that not part of the ball?"

"No, in fact, I wonder how the girls are going to react. My parents will be having their own private dinner just like us."

Gavril doesn't let go of my hand once we get inside like I thought he would. I expected being back in the main cage would make him close off again, but he leads me up the staircase to my bedroom as if we walk hand-in-hand all the time. I can't help but hear a few girls whisper as we go, but I don't see them. Maybe I'm just paranoid.

I smile as I step into my room and close the door behind me, my back to it. I bite my lips to hold in my smile. The realization the day isn't actually over is so delightful I try not to shiver in joy.

Damian smiles at me as I step away from the door, and my maids rush over to help me get ready. Flur makes a face as she smells the tide pools on me.

"What is that?" Vivian asks, trying not to reveal how bad it smells. Funny, Gavril liked it.

"Ocean," I confess.

"He didn't take you to the music hall after?" Flur frowns. Vivian gives her a look.

"What?" I frown.

"Well... he hinted he might take you to the music room again after lunch. You were on the beach all day?" Flur asks in surprise.

"I didn't want to go inside, so asked if there was anything else we could do outside. He showed me the tide pools." I smile at how it made him light up.

"Oh," Flur pauses in surprise, but Vivian is smiling in understanding and amusement.

She gets right to business. "That will need a bath. Drying your hair is going to be difficult."

Chapter 28

The dress they put me in for dinner is not the same as the one they planned for the ball. It's dark blue with a stunning flow to it. It looks straight in line with my body until I move, and it flutters and ripples like water around my body. The sleeves are transparent and cape style, going to the middle of my upper arm. The material is transparent with stunning intricate beadwork with dark blue and silver beads making a beautiful set of circle patterns as if the beads are wrapping across my shoulders. The center of the circle pattern has extra beadwork making a diamond shaped frame around a circle shape with a beaded pennant in the center. Smaller patterns are on each of my arms too. I love it.

When Gavril arrives, he's dressed in a crisp navy-blue suit, soft cravat with a navy pin, and his hair done perfectly. He smiles at me as he looks me over. I'm sure I'm doing the same. He looks good. I don't know if I've seen a suit so perfectly fitted to him, making him look stronger, younger, more like himself.

Gavril leads me to a different room than we used for the chastity date, though not too far from it. This room still has a nice view of the sea. But there is something different in this room. There's a piano shining in a corner.

We enjoy the first two courses when Gavril asks what songs I like best by male performers. I should have known what he was up to as he reviewed the list, got up, and started to play the piano and sing a few for me. I adore it, teasing him about not singing for people.

"You're more than just people," he replies with a soft smile. The look in Gavril's eyes is new; there's a hunger there as well as a tenderness. I smile back softly. "Well, we have a bit of time. Would you like to join me for a few?"

Now he's ensnared me. I join him at the piano, and we enjoy a few duets before it's time to prepare for the ball. But with how the day has gone, even if this were the end of the day, I could go to bed happy.

I return to my room to change. As per tradition I'm sure, I cannot wear the same outfit. And I'm delighted. This dress is stunning. It's mostly a dark periwinkle color that fades to white towards the bottom of the skirt. It's patterned with gold leaves. The sleeves flow from the bust line up and around my shoulders in a beautiful pattern with two folds making me think of being wrapped in the twilight sky. My maids twist my hair into an elegant knot that hangs down the back of my neck in elegant twists, making a beautiful princess-like look. They make my makeup soft yet elegant, highlighting my eyes with just a hint of periwinkle blue to tie the whole look together. They then add soft pearl earrings, and for the first time, a tiara. It's a gentle gold, designed in the same leafing pattern on the dress. Pearls shine at the top of each point of the tiara with periwinkle tinted gems interlaced throughout the gold leafing. But the finest accessory is the shoes, periwinkle and gold with flowers carved into the heel in stunning patterns. Cinderella's glass slippers are put to shame by these.

"If I lose, I'm taking these with me," I tell Damian as I admire them in the mirror.

He chuckles. "Please do." He beams at me which softens to a warm smile. "You look heavenly."

"Thank you." I smile over my shoulder to strike a jokingly seductive look. "Your work is appreciated."

Damian bows his head to me then straightens up, smiling. "I'm glad to hear it. Now," he rests his fingers under my chin, "night angel, enjoy this night and make it yours," he says in almost a hushed tone as his eyes sparkle at me.

I smile and nod, touched at the look he gives me. It's like having all the good things I miss about my father back and none of the nightmare. I try to hold in the emotion as that love and warmth floods me, but I can't. I give Damian a tight hug, trying to hold in the tears and avoid messing up my maids' hard work.

He smiles and holds me tight, wrapping me in his warm embrace. I hold it a moment longer before I pull back. I take a deep breath. "I'm ready."

I take his arm. He smiles and leads me down to the ballroom, but not to the lower entrance I usually come through. We use the upper doors. This is where the royal family normally enters. I glance at Damian with a smile.

Damian smiles knowingly then drops my arm and takes my hand just before we pass through the entrance. As he glides me forward, he slows his own step and lets go, allowing me to glide to the front of the balcony where I can see the rest of the court with their dates or spouses, and the other girls with guards or servants to keep them enjoying the night.

The opening of the top doors draws everyone's attention. I take a deep breath, but for once, I'm not ashamed of the attention. Damian made me a night angel, and there's no reason to be shy about it. And more than that, I earned tonight. I smile and curtsy a little to all of them. I catch sight of Zelda's beaming face, but that's the only other Chosen I notice before I finally spot the royal family.

The king's grin makes me almost giggle; he likes this ball to say the least. The queen is repressing a smile as she looks at her husband as if telling him to behave, but when she looks back at me, her expression is almost proud.

When the king glances to his left with a slight smirk, it draws my eyes to Gavril who's not looking at his father, but he's looking at me with a smile so large it makes his eyes crinkle at the corners. It's a beaming delight I've never seen before. I can see his chest rise as he takes a breath and turns to his parents with a bow of his head, excusing himself before going over to the stairs.

I realize that's my cue and turn to walk down the steps as I have been taught a million times to do right. Head up and hand on the rail as a guide. It's as natural as any other way to me.

I meet Gavril at the bottom of the stairs and give him a proper curtsy, bowing my head, and he bows to me, still beaming. He looks so handsome, happy, and just a little nervous. The gold embroidery on his collar stands out pleasantly in this light. It draws my attention to the fact he's not wearing a cravat, just the collar showing off his stunning figure. I look down at the embroidery on his left cuff, pant legs, and how they oppose the pleated sash that marks him crown prince.

"It's you," Gavril beams at me. "You look…" he struggles for the word. "Heavenly." He takes my hand and kisses it gently, still admiring me with just his eyes over my hand. "My Asteria," he whispers, making my cheeks flush in pleasure. "May I have this first dance, Your Majesty?"

"That's withheld for ruling royalty."

"No one in this wide world is more majestic than you tonight, my Asteria."

He makes my breath hitch once again before he gently leads me to the center of the dance floor. The king waves at the players to hurry up. I can't help but smile as the prince glides me into position.

I have danced with him many times, but this time, his touch floods me with an exhilarating feeling as my heart races in delight. I take a deep breath and dare look up into Gavril's smiling face; his amber eyes rest on me tenderly, filling me with that feeling all the more.

It's magical as we slowly step to the music. We don't speak, just dance at first, but slowly, we step and twirl around one another, taking our time to flow back into a closed hold after each set. It's different than it's been before. It's like he's communicating through the dance more than he ever has, mirroring how awkward our relationship was, slow and unsure, then firm and strong before hot and unsure once more.

When the song ends, we stand inches from one another; his breath on my skin makes it tingle pleasantly. We're so close. But it's in this moment, I feel every eye in the room on us: certain it's the other ten girls who would kill to be in my place. But I refuse to let that break the moment. Even as the nervousness creeps into my heart, I remind myself this is my stage. I won it. Gavril's grip tightens on me slightly as if he senses something unsure in me.

As the next song starts and he leads me right into it, I smile again as the magic of the movement breaks me free of the moment of uncertainty.

"I've never seen you smile so much," he whispers into my ear, his lips inches from my ear. His breath slithers down my neck, making me shudder in pleasure at his touch. "Amazing how much you open up when you don't feel pressured. You'd think an actress wouldn't mind an audience."

I frown a little. "I suppose it has been a bit of a nightmare." We had been a nightmare. We hadn't even known one another a year, yet it feels like I have known him a lifetime. The time when he first tried to convince me to openly accept him was like a hundred years ago and the fights of the delegations were ten years ago. In just a few months, Gavril and I have had more rough patches, good times, and struggles to get through than Jake and I had in a decade of engagement.

The music that plays now is more open and excited, an elegant swing for lack of a better expression. Gavril beams as he gets me into the movement.

"It's been a romantic adventure with as much drama as Shakespeare's finest," Gavril agrees. I laugh. "Question is, is it more of a *Taming of the Shrew* in reverse or perhaps more *Much Ado About Nothing*?"

"Is this all for nothing?" I ask as we let go for our turns before coming back together again.

"No, but there's little I'm allowed to say about what the ado is about," Gavril says as this upbeat song ends quickly, and a gentler piece picks up. He doesn't even hesitate to let us keep dancing, and I like that. I'd rather stay on the floor.

Gavril twists me into a lower cape position. I smile at how comfortable that position is, like coming home.

"You like that," Gavril smiles as he leads me into the back step turn.

I smile and nod, looking down, unable to meet his eyes as I revel in the feeling. I have not felt so comfortable and at ease in so long.

"How are you doing that?" I dare ask as we return to a closed position.

"Doing what?" Gavril asks, his tone low with a hint of mischief as we return to a basic, and he settles me close to him, his lips close to my ear again. His hand holds mine more securely than is typical of a proper dance position. I fight not to close my eyes and fold into his hold.

"What are you doing?" I giggle, liking this romantic teasing.

"I don't know. Trust me. When I figure it out, I'll never stop," he says, securing my hand in his even more.

He might stop. When the day won is done, he will have no choice. My heart falters in disappointment at the impending moment. How did I let this moment go? It had kept me alight. I forgot what it was like without it.

"You don't believe me," Gavril states as we continue our dance.

"I don't believe you?" I frown, unsure what he means.

"You don't think I'd keep doing it, do you?"

"I can assume you'd want to."

The tension that runs through Gavril's body delights and startles me. I easily stop myself backing away from him because part of me likes it, and it also reminds me of how he acts when he loses his temper. I'm able to tell the difference between when he's angry and will lash out and when its controlled. It's wonderful feeling like I'm close enough to him to understand the difference. But it also helps me know when I should speak or give him space.

I dare look up at his face and his closed eyes, his jaw set as he gets his temper under control.

"What would it take for you to believe it?"

"What?" I don't understand what he's trying to say, but he has kept the basic step going so perfectly no one notices the awkward moment.

"Is it me or this life you doubt?" Gavril asks me gently, pulling back to see my face.

"I still don't understand."

A soft smile crosses his lips as he looks me over, spinning me in a way that makes my skirt show off exactly how beautiful Damian's work is.

"You fit this world better than I do," he says as he admires me in our dance. "You're elegant, beautiful, stubborn, more of a queen than a million queens before you. Your tiara is just a tad too small." He gives me a teasing smile.

"I'm fine with its size."

"Exactly." Gavril's face falls a little. "You are more perfect than many who have filled that crown, yet you're afraid of it."

I finally catch on to what he's thinking. "Gavril," I say resolutely. "I told you; I don't want to go. The other night was just... realizing all it entailed." I smile as he draws closer to me again as if unable to resist. I close my eyes for a moment. "If I get this often enough, it will be enough."

Oh flames, did I just say that out loud?

"Will it?" Gavril's eyes meet mine again.

I can't look away as I reply, "It will." If I really win, if I really get this.

We're quiet for a moment, continuing the dance. As it slows to an end, Gavril pulls close to me again, whispering into my ear in the way I'm coming to absolutely adore. "Do you really want this life?"

I smile as his breath caresses my neck. "Yes," I breathe back.

I feel his smile against my cheek. I lean ever closer to him, not fully recognizing how I am drawn to him. I feel so safe, at home, wrapped up in him in a way that feels liberating and empowering. How does that even make sense?

Gavril takes a breath to say something, but the song halts suddenly, snapping us out of the moment and looking around. Something spilled near the players, or more like splashed. A group of servants are already working to clean it up as a group of guests move away.

"Perhaps we should get away from the attention," Gavril says quietly to me and takes my hand, using his body to block the action from the view of the group that made the disturbance.

Attention? I look around the room. Many girls are on the floor too: dancing with staff, off-duty guards, members of court, and the like. The king and queen are still dancing too, looking quietly content in their own moment. Gavril's sharp eyes picked up something mine are missing.

"Or perhaps we should make them sick of us."

"What?"

"If we dance long enough, they'll get bored with old news," Gavril explains as he leads me back into position.

I'd never complain at more time to dance with him. This time though, I try to look around as we own the floor and see what Gavril spotted, but I'm still not sure what it was. His parents are dancing too; Sage is talking with Princess Zelda off in a far corner, away from everyone else. Princess Rose is fluttering her fan and speaking to Princess Amapola, both looking over at us. Jonquil, Bella, and Azalea are by the food table, trying not to look at us, but I see Jonquil glancing over a few times in just the few moments I watch them. Isla is dancing with a guard. Florence is dancing with some member of the court. Ericka and Forsythia are glaring daggers at me. I try to avoid looking at them again.

"Hey, don't worry about them," Gavril says after a dance where I pay more attention to what's around us than the bubble we have made.

"You see so much I miss," I say longingly. I wish I could notice what he did.

"You didn't need to see that." Gavril glances at Ericka and Forsythia.

Would I be jealous if I saw it? Does he just not want me to see how much he looks at them too?

"Can I explain later when they're not looking?" he asks, watching me as I still am looking around the room with each round of the waltz.

"I just wish I could see it."

"Does their opinion matter so much?" he asks with a hint of disappointment in his voice.

"I suppose not." Not today at least.

"How about we break to get some water? We've been dancing a while," he suggests as the latest song ends.

I nod my agreement and slide my hand down his arm, enjoying how smooth and strong the fabric feels. We saunter over to the food table, and Gavril gets us drinks before leading us away from the others to our own corner.

He sighs when he sees I'm still looking around. "Kascia, really, it's fine. They will have to deal with it. You won. I didn't play easy on anyone. I used the same strategy with all of them. I wish you'd stop feeling so guilty for it." There's a hint of his temper hiding under the surface of his statement.

"It's not that." I run my finger over the rim of my glass as I try to think how to explain it.

A slight smile crosses Gavril's face as he watches. "So, what is it?"

"Sometimes it does bother me, but not tonight."

"Is it those kinds of thoughts that made you realize how lonely it will be when they're gone? Don't you look forward to that, even just a little?" he asks, his brows drawing together slightly. "Don't you look forward to being alone?"

I realize how horrible that sounds from his point of view. I am dreading the girls leaving but that also means I dread us being alone if I win.

"Oh no, it's not that at all," I amend. I look down again, holding my glass in both hands. "I guess the reality that we'd have more time together doesn't feel real. It feels like all the time we spend away from you now would just be empty hours then."

"If the court, staff, and my parents are smart, you won't have too many hours to waste, and I'll happily fill those up for you." He smiles gently at me. "I'd give you anything you wanted. I..." He stops himself, clearing his throat and looking away.

I smile. He has a whole speech he is trying not to force me to endure. I want to take his hand and ask him to give it to me anyway, but I don't. I know we're still in public, and to spare his feelings, I avoid looking around again, but I'm sure we're not free from watching eyes. Would we ever be?

"I didn't spike your drink you know," Gavril teases.

I take a drink hastily. The fruit infused water on my throat makes me realize I am thirsty from our dancing and drink more. We're quiet as we finish our drinks. I determinedly watch the dancers, so I don't notice who's staring.

Just as I finish, the music stops, and the conductor calls for everyone to find a partner for the next number, making the largest group on the dance floor yet. Gavril gently takes my glass for me and sets it down before offering his hand.

I smile, more than ready to retreat into the dance that is our special getaway. It's a stunning waltz, and it's one of the special ones where a singer adds lyrics to the music. I love those best.

There are plenty of smiling happy couples. I even spot Fabian with his wife among the dancers, but he's clearly paying far more attention to his wife than any of the Chosen, so for once, I'm not anxious to see him. It's not like he could make things worse for us anyway.

We go around the circle of dance a few times when Gavril suddenly changes directions near the balcony, and in a few smooth turns, we've danced our way out the balcony doors and onto the polished balcony floor. The music still flutters through the open doors as we keep dancing.

I giggle and move closer to Gavril, partly for his warmth as the sudden cold shocks me. But the night air helps clear away all the fears and doubts that suffocated us in the ballroom. Now, it's just us, the night, the stars, the ocean, and the music for us to dance to.

We don't speak for a while, enjoying our waltz around the open space, allowing Gavril to lead us into some steps and lifts we'd never dare do in the crowded room.

I laugh as we come together after a few rather ambitious rounds. "What are you doing, Your Highness?" I ask flirtatiously.

"I like it better outside," he comments on our location rather than his choice of steps.

"You've had me alone outside all day," I point out.

"All but alone," he corrects, "until now." He glances at the doors.

"And now?" I ask, my heart pounding in nervous hope.

Gavril smiles and turns back to me, not slacking in our basic step one bit. "And now they're all busy."

He's right. Sage was pulled onto the floor by Zelda when the conductor invited *everyone* on the floor. Had Gavril planned that? How much had he planned today? He'd orchestrated everything. He had worked hard to make today magical not for him, but me. He must have asked the conductor for this moment.

"And they agreed to all of it?"

"About as much as you did," Gavril says, and his grip on me secures as if he's afraid I'll break away at the confession.

Not only do I let him, I move into his grip, daring to lean in more than I have yet, as close as our dance position will allow.

A large smile crosses Gavril's face as he holds me more tenderly. "It was worth it, even just for this," he says with breathless air to his voice. "Kascia, I..." he pauses.

I stop too, waiting patiently, letting our dance position fall, though he holds my hand in his still and takes my other hand as I let it drop. He looks up at me with a vulnerable desperation in his eyes. "Remember when you didn't fear being the favorite?"

"Did I ever?"

"Alright, when you weren't afraid to let me get close," Gavril corrects himself.

"Sometimes. Other times, I think those moments were dreams." I look down at our hands as Gavril starts to caress them like he had many times before, like Jake had done.

"Then you recall when I broke it?" Gavril asks, looking up to meet my eyes again.

"I broke it," I admit in an intimidated squeak. I ruined it, my pride and fear ruined everything.

"I'm the one who accused you," Gavril says, a new sound to his voice: fear. I look up at him in surprise. "And demanded you prove yourself when I've done so little to prove myself to you. I never thought you..." He pauses again, picking his words carefully. I watch him, letting him take his time as my heart pounds in anxious hope. What is he trying to say?

"I have so little understanding of how this is supposed to work. I've neglected the best thing I've ever had and never realized..." He stops once more. He's really struggling.

"Gavril?"

Gavril meets my eyes again and caresses my cheek. I close my eyes and treasure the warm touch on my face. "I don't know how to say it. A part of me feels certain saying it is useless, empty without actions. But the knowledge of how eludes me and now I know I've been prevented at every turn."

"Prevented? From what? Gavril, what's wrong?" I frown.

"Not... wrong." Gavril pulls his hand back tentatively. "After you saw my father's attack, I thought it all was clear. It seemed so clear in that moment, but then everyone told me I was wrong, including me."

His gaze drops once more. "Yet you kept amazing me. You were the only one who noticed him, noticed what I needed and gave it. No matter how hard I tried to get the other girls to be like you, do what you did, it was useless. I'd give them every chance, both staged and natural, begging someone to be my protection if I was wrong. No one did."

Gavril's mouth twitches, eyes still on our hands as he gently caresses mine; his skin looks so dark in the moonlight compared to mine. "I tried all I could to give them a sporting chance, trying to eliminate you as even a choice in my mind to allow someone, anyone, to have a chance. And in doing so, I lost the best thing I had without realizing it."

His breathing picks up, drawing my eyes to his chest as it rises and falls in his struggle to express himself correctly. "I should have though. It got harder and harder not to think of you, to wish I was with you when I was out with other girls. Every single time, it keeps coming back to you. What I lacked that day and every day since, you filled. You may not believe that, but it's true. You do it day after day, impress me, enchant me, make me better."

His stunning amber eyes meet mine once again. "Even when you drive me insane, or we get stuck in one of our fights where I lose my temper or struggle not to, I'm still happier there than having a lovely evening with anyone else."

I bite my lips to keep my breath under control. I can't believe what I'm hearing. What is he doing?

"And in an attempt to make this game fair with unfair rules, I had no idea I wasn't just keeping my longing in control, I was confusing and depriving you." His gaze is unwavering from mine. "I'm sorry. I always thought when you said you wanted to win it meant you knew and wanted..." He can't bring himself to say it. "I didn't realize you meant you wanted to win because it was winning, if that makes sense."

I nod. "Gavril, I didn't—"

"And of course, you didn't know. I stupidly assumed you knew. How could you when I..." He stops again. Do I dare speak? "I was so sure in my feelings I didn't think anyone else couldn't be. I told you once I'd choose you if given the chance. Do you still think that's true?"

"I...." I cannot lie and say I do. "It was true when you said it."

Gavril bows his head and nods in defeat. I have never seen his shoulders sag like this. I blink to stop the tears that try to spring to my eyes. My heart aches to see it. My reaction surprises me.

"Everyone else thought you were the favorite. I thought that meant you knew you were." Gavril lets out a sigh, looking off to his left into the night sky stretching out to the sea. "And always have been." His eyes return to mine. "Can you believe that?"

I fear believing it, but there is no way to deny the look in his eyes: the begging, the guilt, the adoration. "I can understand the doubts. I challenged you. And you had a leg up with how we met, but it's not that. It's not that the delegations liked you, or that the press likes you, or that you pass each test with ease. That's all just extra to me. No matter what, how I tried to get you from my mind or try to use all those excuses, I keep going back to what I thought that day."

"That this girl is trouble?" I ask with a playful smile, afraid of his intensity.

"No," Gavril chuckles with a breathless smile. "Not that day, though I have certainly thought it many times since." He caresses my cheek again. "That it's you. Even when I say it was the passion of the moment, how overwrought I was, how beautiful you looked that day and since, but it's not that. I know it's not that because when I try to recreate it with someone else, it fails again and again. I fail you again and again.

"Kascia, it's you. I still would, without hesitation, choose you if it finally was my choice to make. And all this time, I was fighting to play this unfair game with fair rules, but I should have known that's not possible, so why try?"

He pauses to study my face, drinking me in as if just looking at me satisfies his soul so deeply it would sustain him the rest of his life. I want to look away, but I can't. "You know what the hardest part was?"

I shake my head.

"How much I wanted to do what I should have done this whole time. I didn't realize that I should or had to prove myself to you as you had to for me because of this contest. All I wanted to do was—" He stiffens like he did in the ballroom, like when he is containing his temper... his desire.

The tension in the air is so thick I wonder if I'll have to push it away if I try to move closer to him. The desire to move closer is overwhelming, but I'm afraid. Afraid that when I accept it, it will be torn away again like it was last time when my father's false pride poisoned it.

Anger floods me as I realize that's been the real thing holding me back this whole time. Every problem that's come up in my uncertainty has been because of what my father's done to me, not Gavril. He's been one of the safest choices in my life. How sad is that?

The rush of anger only makes Gavril's next action all the more delicious as he lets the restraints break and kisses me with all the tension, desire, and apology he had tried to share more purely and perfectly in that kiss than any words he could have picked.

I kiss him back, getting my fingers tangled in his curly hair and shuddering as his fingers get lost in mine too. He holds me tightly to him, pulling me almost into a dip as he presses into me, and the feeling is more wonderful than dancing on air. It's empowering, beautifying.

"I choose you," Gavril says breathlessly as he pulls back just enough to speak, but I keep my eyes closed to hold onto this feeling.

His words strike me like having a bucket of water dumped on my head. "You can't," I remind him, also breathlessly.

"I can't declare you the winner, but I can choose you, and I should have a long time ago." The determination in Gavril's voice makes my heart race. "I know I'm terrible at it. I tried to show it, and you hardly noticed."

"What?"

"I followed some good advice but not well. I sent flowers and brought you a treat, though admittedly that likely looked more like I was just trying to cheer you up," Gavril confesses, but he doesn't let go of me.

I think back. My maids did mention Gavril sent flowers. And there had been little treats or chocolates on my desk, but Damian often had little bits brought up with tea when he and my maids were working as I'd worked on the festival plans. Had they all been from Gavril?

"I should have sent more than a card with my signature on it, uh?" Gavril asks.

"I might have missed them anyway," I admit as my mind races with that realization. He'd been trying to send me favors? Had he sent anyone else favors, ever? He had tried to say something the night after the play. Had that been when he meant to have this conversation? What else have I missed?

"And I've been stupid not to show you I still feel that way. I thought you knew. I didn't... and when I did, I asked, but you said you wanted to win. I thought that meant me," he says the last bit so fast it sounds like he's trying to say it before he loses his nerve. "Not this game. I should have realized."

"I didn't exactly mean I didn't want to leave because I didn't want to lose the Enthronement." I frown. "Gavril, I want to win." I want to win him.

"So, if I threw this whole thing, abdicated and moved to Englaria, you'd still want me?"

I smile but can't hide the sadness and shame in my eyes. "Honestly, you would be the best thing ever to happen to me."

A hope lights his eyes, making them almost glow in the starlight. "Really?"

"I..." I grip his shirt tightly in my hands. "I have always wanted my apprentice."

There's a pregnant pause in which my heart races in fear, and I don't dare look up from his chest to his face. But I get the answer as he swoops down and kisses me again, and again, and again.

I sigh in delight and return it, wrapping my arms around his neck. I'm wrapped up in his happiness, his delight that he tries to share with me in each kiss which I'm all too eager to return.

"So, when you get upset with me for trying to treat you as the favorite?" he asks, pressing his forehead to mine and still grinning from ear to ear.

I giggle in delight, still hanging off his neck, delighting in his arms around me. "I'm scared of how the others will bully me or how much having you now and then losing you when I fail would crush me."

That statement is said in a pleasant voice, but the words bring the crushing reality back down on me. I fought so hard not to give anyone else the power to break me like Father and Jake had. I'd failed.

Gavril kisses me more tenderly this time. I sigh and run my hand across his smooth cheek. "I will be there, no matter what," Gavril promises me.

"You don't pick the winner."

"But my heart chose who I—"

"Don't!" My own cry surprises me.

Gavril pulls back, face filled with confusion and worry. "What?"

"I..." I bite my lip to stop it shaking and hug him, wrapping my arms around his waist under his jacket.

Gavril uneasily returns the embrace. He is quiet for me like I had been for him, and I'm grateful for it. "If you say that and I lose..." I'll shatter. I won't survive it. Even now, I'm riding a dangerous line.

"You won't."

"We don't know that. I won't survive it if..." If he says it and he has to take it back.

Gavril sighs and holds me tighter. "I can respect that." Though I can hear it's a bitter pill for him to swallow. "So, I'm not allowed to? Is that really why you hate me?"

"I don't hate you," I say quietly, still hiding in his chest.

"Alright, that's why you hate being the favorite and the hints?"

I nod timidly.

"So, I'm not allowed to…" Gavril searches for a word. I feel him look up in thought. I smile, picturing the expression I know so well. "I'm not allowed to show it, then?"

"Haven't you already?"

"Badly. If I can do anything to prove it to you, I mean it, I'll do it. I can't call this game off or use my eliminations to narrow it down to you, but anything I can do." Gavril gently pulls back, so he can kiss me again. "I am learning giving into my wants isn't always evil."

I giggle at his tone. That brings another smile I treasure in my heart's collection.

"Hmm, you like that tone," he notes, trying to use it again but ruining it a little with the laughter in his voice. I giggle again. "Oh Kascia, it would be so different if only I could choose."

"No more Ericka and Cuppy to annoy us." I hold to the happy feeling.

"Kascia, it would be over." Gavril gives me a look. "You understand that's what I'm saying, right?"

"Really?"

"Tonight, if I had the power. Please, I will do anything you ask to prove I mean that."

"You really don't have any other girls you like?" I saw how he kissed Forsythia, dated Zelda more than anyone else, and his tender smiles for Bella.

Gavril shakes his head. "No. I tried to keep sane during this insane game. But I understand it's not possible, so I'm going to do what I've wanted, and you've needed. To me, that matters more than anything else."

"Are you going to tell them?"

Gavril frowns. "Tell who?"

"Your parents. Are you going to tell them your choice?"

Gavril pauses in thought as if this hadn't occurred to him before. "Oh." His lower lip sticks out a little as he digests this thought. "I'd not thought of that. I'm not sure it would make a difference," he says the last bit slowly as he processes it.

"So, it's not worth a try?" Didn't he just say he'd do anything?

"Well, it could make it worse. You know my mother. How do you think she'll react?" He smiles in amusement.

That is a fair point. I don't want his admission to get me kicked out or worse. But if he won't confess it to anyone else, does he really mean it? He can't tell the other girls. "So, you won't try?"

"Do you really think it will help?"

"It means you mean it."

"Ah," Gavril says slowly and nods succinctly. "I see. Well, I don't want my mother to use it against you, and I think she would if I told her. However," he adds, giving me a side eye as I open my mouth to protest, "it may sway my father in our favor. I'll tell him, and perhaps if he thinks it prudent, he can tell Mother. Perhaps she'll take it better from him than me."

"Promise?" I study his eyes, begging for the proof my heart needs to trust again.

Gavril smiles and kisses me tenderly, relaxing me. "Promise," he says gently. "But his reaction makes no difference on how I feel. I really would end it tonight, right here, right now. You're my choice, Kascia. No hesitation. I've even tried to talk myself out of it. My guard still thinks I'm nuts, but... I'm sure."

That's when it becomes real. That's when all the protections I'd fought for crumble like they are made from playing cards, toppled by the breath of his promise.

I beam and wrap my arms around him and kiss him in my happiness. I feel the surprise in Gavril's hesitation to react, but he returns it and brushes my hair back tenderly. "And until you win this, my goal is to never make you question again." He uses that low voice that sets my heart alight.

"Come," he breathes gently as we pull apart, taking my hand that rests on his shoulder. "The others will notice if we're gone much longer."

I nod, and he leads me back to the open doors. I smile as I study his face as he counts the beats to make it easier for us to slip back into the dance. The song has changed, but everyone is still on the floor.

Something about this dance is better than the others, and it is not just the lyrics put to music. It's as if having him confess and his promise makes the music finer, the energy of our interaction more powerful and sacred, real. We don't have to talk because there's nothing to hold us back from dancing and acting out our feelings, no inhibitions. And Gavril takes full advantage. It's one of the most beautiful dances we have ever done.

After the song, Gavril leads me back towards the table for a drink. What I don't realize is it's because he's trying to get eyes off us again. He tries to tease me by guessing which of the treats I'd want most, making me laugh, but it does what he wants.

"I have one more surprise," he whispers in my ear as he takes my hand again.

"What?" I frown. What in all creation could he do now?

In a graceful moment, he pulls me towards one of the side exits. He looks back and nods once before we slip out. He's letting me know Sage is watching us.

We take side passages I don't know as well, all dark, and we see only a few guards keeping patrol as they go. None comment, but one of them shakes his head in amusement at us, and another tries to hide a giggle behind her hand as we hurry past.

When we finally arrive, I'm so turned around, I'm not sure which floor it is. Gavril leads me to a door that's pretty, delicately carved with flowers and ocean waves. Gavril carefully opens the door, glancing around before guiding me inside.

It's so dark, I struggle to see. Gavril leads me to the left into a large room. The only light comes from little openings in the curtains that cover the far wall. Gavril finds the light and taps it on.

The floor is the first thing I notice as I look down to protect my eyes. It's fine, covered in dust, but even with the dust, I can see the elegant ocean creatures and themes across the marble. The walls are paneled with a seashell white along the bottom half with the top painted with colors that make me think of the brightly lit sea, not one solid color but somehow painted with various shades. I'd rarely seen such beautiful work on a wall.

The curtains are coral pink with blue and pink island roses done into the pattern. The chandelier above us is a stunning crystal designed to mimic seashells. The rest of the room is hard to interpret when all the furniture is covered with dust protectors. The last detail I notice is a beautiful rug done mostly in ocean blues and whites with coral pink hints making a brilliant collection that stands under the furniture in the center of the room.

"What do you think?" Gavril is beaming at me.

"Where are we?" What is he so excited about?

"I guess it's hard to judge when it's so dusty and covered up," Gavril agrees. "I think we'll leave footprints." He looks over the floor. "But let's see more." He leads me to the right to one of the many doors. He takes me to the one closest to the far wall and opens it for me and waits for me to go in.

This room is even more dusty. A lighter, calmer shade of coral pink curtains cover more windows on the left with more transparent seashell white curtains over them and flower patterns done into them with the same coral color. The walls are much the same as the last room but calmer and simpler. I can't quite put my finger on it, but it gives off a feeling as if to help one relax.

I can tell what furniture is in this room by their shapes, whereas the ones in the last room were too generic for me to guess. One is a four-poster bed. There's a wardrobe, a vanity, and a desk. An odd feeling twists its way into my stomach. There's something familiar about this layout.

"Gavril," I say slowly, "where are we?" My breath has become shallow as I try to take in where I think we are.

"Can't you guess?" Gavril is still smiling.

"Why are you showing me this?" I ask as my eyes go up to a golden chandelier, this time with a fan twisted above it with the blades mimicking long shells.

"You can't believe we're here, can you?" Gavril laughs.

"Gavril!" I give him a look and hit his arm. "Be serious for a moment." Showing me his bride's room is not to be taken lightly.

"I am," Gavril defends, still smiling. "It's the princess's suite. You can change out whatever you like in here. This room is more open to new paintings, so you can take your pick."

"Gavril." He's far too confident in his choice.

"Oh, you'll like this." He guides me to a door near the wardrobe. "Though Damian keeps the inside of your closet amazing, I think he'd like the extra space in here."

"It can't be that big."

Gavril raises a brow then pulls me over. It takes him a moment to get it open. It seems to have gotten stuck after not being used for so long, but once he opens it, my mouth falls open. "That's the study," I insist.

"No, that's the closet," Gavril says, beaming at the shock on my face. He takes both my hands and leads me back out. "And of course, there's your study."

"Gavril," I chide. It's not mine yet. *Yet.* I just thought "yet". The delight of that realization distracts me as Gavril pulls me to the study.

"And the best part is, it's so big it could double as a studio," he suggests. "Perhaps something to help with acoustics, put a music player in here, and it would be perfect for both. We can install a bar along that wall, and the desk can be designed to roll into a corner easily enough."

It's hard not to daydream about what he's suggesting. "It's not mine yet," I remind him. "Should we really act like it's going to be?"

"Why not?" Gavril beams, turning to take both my hands and kissing them. "I see no reason to hesitate." A mischievous smile crosses his face. "Shall we try it?"

I open my mouth to protest, but he pulls me into a closed hold, and we spin across the room. His enthusiasm makes me laugh and hold tightly to his chest as I try to get my head on right. I have never been swept off my feet like this, and it feels amazing. The small twinge of regret I feel over Jake is erased as Gavril kisses me in pure joy.

He's loving every second of this. Each laugh, each stunned look, he's happier than I have ever known him as he spoils me, getting me to smile. He's enjoying this perhaps more than me, yet he's the one giving me everything.

I take a steadying breath as he pulls back and looks around. "Hmm, we could also get something to cover up mirrors. You need those, right?"

"Gavril, stop it." I smile. I must admit it's fun, but this is dangerous. We don't know I'll win. I'm still nothing more than a spy in these walls.

"Why? Too overwhelming?'

"No."

"Excited?" he teases by whispering into my ear.

"Gavril," I laugh. "Just because you said you'd end it tonight doesn't mean it's over."

"So, we plan for the future," Gavril replies, not phased one bit by my hesitation. Then his eyes light up. "Oh, that reminds me." He takes my hand again and leads me out. "There's one more treasure to see." He takes me back into the bedroom, around the curve in the wall to a door near the closet. He opens it, turns on the light, and leads me into the space. "If you think the study was big, this is bigger."

He's right. It's the washroom, and it's huge. On my right is the long, beautiful vanity area with a sink in the shape of a seashell, large mirrors, and decorative shelving for all the bits I'd ever want. Straight ahead, is a wall with a door in it. On the right is a large shower, tub, and a corner where the toilet is. There's also a door to the left of the bathing area with a storage closet beside it.

"Turn it on," Gavril dares me, pointing to the shower.

"No way."

"It's fun."

"No. Not mine."

"Yet," Gavril argues. I give him a look. He needs to stop saying that. "It has many settings to play with. There's a normal spray, waterfall style, steam shower, and a massage feature. I like that one after a long workout. But even better is the tub with the jets and salts." I don't know why that makes me laugh. "What? You get sore getting this strong," Gavril defends. "And Custods weren't always shy to give me a good hit if I couldn't block it."

"I can imagine it feels good," I admit. "A foot bath after a hard show is a blessing."

"There's one in the shared section."

"Shared?"

Gavril nods, takes my hand, and pulls me over to the door on the other side of the vanity. It opens to an area that almost looks like the spa. There's a sunk-in tub with enough room for three or four people, an extra-large luxury shower, and the footbath section Gavril mentioned with two side by side as well as a double sink area.

I am stunned at the luxury and think of how much this all costs, and then pause. Did he say this is shared? This is clearly designed for at least two people. The shower would fit two easily if not more, so would the tub. An uncomfortable feeling twists in my stomach. "Gavril."

"It's not quite as good as the spa room as it only is attended by your staff if you want, but it is nice to have on hand," Gavril says, ignoring the nervousness in my voice.

"Why is it called shared?"

"Because," Gavril walks to the door opposite to the one we entered from, "it's shared. This is my side," he says, opening the door.

I freeze. Something about walking into Gavril's private bathroom feels like it is crossing the line not only with a toe but a good foot or two. "Excuse me?"

"What? You have your suite, and I have mine. They're joined. There's the path through the bathroom here, or the direct door which is the further one near your balcony," Gavril explains. "The king and queen's suite are the same."

That is not what I meant. I am not sure what Gavril thinks he is doing. Doesn't he feel how questionable this is? From his grin, I doubt it. I flush as I think of Sage watching us. That's a line I really shouldn't cross, even if having Sage there makes it feel safe. What if I do not win? I will be embarrassed the rest of my life.

"Well?" I realize Gavril fully intends to show me.

"Gavril, I don't think that's a good idea."

"You don't want to see the other half?"

"It's not that; it's just... this is different," I point out. "Telling me is one thing, and so is the princess's suite, I suppose, but I'm not sure that's exactly... fair," I try to put it delicately.

Gavril pauses a moment. "Well, alright, if you're uncomfortable." He closes the door without a hint of annoyance. He really does not see what is wrong with this, does he?

"But it's not like you haven't been in my room before," he teases.

"I have not!"

"You all have," Gavril says as he leads me back out the way we came in. "Where else do you think you had the match with me?"

I flush as we step back into the reception room of the princess's suite.

"And you can either go through the way we did to get to my room, or you can use the more direct passage." Gavril nods at a door to the right of the room.

"Alright, but that's your reception room, not your bedroom," I point out.

Gavril shrugs. "Not that big of a difference. It's much like the princess's but flipped."

Back in the ballroom, the uncomfortable feeling disappears, and the wonder of what Gavril meant to do floods me. He'd said he'd choose me and acted on it. He did all he could to prove his devotion to me, and it is not just to prove himself. He wants me to feel it. To know how much he wants me. His excitement is for the idea of being with me. My heart lifts, and I can't help but smile.

"Uh, a lot of people took off," Gavril comments, seeing several girls must have called it a night.

"I suppose they have no reason to want the night to last." But I do. I want it to never end.

"I suppose," Gavril says casually. But the silence that follows tells me he has similar thoughts to mine. It is getting late. It is a workday tomorrow. The night cannot go on forever. "But it's not over yet," Gavril finally speaks. "May I?"

"No more surprises?" I check.

"I'll try not to," Gavril says. "I can't promise though."

"What else could you possibly—"

"Don't tempt me."

I giggle and cover my mouth.

"Shall we?" Gavril offers me his hand for another dance. I would like nothing more.

It's nice to dance when it is more private. Gavril takes full advantage. We don't speak much as we dance, letting the music and dance speak for us. Gavril is happy and tender. I am content and still unsure it can be true. I believe it, but it feels too good to be sure.

During one dance, Gavril keeps me extra close as we glide across the room. "Do you have any idea how beautiful you are?" Gavril asks me.

"What?" I giggle. It feels so random.

"You're more brilliant than the stars," Gavril holds me even closer and whispers into my ear, "my Esther."

My breath catches once more tonight. I know what that nickname means, even if I do not know what any of the others do.

I close my eyes as Gavril settles closer, his face cradled into my neck for a sweet moment before we pull apart for the next step. He may think I look like a star tonight, but he's the one who put the stars in my eyes.

We just dance and stay close until there's hardly anyone left. Servants are starting to clean up in areas no one is using.

"I suppose that's our cue," Gavril sighs as the music stops. "We shouldn't have them talking about how late we stayed up." He sighs and offers me his arm. "May I escort you to bed?"

I smile and take his arm, noticing the king and queen leaving. The players start to pack up. We're quiet as we walk the empty, silent halls to my room. I treasure his firm hold on me, wondering when I will get to feel it again.

When we reach my bedroom door, Gavril takes my hand and turns to face me as he kisses my hand. "Thank you," he says, his eyes shining with tender gratitude, "for a day I'm never going to forget."

"Me either," I say breathlessly, giving him a slight smile. I wish it didn't have to end.

"It's not the end," Gavril assures as if he'd read my mind, brushing my hair back, "just the beginning."

"We don't know that," I remind him, feeling like an actor repeating the last line over and over to get my fellow actor to say his line right.

"Don't we? I could just as easily take you out tomorrow. You aren't eliminated," he points out.

"I have a festival presentation to do."

"And I'm sure it will be spectacular." Gavril smiles. "And I'll see you soon. You won't get mad at me for it anymore, will you?"

"No." Or so I hope.

Gavril smiles, squeezing my hand and kissing my forehead. "Soon, my darling. Soon."

Darling. The way he says it makes my heart flutter and the temptation to lure him into my room to make sure the night does not end pops into my mind. I don't dare. But I don't want him to leave.

"What if I can't win?" I ask.

Gavril bends down to kiss me gently. "I'm not worried about it."

I flutter in the pleasure of that moment before I speak. "But I am." I open my eyes.

"They say you perform better with a few butterflies," Gavril replies.

"Not big ones." And when it comes to this "performance", these butterflies are big enough to challenge a dinosaur.

Tonight is over. The protection of having earned it is over. It is back to fighting for his every glance with ten other beautiful women.

"I'll send flowers to soothe them," Gavril says, pressing his forehead to mine, his arms around my waist. "And chocolate to silence the jealous monster." I laugh as I instinctively wrap my arms around his neck. "It's you who has my heart." He takes one of my hands and presses it to his heart, eyes closed, and forehead still pressed to mine. "And if I have to send bits of it every day to prove it, I'll relish creating each one."

"Gavril…" I have never heard him talk like this, romancing and entrancing me a bit more each time.

He softly turns his head to kiss me again. "I should… it's late, and as you reminded me, you have work to do." Gavril sighs, but he doesn't move. "I should get you to bed."

I give him a look that makes him laugh. "Not like that!" His laughter is warm and full, breaking the tender moment, but it had to be done, and if it is going to break, I'd not pick any other way.

"But with that scolding to haunt me the rest of my days," Gavril jokes, "I'll wish you good night, my Esther." He kisses my hand as the name makes the wonder of that title rush through me again.

It helps take away the bitter moment of parting as he squeezes my hand just a little more, as he always does, before he turns to leave me for the night, leaving me lost in the magic of the night.

Chapter 29

Getting up in the morning is one of the hardest things I have ever had to do. I am not ready to leave the warm, happy bubble Gavril left me with which cradled me as I slept. I had been able to settle into dreams that were just as magical as the day had been. I am not willing to leave it yet, and on top of that, I am tired from being up so late.

I arrive at breakfast just in time. The girls mostly ignore me. I feel my heart sink as I think through why. Many might be ignoring me because they are trying not to be envious. Others are trying to hurt me. I am back to having to deal with their drama and Gavril is so far away — well, figuratively. He's not too far from me at the royal table.

I glance over at him. He looks tired, but he's still smiling. He's talking to his father with a smile on his face. The king looks the same. They look so different and yet so alike. The king chuckles and says something that makes Gavril glance at me.

I can't repress the beam that crosses my face at how big of a smile the prince gives me. I look away quickly as the king moves to see who his son is smiling at, bowing my head to pay attention to my breakfast. It helps me hold onto the hope it all isn't just a happy dream. Is Gavril even now trying to get his father alone to tell him he's chosen me? The hope makes a gleeful bubble form in my chest.

I try to distract myself with the other girls, but Zelda looks tired and seems out of sorts too. It's even more apparent in lessons as she fiddles with her tablet or looks out the large windows at the sea towards her homeland.

Lady Keva lets us run our presentation notes past her to help us polish up the presentation. Lady Hydrengia isn't so individual, but instead gives us all a lecture on the most important things to keep in mind to be a good negotiator and talk the royal family into liking our ideas. It makes it hard for me to pay attention to anything other than Zelda's odd behavior or struggling to stop my mind daydreaming about yesterday and wondering what the tide is like outside.

The paper did report on last night's events, but there's nothing too interesting to say. There are some splendid impressions: some of the king and queen, some of Gavril and me, but the article doesn't make a fuss over me being his only date. It explains how there was a contest to win the date and I'd won. I smile, glad for some neutral press for once.

But after lunch, I work out to clear my head (and fail) before I get back into preparing my presentation. My maids are angels helping me with my visuals, getting my charts to look perfect. Flur is really good with fancy lettering.

Nippers comes in to watch for a while, tail curled around his feet when he isn't pawing at Damian for pets which, of course, annoys Damian greatly.

At dinner, the girls are back to their normal chattiness though I notice Zelda smiling at something but I can't tell what she's looking at for sure. I'm so distracted by wondering what Zelda's odd mood means, making sure I'm mentally prepared to present tomorrow morning, and trying to get myself to relax, I'm completely caught off guard when someone grabs me and pulls me into a private corner.

My mind still hasn't caught up when warm lips press to mine. I recognize him and relax, returning it as my mind wanders into the moment of bliss before he pulls away. I blink a few times to get my head around what just happened.

"Gavril," I manage to gasp out.

"What?" Gavril chuckles with a pout. "You don't like it? It's not like anyone can see us here."

The world finally comes into focus, and I see him nod into the hall. I can't see them, so I'm sure they can't see us. That is the rule on stage, right?

"It's not that." I am still a bit breathless.

Gavril grins at his success in surprising me so well. He hugs me, resting his head on top of mine. I smile, closing my eyes and resting my hands and cheek to his chest. "Then what is it?" Gavril asks gently.

"I just... wasn't expecting it," I sigh in contentment. If I was afraid last night wasn't real, this certainly helped me believe it. "What were you thinking?"

"I missed you."

I lift my head to look up at him. "It's not even been a full day."

"So?" Gavril says. "I missed you. What? I didn't do anything wrong, did I?"

"Well, no."

He smiles and holds me close again, and I accept it. "I thought of coming by, but I didn't want to distract you. I know you've been busy." He strokes my hair, somehow causing me to be even more comfortable.

"You missed me that soon?" I tease.

"Yes," he says simply, still stroking my hair.

"You can summon me if you want."

"I know, but you're busy."

"And you aren't?"

"I am fine skipping lessons and other dates are easy to move around."

I frown. "You had one today?"

"Made me miss you all the more." He hugs me tighter. Who did he go to right after me? "I wish I didn't have to. But it's my lot, as you and my mother keep reminding me."

"So rude." I roll my eyes.

Gavril chuckles, allowing me to enjoy the feeling of it against my cheek. "But on that note, are you ready for tomorrow?"

"Yes. Are you worried about any of the tests?"

Gavril pauses to think. "Well, if you want to win." I pull back to give him a glare that makes him smile. "Nope," he shakes his head dramatically. "I don't think you'll have much trouble."

I'm not sure I believe him with his teasing mood. I like it, but it also annoys me. "Will anyone?"

Gavril nods. "Some. But not you. We'll have to wait and see, but I know where I want the winner to be." He kisses me softly. He's so... it's like there aren't ten other girls here. Like I really am just waiting for my win to be official. What is he thinking? "And this test will have to eliminate at least one girl. I think my parents are making that a rule from now on. After last time," he chuckles.

I smile too. "It was a failure."

"And we're running out of time. And I think you're double safe as they worry if they eliminate you now, the people will think it was because of the article. Though to be fair, that's all good for me. Maybe not so much for you..."

I cut him off with a kiss of my own. He's being such a dork. He doesn't mind any more than I mind his kisses. It's kind of nice to initiate it.

"I missed you." Gavril sighs as we pull apart.

"I've been right here," I point out.

"Not like this," he disagrees.

"Well, speed it up. You tell your father yet?"

"Oh, shoot no." Gavril looks sheepish. I laugh. "I actually meant to tell him a few times, but I keep getting distracted. Well, we do."

"By what?" I frown.

Gavril grins. "Work. At the start of the week, he said I'd start joining the meetings in the afternoons. I just observe right now, but it's certainly a step in the right direction."

My face fills with hope. "You're joking."

Gavril shakes his head. "No, and they're mostly about sillier things. Not really war effort yet, but we're on the right road." His smile glows in happiness. I can't help but smile. "But it's kept me busy and away from you."

"We'll have to get used to it if I win."

"When," Gavril disagrees and kisses me again.

"If," I insist. "We have to be at least a little careful."

"Hmm-um." Gavril shakes his head. "Don't think so."

I sigh and shake my head.

The next morning as I get ready, I review my cue cards, complete with notes Damian had given when I'd done the mock presentation. Damian helps me into a ragged outfit that would be like the one I'd wear for the festival. My maids even give me some dirt makeup for effect, and I make sure to do my own hair in one of my most lazy, casual braids, which without my maids taking care of it, I hope will end up looking a bit messy by the end of the day.

I am thankfully picked to go first for once. The girls give me a funny look when they see how I'm dressed, but I ignore them. They are all dressed normally, so I doubt their ideas are as exciting. Unless Florence's is about disorganization as she is fumbling through her notes in pure anxiety and making them messier. I almost feel sorry for her.

I step inside the meeting room with my charts to show the royal family under one arm, neatly clipped together; the larger boards my maids help me put together are neatly organized under the others. I see Gavril's grin when he sees how I look. The king is watching in amusement, and the queen looks nervous. But for once, I'm not at all nervous. I get to share the fun I've had. *Dislike it all you want.*

"I'd like to present," I say once I have the boards set up. "The Rags to Riches Festival."

I explain it all with all my excitement showing as I go over the deals I've made, the lessons and booth ideas, the bathing center, the food stations, the performances, and more. The queen is nervous at first but soon is happily on board with the king and prince. I leave them my notes, beaming in delight at my success.

Breakfast the next morning is one girl short. It is Florence as I feared. Zelda looks happy. Florence's anxiety had really started to bug her, but I'd have rather the elimination to have been someone higher up.

"Do you think they'll do whichever festival it is before more of us go?" Azalea asks.

I think about that. "I don't know. I suppose if they really are doing it to get the people excited, I would think sooner."

"We'll see," Azalea agrees. She giggles. "Let's just hope they don't all swarm us at the festival."

That's true. Girls who live close enough or are willing to travel could easily come. I do not look forward to seeing Dahlia. I would be happy to never see her again. Sadly, Lilly lives too far to come.

My thoughts are cut off by the king standing to get our attention. "Congratulations on getting this far," he wishes us. "You are now officially in the top ten, achieving another level of nobility. Also, we hope you'll all join us for the festival which we'll throw on the Friday after next. We have decided to go with the Rags to Riches Festival with more details to come. Congratulations once again and enjoy the rest of your meal." The king sits back down.

I'm doing my best to hide my smile. They went with my idea. Yes, it may leave me busy, but I'm excited to see my plans come to life.

I notice a few girls exchange glances. For most of these girls, being in the top ten does not mean much. Three of the girls are natural royalty; Ericka will find it easier to marry well, and for the rest of us, it still just means a more respectable position when this ends. For all but one of us.

"Can we just... be out sick?" Ericka asks, complaining again about the festival during lesson breaks.

"What if the festival itself is an impromptu test?" Bella teases dramatically. "Test our humility."

"Willingness to be insulted more like," Ericka huffs.

"Maybe you'd like a good pair of dirty trousers," Forsythia says scathingly. She is lying on a sofa, her feet up on the arm as she reads through some articles on horse jumping. She twirls her dark hair around her finger.

"Better than gross from those animals," Ericka huffs.

"From the girl who lets a rat sit on her lap all day." Forsythia gives Cuppy a look. I thought she liked Cuppy, at least more than most.

"It's more ladylike than those mounts," Ericka retorts.

"So, a picture of Ericka on a horse is the goal of the festival," Azalea decides. She and Bella giggle.

"How are you going to look?" Forsythia asks the two gigglers. "At least you'll look like you belong."

My head snaps over. This is a fight waiting to happen.

Zelda sighs loudly and shuts the book she was reading, though I doubt she'd been able to read much with the chatter. "Some of the most regal ladies ever to live spent more of their lives in rags than ball gowns," she snaps. "So how about we cut down on the dirt and just enjoy getting outside these walls?" I'd never seen Zelda snap like this.

It does the job though. The girls shut up.

Bella smiles and tries to include her. "What do Hyvian rags look like?"

Zelda gives her a look that clearly asks, "*are you that stupid*?" "Like... anyone else's."

I hold in a laugh. Though Zelda is not normally this snippy, I must admit I kind of enjoy it.

"Sorry," Bella says. "Just trying to make small talk."

Zelda sighs. "Small is all we ever do."

I frown a little as the girls go on chattering again. I go over to Zelda once no one is paying attention. "You sure you're okay?" She'd seemed to be bitter lately.

"Yes, I just... am so ready for this to be done," she sighs, turning to the nearest fire. I sit by her, our backs now to the other girls.

"Me too," I admit.

"I don't mind being here. I wish this game was over. This talk is getting old." Zelda glares back at the other girls.

"You normally are so patient. Maybe you need a festival more than all of us put together," I try to cheer her up. "Can't you leave if you want to? You have your own guard. I doubt anyone could outdo your gargoyle one."

"I suppose, but I doubt the royal family would be happy. It would be rude to go against their wishes." Zelda looks back at her book, but I can tell she's not really interested in it.

I bite my lips. "You want to go home?"

"Kind of." Zelda plays with the corner of her book, staring at it unseeingly. "I'm not sure I can explain."

"Well, if we still had the board, you'd be winning."

"Oh yay," Zelda says sarcastically.

I frown. I want to ask but feel it's rude. Zelda can see the question in my eyes though. She catches sight of my expression out of the corner of her eye, and she smiles before she faces me. "One thing you'll need to learn, Kascia, is that sometimes your desire to do the right thing and what you 'really want' often aren't the same. Yes, you want to do the right thing more than anything else, but that sometimes means denying other wants."

"Why will I need to learn that?" I frown.

"Because like the born princesses, you'll need to master it like they have," she says, more cheerful than I have heard her in a long time as she turns back to her book with a smile.

"You talk like I already won."

"You better."

I look around to be sure no one else is listening. "You aren't just giving up."

"No. Well, sort of." Zelda pauses, looking up as she tries to find the right words. "I keep to my word, Kascia. I promised my family I'd see this through. I promised Gavril and the royal family I'd give it a try. And that's what I'll do. And I won't fail on purpose because that would be lying, and I can't just back out. Yet... nothing against Gavril, but no, I don't really want to win. Honestly, he's starting to be more like my little brother than anything." And the smile she gives makes my heart melt a little. She loves him, but not like I do. It actually is really sweet. "But... if it comes to it, it's my oath and duty." Zelda takes a deep breath, playing with her book again as her eyes stare into nothing. "And I'll hold to it."

I wish I had something comforting to say, but I can't think of a thing. I sit closer to her and give her a hug around the shoulders with one arm. That makes her smile. "You'll understand before long," she says brightly. "And it's not a bad thing. I got to come here out of duty and court the prince after all. That wasn't bad. I'd not change that or being here so long, but..." She looks into the fire, going quiet again. "I'm ready to know what happens next."

"Me too. Too bad we can't end it with a vote."

Zelda laughs. "You'd win. If everyone else votes for themselves, but you and I vote for you then, you get the most votes." We both laugh. "Unless the king and Gavril get a vote. Then you win in a four-way landslide." I laugh. I don't know if the king likes me that much. He favored Zelda from the start.

I think our talk did really help cheer her up. She gets more animated with me, taking my arm after meals to chat on our way to lessons or before going about our afternoons.

Chapter 30

The day of the festival arrives, and I dress in the same ragged outfit from before. I make sure my maids dress themselves in clothes as fine as the outfits they put me in. But then the real fun begins on me.

Damian has been enjoying his work almost too much this time. He has made normal pieces, then done whatever it took to mess it up. I think he had Joy use Gavril's clothes as a bed for a while to get them dirty, wrinkled, and ruined. I think I spot a few cat hairs indicating Nippers may have helped with mine. From the look of my shoes, I think he's chewed on them. Damian rubbed them into corners of furniture like my bedposts, rubbing friction between his hands, and even hitting them against things until worn holes appeared that he sewed patches into. He enjoyed making the outfits for all the remaining Chosen and the royal family. I even saw him making all their shoes. I hope Joy or Nippers enjoyed ruining some of those for him.

My outfit is as raggedy as any pauper's attire. The skirt is ripped up and patched in places, but the tears run in long, ragged strands, and I really like how it looks. I wear short leggings that reach just above my knees, just in case. The color of the dress is really washed out and faded looking. There are places where it looks almost threadbare-worn, most of all on the sleeves. The top looks nicer, but it has worn spots and sections that look like someone grabbed it and ripped it. I spot a few small holes I am suspicious are little puppy teeth.

They finish it off by pulling back my unwashed hair into a scarf like I used to wear on cleaning days at home.

My maids giggle that Damian thought it better he dress down too. "I mean, you're her attendant. Makes you a paid servant too," Vivian points out to him as we finish getting ready.

"Well, my brother is a member of the court, so I figured I might as well join him." Damian shrugs as he rubs a bit of dirt-like make-up on his face. His clothes are patched, dirty, and badly fit. His hair is greasy and loose. Damian keeps scratching at it, making it worse by the second.

He's dressed in a dirty, long-sleeved shirt with holes around the neck and sleeve ends, patched trousers, and a worn pair of boots. He also has a thin vest that seems a little too big for him and a mottled blanket-like scarf he's wrapped around his shoulders and hung down his back like a cape. But even with all that, the biggest difference in his appearance is his hair, which usually was no less than perfect. Today, it's dirty and greasy looking, the black of it turned a dark, ashy brown as it mingles with dust.

"You look miserable," Flur says.

"He doesn't look that bad. Though seriously, you'll lose half your hair if you keep ripping at it like that." I frown.

"I'm trying, but I never imagined it'd be this fiercely irritating," Damian says as he scratches faster and harder before forcibly stopping himself.

"Here, this will help it look dirty and not itch." Flur gets some powder from my washroom and has Damian rub it into his scalp.

Damian sighs in relief with a smile as it seems to help the itch too. "Thank you. You are a blessing." Flur blushes her welcome.

We go with the guard to be escorted from the castle to the city streets. I'd never seen them so clean. It seemed they put any punishments on hold for the day too, using the space for some of the workshops and classes I'd suggested. I think they expanded the bathing area. I have to giggle thinking the queen may have asked for that one.

It looks like everyone is already having a good time. There are children dressed in their finer clothes: many with the cheaper little wire crowns or tiaras; some have nicer ones. They're all enjoying playing with various simple toys, ribbon strands, bubble wands in large and small varieties, and the like. I'd never seen such a happy street.

The king is having a great time. He gasps and rushes to bow to every little "princess" he sees, irritating his wife in a rather bemused way. He must have started it long before I got there because the "cuteness" of it must have worn off on her.

The queen looks like she'd stepped right off a play as the ragged lady who became princess. I notice she also has shoes that are a bit firmer than most, but I wouldn't want her feet to get sore either. She likely has never worn anything so simple before. She was born into royalty, unlike her husband who is still almost chasing after little princesses to bow to them.

"No, I missed that one. How can I help it? There are many important princesses here," he insists. I giggle and look around for Gavril.

There isn't any way in all of creation he'd miss this chance to get out and see the town.

As I look around, a familiar hug tackles me from the side, leaving me in a tight vice-like hug. "Takes half the fun of being dressed up," Alsmeria complains when she finally lets go of me.

Alsmeria looks wonderful in a dress I recognize as a princess costume she'd worn for one of our performances. I glance around and notice some of our other castmates doing the same thing. Mother must have thought it a good enough excuse to let them break into the storage.

"I do it every day. Gets old," I tease back.

"Still, normally we're dressed up together," she insists in her bubbly way.

"Just enjoy it," I tell her. I'm happy to enjoy what Damian made.

"So... where are the cuties?" Alsmeria asks, looking around.

"Look for rags," I roll my eyes.

She gives Damian a charming smile, faking flirting with him to mock me. I laugh.

Damian smiles gently then bows to her deeply, the kind of bow that is reserved for royalty. "Good day, lady princess."

She flushes in unexpected pleasure and giggles shyly. "Uh hi," she says lamely. I laugh. It is a good thing she didn't get in the Enthronement. She'd have driven Lady Keva mad.

He smiles and straightens up. The one thing that gave him away as not a beggar is his bright, white teeth. I giggle again. Poor Alsmeria is stammering a bit. "I think I'm gonna... uh, go try some others," she manages before looking at me with a laugh before moving on.

Damian shrugs. "Seems I was not made to impress the court," he jokes.

I laugh harder and shake my head. "You and your brother have the same problem," I inform Damian.

A meow cuts in, and Nippers jumps on Damian's shoulder. He completes the beggar look. "Oh, I need an impression." Why didn't I bring mine?

Flur starts going through a bag she had with her. Of course, she thought of it.

"Well, if you must." Damian gives me a half smile. I forgot he hates seeing himself in impressions.

"For your scrapbook. You won't always have Nippers to complete your look."

Nippers looks at Damian. Damian glances at the cat then bows his head as he tries and fails to smother a smile before looking at me. "Of course."

Flur hands me my impressionor, and I get at least one good impression of the cute beggar scene before Nippers trots off. It looks like he's seen seafood and wants some. I chuckle. A cat is a cat. "Think he'll find his way back into the castle?" I ask Damian.

"I wouldn't put it past him." Damian sighs as he watches the cat leave.

I watch the cat vanish under a table before I turn to the others. "So, what shall we do to enjoy the day?"

No one seems to have an immediate idea, but I notice the queen has given in and greets the girls as princesses too. The first little girl she curtsies to looks up at her with pure awe and delight. She hugs the queen tightly around the queen's knees — the only place the girl can reach — before skipping off. The queen looks stunned for a moment, blinking a few times before she smiles.

I grin. I think she just felt the magic of making a child's day, and soon the king and queen are playing the game. I thought this might be good for her. Although, the king should be careful not to wear himself out running like that.

While the royal couple are at it, Damian starts looking around. "Ah, I think I see your favorite fan, Kascia." He smiles.

"What?" I frown and look over. It better not be Fabian.

"Just over there." He points to a small girl in a pretty purple dress and a faux tiara. I smile. It's Layla, the girl I'd signed a pointe shoe for and showed backstage.

She takes a moment to recognize me as I curtsy to her and call her a "lovely princess". She is delighted. She curtsies back in a way that tells me she spends a lot of time trying to do it like a ballerina would.

I invite her to join me dancing in the street dances and talk to her about ballet. Before too long, Cedrick joins in dancing with us while Damian watches on, beaming as we laugh and enjoy the day.

"Am I too late for a turn?" I turn to look over my shoulder as Gavril joins us.

"To what?"

"Well, dance of course."

"Nope. This one is mine," Cedrick insists as he helps Layla do a pirouette.

Gavril sighs. "Rude hogging the princess." He shakes his head.

Joy barks and runs around with the dancers. She looks cute and dirty from rolling around, and she's wearing a tattered royal blue bandana. It goes well with her red fur.

"That beggar has more class than you," I tell Gavril. Then I notice how he's dressed. His shirt is far too big, making the neck hang low, showing more of his chest than I'd seen since he'd shown me his scars.

His pants are ripped with Joy teeth marks on the ends as well as the ends of his shirt which is so large it doesn't want to stay tucked. His hair is quite the mess, the curls going wherever they want.

I can't help but watch his chest as it rises and falls with his sigh, his shaking head draws my eyes back to his face. "Guess that means I settle for the maiden," he says with his voice dripping in sarcastic disappointment.

The next thing I know, he's taken my hand, pulled me into a closed hold, and we're skipping about the circle in the village dance.

Layla spots us and laughs in happiness as she watches us dance. Cedrick grins too. "Think we can top it?" he asks Layla.

"What?" She frowns at him, and like Gavril had done to me, he pulls her up, scooping her up onto his hip and spinning with her, winning squeals of delight from the little girl.

"Don't give him too many points. It will go to his head," I warn Layla.

"Oh, trust me, it's hard to get real compliments into his head." Gavril nods at Cedrick. I frown. I am not at all sure what he's talking about.

Damian sighs heavily. "Tell me about it," he says, folding his arms with a roll of his eyes.

I wonder how I can make Damian stop standing on the sidelines and join us. Gavril distracts me though by pulling me into some more skips and turns that pull my eyes away from him.

As we finish one twirl, I hear a familiar click. I fight not to let my face fall. Of course, the press is here, doing their jobs. I try not to be sick over what twisted article that impression will go with.

"Don't forget; you have nothing to fear from them, my Esther," Gavril whispers in my ear, taking my breath away before he pulls us into a double turn to help hide my reaction from onlookers.

I'm left a bit dazed as he distracts the impressionor for me by asking Layla for a dance. I smile at the awe and excitement that crosses the young face. She gets to dance with the prince.

Joy is the cutest though. She's running around us in circles, trying to twirl like us and barking as if trying to bark to the beat before she starts "singing". It's adorable but not very good. Rather like the girl who was caterwauling at the talent show.

When Layla gets tired of all the dancing, she happily sits down with Joy to pet her. Joy couldn't be happier. She makes her talking noises at Gavril in a way I've come to take as complaining or asking for something.

"Worry about step one then we'll worry about step two," he tells her.

"You can't really understand her that well."

"Sure, just listen carefully," Gavril says.

"Then what did she say?"

"She wants one."

"One what?"

Gavril nods at Layla. I give him a look. "What?" Gavril smiles. "I told her we'll worry about a spouse first." I roll my eyes.

The other Chosen start to come into the square. Ericka wears a rather disgruntled expression in a tattered dress and hair a flat mess, pulled into a ponytail to try to hide it. Cuppy is on a harness that's looped around Ericka's wrist. Cuppy doesn't look any happier than Ericka.

That does not dissuade Joy though. Her ears go up as soon as she spots Cuppy. She looks up at Gavril and makes a happy sound that even I knew means "friend".

Before Gavril can reply, Joy jumps to her feet and launches herself at Cuppy. She stops several feet away to give the smaller dog his space and play-bows to him, talking in pure excitement to have another dog to play with.

I have been looking forward to this. Joy is going to demolish that rat dog.

Cuppy can sense it because he snarls and barks at Joy. I thought she'd snarl back, but Joy tilts her head as if in confusion and looks up at Gavril as if for help to understand. Gavril watches with an amused smile. Ericka reacts the same, letting the dogs meet and try to be friends.

Joy tries again, barking and giving Cuppy another play-bow. Cuppy barks at her with an aggressive growl. Joy greets Cuppy with a "hello" sound and gets up then back into the play bow in pure excitement. When Cuppy doesn't respond, the sound Joy makes sounds like a "what's wrong" to me.

Cuppy backs away and barks at Joy even more aggressively. Joy tilts her head and makes her 'weirdo' sound and looks up at Gavril.

"Did you just call my dog a weirdo?" Ericka asks in outrage.

Ericka's attention gives Joy hope, and she pants up at her in happiness before saying "hello".

Ericka is not charmed. She picks up Cuppy and turns away.

Joy's happy tail slows then stops in confusion. A light goes off in her eyes. She turns to Gavril, and in an impressive leap, jumps up at him, so he has to catch her. Gavril gives her a look as she pants in triumph and looks over at Cuppy as if she thinks that were the game.

"Joy," Gavril sighs and puts his dog down.

Damian laughs. "She'll make a game even if there isn't one."

"I think she assumed that's the game," I say as Cuppy snarls at Joy again. Joy tilts her head.

"Sorry girl, he's just a grumpy…. pet," Cedrick says. I don't think he can get himself to call Cuppy a dog.

Joy huffs and barks back at Cuppy as if telling him to be more fun. Cuppy barks back and nuzzles into Ericka who huffs and walks off.

"That's a great way to start a marriage," Cedrick jokes.

Gavril's mouth twitches as he tries to ignore Cedrick's comment. "You can try another day," Gavril assures Joy. Joy whimpers a little before she remembers Layla is still happy to play and pet her, so she trots back to the little girl.

"I should go soothe her ego." Gavril sighs. There's a hint of apology to me. I understand it, even if I don't like it. I nod my understanding. "I have to play fair." He smiles. "I'll find you later." He kisses my hand. It doesn't tense this time.

But with Cedrick and Joy keeping Layla happy and Damian watching with that soft smile of his, I decide to leave them to enjoy it and see how the rest of the festival is going. It looks like a hit to me.

Zelda and her gargoyle guard are shopping around. Zelda is smiling wider than I'd seen in a long time. Getting out did her a lot of good. The other born princesses are smiling and giggling as they watch the little girls in their princess lessons with Lady Keva. Princess Rose and Amapola look like opposites dressed in street clothes with Princess's Rose's hair in a stunning mane, and Princess Amapola's hair straight and heavy down her back.

Azalea and Bella are watching Isla perform for the "royals" by showing off her acrobatic stills, cartwheeling and showing off impressive flip tricks to cheers from the children and many adults too. The king and queen have stopped chasing the children. Instead, the king is standing behind his queen, arms wrapped around her from behind and smiling as she too admires the little girls in their princesses' lessons, likely daydreaming of what her own little princess might have been like.

I smile, proud of my efforts in planning it. I may not have been made to do the grunt work, but they clearly used all my plans, including increasing the size of the bathing area where many thankful men and women are getting cleaned up and standing straighter than they had. And the shopkeepers are doing well, or so their giant smiles and thankful attitudes suggest.

I smile and decide to check out some of the other stations. I'm halfway down a side street when a voice cuts into my pleasant mood like dropping a stone into a tranquil pool. "Back where you belong," Dahlia's grating voice accuses.

I turn to her. "Well, as the royals are in rags today, thank you," I say calmly.

"Like the ruddy street performer you are," Dahlia spits at me. "I can't believe you'd sink so low. Doing it to me was one thing, but you got Lilly kicked out? I thought you liked her. Too close to the prize to let even your friends off the hook?"

"So, it was you who started the rumor."

Dahlia scoffs. "I'd not sink to *your* level," she sneers. "Then you pick on poor Florence as she was an easy target. How do you live with yourself?"

"Just because it's what you'd do, that doesn't mean it's what I did," I try to keep my tone proper and even. "I didn't do anything to hurt anyone's chances. They did that on their own."

"Of course, *you'd* say that. He always liked you best, little skank."

I fight not to be offended, but it's not easy. "Think what you want, but it's not true. I didn't say anything to upset the princess. And even before they discerned the truth, it was your pouting that made him eliminate you. Don't blame this on me. Yes, I want to win but not at the expense of anyone: not you or Lilly or anyone. You did this to yourself by treating Gavril like a trophy and the kingdom like just another plaque for your winner's board."

Dahlia glares at me with seething hatred. "You think you can just shrug this all off and be fine?"

"I'm not shrugging off anything. I didn't do anything wrong. I don't flaunt whatever victories I win like some metal. The fact you treated the Enthronement and him like a prize is why you were eliminated. I had nothing to do with it. Trust me. I wish it didn't happen."

"You cocky little brix."

Her foul language shocks me; I can't even reply. Why did I think such insults and vulgarity were beneath her?

"You think because you won that little moment in the safe room, you're already queen?"

I gain a sudden confidence I hadn't expected. "Dahlia, I'm sorry it happened like it did, but you can't come in here and expect to make me feel bad for something I had no control over. I'm not going to apologize for doing well in the Enthronement. I didn't ask him to kiss me. I didn't ask him or the royal family to eliminate anyone. I hope you get a good position by the end, but I'm tired of your bullying, and I don't have to stand for it."

I hold my head high and turn away from Dahlia only to notice Fabian watching us with an impressionor in his hands. I sigh in disgust and turn down a smaller alley to try to shake him.

But no matter how many streets I turn and how far I go, I can't shake the feeling I'm being followed. I stop and wait for Fabian to catch up, but I don't even hear footsteps. Perhaps I'm being paranoid.

That's when a voice tears at me like the claws of some monster ripping at the surface of my heart looms from behind me. "You really are doing better at the look, press, and public persona, but you need to be better at avoiding the spotlight. That was the advice to keep you safe."

I whirl around to spot my father leaning on a barrel next to the back of the store I'd just passed, frowning at me in loving concern.

I back away quickly. "What are you doing here?" I demand. He looks just as he always did, dressed casually, not fancy or in rags, ignoring the festival entirely.

"I wanted to see you. It's been months, and you don't write," Father says, the hurt of that in his tone. I resent it. I want him to miss me, but it's just more manipulation. "I wanted to make sure you're alright. You look good. I was worried they'd do something to you after that impression. Avoiding the press will get harder."

"Why do you care? You're sure I shouldn't and can't win," I reply scathingly. "You admitted it. I haven't changed my mind. I won't let you hurt them. You and your rebels are wrong." The anger that spits out with those words sting. They aren't mine anymore. Nothing of the family I'd loved is mine; it was always lies.

Father's face falls in tender compassion. I loathe him for it. "What have they done to you?" he asks in the same tone he used when he'd ask what my nightmares were about as a child. I hate him! I back away as he moves as if to comfort me.

"You keep away from me!"

"Shh, Kascia, you know I'd never hurt you. I only want to protect you, my cygnet, my princess, my beloved little girl," he pleads with me.

"Beloved," I shoot the past tense back at him. "Not anymore."

"No. Of course I still love you, sweetheart." Father's eyes shine in pity for me. The way he looks down on me — belittling me into being his little, malleable girl again — only makes me angrier. I suddenly think to my last performance of *The Phantom* and how I realized I'd been just as twisted as I'd performed the scene in the graveyard. I am not making that mistake. "Kassie, I'd never hurt you."

"Wouldn't you? You'd do anything for your cause. You already sold me for it."

"Sold you? Kascia, is that what they tell you?"

"No. It's what happened. You can paint it and deny it, but you sent me into this game to play the temptress and murderer. You sent me to play Delilah!"

"It was never like that!" Father snaps back. "You were supposed to go unnoticed. I never wanted you to do the deed. I just want you to let us in, nothing more or less. Be perfect, out of sight, so they'd not have any reason to question you, but it didn't work. I should have known you were too beautiful to avoid their attention, *his* most of all. I failed to recall it was beauty alone that drew the king to Esther."

His use of that name snaps something in me. I slap him. I'd not even realized he'd slowly come close enough to me for me to do that.

My father stands frozen, face turned away from me where my hand had left it from my slap. I back up quickly. I had never seen my father lose his temper like Gavril or even seen hints of it, but if it is in him, I'm sure I have just released it.

Finally, he reaches up and touches his cheek, still in shock. He can't believe I struck him. If I hadn't felt the adrenaline pumping through me, I'd have not believed it either. I never thought I'd strike my father.

He looks at me. I ensure a healthy amount of distance is between me and him, and this time, I won't let him slip into my space.

"What have they done to you?" The hurt in his voice is not what I expected, but it doesn't soften me. It only hardens my heart more as hot tears rise to my eyes. He looks at me as if his five-year-old just hit him. Sad, not angry; in denial, not accepting the reason I hurt him. I am too darling in his eyes for me to be able to make that mistake.

"It wasn't them," I insist. "It's the truth!" I want to throw it at him. Tell him I know his lie about my being a Custod, about our whole life, everything, but that would reveal that Mother told me. She'd hid it for fear of his reaction. He may not be able to accept I'd really betray him without being tricked, but Mother may not have such protection.

"Has being in the king's court turned you from your people, your duty, so easily?" Father asks with a throbbing pain in his tone. "Kascia, what did they do to confuse and twist you so?"

"It was you who twisted me."

"I'd never. I'm your father, Kascia. I love you. I did my best to protect you. When raids weren't your thing, I didn't make you go anymore. I gave you other duties to spare you. I never should have sent you in there. I expected too much of you. You even told me, and I ignored it. I thought too highly of you. I treasure you too much. I'm sorry I put you into that position. I want to take it back. I'd do anything to take it back. Please, just come home, Kascia. I won't make you endure this anymore. We'll find another way for you to fulfill your birthright."

"Is that all that matters?"

"No, of course not. But our duty is bigger. I know that's hard. I was overconfident in your understanding of that. I'm so sorry. It is my fault it's turned out like this. Let me protect you, please."

"You don't think I can win this and fix it?" I demand. I resent that he thinks I can't win. He said he was overconfident in me, but then he can't believe in me enough to trust I see what he can't.

"We've been over this. Their line must end. They've had five hundred years."

"He hasn't!"

Father shakes his head. "Power corrupts. I'm sure most go in with good intentions, but—"

"But you trusted me and Jake."

"Of course, I trust you." He smiles at me tenderly. "I still do, but you just don't understand. This plan won't work. He'd never choose you and hoping will only hurt you worse." The worried crease returns to his brow. "Please, I won't ask more of you. Just come home, please. Whatever it takes."

"No." I step away from his outstretched hand.

Father sighs in frustration, dropping his head before glaring at me. "You really buy they're so good after what you know? You saw what happens out here every day. I can't believe the corruption of the palace could be what blinds you. Is it just the distance that makes it seem like a bad dream? It's what they do, Kascia. They find tricks like the Enthronement, this publicity stunt, blaming the rebels for their problems to lull the people back into a false security. Haven't you noticed it's only gotten worse as people stop resisting?"

I know it's still bad. He's right, a simple festival like this won't fix things, but I have every faith Gavril will. I may not know everything. He still doesn't open up to me about some things: things I'm sure relate to what Father is accusing him of. It comes down to this: who do I trust? My father who lied about my duty or Gavril who admitted he has secrets he cannot reveal?

"Maybe I know something you don't." Will Father trust me? It's all I really want. His reaction to me tells me he had confidence in me but not trust.

"Like how dreamy the prince is?" Anger finally comes into my father's voice. "I'm sure he's done an impressive job wooing you to make you go blind. You never were one to let your mind be swayed over a boy. I can only imagine what he's done to make you forget everything you know is true."

"Maybe I learned how little truth there was in my life," I challenge, wondering if he'll realize I know.

I shouldn't have hoped. He shakes his head in sadness. "When have I lied to you, Kascia?"

I tense in anger and can't reply for how it clogs my throat and makes me tense. I'm afraid of what I'll do if I try to move.

"I didn't want to make you do this, but it's our duty, Kascia. It's what we Custods are born to. Don't you realize you've turned your back on that? On your duty, your people, and Jake, after so long. You promised him."

"You promised me! But you changed the plan again and again. I gave up what I wanted for you when I agreed to be engaged to a man who felt double my age. I gave it up again to join this game while you stood there not understanding why it wasn't 'fun' for me. You lied to me. You never understood me. You painted your version of me in your mind, and I spent my whole life trying to live up to it because I believed you were right. That you knew best and so what you wanted would be what the Maker wanted. I was so deluded."

"And I'm sorry. I should have seen and understood. I'm your father; I should have been better," Father pleads with me. "I'm so sorry, Kascia. Please, let me fix it; come home, please. I'll do anything. Just leave all this behind and come home."

"I can't." Home isn't real anymore. It never was. I couldn't live in the house I thought was home now that I see the crumbling walls.

"You can. No one can stop you. We're alone. Please. We're above their royal rule, remember? You can walk away from all of this, forget it ever happened."

"I can't."

"Please, we love you. Your mother is worried sick." How dare he use her against me! "Please, Kascia. You can have it your way. You win. Please." He offers me his hand again. When I don't do more than glance at it, he goes on. "If it's Jake you don't want, you can forget that. Forget Purerah. We'll have the Head give you a new job. Whatever it takes. Come back to us, Kascia. Please. Whatever you want."

"I am choosing what I want." I step further away from him. I'm fighting not to cry. Why do I have to be an angry crier? At least when it comes to fighting with my father.

"Anything but that, please Kascia!" Father begs. "Kascia, you're a smart girl. How are you falling for his lies?" Father shakes his head, pain and confusion in his eyes.

"He's been more honest about what's going on than you ever were," I say bitterly. Then an idea pops to mind. A way to test his reaction if he knows I know. Mother is not the only person who could have told me. "I spoke to the Custods at the palace about it."

"I told you not everyone is in on it. You're lucky they didn't expose you."

"For what? For stopping you getting in? You're not even a Custod anymore." The tears finally come. "How could you lie to me?" I thought I'd be angrier when I confronted him, but instead, I'm just hurt, broken.

"You don't understand. They don't understand. It's just the cover," Father insists.

That's when the rage comes. I confronted him with the truth, but he's so deluded, he keeps lying to me. Perhaps to himself.

I shake my head, face hardening. "How could you treat me like this? Papa, don't you trust me? I know something you don't."

"Then explain to me. Maybe then we can both understand."

"I did! I may not have all the answers, but I know they're not trying to hurt us. They are trying to do their best by us. I will find out exactly why, but I know this. Gavril isn't going to let it keep happening."

That's when the temper I thought I'd see when I slapped him comes over him. My use of Gavril's name so casually awakens the monster in him more than my strike did.

"I told you about the prophecy. I warned you. How can you ignore that?" Father looks at me with anger yet hurt announce at the same time. "You believe this ill-prepared, pampered, rich boy is going to give a rat's fart about us?" Father demands.

"Yes," I reply firmly. I found no proof it was anything more than Father's lies. I am going to trust Gavril. He's given me more reasons to trust him than Father has. I have found nothing to back up my father. At least Gavril was willing to admit he couldn't tell me everything.

Father's face darkens, and his fists clench. "You are so young. You don't understand.

"I understand more than you know. More than you do. I wish you'd just trust me."

"I do trust you. I know you believe it. But you're wrong. I used to be able to help you see that. And now... I don't know how to protect my little girl anymore." He tries to touch me again, but I back away. "They corrupted you. Hurt you," Father scowls. "I won't let them keep doing it. Just come home. I won't make you do this anymore; just come home."

I shake my head. "I'm where I should be. I hope you believe that."

The rage that came over my father when I used Gavril's name rises to his eyes. I know what he's going to do before I can process anything else. I tense and jerk away from his lunge even before he's started it. I race up the alleyway, unsure where I am going apart from away from the manipulation and lies.

I burst into a main square, gasping for air and realize I need a crowd. If I can find Damian, I can hide. He'd know how to dodge the crowd without question. But I don't see him anywhere.

I pretend my panting is from dancing and put on a fake smile and try to blend into the crowd, my eyes darting around for Damian.

I jump a mile when a hand touches my arm, and I turn, half expecting my father only to meet Gavril's deeply concerned face. "Hey," he says, studying me, "what's wrong? You disappeared for a while. Where did you go?" His amber eyes look from one of my eyes to the other.

I want to hide in his chest and sob, but I can't do that. Yet I seem unable to hide my fear from him now he's spotted it.

Sage comes out of nowhere. "Alley," he says shortly and helps us get into a shadowed alley between two shops; a festival station keeps it further hidden from view. Then, to my shock, Sage goes to keep watch on the street, where he will not be able to see or hear our conversation or interaction.

Gavril gives Sage a small smile of thanks before turning to me. "There, no one can see us here. What happened?" He puts his hands on my shoulders. "Did someone hurt you?"

"No, nothing. I just…" I can't tell him. I recall how he reacted when I betrayed his trust in our fencing date. If he knew this… I want to tell him, trust him with everything. I want the lies to end, but then I'd be thrown back to my father by the man who means more to me than anyone.

I bite my lips to fight the tears. I'm shaking. I let my head fall against his chest. Gavril doesn't question it. He hugs me tightly, comforting and protecting me. He doesn't demand answers. He kindly gives me that space yet is right beside me when I need it. He deserves everything; it's not fair. I don't deserve him. I'm lying to him as Father lied to me.

"I… I ran into someone from home," I confess just a little, hoping the avalanche won't come.

"What did they do to you?" Gavril's tone is dangerous.

"They didn't hurt me."

"They wanted to, though, didn't they?"

"Sort of," I manage. "I feel so… lied to…" And now I'm lying to him. I can't stop the hot tears that rise to my eyes full of guilt, anger, and resentment.

"Shh, I know," Gavril cradles me. "It's hard. I know with your history, it has to be harder for you than anyone else. You trusted them. And now… they act like you betrayed them?"

I smile at his ability to understand without really knowing. He should know, but fear binds my tongue and steals my voice. I want to confess, believe he will not turn on me again, but I can't bear to let

Father be right. I can't survive Gavril forcing me back to him. I have to prove my father wrong. I have to win the only home I have ever really had. It is the safest, yet most dangerous path. Safest if I win, most dangerous if I am wrong.

"Would they hurt you?" Gavril asks.

"I-I don't know."

Gavril doesn't ask more. He nods and cradles me. His soothing presence stops the tears, even as I feel the guilt of how little I deserve it when I won't tell him everything. He strokes my hair a few times, messing up the scarf I wear in my hair, but I cannot begin to care.

After a while, I feel him glancing at the street, making sure no one has noticed us. I can see the headlines now if Fabian catches us like this. I feel oddly smug at the idea. Perhaps it is just because of Dahlia's accusations.

Gavril strokes my hair again before pulling back gently. "You're staying with me the rest of the day, alright?" He brushes a tear from my cheek, drawing a watery laugh from me. He smiles gently. "I know you don't like looking the favorite, but—"

"I understand," I say quickly.

Gavril smiles and kisses my forehead then holds me close again. I don't want to leave. I want to stay there and forget the rest of it. I love this. I haven't enjoyed anything so much as this. I really do love him. I hide my face in his chest. Gavril just strokes my hair then tries to fix the scarf. I want to laugh, but I don't want him to know I've calmed down yet. I want to hide in his arms forever and never come out.

But as always, Gavril's eyes are too sharp. He knows without me telling him. I can't hide from him.

"Are you ready?" he asks as he backs away, putting a knuckle under my chin to help me meet his eyes.

I give him a weak smile and nod. As much as I want to stay, I can't lie to him more than I am.

He nods and kisses my forehead again. I feel him tense before he pulls back. I put my hands on his forearms before he can pull back all the way.

Sage drops from the rooftops. "Fabian is looking," he warns us. "I gave Joy the 'cause trouble' order, but it's not working."

"Of course, he is." Gavril sighs. "At least one day he'll find this kind of thing normal. Why isn't Joy's distraction working?"

"He's picked her up and is trying to give her back to you. She's causing him lots of trouble though, wiggling and trying to lick him," Sage says.

"You should teach your dog not to eat garbage," I tell Gavril. We all laugh.

"Alright, I'll go out and get Joy. Then you can come out while I keep him busy," Gavril decides. He kisses my head before slipping out.

Sage pauses as he moves to follow his charge then turns to me. "Are you alright?"

"Fine." Fear makes me firm. Sage has never sounded so concerned for me or anyone that I'd ever heard.

Sage nods shortly and follows Gavril with a flick of his cloak. I wait a moment before I hear Joy making a lot of talking sounds and follow them.

Joy is still wiggling in Fabian's hands, making him squirm to keep holding her as he tries to hand her to Gavril. I think Gavril is letting it go on just to annoy Fabian. I smile. At least I will get to enjoy that the rest of the day.

Or so I think. It's not long before Fabian spots me, and I remember about Dahlia's conversion. He heard it. "Good to see you're alright," he says to me. *Oh, don't say it.* "Most of all after that fight."

Gavril turns to me so fast, I wish he weren't so protective. Fabian beams to see his reaction. I bite my lip. I didn't even think to warn him. Gavril is trying to hide the question and worry in his eyes, but I can see it. I hope Fabian cannot.

"It was nothing," I insist. "Dahlia was just upset."

"She made it sound like she thought you were causing eliminations on purpose," Fabian says.

"Your article made a lot of people think that," I point out.

"But the castle said it wasn't true, and it was after she left."

"Dahlia likes herself a good rumor. She'll believe them for the fun of it," I state flatly.

"I see." Fabian nods. "Well, hopefully she'll keep out of trouble."

"I hope so too."

Joy spares me more by wiggling suddenly and making Fabian drop her. She turns to him and clearly huffs "catch me" then runs off.

"You lost my dog," Gavril says in mock offense. But that does mean Fabian has to chase Joy until she runs over and sits by Gavril to take a break. The chase takes a good ten minutes or so. Fabian is worn out. I smile and stroke Joy. She is a good guard dog, even if she's not very traditional.

My stomach twists as I see signs of Gavril fighting not to ask me about what happened. I am in for it when we get home.

Chapter 31

"No, really, I'll call you," I insist to Vivian who's looking at me like she's worried I'm ill. The royal family thought we'd like a break after being in public all day, so they let us have dinner in our rooms. I let my maids change me into a day dress for dinner, but when they propose getting me ready for bed, I tell them to enjoy a rest until I call them. Truth is, I know Gavril will show up at any moment, and Damian is more than enough to chaperone. I'd rather be as alone as possible for this dreaded fight.

"There's no reason for you to have to wait, my lady," Vivian insists.

"I would much prefer to be alone awhile."

"Then why not prepare for the night?"

"I can dress myself, thank you. If it's that you don't want to be called back, I'll have Damian fetch the tea for me."

I realize in the way Vivian and Flur glance at one another that they feel something is wrong, and that's why they don't want to leave.

"Really ladies, I'm fine. I'll call you if I need you. I promise. Spend a night with your families for once. I would really much rather that tonight."

"Are you sure?" Flur's frown keeps growing.

"Yes. Please, I don't want to demand, but I'll be fine. I'd rather have the night."

The two women are clearly apprehensive, but Vivian can sense I'll make the order if I must, so she gives me the proper curtsy before doing as I asked. Flur follows but is not as sure in her step, still frowning slightly.

I sigh and flop onto the bed once they're gone, staring up at the canopy. I'm not sure I'll ever get used to having to do that.

I don't have long to feel guilty. The knock I'm waiting for comes soon after. I stand and move to get the door, but Damian is there first. I should have known he'd still be the perfect attendant, even when I want to pretend he isn't there. Once I give him the nod to let Gavril in, he vanishes into the shadows as well as Sage ever could, if not better.

Gavril nods his thanks to Damian as always, but he clearly isn't really thinking about it as he turns to me as soon as he's in the room. "Are you alright?" he asks first.

I had tried to plan for everything he might throw at me, but his concern upfront surprises me. It shouldn't have.

"I'm fine," I insist, hugging myself and struggling to meet his eyes.

He doesn't find it odd. He comes over and puts his hands on my shoulders as he studies as much of my face as he can see. "What did she do to you?"

"It wasn't Dahlia."

"Fabian was lying?"

"No, I did run into Dahlia, but it wasn't her who upset me."

"What did she do?" The anger radiating off him is oddly attractive. It never has been before. Perhaps it is that he is locked and loaded to launch that frightening power at someone else for me, someone I must admit I dislike.

"Gavril, I swear she didn't do anything. She didn't hurt me. She tried to make fun of me and accused me of being what the paper said. It was nothing. I told her I hoped better for her, and when I turned away, I saw Fabian was watching. I ran into my... friend when I took the side streets to stop Fabian bugging me about it." I still can't meet his face.

"You're sure?"

"Yes." I finally meet his eyes to assure him of that much.

Gavril's observant eyes flick between mine as he calculates what my words and reactions mean. He's so good at that.

Finally, he nods. "And you're not just saying that to comfort me?"

"I was worried she'd jump at me like last time, but no, she didn't hurt me."

Gavril sighs, nodding, but his anger has not abated. That was what I feared and expected from him. If it wasn't Dahlia, he knows it was someone else. How do I tell him? What if that breaks what we have built?

"So, what *did* happen?" he asks with a frightening coldness. It is worse than if he raged. A quiet, controlled anger is a better weapon than explosive rage.

I swallow. "I-I ran into someone from... before."

"Whatever rebellion your friends were in?"

Tears flood my eyes. He knows. He does not know who my father is, but the way he said it, he knows I was one. He knows I wasn't just surrounded by them. I have been foolish to think he wouldn't figure it out. Is that really why he was upset after our fencing? That bit of evidence is all it took for him to lose the power to deny it? Gavril isn't stupid. He's smarter than anyone I've ever known.

I nod, trying to force down the heartbreak. "Yeah, from before." I hold myself tighter, telling myself shrugging off Gavril's arms will not help.

"Did they try to hurt you?" He rephrases his question.

"I don't think so."

"What did they do?"

"They wanted me to come home, forget this whole game and come home." My lips shake.

"And you don't want to?"

"No!" Why does he keep asking?

"Shh, I know." He hugs me, and I bury my face in his oddly coarse shirt. "Not like that. Sorry, bad phrasing. I meant you told them you didn't want to?"

"Not in so many words." I suppose I never said that to him. I said I can't. Did that give him the hope I wanted to?

"What did you tell them?"

"Does it matter?"

Gavril thinks that over, still holding me, rocking me ever so slightly. It is soothing. "It might affect how they reacted, what they did, or would try to do to you."

"I said 'I can't'," I say quietly, so quietly I'm not sure Gavril heard it because he bends lower as if to hear better.

"You can't?" he repeats.

"Yeah." I wish I'd said more. I wish I'd been firmer and more eloquent with my father. That I didn't crumple at his mere presence and stood up for what I believed. Maybe then I'd not feel so unsure and so ashamed. I am painfully reminded of the thoughts I'd had performing *The Phantom*. My father had been my phantom in more ways than one.

The increase in Gavril's breathing pressing against my cheek sends a twinge of panic through my body. He's becoming angry again. He is still there with me, but what he wants to do is give my father a bit of his mind. I hold tighter, afraid of what would happen if Gavril did. If Father ever got close enough…

"Hey, shh, it's alright." Gavril must feel the change in me because his body softens, and he bends gently and pushes me back just enough to see my face but doesn't let go of me. "What is it? Kascia, please, I just want to understand. I hate seeing you like this. You're shaking like a squirrel being chased by Joy."

I laugh at the idea.

Gavril smiles at his success, but his eyes are still concerned and tender as he studies me. "What did they do to you? You're sure they didn't hurt you?" He does something odd. He strokes my hair back as usual, runs his hands down my arms to my fingers, which is also normal. But when he takes my hands in his, he only takes my left hand, and instead, runs his other hand to my shoulder, across the back of my neck then down my back before taking my other hand. I pause at the strange action. It does not hurt or feel uncomfortable, but it was odd.

But once he's done it, his shoulders lose their unnatural straightness. He holds my hands tighter then lifts them to his lips to gently kiss my knuckles. "And it wasn't Dahlia?"

"No."

"Will you tell me who they are?" I can't meet his eyes. I can't say no, but I also can't tell him. "Afraid what I'll do to them?" I nod. Not to my father, but to me. "Do you think you'll ever tell me?"

"I don't know." I will have to someday if I win, but what happens then? We're alone one night, perhaps our wedding night, and that's when he learns everything. Then what? This is why royals have separate bedchambers. I shudder at the idea of getting myself into that, but what other choice do I have? If I speak too soon, my father will take me once again.

"Do I know them?"

What an odd question. "No." He's never met my father.

Gavril nods, his jaw still stiff.

"You're mad at me."

"No, no, not at all." Gavril strokes my hair and kisses my forehead. "I don't know what it's like to be in your position. I wish you didn't fear to tell me." He stops. What is he holding back from me?

I shouldn't be afraid. After all, he knows quite well I am holding something back from him. I trust him, but there's still part of me that worries, but I choose to let it rest. It is an unsettling yet peace inducing thought.

"I suppose I can't imagine anyone meaning that much to you that you wouldn't want justice done, is all. Is that strange?" His eyes meet mine. "You're so much my better. I cannot imagine caring for anyone so much that I wouldn't want them to pay for the harm they'd done to me."

I bow my head. I'm not better. I'm scared of their retribution far more than anything. I have not let myself think of what it would mean for my father and Jake to face justice for what they'd done to me because I do not believe they ever will. Even if I win, I will only be punished for what they did to me. Their secret is mine. And for them to be justly served, I must too. We will all go free or all hang together. And I hate them all the more for it.

"Kascia?" The worry in Gavril's tone doesn't help. He's far too good at this. "Darling, what is it?"

Darling. My mind can't help but relish how that title feels. So intimate, like I am already his. Now I know why the others boasted of their nicknames. It gave such a feeling of intimacy. And I have gotten so many now.

Yet his question makes my stomach twist. I bite my lips to stop myself throwing up. How do I explain? I can't. I am as guilty as they, so to confess means to be burned with them. I have no hope of feeling it all made right because justice will claim us all.

Gavril takes a deep, steadying breath and just holds me, but I can feel his reactions in his grip. He's filled with hatred for whoever hurt me, pain at how I ache, and helplessness. He can't help me feel better. He can't fix it. Yet I can feel how badly he wants to.

I don't want him trapped in this mixed-up bog that is this pain. I pull back a little. "It's late. If someone finds out you're here..." I can't think of anything to add.

Gavril's mouth opens slightly, brows pinched in helplessness as he looks at me. A jolt shakes me as I realize he's fighting tears. Why does that feel so strange?

Gavril shakes his head and closes his eyes, pressing his forehead to mine. "I-I can't leave you like this." I have never heard such a broken voice before. His warm hand caresses the back of my neck, holding me, trying to protect me.

I take a deep breath and shake my head, my eyes closed too. "It's fine," I insist and put my hands to his chest. "Really, I'm alright. Just shaken; it's alright."

"It's not," Gavril disagrees, "and you know it."

"I just need to calm down. I'm fine. I'll be fine." I have dealt with this pain since the Enthronement started. I've managed so far.

But I wished I hadn't said it. Something inside Gavril snaps and not in the way I'd expected. He becomes oddly firm, proper. He stands upright, still holding me, fingers still tangled in the hair at the back of my neck.

"Alright," he says, eyes still closed before he opens them and looks down at me. He's reminding me of something, but I can't think of what. I have seen him like this before. No, it is that I normally see him like this. He is this way around many others: the Chosen early on, Lilly, the princesses, his mother. I am not sure what this is. He has never done this to me. "Sorry if I intruded. I know it's hard to say 'no' without feeling like you'll get in trouble. Thank you for humoring me."

He takes my hands and kisses them again. "It's been a long day. I should have known better than to wind you up more."

"What?"

He smiles tenderly and strokes my cheek. "It's alright, my Esther." He kisses my forehead. "I wouldn't have you in trouble for the world." He then turns to leave.

"Gavril, wait."

He stops and looks down, patiently waiting for me to go on. But what did I say? "Don't go. You're acting weird"? I'm not sure what to say.

"What do you need?" he asks sweetly, brushing my hair back again.

"I-I don't know." What is he doing?

"That's alright. You have plenty of time to figure it out, and you have many people expert at meeting your needs," Gavril chuckles, and I don't miss him glancing in Damian's direction. But that isn't it. I wish I knew what it was, so I could address it.

"Do you have to go?"

"No. What would you have me do, my Esther?"

"Explain what's wrong." My brows draw together, struggling to understand why something feels so sick.

"You had someone you trusted attack you," Gavril says simply. "Who wouldn't be hurt and confused by that?"

"Not that... you." I wish I knew how to explain it to him, but I can't, even to myself.

"Esther, I'm fine."

"You're not." Or maybe he is, and I'm the one seeing things.

"Well, neither are you." He smiles again. What is it with that smile? What is he doing?

"I suppose not." I hug myself, so confused I don't know what to do or say.

There's a pause between us before Damian loudly slams the book he's been reading. "Alright, I can't watch this anymore," he says as he rises to his feet.

I jump and step back. I look at my feet, still holding my arms as if holding a blanket around myself. Gavril just looks up at Damian, mostly expressionless. Why does it feel so odd, yet I know this isn't odd for Gavril at all. Perhaps I am overreacting.

"Watching you two is like looking at a mirror when my brother can't figure out what's wrong with me, or vice versa." Damian sighs with a shake of his head then tilts his head to meet my eyes while my head is still bowed. "Kascia," he says more gently, "you remember how I told you that anything you told me would be kept in confidence, except that I would have to tell my brother? Well, this is why." He waves between the two of us.

"What?" I frown, confused as Gavril nods as if he gets it.

"Well, to be frank, it is unsettling to be helpless," Damian explains, "but it is worse when someone we love is in trouble, but we can't do anything to help them. If I can't or won't tell Cedrick things and allow him to help me, he closes off and becomes distant. I can't blame him for it because I often do the same. But do you see the correlation?"

I think it over and drop my head again. I nod. So, I'm stuck no matter what I do. How did it become so hard not to hurt someone? Gavril just watches me with that sad yet understanding half smile.

Damian lets out a sigh and nods. "However, there is more than one way to skin a cat. I think it is fair to say that Gavril respects your choice not to say anything. He just wants to ensure you are alright and protect you from further harm. Can you let him do that?"

"Of course..." Maybe I don't understand.

"And you're not trying to get rid of him, right?" Damian wears a small smile.

"No." I really am confused.

"So, when you said he had to leave, what was your intention?"

"I didn't say..." I don't know if I should say "he" or "you" as I mean it for Gavril too. "Didn't mean it was a requirement," I struggle with the phrasing.

"So, is it alright if he looks after you a bit longer? Or simply stays a while?"

I nod, wishing I had words, but it seems to be my lot today.

Damian nods but more to himself this time. "I apologize for the interruption, but when I see Cedrick wall up like this, it annoys the bloody hell out of me. I hate to see it happen to others over a simple miscommunication."

Gavril nods that elegant thanks of his. I smile a little at him then at Damian. Gavril seems to get it more than I do.

Damian looks at Gavril. "But I think it was a mere lack of words that brought it about this time and was nothing against you."

Gavril nods at Damian in a way I understand is "I know". He's still smiling, but at least it's real. Damian returns the gesture then sits down again as if that alone will make us forget he is there.

Gavril chuckles and looks at me, clearly giving me permission to decide what is next. I swallow and look at him and manage a weak smile. With a sigh, Gavril steps back to me and hugs me gently. "I know," he says quietly. "I know."

But he doesn't, and he can't. And I hate it. There's nothing I can do about any of it.

Yet he doesn't seem to mind. He doesn't speak, just lets me hide there, but how long can I just hide? I'll have to let him go sooner or later. And he'll know it's not over. Will it ever be over? Or did I unknowingly make this the rest of my life?

I don't want him to go, but with nothing else I can tell him, there isn't much for either of us to say. He calmly holds me, stroking my hair now and then or kissing my head.

"Will this ever be real?" I ask.

"Sure, it will. I'm confident," Gavril says softly. "There's no reason it doesn't have to just be a matter of time."

I shouldn't have asked. I have lots of reasons and none I can tell him. I wish his shirt wasn't so stiff. Godwin needs to starch them less. I smile at the idea of Vivian telling him off for me.

"That's better." Gavril must have felt my smile because there's no way he saw it. "No storm can last forever." Neither can the sun-filled days. "It's going to work out in the end. I only wish... it wasn't so hard." Though he didn't say it, I could hear the "on you" in his tone.

I stay hidden there for as long as I can get away with, but both our feet are getting tired after being on them all day.

"Well, I can at least promise as long as you're in here, they can't get to you," Gavril promises when he feels me adjust my weight to help my tired feet. "Should I send extra security anyway?"

I laugh, knowing what he means. "I'm fine." The only one I want, I can't have.

Gavril watches me sadly then leans in and kisses me gently. It is overwhelmingly assuring, and tears of gratitude rise to my eyes before I wrap my arms around his neck. I hug him tightly, and he returns it, holding me up a little before I slide back down.

"You'll be perfectly safe tonight." He kisses my hand. "Assured the night is your domain, after all." I flush at the hint of a flirt. "I'll see you in the morning. Perhaps we can find something more relaxing to do."

"You are asking me out?"

"Oddly, I hate it when they make it sound so formal, but sure."

I giggle and nod my agreement that sounds nice. "Thank you." It's not fair to him.

"There isn't anywhere else I'd rather be." He kisses my hand again. "Good night, sweet Esther."

"Good night," I manage and can't look at him as he leaves. Would he ever not have to leave?

I take a deep breath and hug myself again. Damian stands with a soft smile. "Again, I apologize if I overstepped."

"It's alright." I give him a smile. It's not like I had a clue what to do. It did calm Gavril down, or I think it did. "Not like I could fix it." Let alone understand it.

"To be honest, that was Gavril's frustration too. I simply hoped the understanding would help."

"It seemed to help him. I'm still not sure I understand. I don't... I've seen him like that, but..." I sigh. "It's not fair, but it's all I have."

"What isn't fair?"

"That I can't tell him. I can't..." I shake my head and take a deep breath. I'd come to accept this. Why is it back? "It's just so hard."

Damian nods. "It is, but you won't have to hide it forever. To be perfectly honest, I don't think you should."

"I know. I want to, but... well..." How do I?

"Kascia, you have done nothing that is a punishable offense. And Gavril has proven himself to be an open-minded and understanding man, hasn't he?" Damian tilts his head as he watches me.

I nod. "He has."

"Then don't be afraid. He cares about you, and that means he will more likely than not forgive you of your past, but you have to trust him."

"I'm scared he'll shut down like... the last time my past showed. Not to mention what Sage might do when he learns h-he-he's right." I swallow.

"But he isn't right. You are not a traitor, and what your father has done does not fall on your head," Damian says firmly then sighs heavily. "I wish I could help you see what I see in you. You are much more than the girl your father made you to be. I don't expect you to accept my words simply on my say so, but I do hope that someday you can see yourself without the weight of that burden."

I nod. "I hope so too." I just can't believe it when I feel the truth of what I was so heavily. "But he's right." My father is right. "I haven't gotten them to change anything. I've not even tried." I've not helped anyone yet. "I didn't try to get the king or queen to change anything or do anything. I've just... taken advantage too."

Damian shakes his head sadly. "How can you see so little of yourself that you fail to see even the smallest of your successes since you have been here? Is not the king giving his son the chance you encouraged him to give Gavril? And have you not opened the eyes of the prince to a people he could not see for the protective walls around him? You do so much for this people and the royal family. Just because your father cannot see it, that does not make it untrue." He takes a moment to pause and meets my eyes. "They trust you. But I suppose the real question is: do you trust them? Do you trust the prince?"

I take a deep breath and nod, looking up at Damian. "Yes."

"Even though there are things he can't share with you?" he asks, watching me carefully with those emerald green eyes of his.

I swallow then smile in confidence and nod. "Yes."

There is a long pause as Damian continues to study me carefully. He glances at the door then looks back at me and nods. "Perhaps it is time you knew then," he says and moves to his work bench.

I frown. "Know what?"

He glances back at me as he pulls a drawer open. "I never showed you the monthly budget you are allotted for this competition, have I?" he says as he takes something out without looking and closes the drawer.

I shake my head. "No, never really needed to."

"Well, I think it is time you learned." He walks back over to me. He takes my hand then places a coin purse into it.

I frown a little and open it up. I blink. There isn't as much as I'd expect, but I suppose Damian knows how to use it. There are mostly lighter gems, which just make it worth less. "There's hardly a hundred gemlets in there." Damian is good with money, and sure, it's almost the end of the month, but they haven't made much of anything new the last month.

"I know." He nods. "I haven't taken anything out of that purse since it was given to me. And... that is double what it was when I first started working for you."

My face falls. "What?" How has he made what he has with less than this?

He smiles softly. "Well, as girls left the Enthronement, the money disbursed to their teams was equally divided among the remaining girls, but I imagine ladies such as Princess Rose and Zelda have their own funds, so they have little use for the royals' money. Ericka and Forsythia are likely the same, though I'd wager they spend their share plus their own. After, of course, their attendants take their wage from it as instructed."

"How?" I can't imagine they'd skimp this much. "Why?"

Damian smiles sadly. "Because they must. Kascia, though it is in my right to take a wage from your budget and to use it to create gowns and dresses for you, I have never taken a gemlet from that purse. Every month they give it to me, and at the end of every month, I give it back, not one gemlet shy of what it was when I received it. Save for the times you have made use of it, of course," he says with a warm smile to me.

I shake my head a little. "But why would you do that? Why do they have to pay the servants in this way?" I've seen this place and the taxes they take. There is no way they can't afford it... is there? Damian wouldn't lie to me.

He closes his eyes and lets out a deep sigh before opening them. They meet mine straightly, and his face is stone serious. "I will tell you, but what I am about to say does not leave this room. This conversation *never* happened. And I mean that. You must never tell anyone what I am about to relate to you. Not Jake, not Zelda, not even Vivian or Flur. You can't even hint to Gavril that you know. Doing so will mean immediate elimination because this is extremely sensitive information, and the mere fact that you know will make you a high-risk security threat, even greater than knowing of the king's illness. Do you understand?"

"Uh, yeah." I nod. What could be worse than knowing about the king's illness?

"Alright then." He nods, his face lightening a little. "Though you may want to sit down."

"Okay." I sit on the end of my bed, hugging my knees and looking at Damian nervously.

He sits on the edge of the work bench table and folds his arms. "Now then, if you were to multiply that amount by ten, then add about four hundred gemlets, the total would equal that of the entire royal family fortune."

"You're kidding." There's no way. "They take at least that much from one show, not the whole running, just the one performance if we're lucky that's all they take. There's no way."

"Yes, but you really think it all comes here?" Damian cocks his head and arches his brow with a smart smile.

"Well, of course. Where else does it go for them to budget it out?" I ask.

"Believe it or not, the majority of it goes straight to the war effort."

"All of it?" That seems insane. How much could it cost? "What are they doing with it?"

"Well, let's take an accounting, shall we? There's the pay for the soldiers and their commanders, who have a high wage," he counts off as he goes through them. "They each get paid monthly. Then, there's the care for those soldiers such as uniforms, bedding, tents. And the non-reusable items like food, water, toiletries, not to mention medicine and bandages. And let's not forget that each squadron or group of squadrons is going to need a doctor, plus the tools he or she will need like a bed for himself and spare beds for the sick or wounded. He also needs tools to set bones, to stitch up injuries as well as ointments to clean wounds and possibly treat burns, and other such things he must have readily on hand.

"Then, there's the livestock such as horses, which never come cheap, and the food and water to care for them. And of course, you'd be a fool to go to war without a weapon. And even if you only gave a single sword to each member of your army, that is still tens of thousands of swords that must be well made and kept in good repair, which means you'll need a blacksmith and the tools he'll need because you can't have the soldiers waiting to get their sword back from the castle blacksmith, especially if you've only given them one. And I haven't even mentioned how much it costs if someone actually dies in your war."

"But they've been... well, used to those costs for a long time." Five hundred years in fact. "Does it really change that much?"

"Oh yes, and not for the better." Damian frowns. "The longer a war persists, the more expensive it gets. There are less people working fields or performing in the arts which you can tax to gain revenue for yourself or anything else you want to put money into. The royal family makes no money themselves because their lives are dedicated to being servants of the people. They spend all day governing the affairs of the kingdom, so you can live peaceably, so they have no time to work for themselves. This means, none of the war is or can be funded by them. But they must oversee that every soldier is paid, so the soldier's wages come from tax money, which he likely sends to his family, so they can continue to support themselves.

"And if that soldier dies in the line of duty, the costs do not just stop because the family is guaranteed a pension for a set amount of time after the death of the soldier, either until a year cap or one of their children comes of age to make their own living and support the family. And on top of that, you are still down a soldier and must recruit another to replace him in your army. War costs are always building on themselves. In fact, it is extremely rare that at the end of the war, a country does not have a heavy debt to pay, even years after. And when your war has been going on as long as this one has... Well... Gavril will be lucky if his great grandchildren are able to finally pay off the debt. And that's *if* he is able to end this war in his lifetime."

"But... why hide it?" I ask. "Wouldn't they need people to know to even go into debt?"

"And what do you imagine their enemies will do when they get wind of it?" Damian leans back a little with his head tilted to the side. "You think Dragia will show them mercy? Or any of the other neighboring countries? The high king could even see it as his duty to swoop in and conquer a nation that is on the verge of financial and physical ruin. Then the Custods are left to decide if he was right to do it or not. And another war breaks out. Fighting continues but on a much larger and grander battlefront while what is left of this nation withers, forgotten, no one really understanding why it all even started."

I frown a little. "So, they wanted money so badly they ended up with nothing?" I just can't understand that level of stupidity. If they'd let up a long time ago, it wouldn't be here. Not that the current royal family could do a thing about it.

"If you want to say it that way," Damian says, straightening up more. "But don't you at least understand now? Gavril and his family want desperately to help their people. They put up the charade of wealth to protect their nation from an end that many have already predicted, but the signs are clear enough, if you look for them. For instance, why would a pampered prince need to teach himself how to play the piano? It isn't like it is dangerous, so the queen would have no reason to object to hiring a tutor for him. And you must have noticed the fake jewelry the queen wears or her limited number of dresses."

I nod. I had noticed the dresses. And I'd seen Gavril whisper something to his mother about her reacting to something, and she started to rub her neck. "She's allergic to it." I hadn't quite put that together. When we first arrived, they asked us if we had allergies like that. They asked because they know; they deal with it all the time.

Damian nods. "That's why she'll often wear shells. They're beautiful but cheap to make and readily found on the royal beach. The few real pieces they have left are kept safely in a vault and rarely used. Though, I once took pity on the queen and made her a few dresses and fine pieces and placed them in her room. She was too embarrassed to ask for them, even when I offered," he says, smiling thoughtfully then looks at me. "Don't tell them I don't take a salary."

I nod. "I won't." Then I would have to explain how I know. "That's why Gavril didn't have a clue on how to help the Japcharian delegation when they're starving." It makes sense why he couldn't tell me and why he hesitated. They pretend to they're financially stable. But all they are doing is getting by.

Damian nods. "It isn't much that makes it to the palace, especially after rebels raid the amount of the ration for castle expenses. What's left pays for the food, the necessary upkeep and repair of public rooms, and the servants that work here who are sadly underpaid, though I know the family would like to pay them more. And of course, the medication for the king isn't cheap." He sighs.

I flush. "Right." I am just going to pretend I hadn't helped with that before in this moment. But that does make the rebels' plans rather wimpy. Sure, put a new ruler in, then what? It's not like the stockpile they expect to dish out to make everyone equal again is even here. It's so strange to think it is just... going to the very fight they are pressing. "Wouldn't people stop if they knew?"

"That would be the hope, wouldn't it? But there's no guarantee of it. And they fear other countries learning of their weakness. It is much easier to put up a fight when your opponent doesn't realize they have you backed into a corner," Damian says. "Which is just one of many reasons they hope to end the fighting with Gavril."

"Like they likely hoped it would end with his parents." It sounds like a hopeless cycle.

"It's a bit more than that." Damian smiles gently, an odd hope in his eyes before he blinks and shakes it off. "But I hope this has helped you understand. It isn't that they want to take from their people, but they have to keep pace with the very ones who are fighting them to get it back. Ironically, they have to tax their people to protect them from... frankly, themselves. And it's sadly a fight they and their ancestors have been fighting for five hundred years."

"But how did it even get here?" I ask. "Surely it couldn't have run out so quickly. Did they really just get greedy, and it spiraled out of control?" That just doesn't make sense to me.

"Ah." Damian smiles and stands up with a clap of his hands. "Yes, of course, you must know that too. But unfortunately, that is a story that will have to wait another day."

I frown. "What?"

"Frankly, I'm not sure there is enough time to explain. You see, I received word that one more person wants to see you tonight, and I want to be here for it."

My face falls. "What?"

"They assured you aren't in trouble or anything of the sort, but they did want to speak with you once they have a moment tonight," Damian says carefully.

"So... I should wait?" I frown.

"I would, but I can bring up the tea, so it is ready once they leave."

"Alright," I nod. "I'll stay here then."

Damian nods then excuses himself to fetch the tea, promising he'll be back shortly. I'm now extra glad I dismissed my maids as I sit on my bed and dim the lights so at least I can start mentally preparing for sleep, even if my heart is racing in nervousness.

As promised, Damian returns shortly with the teapot on a warmer to have it waiting. He then goes to his bench as we wait for my visitor. I'm not made to wait long. But this visitor is even less of what I expected.

I hear a click and jump back when I realize the balcony door is opening from the outside. I know only one person who comes in like that. "Sage, good grace!" I snap. I'm not in the mood for whatever he wants.

"Sorry, sorry." Sage holds out his hands defensively. "But if anyone saw me coming here, it'd be much worse for you; I can promise that. Geesh..." He sighs. I don't think he expected me to be waiting for him.

"What do you want?" I demand, defensive and annoyed. He never has anything nice to say, and it has been a rough enough day.

"Are you alright?" His tone is brand new to me. He's concerned, watching me with almost the same level of concern as Gavril.

I gape at him then shake my head. "What do you want?"

"He didn't hurt you?"

"He... No, of course not."

"Not Gavril." Sage rolls his eyes. "Your father."

My face goes white, and I back away. "It's okay," Sage says quickly. "I'm not going to hurt you." I don't believe him and keep moving away. "Look, look." Sage rolls up his sleeves, showing his signature assassin weapons, the wrist blades. He presses a few buckles that snap the straps open, and he slips them off and puts them on Damian's desk. "I promise, I'm not going to hurt you. I'm... Well, hold on, this will take a while."

I knew Sage was heavily armed, but the number of weapons he takes out and puts down shocks me. A dazzling dagger from his boot, some odd snowflake looking disks, a blow pipe, a whip, odd round objects that must be various kinds of bombs, tiger claws, throwing daggers, a rope with a metal dart tied to one end, a small red tubular device, and of course his sword, all of which he tosses onto Damian's desk while Damian pretends not to notice over his book.

"There, now you believe me?" Sage asks, still holding up his hands as if I was the threat to him.

"No." He is well trained enough to do anything he wants to me even without them.

Sage sighs. "I just... wanted to make sure you're alright and say I'm sorry." I stop at the sincerity in his deep green eyes. "I had no idea who or... what made you do this. I noticed you were gone a while at the festival, and something told me to find you. I left Gavril with the other guard. He doesn't know I tried to find you or what I heard. I heard your fight. Well, saw it."

He pauses, watching me as if making sure I'm alright. "If I knew Peodrick Custod was your father, that would have explained everything, *everything*. And I can't ever apologize enough for how much harder I made this." He's still holding up his hands to prove to me he won't harm me. "You have to understand; you were so... strange. You clearly hated the royals but then... you didn't. Now, it all makes sense, so much sense. He lied to you. You thought this was your mission, didn't you?"

I bite my lips and look away. I'm scared of the fact he knows, yet his understanding is overwhelmingly comforting.

"You poor thing," Sage says gently, lowering his hands carefully. "He told you to let the rebels in at the ball, that it was your duty as a Custod to be the Custod on the throne. He pressured and twisted you into his weapon. How long has he been grooming you for the Enthronement?"

"Almost the moment it was announced," I admit.

"And for the throne?"

"I realized it when I was very small but didn't feel it affect me much until he... made... arrangements for the kingship too."

"The boyfriend?"

I nod. It's hard to look at Sage, but when I do, it's hard to look away from his compassionate expression. He understands. He perhaps knows better than anyone could.

"And so, you learned to love this boyfriend out of duty. Then he took that from you. He made you come here to be his infiltrator, and you quickly learned all his indoctrination was a lie. When did you realize you weren't a Custod?"

"My mother told me at Christmas. He was d-disinherited before I was born." My voice is shaking. It's comforting, yet part of me is resentful. I do not want to talk to him about this. I want to tell the man who left.

"So, you never knew?"

"No."

Sage nods, looking down. "He's... kind of a horror story among Custods to this day. I had no idea he had any children, let alone that he'd be able to... do they know you exist?"

"What?"

"The Custod Council. Do they know you exist?"

I blink. I'd never thought of that. "I-I don't know. Father spoke of them often, but..."

"Of course, he used them as the bad guys when you didn't like what he told you to do," Sage huffs and paces a little. "If... I wanted to make sure you got away from him, but..." I look down. He, like Gavril, would love to rip him apart. "I'm sorry, Kascia. There's no excusing how I treated you, and there's no excusing what he did to you."

"Doesn't mean it didn't happen." I fold my arms and look at my bedspread.

"I take it Gavril doesn't know?"

"How could I tell him when you'd hear, and you'd have me done away with for being here only to assassinate him?" I challenge, glad to let at least a little of my anger and fear out.

"Understandable. Once again, I apologize. Over time, I realized you weren't a threat, but you also didn't make sense. In my role, what doesn't make sense has to be kept an eye on or it's what gets you killed. I'm glad what it was turned out not to be dangerous. He was right to feel confident in you when I did not."

"But he's not!" I burst out. "I am what you thought I was."

Sage stares at me. "My dear girl, you are nothing of the sort. You've overcome and given up more for our prince and this people than perhaps even some current rulers have. You came here deceived and have turned your back on all of it. That's why Peodrick isn't happy with you. Why you're scared to go home. You have every right to be scared. I'd be petrified in your shoes."

I laugh at the idea of Sage being afraid of anything. I can hardly believe it.

"Oh, dear sister, he truly has poisoned you." Sage frowns in sympathy for me. "You really think it's that bad?"

"You were right. I am a traitor."

"To a rebellion so full of itself, it will reject people happy to help them," Sage scoffs. "You have done nothing to your kingdom. You've committed no treason. You've kept national secrets. You've defended the royal family more zealously than anyone here ever has and against more frightening and personal foes. I admire the courage it's taken."

I shake my head. I can't imagine Sage admiring the horrible mess I've made of myself. "But you're right. So is your father."

"What does my father have to do with this?" Sage frowns.

I sigh and explain how he'd pin me. "And… I may have hit him a few times."

"Really?" Sage sounds surprised. "He didn't mention it. He must have been too embarrassed to admit you got the better of him." I did wonder why I hadn't gotten into trouble for it.

Then Sage meets my eyes. "But I was wrong, and now I'm right. Glad you're following."

I glare at him. He knows what I mean, but he just smiles gently. "Lady Kascia, I came here to apologize and assure you no harm will come to you. No call of treason will be laid on you, and I promise anyone who tries answers to me." His expression is tender, but not the way Gavril looks at me, and not quite how Father once looked at me. Almost like how Damian looks at me, but not quite. "Although, I am almost positive how this is all going to go, if it doesn't, I'll make sure you're protected beyond what this royal family could give you.

You're not Custod by oath, but you're still my Custod sister, Kascia. And come hell or high-water, I'll make sure you get through it. So, with that in mind, I'll ask again, did he hurt you?"

"No. You saw it. He didn't touch me." I fold my arms again.

"I guess I should ask if he's okay. You hit him pretty hard." He smiles.

I bow my head. Maybe I imagine it, but I swear I hear Damian choke on his tea in laughter. "I shouldn't have."

"I wish you'd done more. He's worked so hard to delude himself; he honestly buys his own lies. Anyone would feel hurt. You acted with more dignity than I ever could have. You acted like a lady when he besmirched you. If the king and queen saw and knew what I do, I have no doubt the prince would get his wish this very night."

"Oh please, if you breathe a word..." My eyes widen in fear.

"I will keep your secret, dear sister. But if it's any consolation, even in keeping your secret, I'll be ensuring you win this thing."

"Don't cheat."

"I won't cheat. But I know a true princess when I see one so obviously before me. You do your ancestors and any royal line you joined prouder than you can imagine, my lady. I doubt you believe it from the distrust in your eyes, but perhaps in saying it enough, it will get through to you. Do not hesitate to call on me if you need anything. I'll keep your secret even from Gavril."

Sage hesitates as he debates how to phrase it. "But... you should tell him."

"The one time my 'Custod' past showed he started looking for a new favorite," I scoff.

"Ah yes, the fencing date. That is partially my fault. I knew something was not as I assumed then." Sage nods. "Your reaction... but that now makes sense too. You thought he should be easier to beat if you were a blessed Custod." I nod. "But for someone who isn't, you held up well. He's pretty good because he fights those who are blessed all the time. I hope you know that now."

"My pride was stupid." I glare at him.

"Well, it was taught to you by someone stupid. You've learned better," Sage says confidently. "But it will be better coming from you. Gavril will suspect if I suddenly let you be alone together, so I can't just back off completely, but if you need the moment to tell him, give me a hint I'll give it to you."

"He'll make me prove myself again." Just like last time.

"Hmm, you really think so?"

"I'm afraid of it. He'll be angry who he thinks I am is a lie and throw me back to my father." I can't stop my voice shaking.

"I won't let him do that. On my life, you'll never be forced to go back to your father," Sage promises. "But you shouldn't need my promise. I hope you see what Gavril sees in you soon. He really does believe you'll win. He grows surer every day."

"And I have to take the illusion away."

"No, he's right. Perhaps the tests will be more about proving it to you than anyone else." Sage watches me with a smile. "Oh, if only I could tell you." He chuckles. "But for your safety, I'll refrain. Let's just say... I know he's right. And I doubt I'm alone." Sage nods at Damian. "He's so smart he knew I was coming. I didn't think anyone knew. He's smarter than you realize."

I laugh. I doubt Damian can be smarter than I already think. I doubt there isn't a thing he doesn't know.

"Hmm, we shall see." Sage bows to me. "But... as I've said my piece, it is quite late, and I know you struggle to sleep. I shall let you rest. Your Hi— well, my lady." He bows to me and his teasing like he was going to call me 'Highness' only annoys me. I think he likes it annoys me. He has to take a minute to put all his armaments back on before he slips back out the way he came.

I wait to be sure he's gone before I sit heavily on my bed, mind reeling with what just happened. Sage knew, and he didn't... I'm safe from Sage? And the royal family is broke? Did I fall asleep and dream it all? It can't be real, can it?

Chapter 32

I sleep later than I normally would, even on a rest day. My overwrought mind must have really needed the shutdown. My maids help me dress and go to breakfast. There are signs of the staff preparing for the small New Year's Eve ball that will take place tomorrow night. With so much going on in the palace, I'd almost forgotten about it.

Once in the hall, I'm pleasantly startled when Gavril pulls me aside and kisses me softly. "Better?" he asks me gently. He loves this little corner. I'm going to have to be careful every time I pass it.

"A bit." I've been feeling mostly neutral all morning. Not bad but not great, just another day in the life of a Chosen.

"Well, getting away with more outside time is near impossible, but perhaps around the conservatory would be nice?"

I like that idea. It's nice to just walk around the familiar setting, talking about everything and nothing all at once, just enjoying the morning sun through the glass.

"Hmm, hope it stays clear. Wonder if the new year will bring more sun or spring rains." Gavril smiles at the surprisingly clear sky.

"It normally rains just after the new year," I shrug. "Is there something wrong with that?"

"I like clear skies," Gavril smiles.

"I like the rain," I say playfully.

"Ah yes, to dance in it," he recalls.

"You just have never tried it."

"One day, but this New Year, I'd like it to stay clear. You'll find out why."

That piques my curiosity, but he deflects all my attempts to find out what he's talking about. It does help relax me. Gavril has to go after lunch, keeping the other girls content and his parents off his back, but it is nice he risked getting into trouble over me after he spent most of the festival with me, and the girls haven't gotten over my win on Celeste Day either.

On my way to dinner, Gavril pulls me aside and whispers in that low voice that makes my heart flutter, "I may come pick you up tonight if I can get away. Wait for me." And he's gone before I can react. It leaves me in a blissful flutter I have to shake myself out of.

When I tell my maids I am not ready to dress for bed yet, they act overly disappointed. "What?" I smile at them. They'd never been this disappointed.

"Well, we thought you'd want to try your new nightdress," Vivian says in her mock complaint.

"Gavril might come by."

"He'll like it."

That catches my interest. They know? Maybe there is more to this than just their wanting to share nice clothes. If they know Gavril is coming, they planned the outfit for the date.

I give in and find the outfit is far fancier than a dress for bed should be. They don't wash off my makeup, and they put my hair into a tight braid, nicer than my normal overnight one. The super soft nightdress is cute and goes to my knees, though warmer than I need. It's dark blue with star-like specks across it. Then I pull on a pair of dark blue night pants like I normally wear. They even present me with matching slippers.

"How long has this been planned?" I ask suspiciously. "We don't know he's coming for sure. He said, 'if he can get away'."

"Hmm, hunch," Vivian says, smiling at Flur who giggles.

"You two are trouble." I love them.

"We just want you comfortable." Vivian smiles gently.

"Well, whether he comes or not, I'm more than ready for bed. Why don't you go on to bed or just relax? I'm sure someone misses you." I give Flur a look.

Flur laughs. "Are you sure?"

I nod. "I'm alright. It's not like last night. Go enjoy yourselves. We'll all be up late tomorrow, I'm sure."

"Alright, enjoy your night," Vivian teases, making Flur giggle before they leave.

Damian, on the other hand, is sitting back reading again, as if trying not to be there. I try to excuse him too, but he smiles and leans back. "I'll wait up. I don't mind."

I shrug. "Suit yourself." Gavril may not show up at all.

It's about twenty minutes later I hear the quiet knock. I smile. I go to get the door, but Damian beats me to it. Gavril just gives Damian a smile. It's as if he's telling Damian something, but I can't tell what.

Damian returns it with a slight nod as he steps aside and turns to me. I smile as Gavril looks back at me. "Oh good, nice and warm." Though

Gavril is dressed casually, I don't know if I'd say warmly, in the most casual shirt I've seen him in yet. I think it might even be a nightshirt. It is short sleeved like they often are. I am almost certain his bottoms are night pants.

"Warm? Are we going somewhere?" I ask.

Gavril smiles. "Kind of. Shall we?" He offers me his arm.

I look at Damian. Of course, he knows. Is there anything he doesn't know? He smiles. "Have a good evening, my lady." He bows to me.

"Good night, Damian." I shake my head. He's impossible.

Gavril gives Damian a last nod of the head before we head out. "What are you up to?" I ask. "It's late to be going out, isn't it?"

"We need late," Gavril replies. But he gives me no other answers as we travel up a few floors, almost to the royal floor, when Gavril turns down a side passage and unlocks a door with a key he pulls from his pocket. It leads up a dark passage that's utilized a gentle, upwards slope rather than stairs.

The darkness soon swallows us, and I can't see a thing. "Gavril, how do you know where we're going? It's too dark."

"We need dark. We're almost there. It's not hard."

We stop after a minute or two, and I hear a click and a glass door opens, showing a faint light from outside, but it's not much. Gavril steps up first then reaches back to help me.

We step out onto a platform on the roof. The dome that covers the ballroom and throne room is behind us. We're standing on one of many small little walkways around the dome for cleaning and possibly defense. Perhaps there is more, but it's so dark I can't see around us very well.

On our right, leaning on the lip around the dome, a thick blanket is laid out with pillows and cushions as well as extra blankets resting against the slope, making a natural recline.

"What is this?" I ask Gavril with a smile, shivering as the bitter late winter air cuts across the high rooftop.

"The best place in the palace to get a good view of the stars," Gavril says. "I told you if you looked to the stars, you'd find more things to count down to." I look up at the reminder. He's right. I've never seen so many stars. "I've been looking forward to this for a while." He smiles at me.

Sage really did get over himself if he let us have this date. I wonder which of the hundreds of dark shadows around us he is hiding in, but I'd rather not know where he is or think of him watching us.

I shiver as the wind cuts across my skin again. It is a weak wind but cold enough to make me shiver. "It's beautiful," I admit, hugging myself. "The sea is so dark."

"Until deep sea creatures pop up with their small lights," Gavril agrees. "But the real magic is above us." He takes my hand, sending warmth through me that makes me shiver in a different way. He steps behind me, wrapping his arms around my waist and putting his lips near my ear. "Look up." His quiet husky voice makes another tingle run over my body as my eyes follow his direction.

I'd never seen how many colors there are in the sky. There are pink, purple, and yellow patches of color streaking across the sky, speckled with the millions of stars glittering, stretching endlessly above us. I gasp at its wonder; its vastness fills me with wonder and a sudden sense of smallness that overcomes me. How have I never seen it? This sky is visible from my home on nights like this too. How have I never looked? How had this wondrous magic eluded me?

"Your true kingdom, my Esther," Gavril whispers in that dreamy whisper of his.

I close my eyes as the humble joy of that statement courses through me. That's how he sees me. He sees me and thinks me just as wonderful and full of beauty as that night sky. I am his Asteria, starlight princess, Esther. What does Esther have to do with stars?

"I'm nothing compared to this," I whisper, shaking my head.

"I bet you that's what some of those stars think too. They look close, but most are so far away from one another, I doubt they'd be able to see each other. But without each one of them, this wouldn't be possible."

He settles his cheek against mine, looking up at the view. I enjoy his warmth close to me, most of all when another hint of wind makes me shiver again.

"Come on," Gavril smiles, pulling back, "standing up all night will wear out our feet." He leads me over to the thick blanket, more like a large cushion spread over the wooden platform. He helps me settle down before he sits to my right and leans back on the cushions that provide a perfect angle to view the stars above the sea.

"This will help." He takes one of the blankets and wraps it around my shoulders. "Wait until your eyes adjust; you'll be able to see more."

"More?" I look up, unable to believe it as I sit back too, hugging the blanket around me.

"Yeah, as your eyes adjust, more will be visible. Why I tried to plan this on a new moon. Lucky for us, the clear night didn't fall on tomorrow night. We'd have trouble getting away from the ball." He smiles; I chuckle. "But it's called dark adaptation. It can take up to thirty minutes for your eyes to fully adjust to see all that the naked eye can see."

"Do you have a telescope?"

"Not one that helps much." Is it the darkness or is he flushing? Why would the prince not be able to buy a good telescope when he liked stargazing so much? Another sign of how little money they have. What else had I missed? "And it's more romantic not to use it, right?"

I let him change the topic, afraid of breaking my promise to Damian not to let anyone know I knew.

"I've never used one. I wouldn't know," I say, trying to get my mind back in the moment.

"Well, they don't really allow for two people to use it at once," Gavril says, putting an arm around me, so I can sit closer to him. He is warm. I curl up a little and look up at the stars. I spot one star I know, but everyone knows that star. "There's the Southern Star." I point at it on our left.

"Yes, the anchor," Gavril smiles. "It's said to bind people together who are far apart."

"Does anyone not know that romantic reference? It's in more stories and plays than any other, I'd bet."

"Know any others?"

I'd heard of a few, but I do not know many. Gavril doesn't mind, and he points out the late winter consolations like the Archer constellation. "The tip of the arrow is the Southern Star. It moves around the Southern Star throughout the year."

"I thought most consolations changed throughout the year."

"They do." Gavril nods and points out the ones that are visible. With spring coming, a lot of them are only partially visible from our vantage or not quite as easily spotted: The Swan, The Tiger, The Flower, and even one called The Eye I'd never heard of. Then he points out another one that appears year-round: The Phoenix.

"Looks a lot like the Swan," I joke.

"The Phoenix has his wings out and long tail; The Swan's wings are folded in with a smaller tail," Gavril teases back.

As we sit there, nuzzled together for warmth, Gavril explains some of the stories about the constellations, and I notice more stars appear as my eyes adjust. The colors in the night sky also become brighter and more plentiful. There are blues and almost greens mixed in with the pinks, purples, and yellows. It's easier to see how the stars twinkle. A few don't, and Gavril explains that those are actually planets.

"Who got to name them all?"

"No one knows for sure. Those we do were mostly named by sailors who used them to navigate, and those were passed down from crew to crew until they became officially accepted in general," Gavril says. "It seems astronomy and sailing have always gone hand in hand. Most astronomers were sailors or from sailing families."

"Is that how you became interested in the stars?"

"No, I liked looking at them through my window. In my room, the balcony is visible from my bed when you roll onto your left side. I used to look out and notice the longer I looked, the small part of sky I could see would get more stars. So, I'd get up to see more, and then I just... liked to do it each night after my staff turned out the lights. The idea there were people and animals with stories up there fascinated me. There was a world I could see with life in it."

I can see a little Gavril being excited to be a part of a world he could experience himself from within his locked cage. The same one who played "king" and stole and doodled on important paperwork. I smile and curl closer to Gavril, feeling overly fond of that little boy, and even more of the man he'd grown into beside me.

"The crazy part was I figured out there are some stars you can't see if you look right at them."

"What?"

"I'll show you." Gavril takes my hand and holds it up, so he has my finger pointed at one bright star in the Phoenix constellation. "Now don't move your eyes but use your peripheral to look to the right. Do you see that other star?"

It's hard to resist the temptation to move my eyes there, but he's right. There's a star almost as bright right next to the one by my finger. When I try to focus on it, it disappears.

"Wow," I breathe.

"We call that averted vision," Gavril explains. "And it must have something to do with how our eyes perceive light, but some stars you can't even see unless you do that. That one is known as the Hidden Brother."

"Why?"

"It's right next to the star we call the Phoenix's Heart," Gavril says.

"So, like the Phoenix has his brother with him but often unseen, the constellation has a shadow heart star?"

"You got it."

I giggle and put my head on Gavril's shoulder without thinking, looking up at the star and enjoying his closeness. His arm around me secures as he lets my hand drop and tells me more tricks to see more of the stars.

After a while, my mind catches up to what we're doing. I'd spent many a date in my past nuzzled up to someone, but we weren't ever this relaxed. If Jake and I tried to do this, we'd not be able to keep our hands off each other. What does that mean for me and Gavril? Was what I had with Jake more real, or is this joyful moment more real?

With Jake, being this close and not doing more felt odd, bad. Being this close to Gavril, feeling his breathing against me, listening to the soothing rumble of his voice in his chest, slowly settling into his support is wonderful. Not that I didn't want more or wouldn't be happy to do more, but I am perfectly happy here too: content, peaceful, joyful just sitting peacefully with him, my fingers playing with the hair at the base of his neck, alone in the dark with nothing but the stars and hidden guard to break this private moment.

I quickly push down wondering what it would be like spending a night with Gavril the way Jake and I often spent our nights by the river. I don't want to lose the contentment in this moment by daydreaming about more.

"Sadly, in one night there's only so much to see." Gavril glances down at me then smiles. "What?"

"What?"

"You've got a strange smile."

"I do?"

"Yeah, hard to describe it, but you had a happy, peaceful, yet... mischievous, guilty? Not sure. What were you thinking?" He's giving me one of his teasing half-smiles. I love those smiles.

"I can't believe how good it is to just be here like this."

Gavril smiles and pulls his right hand from behind his head to take my hand that I'd not realized was resting in the middle of his torso. He started rubbing his fingertips across my knuckles. "I couldn't agree more. Though I'm sure, this is boring. You've hardly said a word. I likely should shut up."

I relax just a bit more as the fingers of Gavril's right hand start tracing figure eights on my left arm. "Not at all." I am having a wonderful time.

My fingers continue to play with Gavril's hair. The curls are slightly damp. I smile, recalling he showers at night. Gavril enjoys the feeling by how I feel him relax, but he doesn't react to my subconscious playing otherwise.

"Well, that's just the highlights, and of course, just the basics of the stars here at this time of year. We'd have to do it more to get it all. But we don't have to if you hate this." The little flickers of touch between us are so innocent, sweet, tentative, playful.

We're both silent a moment. It's nice, settled next to him, looking up into the night sky and seeing things I'd never seen before. I really had been blind to the truths of the world before.

"Gavril," I say quietly. He turns his face back to me. "As stupid or corny as it might sound, I honestly don't think I'd rather be anywhere else," I confess nervously. "And not just up here with you tonight;

though trust me, I'd not trade this for anything. I mean in the Enthronement. I've learned so much. You spot things I always miss. These stars were above my home just as much as here. I lived just as close to the sea and never paused to see those amazing animals. I saw the whales or dolphins from a distance or the seals and otters, but I never looked closer. I just saw the ugliness I was told to look at. I wish I saw things like you do."

"Easier to see it all when you have a limited window. I wish I knew the things you did. Maybe then I'd know what to do about it." I shudder in pleasure as Gavril's right hand moves from playing with my arm to dropping down to my elbow and starts tracing circles around it. "My limited scope makes it easier to see the small things as well as the big things."

"It's not that much smaller than mine. I walked the same streets most of my life. I went on a few tours, sure, but I've lived in the same home, same city, my whole life. I had a limited window and still never noticed the details. I never paused to look or even to learn what lived in the waters I heard every day. I hardly even noticed the soothing sound of the waves that often."

"I doubt you were that blind," Gavril says. "Maybe it just seems that way."

"Maybe." But I was blind to the truth of my whole life. I thought I was a Custod, to my detriment. Yet it did get me here. And though I'd think myself insane if I told myself I'd feel this way when the Enthronement was first announced, I really am glad I'm here.

Subconsciously, my right hand moves from Gavril's hair to his right shoulder, fiddling with an oddly smooth patch of skin. Gavril closes his eyes for a moment. His knee bushes my leg as he adjusts his position slightly, making it more comfortable for me to lean against him.

I close my eyes and fight not to let the words I long to express pop out of me. If I lose him and I had said them, I'd shatter, crumple like a puppet once its strings are cut. I adore him, but I can't be that open. We're flirting with a dangerous line, letting ourselves play a committed couple, but the truth is, he still has ten other girlfriends sleeping somewhere below us.

But he amazes me, this man who I thought little more of than a spoiled rich boy who was happy to take and take and take. Instead, I found Gavril, a prince willing but afraid of his own lack of ability to help the people I thought he just wanted to rob. This man who saw the little people, the little things, and took it all in. He could read the aftermath of a battle and solve its puzzles in a way I don't think I ever could. He's exactly who this kingdom needs on the throne, not me. I didn't ever pause to take a closer look to find out until I had to. I blindly followed like every other rebel. We thought we knew better and were smarter. But just because it was a minority opinion, it didn't make it truer or more forward thinking.

"Are you cold?" Gavril's soft voice makes me smile, and he caresses my cheek with the back of his free hand.

I smile and close my eyes. "No, just thinking." I soak in his touch. "This is amazing." *He's amazing.* "This moment... thank you." They are not the words I long to say, but it is as close as I can get.

Gavril smiles tenderly, kisses my head then hugs me closer. We both look back up at the stars, glittering just for us. How funny it is, we can sit so happy and peaceful together like this. Jake and I would have been lip-locked by now and missing the chance for this beautiful moment. I don't feel the mad desire to break it like I did with Jake. Gavril and I are enough: perfect, beautiful without the needed extras. Not that they wouldn't be wonderful. I brush my leg against Gavril's as I move closer, wondering if I dare.

Would it be worth it? I am so happy in this bubble; do I want to break it? But if quiet moments were this much better with Gavril, how much better would more be with him than Jake?

"You're welcome, but I think I owe you that more than you owe me."

"You're joking." I sit up a little to look down at Gavril incredulously. "You've done far more for me than I ever have you. You've been patient with how stupid I was in coming here. You've shown me worlds in my own backyard I missed. You've stayed with me even when I tried to push you away. You've given me a life I'd never have had otherwise. You made me nobility."

"You did that yourself by signing up," Gavril says, smiling at me in amusement. "I didn't offer that."

"Yes, you did. You brought me up here without the rules saying you had to. You could have dismissed me after I spoke to you so rudely that first night or any of the times since."

"Well, that part might be true, but in reality, I've not given you much." There's a sadness or, perhaps, a disappointment hidden in his eyes.

"Yes, you have," I insist. "Let's just talk about the insane wardrobe in my room to start with."

"That's aaaallll Damian," Gavril laughs, tilting his head back a bit in his genuine laughter. I roll my eyes. "You really don't have much I gave you."

"Maybe not things I can hold, but you have. You have no idea how you've changed how I get to see the world. All in good ways. It's you who gets all the thanks."

Gavril shakes his head, eyes dropping in that sad disappointment. "Not exactly. You've given me far more. If you want to talk 'gifts' in the more traditional sense, you've outdone anything I could ever do." I don't miss a hint of bitterness in his voice. I can't understand why.

"One of them barks at me to let her eat squirrels." I laugh.

"You got me through the first public event. I'm not sure I'd have made it without you. You got me out of the palace to see a magical world you created. I sometimes still can't believe that wasn't a wondrous dream. You gave me support I'd never found before. Gave me some relationship skills I sorely lacked, even just the patience to get through my temper." He chuckles. "I'm still working on that."

"You're getting better," I assure him, settling back beside him. My fingers brush his hair again, enjoying the dampness, the reminder of how comfortable and candid and casual he could be with me.

"Thanks to you mostly," Gavril says as I settle in. "I didn't choose you just because I like you best. You really do the job better than the others, not just in the test or political sense. This job requires a lot of help and confidence and teamwork. You've proven better at that part than anyone else too." He starts tracing shapes on my arm again.

"I thought that's why you liked me," I say in mock offense.

"It's a big bonus." Gavril smiles.

"Then why do you like me, even without my skill in court?"

"I keep wanting to ask you that, but I'm scared of the answer," Gavril admits.

I blink and look at him. "What?" That took a more serious tone I wasn't expecting.

"Well, you came here at the pressure of your friends and to escape a bad boyfriend. I... I'm still just a rebound."

"You are not a rebound," I say stubbornly, wanting him to understand. How can I explain without breaking the magic of this moment? Sage and Damian said I should tell him. Is now the moment? Would I ever get him in a better mood?

But I don't want tonight to end like the fencing date. I don't want all the glory of tonight ruined by that. I have time. Plenty of time to explain the full truth. It does not have to be tonight, but I at least have to explain in part.

"I don't mind." Gavril takes my hand on his chest and brings it to his lips. "If it got you here, that's all that really matters."

"Then why are you scared to ask?" I ask in my own worry for him. I wish I could see his face better in the dark.

"Because sometimes, I still am worried you want to win the Enthronement, not me, you know? I know you said you want me, but I suppose after I realized my words weren't enough for you, sometimes

I worry it's never enough. Everyone else came here for that reason. You came not expecting or really wanting to win. They wanted a prince, a crown, a way out of the poverty of the kingdom. Did it turn into that for you?"

"I didn't come here for you, no," I admit. "But it's the reason I stay." I press closer to him. "Honestly... when I didn't know you were the prince, the possibility of escaping with my apprentice was really, really appealing. Unrealistic, but it was the only hope I had once locked in these walls."

Gavril pauses. "I was?"

"Did you not believe me when I said all I wanted was my apprentice?"

"No, I believed it. Thought it was a cute way of saying you wanted me, not the title. You wanted... even thinking I worked for the slave masters?"

I nod. "I even joked with my mother that if I took her suggestion of finding my own way out of my mess, I was running off with the boy I met in the garden."

"What did she say when you found out?"

"I... was too embarrassed to admit it then." I flush pink. "I was so confused. That's the real reason I was upset when I learned who you really were. You weren't safe anymore. I guess the apprentice was the rebound. You were a choice."

Gavril smiles and kisses my head once more. "Even though I'm dangerous?"

"Even though you're dangerous," I confirm.

"Knowing how it's gone, would you still go?"

"I'd do whatever it took to talk my past self into it." I nod. "You?"

"I'd not feel sick at the idea of the game if I knew it would go this well." He smiles at me.

I laugh. "Sick?"

"When I saw those thousands of applications, sometimes I wanted to vomit. I was petrified of fifty girls. I'd never really dated anyone. Now I was... the star of some kind of dating game." I chuckle. "It was terrifying. I was sure I'd not find anyone I'd really love. Maybe we'd find someone who could do the job, but I'd end up with the smartest choice as my parents saw it. If I had any idea what I would find, I'd have been too excited."

"Me too."

"Liar."

We both laugh.

"So how did I win your interest the first night?" he asks. "I doubt you were in love yet but interested."

"Yes, I thought it was a possibility," I admit. "I liked that you were relatable. You also were humble enough to admit you didn't know everything, but you were so desperate to understand. It was the first time I felt I wasn't alone in these stone walls." I turn and smile up at him. This isn't a bad angle for him. "How did I charm you that night? You wanted me to stay?"

"I told you. You were a way to understand my people. I still feel that way, but that's become less and less important as our relationship has grown." Gavril smiles, still rubbing my hand. "And when I think about it, when I tried to get the other girls to be as appealing, it often was the little things. I like that you're like me. You like to be moving, dancing, pacing. You think better when in movement but not so much that you try to run me into the ground."

"Like Dahlia?"

Gavril laughs. "You read right through that one."

I smile at the feeling of how his laugh feels against my cheek. I love it, all of it... him. The bounce and rumble of the sound fills me with warmth and excitement. I close my eyes to enjoy the feeling, forgetting our conversation for a moment.

Gavril doesn't comment though. He lets us slip into silence once more, watching me with a soft smile as I enjoy the sound of his heartbeat and the steady rhythm of his breath. It's so soothing, relaxing. I'm just about ready to fall asleep.

"I like that you trust me," Gavril speaks after a while, watching me with curiosity in his eyes. "You keep a respectful distance, but you care. You're the only one who didn't let me choose a favorite to keep me sane."

I nod, listening but not really listening, just enjoying the sound in my ear. The purr of his voice is the most comforting sound in the world.

"You seem to like doing the things I like with me, but you push me to try different things too. I love the way it feels to dance with you. And yes, you are the prettiest of the bunch," he teases.

I don't nod this time, soaking in the perfect sound. He's so wonderful. I'll stay here all night, if allowed.

"And you're so happy and content doing nothing, you're not even listening anymore." There's a slight laugh to Gavril's voice.

It's too perfect to interrupt. I want him to keep talking, not caring what he says. I get something even better as Gavril laughs heartily. "I'm putting you to sleep."

"Hmm-um," I say, not listening at all.

I get another delightful chuckle. "Are you lying about that sleep disorder? First you fell asleep at the tree decorating and now you're about to fall asleep out in the cold against me in the starlight."

"Delightful," I purr.

"Kascia!" Gavril laughs and hugs me close. Yes, please, let's just do this all night. "I think we might get into trouble if we're found sleeping up here or if I literally have to carry you to bed."

"Sure..." I mutter.

Gavril laughs again and kisses my head. "Kascia," he says gently, "you have to wake up."

I don't like that idea. "I'm awake," I insist.

"No, you're not." His voice still has that hint of laughter I enjoy listening to.

Suddenly, I'm all too awake as a hard tickle attacks my left side. I let out a shriek and curl away from it, which means into Gavril.

He's laughing again; his head leans back in his laughter. "I told you to wake up. I thought you were the one telling me we're not there yet. Caught asleep on the roof?"

He has a point, but I don't want it to end. "I suppose you're right." I close my eyes as he brushes my cheek tenderly.

He reads what I really want. "Maybe if you keep awake."

I settle into him again, rubbing my head into his shoulder.

"Well, there are still a lot of stars up there," he jokes, watching me warily. "Don't go back to sleep."

"I wasn't asleep," I retort.

"You don't sleep talk?"

"On my honor, I don't."

"Hmm, you still were more asleep than awake."

I sigh dramatically. "What's so wrong with being that comfortable?"

"I'm not a bed."

But he could be. Gavril must have read what I thought in my expression because he bursts out laughing again. "You are trouble, my darling." He kisses my head. "However, it is quite late, and you clearly cannot keep awake. This doesn't have to be our last time up here you know."

But I don't want this bubble to burst. I groan and shake my head.

"We have the ball tomorrow, Kascia. Come on," he urges me.

I sigh and nod my agreement. I sit up, so he can get up. To my surprise, he doesn't load everything up into a bag to take down. He does pack them into a bag, but he opens a closet I hadn't noticed.

"You do this often?" I ask as he takes my hand.

"Never with someone, but yeah," Gavril says as we walk down.

The light hurts our eyes at first, but thankfully, we adjust to it faster than the dark and can navigate, no trouble.

The castle is oddly quiet. It's late I know, but something seems stiller than normal. It's more than silent. It's still. I suppose that's normal for nighttime, but it is slightly off-putting. I wonder if Gavril feels it too as we quietly make our way along the dimly lit passages.

"Hopefully we can catch up on enough sleep tonight," Gavril says to me as we finally reach my room.

I smile, wishing it didn't have to end, but now we're inside, the tiredness has struck. Gavril smiles, seeing the tiredness in my eyes and kisses my forehead. "Good night, my Esther. I'll see you in the morning or afternoon if you sleep late enough." I smile. "Rest well, sweet Esther. Until then." He kisses my hand.

"Good night," I breathe out, wishing for more but unsure how to ask.

Gavril feels something off and pauses. I smile and lean forward, testing it.

He kisses me, reading what I want. It feels so good and doesn't last long enough as he feels me relax. "Sleep well, my lady." He smiles.

"Good night, my prince."

He chuckles at the name and turns down the hall. I smile and go into my room to stop myself staring after him.

The light in my room is on which normally means Damian is still there, but I don't see him anywhere. I do notice there's a note on my desk. I hadn't seen one of those in a while.

I frown and walk over to it, picking it up.

Kascia, I'm so sorry! I think I let them in. I'm trying to stop them now but know I didn't mean for any of this to happen. Please make sure he's safe and stay safe yourself.

My frown increases, and my brows draw together. I look around. Who wrote this? What is it talking about? Let them in? Is there an attack going on we don't know about? I would think we'd hear the alarm.

I scan the room but don't see anything else out of place. I wonder if I should try getting a hold of Damian or someone about the note. I don't know who left it or when.

Then my eyes land on something green sticking out from between the two mattresses on my bed. It stands out against the colors of the sheets. I carefully walk over and pull it out. It's another note, this time written in green ink.

I did it. One down. Two to go. Your turn.

This one isn't signed either, but the handwriting is different, yet familiar. I can't place it. I frown, but now my heart is racing. Something must be wrong. I look around again, but there's nothing else I can see out of place.

"Kascia."

I jump, causing the paper in my hand to fall as I turn to see Damian. Had he already been in the room, and I'd missed him? Or had he come in when I was looking at the notes?

I force a smile for him, but I'm still nervous. I open my mouth to ask, but Damian speaks first. "Kascia, there's something I have to tell you. And... I wish I didn't have to."

He closes his eyes as a pained expression pinches his face before he takes a breath and opens his dark green eyes with the saddest look in them I've ever seen. Whatever he has to tell me is causing him great pain. "Something's... happened," he says slowly as if the words weigh as heavy as a boulder.

"Damian, what—" I start to say when there's a loud noise from the hall.

Someone is yelling, trying to announce something. It takes a moment for my ears to figure out exactly what it's saying. But when they do, an icy boulder drops into my stomach.

"The king is dead!"

**What has happened to the king?
Read *The Consort* today!**

Review Now
And if you haven't yet, join our community for exclusive content, updates, and more!
Sign Up

Character Guide

The Chosen Candidates (In Chosen Order)

1. **Princess Rose:** High-Princess heir to the high throne of Emilimoh.

2. **Princess Amapola:** Princess of Spearim, elegant, fiery, and passionate.

3. **Princess Laurina**: Princess of Bruag, she loves her dragon, exploring, and is the boldest of the born princesses.

4. **Princess Zelda:** Crown Princess of Hyvil, curious, inquisitive, and will take any excuse to use her Magus tablet. One of Kascia's closest friends.

5. **Bella:** A dreamer, high in the ranks but friendly with the other girls, most of all Azalea. She's also close to Kascia.

6. **Dahlia:** The most competitive of the girls. She's used to winning her matches. And she's ready to do whatever it takes to beat those above her.

7. **Jonquil:** Is one of the friendliest girls, yet judgmental of the others. But there are hidden struggles inside her ready to come out at any moment.

8. **Lilly:** Is the youngest Chosen. She's very shy and sensitive. She wants to do her duty but wants to get out of the Enthornement.

9. **Kascia:** Came here out of loyalty to her family but now she's desprate to prove to herself and others she should win this dangerous game.

10. **Azalea:** Tries to look after the other girls like she looks after her younger siblings at home.

11. **Ericka:** Is sure she's already princess and should be treated as such.

12. **Forsythia:** Is clever, and happily aligns herself with Dahlia and Forsythia in a click nicknamed "the elite". Her true colors are showing in her snake like charms to win the prince's attentions.

13. **Isla:** Is a woman of faith. She's shy and quiet with the other girls, often studying cannon.

14. **Kamala:** Is proud of her island home and sure she'll do them proud as princess.

15. **Florence:** Elegant as a princess and as a lawyer, the best versed in law. But that skill fails her when she sees how far she has come.

The Royal Family & Staff

- **King Aster**: Is friendly and likes a good joke, but his borderline humor makes some girls nervous.

- **Queen Dalilly**: The elegant queen who plays her role faithfully. Is an anxious personality.

- **Prince Gavril**: Only son of King Aster and Queen Dalilly. He's ready to prove himself worthy of the power to help his people but his blind, over-protective parents still refuse to see it.

- **Sage**: The prince's Custod guard. Here on a six-month assignment that was up a long time ago. There are rumors about why he stays, but no one knows for sure but him and the prince.

- **Hydie**: The castle's head of staff

- **Vivian**: Kascia's head maid who keeps everything orderly. She hates the rebels for their hypocritical methods.

- **Flur**: Kascia's second maid who is rather shy. She married Kerrigan, a castle guard.

- **Ro**: Kascia's third maid who always is ready with a questionable joke. She hasn't been heard from or seen since the rebels took her during a raid.

- **Godwin**: The prince's faithful and playful valet.

- **Reinold:** The prince's new court liaison. He's Godwin's twin brother.

- **Maryum:** The queen's faithful lady-in-waiting.

- **Porteous:** The king's loyal valet.

- **Lila**: Kascia's head of security. She's a Custod.

- **Keva:** The royal etiquette teacher

- **Gentian:** Sage's father who comes to provide back up of his own volition.

- **Hydrengia:** The royal political science, economics, and history teacher

- **Grand Duke Aldgrone:** The grand duke of Purerah. Heir second to the royal family's line of succession

Other:

- **Joy:** Prince Gavril's red husky puppy given to him by Kascia for Christmas.

- **Peodrick**: Kascia's loving father who pushes her to fulfill her Custod duty

- **Chryasinth (Chrisa)**: Kascia's loving mother who runs the theater and helps her daughter make her own choice.

- **Jake/Jacek**: Kascia's fiancé in a marriage arranged when she was young.

- **Alsmeria**: Kascia's best friend and first soloist at the theater.

- **Jashon**: The cobbler who makes Kascia's pointe shoes and a friend of Kascia's.

- **Yarrow**: Kascia's first attendant who wants to lead the cutting-edge fashion world.

- **Damian**: Kascia's new attendant with an unknown past. His skill with magic is greater than anyone expected.

- **Adam**: The impressionist the royal family trusts most.

- **Omran**: The leader of the Loyalist rebellion. He's Jake's father.

- **Nippers**: The black castle cat.

- **Marlon**: Omran's falcon that has a soft spot for Kascia.

- **Fabian**: The lead reporter for the Purerah Chronicle

- **Cuppy**: Ericka's little curly haired dog

- **Duchess Clarisse:** Head of the Purysian delegation, wife of Duke Cedree
- **Duke Cedree:** Head of the Purysian delegation, husband to Duchess Clarisse.
- **Marquise Loretta:** One of the delegates from the Alalusian delegation.
- **Grand Duchess Kira:** The head of the Japcharian delegation.
- **Princess Tsikyria:** Crown princess of Japcharia hiding some dangerous secrets.

The Rebellions:

- **Loyalists:** The oldest rebellion. The seek to put a common man of Purerah on the throne.
- **Potentates:** Almost as old as the Loyalists rebellion. They want a properly endowed Potentate to take the throne, but not the direct Purerahian royal line.
- **Custod:** The Custod rebellion seeks to have a Custod turn Potentate to rule

Other Books by Charity Mae

To see the complete works of Charity Mae use the link below:

Complete Works of Charity Mae

About the Author

Lives near Mt. Shasta in Northing California and loves the nature there (though she'd like some more snow and rain). She wrote her first 700+ book when she was eleven-year-old and published her first book when she was twenty-one.
When she's not reading and writing, she enjoys making and watching YouTube videos, gaming, hiking, swimming, and sitting outside while working on projects.
Sign Up for her newsletters for updates and exclusive content:

Sign Up
And see sneak peeks, enjoy some memes, and more on her social media platforms.:

Instagram@charitymaeauthor

TikTok @charity_mae_author

Facebook@charitymaeauthor

Pinterest@charitymaeauthor

Website:charity-mae.com

Copyright © 2023 by Charity Mae

All rights reserved.

This book or any portion thereof may not be reproduced or used in any manner whatsoever without the express written permission of the publisher except for the use of brief quotations in a book review or scholarly journal.

The character of Damian Lexus was used with the permission of Raye T. Watson.

Knighted Phoenix Publishing

Chairty-Mae.com

No portion of this book may be reproduced in any form without written permission from the publisher or author, except as permitted by U.S. copyright law.

Made in United States
Troutdale, OR
03/15/2024

18503490R00257